Melanie's Song

Melanie's Song

JOANNA BIGGAR

Alan Squire Publishing
Bethesda, Maryland

Printed in the United States of America.
ISBN (paper): 978-1-942892-10-6
ISBN (epub): 978-1-942892-11-3
ISBN (PDF): 978-1-942892-12-0
ISBN (mobi): 978-1-942892-13-7
Library of Congress Control Number: 2019936747

Jacket design and cover art by Randy Stanard, Dewitt Designs, www.dewittdesigns.com.
Cover photo by Rebekah Littlejohn Photography.
Model: Bianca Corvi.
Author photo by Reenie Raschke.
Copy editing and interior design by Nita Congress.
Printing consultant: Steven Waxman.
Printed by API/Jostens.

First Edition
Ordo Vagorum

To my old *copines* and *copins* Josephine Jenkins Mitchell, Christine Berardo, the late Patty Kenny Immel, Bob Biggar, and Garry Lambrev whose shared lives and adventures during a very special time found their way into this work of imagination.

Acknowledgments

First, a note of huge gratitude to Rose Solari and James J. Patterson, the incomparable editors/publishers of Alan Squire Publishing, whose excellence permeates all that they do, and who make the process of writing and publishing a joy.

Further thanks to ASP partner Andrew Gifford of the Santa Fe Writers Project, and the fine ASP team, notably: Randy Standard for the beautiful cover design and layout; Nita Congress for the highest standard of copy editing and interior design; Max Barton for creative ideas and web design; and Susan Busada for great assistance with marketing.

Many people helped me ground this story in the realities of the era. My sincere gratitude for their time and insights, in particular: Karen Carlson, former director of Caltech Alumni Association, and the extraordinary group of women—both students and faculty—she gathered together for me, who experienced Caltech from the late 1950s–1970s. They include the late Marjorie Davisson Dwight, Iris Schroeder Ted, Susan Murakami, Louise J. Wannier, Debra Dison Hall, Peggy Otsubo, Louise Kirkbride, and Anneila Sargent. Arnold (Skip) Isaacs, colleague and friend, whose experience as a war correspondent for the *Baltimore Sun* during the last three years of the Vietnam War and whose detailed information was invaluable for understanding the realities of the war at that time. Shelley Conrad, midwife, whose descriptions of rural life and the practice of midwifery in Mendocino County during the 1970s grounded my depiction of it in reality. Katie Burke, attorney at law and friend, whose network of family practice lawyers helped me understand how family and adoption cases were handled in rural California in the 1970s. Jonathan Chase, attorney at law and friend, who provided great insight into the workings of the judicial system, including whether cases are tried in state or local courts. Sheriffs in both the Mendocino County Sheriff's Office in Ukiah and the Coroner's Office of Fort Bragg, who generously shared their time, knowledge, and personal experiences. Ron Wallace, whose first-hand knowledge of the music of the era was very helpful.

I also owe a big debt of gratitude to the many readers I have had along this journey whose suggestions have been crucial in shaping this book. In particular, thanks to Antoinette Constable, Skot Davis, Ann Harleman, Barbara Milman, Claudia MonPere, and Molly Walker of my writers' group; the encouragement and support of Left Coast Writers, and of its founder and my close friend Linda Watanabe McFerrin; the wonderful structural editing of Hugh Biggar, and copy editing of Laurie McAndish King.

Finally, a most special thanks to my husband, Doug Hale, whose encouragement, support, feedback, supplies of morning coffee, evening wine, and the great gift of time, have made everything possible.

Contents

Chapter 1

T.J. drew in a deep breath, ready to give herself up to the sun. Sea breeze blowing through the open car window whipped strands of dark hair across her face. Below the turnout along the coast road, rocky cliffs disappeared into a tumult of white waves, the ocean stretched endlessly in symphonies of blue, and gulls rode crests of air past islands of seaweed searching for life beneath. Closing her eyes for a moment she could still see the colors, the contours of the sea. The gulls cried out, while the pounding and receding waves thrummed like her pulse. Calm down, she told herself, trying to let the beauty around her erase the fright that had just made her heart pound, willing the lingering smell of smoke from the remains of the Hi-Diddle House to clear from her nostrils.

She tasted the salt air even before it made a delicate crust on her skin and relaxed a little. The California coast was her native place, imprinted on her since before she could walk,

1

and she felt that imprint even hundreds of miles north of her childhood beaches. No matter what she discovered about Melanie, she could cope.

As her breathing returned to normal, she pulled down the visor to stare at the sea, and caught a glimpse of herself in the vanity mirror. "Damn," she said aloud. Her dark blue eyes rested on smudged half circles, like wayward moons, and her black brows seemed to point at the small crinkles that had crept in at the corners, appearing overnight, like fault lines. "This babe sure looks older than thirty-two," she thought, wondering at the loss of the child she had been, then snapped the visor shut.

The old questions started up again. *What am I thinking, anyway? Why am I doing this?*

Like the last decade, and the nagging restlessness that had driven her—drove her still—to seek that maddening, elusive thing, a kind of truth. It was the same force that had sent her from poetry and its eternal questions to journalism and its fact-based resolutions.

Answers. That is what she wanted, and now more than ever. For the last two years the quest for stories of her oldest, truest friends—the ones she'd journeyed to Paris with a dozen years before, in 1962, a lifetime ago—had kept her going. That was also when she realized she'd lost track of Melanie. Now, going over what had just happened, she was hell-bent to find her.

How she'd learned from Ivan that Melie had almost certainly been seen nearby not long ago at a small commune, Hi-Diddle House. How she'd left L.A. for a long weekend to see what she could find out. How she'd followed Ivan's hand-drawn map with an arrow pointing deep into the redwood forest.

As her small Datsun headed up the coastal highway, as she'd glimpsed the shimmering, endless sea to the left, her spirits had lifted. And finally, turning inland to follow a winding road along the tumbling Little River, where the sunlight fell in strands of gold through the towering giant redwoods, she'd felt ready to succumb to magic. Then there was that first rough hand-painted sign saying *Hi-Diddle*, with an arrow pointing to a narrow twisty road, and the first jittery sense of foreboding had set in. The worry that she was treading a path where she ought not to go. She'd remembered the packet of Melanie's letters and journals carefully tucked in her bag. *Didn't Melanie almost invite me here?* "For J.J." the note on top of the journals intriguingly said, in Melanie's neat hand.

As Ivan's map instructed, she'd driven the requisite five point three miles, then slowed to find the dirt road that veered off to the right leading to the Hi-Diddle House, less than a mile into the forest. The redwoods nearly closed ranks at the top, creating a roof over this small piece of the world, and large ferns graced both sides of the path, seeming to wave her on. Soon she saw the crooked wooden sign with faded Day-Glo paint nailed to a tree.

HI-DIDDLE HOUSE
ALL PEACENIKS WELCOME.

The road widened slightly beneath the sign. A sign for me, she'd decided; time to get out and walk. Standing by the car door a moment, letting her eyes adjust to the deep forest light, she'd walked slowly around a bend. A hundred yards ahead, the ghost buildings appeared, and she'd frozen in place. For a long minute, her feet had refused to move farther. What had been the Hi-Diddle House was now the charred remains of a good-sized building, its roof and most walls gone, its foundation blackened. The debris from smaller buildings on burnt foundations was scattered beyond the clearing and into the forest.

Suddenly flames from that day in 1962, when fire had consumed her own house and much of the west side of L.A., had jumped into her eyes.

I can easily see this forest going up in flames, she panicked. *Can even smell it. God, it's choking me.*

That's when she'd run to the car, jerked it around, and driven as fast as possible back down the dirt path toward the coast. Then she'd pulled into the overlook and rolled down the window again to breathe in the sea air.

Remembering her purpose there, overlooking the glittering sea, put the image of Bud Purvis in mind. Bud Purvis, that idiot, *and my very own managing editor,* she kept reminding herself, had not only agreed to the short profiles of her *vieilles copines,* her friends, but it was *his* suggestion that she do them—along with all her other reporting, of course.

"You know, those little rich bitches who'd ventured off to Gay Paree long ago, how about a follow-up, something frothy and titillating, like tales of 'Life after *La Vie en Rose.'* Our highbrow *Star* readers could use some comic relief, don't you think? After all these years of bad news—Jesus Christ, they deserve some. I deserve some myself."

She remembered handing her copy to Alice, editor, mentor, and often her personal savior. "Ah, stories of the *demoiselles,"* she quipped. "Can't wait."

"Hey, these women are really gifted, and their stories really surprising—nuanced, complex…you know. The public loves this kind of stuff," J.J. insisted. "He'll love them."

"Wrong," Alice smiled, pencils sticking out from her bun.

Indeed, when the stories about her old friends came in, Purvis was furious.

"We got Vietnam, corruption, Watergate, revolution in the streets, bombs going off everywhere, crazy-assed feminists running all over the place, and a kidnapped heiress who's robbing banks for terrorists. I didn't want this psycho-femme liberation crap. All I wanted was a little light relief, you know, the rich bitches who fell into place like a line of cheerleaders dancing on the page," he said. "A little sweet-faced, innocent, verbal nooky. Is that so much to ask?"

The hard news issues he catalogued were ones J.J. had managed to cover even under the guise of writing for Travel. "Actually, I have done pieces about all those 'bad news' issues you listed, and the public seemed to like them, if responses to my clips are any evidence," she shot back, voice rising. "So my guess is that they'll really like positive stories of amazing young women, as opposed to mindless dancing cheerleaders." She was close to yelling.

Purvis shouted back. "Yeah, you sure as hell did write those pieces, way, way out of your territory. J.J., I'm sick of you always pushing the boundaries. Fine, so you want to write girl stories. I've had it. As of today, you're done with Travel. I'm moving you into Women."

Even now, remembering that moment was like being slapped in the face again. Instead of getting a News assignment, as she deserved, she'd been sent to the Women's Section. A demotion.

As these memories raced through her head, sea air blowing into her face, she thought, *Of course, I should have known.* No shock that Purvis was enraged, for reasons so deep, so obvious, they were embedded in him at an evolutionary level. Easy to dismiss him with a few swipes of the cliché-difpped pen: An old-time hard-drinking, hardheaded knuckle-dragger reveling in the scores of football, war, and bedding women. No surprise, really, that he said "This blather pisses me off royally."

Now her ears were closed to him. She knew she had determination, and she knew she would get the story. *Okay, I've also got a talent for telling it. My gift and maybe my downfall. And I've got Alice.*

With Alice at her back, despite misgivings, the paper had published those short pieces on Jocelyn, Gracie, and Evelyn. Only Melanie was missing.

Then there was Guy. *Guy, Melanie,* even saying the names to herself caused a jolt of pain in her gut. She twisted on the seat, pulled the visor down again. "Champion of civil rights, peace, and the Peace Corps," one caption had read. Guy, her first love, had also disappeared. *Long since from my life,* she thought with bittersweet regret, then, suddenly, gone to Vietnam.

One cryptic note from him that had cleaved her heart in two, followed by the news that he was missing in action. She had to find out what had happened. Without assignments from Purvis, who fumed about women messing in men's work, nor press credentials of any kind, she took a leave of absence and went on her own to Vietnam determined to learn Guy's fate. She had imagined it, but hadn't found it. That's when the dream of empty graves had begun.

One of those can't be Melie's, she told herself each time upon waking. *I can't let it be.* Finding Melie was the only thing that got her up some mornings. Finding Melie was what brought her here. How she came, with Ivan's help, to find the creepy, charred remains of the Hi-Diddle House.

———

J.J. SHIFTED IN the striated light created by the long strands of crystal beads that separated the front section of Bread & Beads Café from the small back room, where she occupied the first of four round plastic tables. The smell of incense and highly perfumed tea wafted in, filling her senses, and telling her, as if she needed reminding, that this was Mendocino.

The café was only the fourth place in town she'd hit on her initial inquiry about what had happened to Hi-Diddle House and its inhabitants. A baker, a gallery guide, even the

guy with the Gold Rush–style beard sitting on the boardwalk peeling an apple — all seemed reluctant to say much
except "See Mama Cass."

Now I'm getting somewhere, she thought as she'd pulled
open the door to the Bread & Beads. There, hands on hips,
its proprietor, a large and loud look-alike for the folk singer
of the same name grunted and looked her over suspiciously.
But when J.J. stated her business, Mama Cass's voice
dropped to conspiratorial. She quickly whisked J.J. to the
back room behind the bead curtains.

"I'm just trying to find an old friend," J.J. said, also in
hushed tones. "I finally got to the Hi-Diddle House, where
she was recently, and well, you know, it's burned to the
ground. So now I'm trying — "

"I hear you, woman," Mama Cass interrupted. "But
there's been inquiries, police sticking their butts in over there,
and folks around here don't take well to police investigations."

J.J. nodded.

Mama Cass moved her round face almost into J.J.'s and
scrunched up her eyes. "Somebody died in that fire. Body
of a young woman found. Or so they say. Who's to know?
You see where this is going? And like most folks up in the
woods, when trouble comes, they scatter. But if you're needing to find out about a friend, I can get the word out. Moon
might know, might be willing to help you out. Provided of
course you don't squeal, don't help out the pigs." She paused
and looked J.J. over with a practiced scrutiny. "I'm a great
judge of character. You look honest." With that she turned,
her very large derrière brushing the bead curtains and caus-
ing them to jiggle in a frenzy of air current, and J.J. to
shrink in her chair, holding tight to her mug of tea, hoping
that the word "journalist" didn't suddenly break out in neon
on her forehead.

It was hard to know how long she sat, hands clutched
around the cup of tea. The words "body of a young woman"

worked through J.J. slowly, chilling her pore by pore even though it was warm in the back room behind the beads where ventilation was barely an afterthought. Suddenly Mama Cass was standing beside her again. She had arrived stealthily, like a cat, with surprising agility for such a big woman. J.J. looked up, saying nothing, while Mama's dark eyes peered into her, as if getting another read.

"Word's in that Moon will see you. Breakfast tomorrow. Here." She paused, exhaling. "Don't fuck this up, will you?"

J.J. nodded. "When's breakfast then?"

Mama Cass let out a noise that sounded to J.J. like a cow in distress. She saw it was a laugh, one that began somewhere in Mama's depths and erupted through her nose.

"Let's just say he's not an early riser."

Chapter 2

J.J. pushed past the beads and half stumbled into the street, blinking in the light. Even an uncertain rendezvous with the mysterious Moon now seemed like a solid lead. But her instincts told her to get out of sight and lay low until the next morning. "Eleanor Rigby died in the church and was buried along with her name, nobody came," she hummed the Beatles' tune low, kicking a stone aimlessly toward her car. *Relax, kiddo*, she reminded herself, *but get your ass out of sight.* Instead of trying to find an affordable room in one of the town's swanky B&Bs, she headed the Datsun back down the coast toward Little River and the old inn, which provided cheap cabins for rent out back and at least the illusion of cover.

Winding back down the twisty, sun-splashed road from Mendocino, J.J. glanced at the packet Ivan had given her only a month before, thinking of the day she'd come home from work to find him. Like a guardian angel, just appeared out of nowhere. Dear, lovable, radical Ivan, among her oldest friends—and Guy's old roommate—now a liaison with the tie-dye underground of Northern California.

She remembered how Ivan, bearded and wearing a buckskin vest with a single feather stuck in his dark hair, was sitting on Gran's front porch swing. He'd grinned to see her, and she'd embraced him hard before he began speaking. "The feather, you know, it's a symbol of my solidarity with Native American rights." The talking and joking followed, and they had connected, in the deep, inexplicable way they always had. She'd poured tea from a delicate porcelain teapot while they sat at Gran's round kitchen table. She had long ago—since their Paris days a dozen years past—given up being surprised by Ivan.

"So what brings you off the reservation this time?" she asked.

"Instructions from the cosmos, I think," he answered. "I come bearing gifts." Then he withdrew a bundle of journals from his vest, laid it on the checkered oilcloth, and commenced his story.

"You know, I've been doing community action work in the northern counties, I'm working with the Hupa tribe now, trying to shake some bread down for them from the feds, and I had business down Boonville way. Got the name of a crash pad near there in the forest and was cool with that because the place came highly recommended." He paused, pulled out a pipe, lit it, and inhaled before continuing. "This dude, some faux mystic, owns it, and the rumor was he had first-class weed to share if he took a liking to you. He liked me…and after enough time to get mellow, shooting the breeze about this and that, mentioned that a blonde chick with see-through blue eyes had passed through a few months before and had left behind this packet, all held together with rubber bands. He found it in a bed-stand drawer. Said, 'You should check this out, man. I've been reading this stuff.

Chick must have been a maven, you know. Some heavy shit in here. Must be a sign.'"

Ivan, who had a few years before given up his Fulbright and master's in history at Stanford to become a "deep space astrologer," was moved by the prospect of signs. "The package was one thing, but when I saw the note still stuck on top—'For J.J.'—I nearly freaked. Melanie. Of course. It had to be."

He patted the note, still attached with Scotch tape to the packet. "So that's what brings me from the woods, old friend."

He offered J.J. the pipe. She declined. "Working girl, you know," she shrugged.

When midnight turned the sky inky, when dawn lifted the edges of night with a trace of blue, they were still talking. By tacit agreement, they did not speak of the hole in their lives left by Guy. But they did talk of commitment, passion, love, the need to make a difference in a wretched world. Of endless war, revolution, the idiocy of politics, street theater, and the surprising conversion of Patty Hearst, the kidnapped heiress, into Tania the revolutionary. Of Nixon and Watergate. He brought up poetry, the need to read it, the need to write it. She listened silently. When Ivan said, "It's the moral imperative of our generation to bring down the corrupt System," J.J. responded with, "Well I assume head-butting the patriarchy in the person of Bud Purvis counts."

"What I don't get is why you've stuck it out so long at the *Star*. Shit, J.J., there's a thousand papers would love to have you. You could see the world…" Ivan smiled teasingly.

J.J. closed her eyes before answering. "Easy one-word answer, *mon vieux*. Gran."

She could not explain further, and he didn't press.

They came, at last, to Melanie—to where she had been and where she might be. J.J. recited her litany of facts to Ivan, just as she had gone over them so many times in her head. "You know I had an extensive correspondence with her, so she always seemed present to me. It took me a long time to understand she'd really disappeared. I guess that occurred to me a couple years ago, in '72, not long after I got the journals she sent me."

"When did you see her last?"

"Funny you should ask. I've just been thinking about that, trying to pin it down. It would have been the year before, spring sometime, and she came by on what she called a 'peace mission' to her family. She seemed pale — I mean not just pale like she always was, but as if a blizzard had caught her from the inside. Really quiet, her eyes bobbing around more than I'd remembered. There was so much to catch up on, so much I didn't know about what she'd been up to, that I'm sure I was more than usually persistent in my interrogation."

Ivan smiled and stroked his chin, not mentioning what they both knew about the hazards of her profession.

"Melie just kept saying 'I know, J.J., there's so much to say, but I'm in such a rush now. I just wanted to see you. We'll catch up soon.' I can still feel how tight she hugged me when she left." Tears trickled from J.J.'s eyes. She made no effort to wipe them.

Ivan handed her a kerchief from his pocket, and she continued.

"But it was when I went back to the college to talk to the coeds who were thinking of going to France that it really hit me: I did not know where she was. I'd asked for, and gotten, letters from the others with advice for these darlings, but nothing from Melie. So I made up her letter."

Ivan inhaled deeply, then laughed. "No way."

"Really. That was so out of line. But I sort of admitted it, and I had good source material. From way back when Melie was still in Rochester, I had all these letters. Then she actually sent me a few of her journals. They were mailed from someplace in western New York, and they came with a note saying 'Dear J.J., I'm sending these to you to safeguard for me. Love always, Melanie.' I had no idea that would be the last thing I'd receive from her. Weird, isn't it?"

"No." Ivan sat up even straighter in his cross-legged position. "Mysterious yes, but not weird. It's a sign. She was definitely sending you a sign."

Suddenly very fatigued, J.J. declined to ask Ivan what the hell that was supposed to mean. But he answered anyway.

"I mean, J.J., you're the writer, right? She means for you to tell her story. She's sending you the goods."

Chapter 3

"Just deal with it," J.J. said out loud to herself, thinking about the upcoming meeting with Moon. Whoever he was.

She had taken a long time adjusting her feet on the wooden floor of the cabin. A faded calendar on the wall reminded her it was 1974 and already June. The transition month between the budding season and the simmering heat, and momentarily she was a child again splashing water from a bucket in her grandmother's garden. Wandering far in her imagination was a mind trick to escape the long night of Melanie dreams and a rising dread of what the day would bring. A glance out the window showed a stand of redwoods framed by a blinding blue sky. The summer coastal fogs had not set in yet, the early mist had burned away, and the North Coast in June, dotted with wildflowers, was intoxicating.

Still, her stomach churned. By the time she backed the Datsun down a pitted drive behind the inn, she wasn't sure what to blame. The trial of perfect weather when all she felt was gloom? Trying to absorb the idea that Melanie had been in that burned-out pad? Or just nerves about meeting Moon? *I can't blow this,* she told herself, adjusting the mirror. *What do I say?*

J.J. FIGURED THAT ten thirty was a good hour for a breakfast meeting with a guy famous for not being a morning person. She figured wrong. After two hours behind the beads in the back room of the Bread & Beads Café, she felt drowsy from the heat and the commingled smells of incense, tea, and leftover smoke from the previous night's reefers. She'd tried coffee to clear her head, but it had only made her stomach burn more. After a night of little sleep, she just wanted to put her head down and rest—or cry. She felt like yelling at Mama Cass for setting her up with a no-show, but Mama Cass evidently didn't do morning duty either. The only employee on duty was a wispy-bearded skinny young kid in a knitted Rasta cap, who was tasked with opening the café at ten, making coffee, and serving whatever breakfasts were ordered up at that ungodly hour. From the sounds of slamming, crashing, and the occasional curse from the kitchen, they must be preparing for an army of patrons.

"I'm Pigeon," the skinny one announced as he slammed a coffee cup in front of her and turned away, making it clear that that was all she needed to know, without asking if she wanted to order. Evidently he'd been informed that she was there for a meeting. By twelve thirty, she decided to ask Pigeon if the breakfast moment had passed and they were serving lunch yet. If so, she would order lunch, take her throbbing head out the door and split. But just as she rose to find him, the bead curtains parted with a rush.

J.J. looked up, startled, and wondered if this was her own version of a bad trip, for what looked like a bear was heading straight for her. An immense creature with bristle in every direction, wild red hair streaked with gray running into an underbrush of gray-striped beard, a plunging mustache, and huge hairy arms, waving. "Moon," he said, nodding his head slightly in her direction before crash landing on a wooden chair opposite her. The glass beads quivered.

"God damn, I hate early risers," he offered. Then the mustache parted above the beard, and his face split into an enormous grin. J.J. scoured the landscape of his face to see if she could find eyes. They were small, dark, darting, impossible to decipher. At the same time, they were trying to read her.

"God damn, girl, you look like you could use a meal. Need to eat to keep your strength up. Where is that woman anyway?" The mammoth shaggy head turned marvelously on an unseen neck to peer at what lay behind the beads. "Woman," he bellowed, "where in the God damn hell are you, anyway? We need some grub in here."

Mama Cass parted the curtains and entered as silently as she had the day before. The long multicolored muumuu she wore danced around her heavy ankles. Without seeming to stir the air, she was suddenly at the table. "Top o' the morning to you, Moon," she said, without actually looking at him.

"And to yourself, Mama. We'll be taking two specials. And plenty of coffee."

She left silently. Before J.J. could gather her thoughts, the taciturn Pigeon appeared, bringing more coffee, silverware, water, fluttering noisily between her and Moon.

She opened her mouth at last, but too late. The small dark eyes were boring into her. Moon was speaking. "Like I was saying, like we didn't have enough trouble, the fucking pigs are everywhere up in our business now. Hi-Diddle gone, everything up in smoke, folks scattered, chicks gone... missing."

"Chicks?" J.J. tried to compose a coherent thought as she surveyed the mess of ham, eggs, flapjacks, and biscuits that Pigeon had begun slapping down on the table. She sipped her coffee again. "What chicks?"

"Look, Bones," Moon said with his fork poised in the air, eyes drilling into her, "I'll be asking the questions first, if you get my drift. I don't know who you are and what your game is. All's I know is that Mama took a liking to you, said her vibes were that you're for real, and Mama carries a lot of weight with me." The eyes closed for a moment, as he shook with pleasure at his wit. They opened again just as suddenly. "You got a missing friend? Tell me about your friend."

Unused to being on the other side of questioning, J.J. paused for a moment, searching for what to say. "Yes, I've got a friend, a dear friend, who's...lost. I have reason to believe she was at Hi-Diddle... I, that is, we were friends in college, and we traveled to Paris together, and I have letters from her, from, I don't know, ten years or more—and her journals, and..."

As she spoke, J.J. realized how difficult it was to actually visualize Melanie, just Melanie alone. The images of her always seemed to be in shadow. The impossibly overwhelming shadow of her socialite mother. The vague shadow of her absent doctor father. Hans, her husband—so pale it was hard to believe he could even cast a shadow—yet J.J. knew that, ever since he had seduced her by playing his violin and playing himself into her life, Melie had lived in permanent semi-eclipse.

Take care here, J.J. reminded herself. *Don't reveal too much to this shaggy dude until he shows his hand.* She could feel in her gut that he knew Melanie too, and in ways that she never had. "She always wanted..." J.J. stopped herself before saying *to be taken seriously.* "I guess you could say she is sort of...fragile."

Moon gave full attention to J.J.'s account and full attention to breakfast at the same time.

"You say she was small and blonde?" he asked finally.

"Yes," J.J. answered. "Her name is Melanie Hart. From Pasadena originally. Dad's a big-time doctor there, so she... she had some means. Here's a picture." She pulled a well-worn photo from her bag showing Melanie in a full-length coat next to a snow bank overlooking a frozen Seine. Winter light caught her hair, making it glow. Melanie was smiling in the way she did only in deep winter, her true season.

"It's old, but—"

"God damn," Moon cut her off. "That's her all right. That's Fiddle."

"Fiddle? Okay, Fiddle, whatever. Tell me—"

He cut her off again. "Fragile?" He frowned. "Rich bitch, you say? Well, I'll be damned. Never know it. She's got the spirit, woman, she has the goods. A witch if I ever saw one."

"Witch? What are you talking about? Where is she? What happened?"

"God damn if I know, Bones." Moon's hands, manic a moment before, suddenly stilled, as if limp with remembering. "See, I wasn't around at the time, been doing what had to be done up-country at Diddle Farms. I'm, like, the CEO, you know? And like I said, there was plenty of chicks down at the pad. Chicks coming and going—dudes too of course—because it was, like, our philosophy. Peace. Easy come, easy go. And witch? Oh yeah. She had the magic, could fix anybody."

"Then the fire. God damn! Could have been from anything, anyone. Folks cooking, lighting up, you know, just a careless thing. Could have been the God damn fucking pigs themselves, wanting to root us out, destroy our inventory. If you get my drift. But a body! Now they're saying somebody died—a woman—and they all over us, all over the whole community, wanting to bust our asses, shut us down, make us *criminals*. Which they been wanting to do for years."

"The woman, was it Melanie — Fiddle, that is?"

"Folks scattered so much, hard to know who was there, what was what." A large hand reached out to cover J.J.'s with surprising gentleness. "I hate to say this, but most likely was Fiddle. Sorry, Bones. She was an angel witch, you know? Love enough for the whole world. God damn! Hard to wrap my head around that sorrow. But we just don't know for sure, and now the pigs everywhere."

Moon's eyes appeared to mist over. J.J. held her breath, not wanting to let in the words he had just uttered. It was easier to keep on playing the investigative reporter. "So, if you don't know, who would? Somebody must know who was there, must be able to tell you something."

"Like I say, they all scattered to the four winds. Especially the chicks. By the time I got there, it was all over but the smoking, like the inside of hell. Only one who would know who would talk is Cat. Haven't found her neither, but got word that she was up Cleone way. Have a mind to go up there now. Want to come along for the ride?"

Moon suddenly looked down at the plate heaped with breakfast that J.J. had hardly touched.

"What's the matter Bones, you didn't eat nothing. And you such a morning person, too. God damn, I HATE that when a chick drags your ass out in the middle of the night for breakfast and then won't eat a thing. You going need your strength, woman, you know that, don't you?"

⌣

AGAINST HER BETTER judgment, J.J. climbed into the battered Ford truck with Moon. Journalism 101: Never, ever put yourself in the control of an unreliable source. But this was hardly standard operating procedure, J.J. knew, this was closer to…Moonscape. Moon turned his old wreck on a dime, and soon they were back on Highway 1, heading north.

"Where'd you say we were going?" J.J. shouted. The rattling of the open truck bed behind and the wind rushing through the open windows required high volume.

"Cleone." Moon's beard and hair were flying everywhere, making it hard for J.J. to even see him. She wanted to know who Cat was and what she had to do with anything, and what she was doing in a place named Cleone, anyway. But it was pointless to ask. Moon was one of those sources who are going to go where they're going to go, do what they're going to do. If you push them, they'll just push back and leave you behind in the dirt. Still, she watched carefully where they were going, wanting to memorize the details — road signs to the Noyo River, Fort Bragg, Highway 20 heading over the coastal mountains to Willits — and formulated all the questions she wanted to ask in her mind.

Unaccountably, Moon began to whistle. J.J. caught pieces of what she privately named Moon's Weird Medley. Snatches from "Yellow Submarine," "O, Shenandoah," "My Darling Clementine," and what she was pretty sure was the melody from Brahms's Symphony No. 1. As the truck went flying across the Noyo River bridge overlooking the harbor, she took in the scene of fishing boats crowded together at the docks, nestled contentedly below white frame buildings sporting signs saying *Seafood & Bar* and *Tackle Shop*. Ahead was the road, bordered by redwoods, and the town of Fort Bragg. It all seemed reassuring, knowable, and J.J. relaxed. In a moment, her eyes fluttered closed.

She didn't know how long they were shut, but when they opened she had a distinct sense she had been with Cat, a slim young woman with long, dark hair sitting in what seemed to be a cabin. She wore a full-length gingham dress, like a vision from the nineteenth century. Appalled to have let down her guard like that, J.J. glanced over at Moon, who continued pushing the rattling truck at a mighty pace and was no longer whistling. With his hair and beard still blowing, J.J. wasn't sure he'd even noticed that she'd nodded off. She wondered where exactly they were. As if in answer, Moon began to speak.

"That turnoff up yonder, you see? Well, that's where Diddle Farms is, up in that mountainy territory. And you may be wondering why I was up here, rather than down at the little house in the forest when all this was coming down. And I wouldn't blame you for asking, seeing as how Cat was my old lady at the time. Well still is, by my reckoning. It's like why wasn't I minding the store, so to speak, taking care of my women and my people—of course, I do come up to the farm regular like anyways, because we've got cash crops that need attention, and I'm not talking peas and beans, if you get my drift, but I admit I'd been away awhile. I—" Moon cut himself off abruptly and suddenly turned toward J.J., those dark eyes visible and searing.

"You ain't working for the pigs, are you, Bones? Like undercover or something?"

J.J. shook her head vigorously.

"Because I'm about to level with you, and God damn, woman, I don't take kindly to being messed with, you understand?"

J.J. nodded in the affirmative.

"Cat could tell you how I feel about that," he snorted, then went on. "There was like some, um, difficulties between me and Cat. I'm as open-minded as the next honcho—we're all sworn to complete openness you know—but I just didn't like it when that young black hipster came, kind of moved in on her. Wasn't the black thing that bothered me. I'm no racist, anybody'll tell you that, 'Old Moon, he gets down with everybody, man,' but it was, well, like he didn't fit in. Just wanted to smoke free joints, party, mess with the chicks— well Cat to be precise—and do nothing in return. Couldn't work out that way at Hi-Diddle. Nope. Everybody has to go with the same flow, you know, contribute? But Sport, he was just doing his own thing, too much of a city cat."

Moon turned to look at J.J. again. "So I just decided to, you know, chill for a while on the farm. Need to keep my eye on things anyway to keep turning a profit. I figured in good time Cat would get around to missing old graybeard here and send me a sign, and we'd, you know, pick up where we left off. So I kind of let things drift there, don't know who was there, who not. Heard new chicks moved in. Maybe old Sport just wanted a chorus line." Moon snorted again. "Don't know how Little Dog and Dish and all would have taken to that, but... anyhow, before that happened, well the fire. Whole thing's gone. And I don't know who was there when it started, don't know for a fact that Fiddle was there, that she's the one they found."

J.J. finally broke in. "Actually, do you know for a fact that Cat was there?"

"That I do. She's been seen around, like the Cat she is, in the shadows of things. Hope the last intelligence I got is for real, and that she's up here Cleone way." Nearly as soon as he said the word, he wheeled the truck into a side road and began up it, slowing down to look at mailbox numbers. There were small tin-sided houses and cabins tucked into the trees on either side of the road. He came to a stop in front of a mailbox painted "12."

"Intelligence says she came here and holed up with Sport. Don't know what in the God damn that city hipster would do up in here. You stay here, Bones. I'll do reconnaissance."

J.J. waited impatiently for about ten minutes.

Then, before she heard him come, Moon was at the truck door again, pulling it open. "Well what in the God damn do you make of that? She split and..." he paused, drawing in his breath. "Must have left in a hurry. Must have had a kid with her. There's baby junk all the hell over the place."

⟶

THE RIDE BACK to Mendocino, to the Bread & Beads Café—and J.J.'s car—seemed interminable. She couldn't wait to get out, although Moon was oddly quiet or pensive, or…the word deflated came to her mind. Perhaps he wanted sympathy? Lost in the whirlwind of her own worries, she hardly knew what to say to him. It was easier to revert to journalist mode. "Look," she finally ventured, "these cops you're so worried about, are they local?"

"Hell yes. Sheriff and his kiss-ass cousins who been pissing themselves for years for something real to nail us with."

"Why?"

"Why?" Moon suddenly faced her for the first time on this leg of the trip, animated again, his intense dark eyes finding their way through layers of facial hair to bore right into her. "Ain't that obvious, girl? Macho red-meat flag-waving war-mongering uptight motherfuckers do anything they can to bust us. Why? Because we're peace-loving, fun-loving, pot-smoking, free-loving hippies, that's why. Because they hate our guts, that's why."

"That's it?"

"That's it."

"Well then, why don't they? I mean they could get you on something, housing code violation, taxes, jaywalking… something."

Moon snorted. "It's bigger than that, Bones. It's like a war thing, a generational thing, age not being chronological if you get my drift, but any violation like that, yeah, they could do it, but what would be the point? The woods is full of hippies like us, you dig? They get us somewhere, we just crop up somewhere else. Like mushrooms." Pleased with this analogy, he snorted again.

J.J. sighed. She couldn't tell him to what degree she "got" the generational thing, or that what she'd written—what she was writing now—was all about that. Finally she said, "So, in order to 'nail' you they have to come up with something big. Like a house fire. With a body in it?"

"God damn right."

"But even so, even if they identify the person, having a house burn down isn't a crime, is it? Even if somebody dies in the fire? I mean it happens to lots of people. Unless…" J.J. stopped there, not knowing how to phrase her thought.

Moon, evidently amused, laughed loudly. "Plenty in that unless, Bones. Unless lots of things. Point is, they don't find our lifestyle savory, if you catch my meaning. They get a chance to shut us down for real, they'll shut us down good."

They rode on in silence.

"Look," J.J. said, relieved when they finally pulled up alongside her Datsun outside the café, "like I was saying, Melanie was my close friend. What's happened to her, it's really important to me. Would you let me know when you find out something?" She reached inside her bag for a piece of paper, careful to not let slip her *Pasadena Star* business card identifying her as a reporter, and wrote down her address and phone number. "Call me any time you want, collect," she said handing him the paper. "And how could I get in touch with you? If, you know…"

"If something comes up about Fiddle," he finished her thought. "Mama handles my business matters," Moon gestured toward the Bread & Beads. "You want to find me, tell her. Long as she still trusts you, you're good as far as I'm concerned."

Chapter 4

*D*amn it, Melie, I came here to find you. Retreating to the wood cabin after her strange ride to Cleone, J.J. longed for the comfort of solitude and a place to rest her weary head. More than that, she longed to have some tangible news of Melie's well-being. *This is not the story I meant to discover.*

My God, she thought, after all the years of shifting through other people's lives to find just one true thing, *I end up here, a fugitive on the Mendocino Coast, placing my bets on some caricature named Moon. And Melanie, you were here so recently, the ashes in the woods still warm. Now you're gone again. Were you in there? Where the hell are you?*

She shut her eyes then, ready to weep, or to sleep. Sleep more than anything, for suddenly she felt bone weary. Or, worse, sorry for herself. Heavy limbed, it seemed as if her body had been taken apart and reassembled incorrectly. *Solitude*, she said to herself, *a prerequisite for thinking.* For grief.

Flopping on the lumpy mattress upheld by an old iron bed frame, she pulled up a comforter, at last free to give herself over completely to despair. Melanie's packet of letters, now tied with string, sat beside her, while the bundle of journals perched on the dresser like a reproach. Ivan's gift—or was it Melanie's?—reminded her of how far she was from writing Melie's story, if that indeed was what she was meant to do. How far she was from knowing the truth about Melie—and how afraid to learn.

The note was no longer physically there, but in her mind was still attached. "For J.J." Maybe Ivan was right. Maybe Melie had intended in time to send these to her and had just left them by mistake in Boonville. But writing? That was a reporter's game, but now J.J. felt more friend than reporter. Above all she felt heartsick.

Still the letters taunted her from the dresser top. Throwing off the comforter, she sat upright again. *Do the one thing you know how to do well, damn it. Be a journalist. Figure it out. Begin at the beginning, put it all together, don't miss anything.*

At a small table by the window with a view to the sea, she stacked together the letters Melie had written in such profusion, then took the packet of journal entries that Ivan had recently given her and determined to sort them all by date, to make a logical, cohesive narrative. They began with those early years after Melie's secret marriage to Hans—celebrated on the sly at the other wedding, that of Evelyn's to Jay Greene on November 21, 1963.

The date still had the power to give J.J. a sharp pain in the pit of her stomach. The eve of JFK's assassination, the death of an era and of her youth, just as she was to celebrate her twenty-first birthday. The moment she saw Guy again after so long a time, his new woman at his side.

For J.J., the word "innocence" would no longer have a place in the world. Like virginity, it could be tossed on a list of overthrown archaic concepts. Still, it was the first word that came to mind when she read those early letters from Melie.

Aug. 14, 1965
Rochester, N.Y.

Dear J.J.,

It's hard to believe we've been here nearly a year—and that Hans has done so well so fast. He's on the violin all the time of course, but his professors at Eastman think he has a real gift for composition and should specialize in that. It takes so much of his, well his energy, his soul I guess, that for a lot of months I felt I hardly saw him. But our world is still filled with sound, though more Shostakovich now, less Bach. That's strange in a way, too, because Shostakovich was so rebellious, so revolutionary—which Hans definitely is not—and yet for him going deep into that other, now faraway revolution may be his way of handling our own time. Not that living in Rochester is really living in our own time.

Anyway the summer has been different, with so much light and such long days, we seem to be in them more together. Funny, you know how I was always avoiding the sun because my skin can't take it and kind of dreading summer, but this summer has been so full of light, and a kind of airy lightness, I'll be sorry when it passes. You know I never was much one for the beach, but last weekend we went on a picnic to the nearest lake called Honeoye (these Finger Lakes do spread out like fingers!) with a few of the other students and their wives. Somebody even had this little Styrofoam sailboat, and I loved blowing around on the small lake in it and certainly didn't mind getting dumped in the water. We had a cookout and sat on the beach so late until it actually got dark and a million million stars came out. Funny. I wondered, too, what Pascal would think at that moment because just then they didn't look so distant, nor scary, as they usually do, not the way he described them.

Somebody had a guitar and we all sang just plain old songs, "Shenandoah," "When Johnny Comes Marching Home Again,"

"Clementine," "Blowing in the Wind," things like that, and you'd never know these were the future great musicians of America. Except me who can't sing worth beans nor play anything, of course, but somebody has to be a regular citizen.

I know this must sound strange and, well, like another country to you, J.J. It seems that way to me, too. The war, the riots, the bombings—all the things you are learning and writing about and I know affect you—and the others of us too. I hear or read about them, but they all seem distant as those stars from this world of graduate students and music so far from where the rest of life is happening. Is that real, or is this? Tell me which.

I do love hearing from you when you get a chance and learning about how things are for you. I know you're in school, too, but it sounds so different, so...is vital the word?

All for now,

Love, Melie

July 28, 1966
Rochester

Dear J.J.,

I've not heard from you for a while and I wonder how you are. I got that postcard months ago from you and now things are so terrible with all the riots in Cleveland, which somehow seems more real to me, maybe because it's closer, and L.A. has receded into a hazy (smoggy?) past. But it's almost as if what you wrote is happening there in Watts is on my doorstep now (absurd, isn't it?) and I can grasp what you experienced. Or maybe I mean the greater world—apart from the sheltered, idyllic life we live here— is closer. I do know, of course, about the greater world and its passions, obsessions, poverty. I guess that was the great lesson for me from Paris. But in some way, the troubled present you are living in seems as distant from me here, as Paris does in time.

Then as soon as I say that, all I want to do is tell you the good news. We left that dark basement apartment and have found a great little Victorian cottage close to downtown. It's an old neighborhood, but new in the sense that it's full of young people like us. And music students! Oh, J.J., now that the nights are long, you can see light close to midnight and everybody has the windows open and it's a symphony on our street. Jazz, blues, classical, guitar, even some opera singers exercising their pipes—it's glorious. It's hard not to tap, or dance, or want to sing along...

Hans thinks it's glorious too. He has fewer classes in summer and is turning back to his composing, which always makes him happy. I'm hoping now with the summer months of good weather we can go to the lakes, take some picnics, you know... have fun. Is it too frivolous to wish for, when the world seems to be blowing up, falling down, or plain old coming apart?

Our little place needs a bit of paint, and some curtains, so I'm setting about doing that myself. Can you imagine? So domesticated now. My mother would be amused. Maybe pleased?

Journal—October 10, 1966: Nearly Hans's birthday and even though I'm not, I feel older than he is. Guess I can feel the season turn too quickly now. Days shorter and darker again, cold soon to come off the lake with the winds bringing winter rather than the glorious tastes of fall. Red leaves, and yellow, apples everywhere off the farms, and grapes, and even that slightly ridiculous upstate wine, and geese on the ponds not yet frozen. But I am, if I admit it. A small glacier inside that didn't melt even through summer. We did get to the lakes, too, even if not as often as I dreamed.

Now that Hans has turned back to composing—composing me, I should say because the song he wrote a few years ago that was so acclaimed he now is trying to turn into a symphony. "Melanie's Song" into "Melanie's Symphony"? I don't know why I find a little corner of dread in this.

Sometimes I dream of France, although I try not to. Never the terrible visit to his family that Christmas with J.J., nor even the unspeakable encounters with Prof. A. Saint-Georges, just ordinary things. Walking along the river, buying bread in the boulangerie across the street, meeting Gracie or Eve or anyone *at all in a café. Especially the way the sunlight falls winnowed through the leaves at this time of year. As if I were happy.*

Nov. 20, 1966
Rochester

Dear J.J.,

How good of you, and how amazing that you remembered our third anniversary! How do you manage to keep all this straight with all that you're doing? And no, you weren't far off the "real" date, although we count Nov. 21 as the official one, it being the party and all—and Eve and Jay's actual wedding of course. How are they? Isolated as I am here, I seem to have lost track of them. News, please!

Speaking of that, I have some. When I think about it, and then think what you are doing at the center of things—reporting on racism and riots and everything explosive and dangerous—what I have to say is so, well, trivial. But somehow I don't think you'll see it that way, because you do have this ability to see things through other people's lenses (maybe that's why you are becoming a journalist?) and you'll take me seriously. More so than I deserve. But anyway, here it is. I'm going to start working mornings in a nursery school! The winter months are so long here and I need to have a more rigorous schedule now that Hans is in composing mode. Also, even though it's a pittance, I need to earn some money...

Journal—November 22, 1966: Hans actually forgot our anniversary. I waited until late at night to give him my little gift letting him have a chance to do whatever he wanted to do without me going first. But he came in so late, he just fell into bed and rolled over mumbling "Good night." I can't tell if I'm more shocked or hurt. But I do know that at some level this is my fault. He is so deep in the world that matters to him, and I know nothing about it. It's as if I can't speak—or read—his language. Music. I know now what I have to do. I have to learn it.

Journal—November 29, 1966: J.J. sent me a copy of the <u>Star</u> to see a story she'd written about "The Rebellious Generation"— ours—and how we're supposedly shaking things up. Even mentioned Jocelyn as part of the "new young Hollywood," though I confess I've not seen her new movie and don't really get what that means. I suppose J.J. didn't realize she'd included the society pages too. So weird to read that my parents actually were having a "bash" on Thanksgiving Day, the day of the great family feast. There was no mention of the fact that "Dr. & Mrs. Hart" have a daughter who seems to be missing from their lives. And their hearts.

Nov. 31, 1966
Rochester

Dear J.J.,

Thanks for the great letter and your newspaper. Amazing to see your name in print and to read your well-chosen, well-thought-out words. I confess I don't know nearly enough about our generation, being caught up in the world of music students, to get a lot of what you're saying. But it did make me think, and I hope it's OK to ask, whatever happened to your old friend Guy, anyway? Talk about people breaking and shaking the ground!

And as for that music school world, I just have to tell you. After Hans taught me some little tunes on the violin, like ditties or folk tunes, I realized the way to really get closer to his world is to learn music, although clearly not the violin. The way I play he jokes is just "fiddle" music. But I'm secretly taking music lessons—piano, actually—so one day I can surprise Hans by playing something for him. Isn't that great!? And the nursery school I told you about. Honestly, I never thought I'd be so at home with tiny children, but...

J.J. rested her eyes before continuing the now familiar letter, and the ones to follow that documented Melie's small triumphs and hurdles through the dark, cold mornings in the preschool, with the darker and often bitter evenings of

Rochester winter closing her days. The letters, intended to be upbeat, were shadowed by the journals, which leaked with a different version of Melanie's story, a creeping sadness at Hans's preoccupation with music and indifference to her; a growing sense of inadequacy as she struggled to find meaning in her own life.

Reading the letters from '65 and '66—time she herself had spent at the Journalism School at Berkeley—brought back a flood of memories to J.J. Yes, there had been that piece, the first she'd ever written, about Watts, which had been published and gotten her into Berkeley. Fateful decision, she thought, starting her on the road to journalism. Those days in the Bay Area had been so tough in terms of work, but also magical—crazy, music-filled Peace and Love days. Writing some sketches about that scene had gotten her the intern job at the *Pasadena Star*, her hometown paper. It's been a long ride, she thought to herself. Starting in late '66, going back to cover the Summer of Love in '67.

Restless, she pulled herself into the present and knew it was time to head back down the coast to home. Just before leaving, she reread Melanie's letters and journals through 1967. The sensation washed over her that she was in the presence of two different people.

Chapter 5

J.J. knew when leaving Mendocino it was best to head inland, go over the coastal range to Boonville, where Ivan had found Melie's journals, and crash there for the night. Boonville was, after all, part of the story, the place where Ivan had discussed Melie with that guru in his flophouse. The reporter in her said it was a place to check out further—and it also put her on the way to Highway 101, the fastest route south from the Mendocino coast. But Melie filled her head. Going into the dark forest and poking about in the spot Melie had once stayed seemed a bleak and forbidding prospect. As sorrowful friend instead of working reporter, she took the coast road. *The light will last longer*, she told herself for justification, keeping to the winding road by the sea.

I really don't want to be in charge of this disaster, to think about who to call, who to tell…who to question. With that thought, J.J. jammed a Joni Mitchell tape into the cassette player. *Perfect,* she smiled to herself as the clear voice called out the warning, "I couldn't let go of L.A., city of the fallen angels..."

By the time the Datsun pulled into an oceanside motel south of Gualala, it was dark. Once inside her small room, J.J. opened the window and let the sounds of pounding waves lull her to sleep.

It was still early morning when she turned inland at Jenner to follow the Russian River and reluctantly parted company with the sea. Glancing at herself in the rearview mirror with windblown hair full of salt, she saw her face shining pale beneath dark brows in the reflected light. God, she thought, frowning and reviewing her nondescript loose blouse over a long, creased jean skirt. What a mess. Bones? Hah! More like lumps and wrinkles. No lady reporter look going on here. With hours of freeways stretching numbly in front of her, J.J. willed herself not to think of Melanie, her notes and journals, her fate—and also what a potentially big story she had stumbled into.

She just wanted to lean into music, for her mind to be quiet, blank, and "to fix on something nourishing," as Gran would say. Suddenly Gran's garden, with its crazy juxtapositions of palm and avocado and orange trees, its ferns in huge urns and trellises with sweet peas, its flat beds of daisies and nasturtiums and ranunculus, its sunny side porch where terra-cotta pots filled with lavender and red geraniums made visible Gran's Provençal roots.

She saw a child running barefoot through the sprinklers, making wet footprints on the smooth cement paths, watching butterflies drift lazily around bright petals. Herself.

Gran's back fence, Gran's house. Gran's kitchen, with its aromas of herbs and olive oil. The past. For all practical purposes, Gran's house was her house now. Or more accurately, Gran's house without Gran, because Gran lived nearby in a "residence" but didn't really reside there either, because she didn't reside inside herself anymore.

J.J. clutched the wheel tighter as she headed toward the inevitable, dreary I-5, trying forcibly to prevent herself from thinking about the grief of losing Gran piece by piece, of the awful decision she had made—*they* had made, for when Gran was lucid enough, she'd agreed that she couldn't remain at home any longer. She needed more attention than J.J. could give in the time left after work and travel. Gran needed more than help with dressing, meals, the every-day things of daily life; she needed someone to watch her every minute, someone to keep her from wandering. J.J. had wanted, at first desperately, to hire someone, to have a "keeper" full time at home. But it would have been just that, a keeper, and Gran would have been a prisoner in her own house.

When Gran was lucid she knew, far better than J.J. could understand, what needed to transpire. "There are times in one's life when it is the moment to leave one place, one phase, and move to the next, *n'est-ce pas, chérie? Non, ma petite,*" she went on, "it's no use to rattle about this big house alone, and *non, non* certainly not with a pair of strange eyes watching me all the time. It is best now for a place that is...cozy, *non?*" She smiled that soft, dreamy smile that had always calmed J.J. and as a child had made her think of faraway places. "Besides, *ma petite chérie*, it gives me such comfort to know you are here, and to think I can come home whenever I wish. When you are home too."

J.J.'s heart had missed a beat, for then she knew. Gran had never once said it in so many words, she had never even faintly complained at her granddaughter's long hours and absences since J.J. had given up her apartment to move into Gran's house more than two years earlier. But with that phrase J.J. at least glimpsed the loneliness of Gran's isolation as she lived more and more within the confines of unraveling memory. *I am her world now,* J.J. had acknowl-edged. For reasons J.J. never fully comprehended, she and

Gran were close in ways that Annie and Gran never had been. *I am what she hangs on for. I am home.*

Facing the hot barrenness of the highway, J.J. needed to make a plan. Gran first, she thought. *I'll go to the residence, sit and have supper with her, or tea after dinner while she rocks in that wicker rocker we brought from home.* If Gran was up for it, maybe she could come home for the night, stay for a spell. Of course, Gran might not be up for it, might be in that vague space where the old familiar smile seemed to mask an entrance to a new, unfathomable place, or she simply might not communicate at all. That's how it was now, you never knew where Gran might be.

Then another idea came to her. Drop in on Mom. Or Annie, as she always insisted, Annie, short for Antoinette, and mother not a concept or a name she had ever been particularly comfortable with. *Okay, drop in on Annie...whoever.*

Especially now, with Gran in some sort of permanent twilight, it was important to lessen the gulf that had always existed between her mother and herself. After a bout of what J.J. knew had been reckless complaining, Alice had once chimed in: "Despite herself, despite her obsessions and possessions, your mother does have a streak of empathy, you know." Maybe now was the moment to test it. Maybe Annie would be the one to offer comfort for the stress of confusion, loss—of losing Melanie.

But getting to Annie's, all the way in West L.A., was the problem. And a crap shoot as well just to go to that jumble of a house, which never seemed to unclutter despite the fact that so much of the junk—"unique collectibles," Annie called them—wound up in her trendy shop in Brentwood. "It's all the rage with the rich, famous, or aspiring to be. Annie's Ark, the place to see and be seen, like a club along the strip. It's even turning up in the gossip columns," Annie had reported triumphantly.

Okay, J.J. reasoned, maybe not Annie's. *Maybe I should*

see Dad first instead? Or would he be with Annie? If so, would they still be fighting about the fact, still quite incredible, that her middle-aged, mild-mannered father had moved an acting student who looked hardly a day over eighteen into an apartment in Santa Monica? The fact that he had met her at a sleazy bar where she worked as a hat check girl in a costume leaving little to the imagination hadn't bolstered his case that she was just "a sweet kid who needed a break."

J.J. recalled the aftermath with a shiver. Annie, her empathy button definitely turned off at that news, had yelled: "To hell with all this peace, love, go-with-the-flow shit," and things began flying. An empty picture frame, a milk glass pitcher, and a few Chinese rice bowls barely missed him as he ducked. Later, his listed crimes included "the loss of irreplaceable precious objects."

After slinking back to the apartment and assuming his absent posture, he had tried to tell his version of the story to J.J. "Annie," he said, summoning his worst epithet for his wife, "has been acting French again."

Remembering all this, J.J. shifted her weight in the seat. Joni Mitchell sang "Black Crow" on the tape deck. The possibilities racing through her head finally turned off. Checking in with her crazy relatives wasn't going to bring any relief from her angst about Melie, and she knew it. She also knew what she really needed to do. See Alice.

J.J. KNOCKED ON the beveled glass door of Alice's small office, feeling as if her head would split.

"Come in." Alice's eyebrows arched in anticipation over her tortoise-shell glasses, pencils stuck in the bun atop her head. Alice looked like a school principal, and J.J. had long concluded it was impossible to know how old she was. Old enough at least to have come up the ranks before the word "feminism" was uttered with meaning, old enough to go head-to-head with the likes of Bud Purvis and walk away with a tight victorious smile on her thin lips whenever required.

Uninvited, J.J. sat, and Alice, sensing something more than usual amiss, pulled her glasses down on her nose and ceased her normal twitching, ready to listen in silence. "Okay," she said, "let me have it."

There were a few clarifications as J.J. spilled out the entire story.

"Wait, so there was yellow police tape around the fire site, but nobody present?" Alice wanted to know.

"Correct," J.J. answered.

"This Moon character, no other name?"

"Not that I know of."

"Wait," Alice raised a hand to stop J.J. at one point. "Tell me I didn't hear what I thought I heard, that you got in a truck with this creature."

"Actually, yes," J.J. replied. "But he was harmless. I've got a good sense about these things." Alice rolled her eyes.

The recitation finished, Alice's eyebrows arched like a cathedral spire. "Oh my God," she said, in a quiet monotone.

"Let me get this straight. We have a missing friend, who more than likely has turned into a missing person and quite possibly a body in a mysterious fire in a hippie commune. We've got a bear-like creature named Moon, a fat-assed café owner and possible conspirator named Mama Cass, a missing—this word keeps coming up, I notice—witness and source named Cat, who somehow has come down with a baby. Am I forgetting something?"

J.J., noting Alice had switched to "we," shook her head no.

"Well, of course I am. I need to say it loud and clear: we've got a hell of a story, J.J., you know that, don't you?"

J.J. nodded, not wanting to get into how it was so much more than that for her.

"Mind you, breaking news in Mendocino is slightly beyond the normal interest of the *Pasadena Star*."

"Yeah," J.J. agreed. "There is a local angle, though. Melanie is a Pasadena girl. Her parents still live here."

Alice sat uncharacteristically still for a moment as she knitted her eyebrows into a question mark. "So what do you want to do?"

J.J. took a long time to reply. "Same as I wanted when I went up there last weekend—to find out what has happened to Melanie. To know the truth before I begin writing it."

"Okay. Fair enough. So what we need is to figure out a way to keep investigating this without having a dragon breathing down our necks," she gestured to Bud Purvis's office, "pressuring us to publish before we're ready. What if somebody else breaks it first?"

"That's a problem," J.J. acknowledged. "But it's necessary to have whatever time it takes to get this right. More than I can ever remember, I want certainty of a high order on this one before going into print."

"Right." Alice shoved her glasses back up in front of her eyes. "What we need is a strategy." She thought a moment. "What are you working on now?"

"That Hollywood fashion show thing." J.J. sighed.

"Aha, got it!" Alice slammed her palm on the desk in triumph. "We go with some 'homespun threads and hippie trends piece' prevalent on the North Coast, pitch it as a counterpoint to the Hollywood style. So go to Hollywood, my dear, make it sparkle, and I'll take care of the other end." She jerked her head toward Purvis's door once again.

～⌐

J.J. HEADED WEST on the narrow entrance lane to the Pasadena Freeway—First Freeway in the Nation, the city fathers boasted—with a familiar well of restlessness rising in her. She blocked out the press briefings she'd scanned earlier that would define the day ahead: bimbos in grotesque makeup parading around in miniskirts and versions of go-go boots that had been around already for nearly a decade, at least since Nancy Sinatra had immortalized them in song. Then some radical "protester chic" thrown in for counterbalance. And of course, interviews to arrange, and a photo shoot. She glanced at the freeway signs and saw the turn-off for Melanie's parents' house. The whole fashion charade seemed even more grotesque now that Melie was missing, and perhaps… She couldn't finish the thought. Her mind drifted to getting in touch with the frosty, difficult Harts.

Nearing Hollywood, the image of Jocelyn—clad in the very miniskirts and high boots that J.J. had to cover now—jumped up at her from a large billboard. For an instant, J.J. fantasized about bagging her studio fashion show assignment and heading for Jocelyn's house and demanding to be let in. Then she remembered what she had to do and gunned the motor.

By midafternoon, back in the office banging out her notes on the newest model IBM Selectric, she felt nervous indigestion. The typewriter had been a peace offering, of sorts, from Bud Purvis when he had first pulled her from Travel, declaring that he would give the Women's Section, for God's sake, one of the first new expensive machines with its signature instant correction feature, no erasures, no mess. "No excuses for any fuckup now, J.J.," he had said with an unrepentant laugh. But at least he no longer smoked cigars in the office, and he no longer called her sweetheart. What was he going to do now, when Alice hit him with their scheme?

A week later and the first draft of "Hot Styles among Starlets" was done. With enough time to go before deadline, J.J. drifted from her uncluttered desk to the window. Fidgety, and knowing Purvis was stingier than ever these days about travel money—he himself was being squeezed by the money boys, as he called them—J.J. worried that he'd cut her funding for travel. She paced, watching the mindless traffic of Colorado Boulevard move back and forth in the afternoon smog. She tuned out the clacking of typewriters, the ceaseless jangling of phones, the banter and jokes of the newsroom to peer out the dirty window. Images of boots and miniskirts and outsized belt buckles and flowing bell-bottom pants blurred her reflection in the glass. It all seemed so banal, Hollywood and fashion crazes and movie star worship. She swallowed with a trace of bitterness. People were out there dying, in wars, in the streets. People out there were disappearing.

Finally, she settled down enough to polish her piece, then presented herself at Alice's door. "I have copy," she began.

Alice skimmed through it quickly. "Fine, okay," she pronounced. Then, with a sweeping movement of her hand toward Purvis's door, said, "I'll handle this now."

J.J. returned to her desk in time to hear, "Jesus H. Christ, Alice…" erupt from his office, and plunged into her files, trying to look busy. A few minutes later, she felt a hand on her shoulder and looked up to see Alice.

"Well?"

Alice greeted her with a tight smile. "You've got to the end of next week and the weekend's your own. Be back Monday. Two pieces on the raggedy-muffins and their rainbow rags. So go for it." J.J. blew a kiss as Alice waved, turning on her heel.

On impulse, J.J. picked up the phone to call Bread & Beads before leaving. If Purvis objected, she could justify the expense by claiming she needed to consult Mama Cass about "full-figured fashion."

After dialing the operator and waiting impatiently for the long-distance wires to connect, at last the repetitious honking sound began to reverberate in the receiver. "The line is busy," said the operator in the requisite nasal voice, "would you like to hold?" J.J. held.

"Bread & Beads," a voice suddenly squawked on the other end of the phone she still clutched, sounding a thousand miles away. "May I help you?"

"Hello Pigeon," J.J. answered, hoping the familiarity would disarm the skinny-ass waiter. "J.J. here. We met recently when I was visiting and I'd like to speak to Mama Cass. Please."

"She's not available right now," Pigeon sniffled.

"Well when might she be?"

"How should I know? She's a busy woman."

"Right. Well, how about Moon? Is he around?"

"Look, you're the one he calls Bones, right?" Pigeon was whispering conspiratorially now. "I don't mess in any business but my own. But I'm giving you my professional advice, free. You want to talk, you get on in here, and don't say you heard it from me." Then the line went dead.

Chapter 6

As Jocelyn pulled onto the Hollywood Freeway, her eye caught the billboard. *Oh God*, she thought, *really?*, and tried turning away from the image of herself beckoning with half-closed eyes and a pout. Old P.R. for the release of *Walk on the Woman Side*. A glance in the mirror reminded her of what she looked like now. Hair covered in a Hermès scarf, eyes covered by Mary Quant sunglasses, a tanned arm resting on the open window of a gold Jaguar convertible—P.R.'s idea of what she should be driving. *I look like a goddam movie star, that's what.*

Maybe the next shoot will improve things, she thought, remembering why she was heading to Pasadena—the series of publicity pictures for the upcoming *Pacific Blue: The Louis Dubois Story*. "A World War II romance based on the best-selling novel," as the ad guys put it, and she, playing Edna, "the beautiful, stoic young American who falls in love with a dashing French pilot." *Supposed to widen my appeal. Expand my image. Push me into the mainstream.*

She sighed, thinking of how the new billboards would look. The Hollywood Freeway would soon light up with Edna, hair upswept, scanning the sky for her hero's plane as she looks up from a bed of roses. She wondered if she'd like that any better than she liked the trendy, booted image. *She's still not me*, Jocelyn told herself before closing down that line of thinking.

Restless as usual in the morning, she had left early. Dru joked about her being the opposite of most stars he had directed. "You always arrive before those birds catching the worms, darling." With his voice in her head, she smiled, translating the words into the way he said them in his heavy Polish accent, which sounded German to her. "You alvays arrive before zoze birds catching ze vorms, darlink."

Dru. Silver-haired, charming, continental. She was happy to fall into his passionate embrace, as she always did when they worked together. Living briefly in a world of their own creation was so consuming, she relished having someone to share the experience with. They both knew they would drift away from one another sometime after the final credit.

Signs for Pasadena loomed overhead, and her thoughts shifted from Dru to J.J., her oldest and best friend, who lived only blocks away from the Tournament of Roses Headquarters, where the photo shoot was to take place. There would be plenty of time to drop by. They hadn't been in contact for over a year—ever since J.J. had written that awful piece, "Superstar a Virgin Still."

Okay, Jocelyn admitted to herself. *I haven't exactly been in contact with her. I know she's put out feelers to me.* Maybe it was time. She could go just down the street to Gran's big old loving house—J.J.'s house now—check out the garden and say hello. Turning from El Molino, Jocelyn slowed onto a side street, entering the neighborhood of turn-of-the-century houses, wrap-around porches, and old shade trees. *It's a set from another time*, she thought. Like the one she was temporarily living in, which happened to be the 1940s, another place to escape to.

As she pulled in front of Gran's and parked, a rush of memories flooded over her. The days during college when the fire had consumed both her house in Hollywood and J.J.'s in Mandeville Canyon, West L.A., and they had both found refuge with Gran. Gran's wisdom and kindness to her. That memory unlocked others. Life at La Maison Française, where she lived with her *copine* before they all sailed off to Paris together. They were all so scattered now.

I can do this, knock, say a quick hello, then leave. Before I lose my nerve. Jocelyn walked up the drive to the familiar covered porch with its huge old-fashioned pots and pressed the doorbell. When the bell stopped chiming, she tried again. Maybe Gran was home, but hard of hearing. As Jocelyn looked around at the flowers, the clipped lawn, the porch swing, she took in the stillness, so different from the throb of Hollywood. She waited another minute for someone to open the door. Then it occurred to her. Of course, J.J.'s at the paper now. Maybe Gran wasn't there at all. Nobody home.

Typical, she thought, pulling away from the curb. How often had she wanted—needed—to be with J.J., but J.J. was too busy, too wrapped up in some love affair, too focused on some damn writing, that she wasn't home? *Maybe it's just as well I didn't see her now. I've got enough to worry about at the moment.* Okay, she hadn't answered J.J.'s last few calls. But what was she supposed to say, after that story about her? Just thinking about it made Jocelyn mad.

Slamming the Jaguar to a halt, she reached for a folder, thrown with others on the backseat. Pulling out the offending piece, she knew it wasn't really necessary. She had memorized the damn thing—the curse of being an actress. J.J.'s horrid headline jumped out at her.

Superstar a Virgin Still

Jocelyn, with a single-word sobriquet that only the stars highest in the firmament of fame can attain, at 31 has reached those celestial heights. The name alone conjures for multitudes of fans her image, one of long-limbed, slender perfection, of a classic oval face framed by trellises of golden hair and eyes that shift in color and mood so completely, she exudes perpetual mystery even while intensely exposed. Think Botticelli's Flora. Think Aphrodite or Isolde or any goddess of myth and you will find her. In particular, think Sainte Geneviève, that beautiful young woman, a nun from the age of seven, who liberated Paris from an attack by Attila the Hun and helped barges filled with food and probably wine to escape down the Seine. Jocelyn is a passionate Francophile, and Sainte Geneviève is her saint.

Even as fans and critics have watched her evolve from ingénue to femme fatale to hard-core feminist babe (I'm thinking of the storm released along with "Walk on the Woman Side," that blockbuster of 1971), Jocelyn, the woman off the marquee, far from the lights, costumes and make-up remains infinitely more interesting than any of her roles. I know. I was her room-mate in college and in Paris. I am her oldest friend.

She still felt betrayed by J.J.'s "honest" reporting, making her into a cliché.

Best J.J. wasn't home, after all. Best not to open that can of worms. Or *vorms*, as Dru would say. She stepped out of the Jag, closing the door gently, as he had taught her, and walked toward the old Italianate mansion on Orange Grove in search of the shoot.

It was easy to spot the camera and crew and small portable changing/makeup cabana already in place. She studied the arbor, caught the scent of the roses, and tried to imagine how they intended to place her in them.

"Darling, there you are."

Jocelyn started, then felt Dru's hand on her shoulder.

"Dru! You didn't mention you were coming." She relaxed immediately under his touch and turned to face him. His silver hair shone in the full sunlight, and she felt like kissing him. Although everybody knew about their relationship, they were discreet in public.

"So not even one small welcome kiss, darling?" he whispered, teasing.

"No, but why don't you tell me what you're doing here?"

"Ah, my curious beauty. For one thing, because even though I'm not needed here, it's always such a delight to see you. And, for a second, at the last minute I decided to go further east to that range of mountains. I want to check out another location. I was hoping to persuade you to take me in that wonderful convertible and spend the rest of the day with me."

Jocelyn smiled in agreement, then headed for the costume tent.

HOURS LATER, THE makeup finally removed, Jocelyn found Dru alone for a moment. "My car is parked by the curb over there," she whispered. "Come get in when it doesn't seem too obvious."

He slipped in beside her. "You make us seem like, how do you say, 'sneaky kids.'"

"But we are, don't you see?" Jocelyn laughed. "Okay, I'm ready to roll, just tell me where you want to go."

"Well, to the mountains, of course. But not too fast. First just go down Colorado Boulevard. I want to show you something. Turn here."

"What is this place?" Jocelyn asked as he took her by the hand, leading her up the steps of an ornate Spanish-style building, whose beauty she could make out despite its being boarded up, with all access denied. "It certainly has good bones," she added, stopping to admire the red roof and ornate tile.

"Yes, darling, good bones, like all the classic stars who last a long time. This is the Pasadena Playhouse, a breeding ground for theater—real theater, on stage—and for so many who got their start here. They put on the newest plays by Eugene O'Neill, Noel Coward, Tennessee Williams, talent like that. And the actors who trained or got their start here—Tyrone Power, William Holden, Eleanor Parker, Robert Taylor—you see darling, it really was, how do you say, star-struck. I taught film directing for a couple of years when the Acting School was still going, and even though I always will be in the world of film, I caught the magic."

"What happened to this place?" she asked, the names of the stars he mentioned swirling in her head, as she tried standing on tiptoes to peer in.

"The usual, unfortunately. Money problems, studios training their own actors. Still, they never compared with the Playhouse as a real, what is that word, nursery? And being here, I felt that wonderful mix that takes place on stage, the daring of playing live to an audience."

"No safety net like retaking the scene, you mean," Jocelyn said.

"Exactly, no safety net. Sorry we can't see much from here, but I have some wonderful pictures I promise to show you. It's all done in the best Spanish-Moorish style, lots of gold and painted ceilings, fit for, what do you say, the sultan's palace."

They both laughed, and he grabbed her around the waist.

"Will it ever come back?"

"I don't know, darling, but it should. It was so respected, and especially famous for highlighting Thornton Wilder's *Our Town* that it is an American classic in itself. They ought to, you know."

When they took off down Colorado Boulevard again, Jocelyn fell silent. Her head filled with images of what Dru had shown her, and what she imagined inside the mysterious building. She glanced up at the *Star* offices as they passed, but Jocelyn didn't want to discuss what she had been thinking about that morning. Then, when signs for Cal Tech appeared, she slowed slightly, imagining Gracie was somewhere inside, almost tempted to turn in, but pushed on past.

"So quiet, darling," Dru finally said. "A nickel for your thoughts?"

Jocelyn adjusted her big sunglasses and looked at him, smiling. "It's a penny, Dru, just a penny. And mine probably worth just that."

"Well, that could be managed by the budget then." He grinned at her, placing his hand over hers on the wheel.

"It's just that this town is so full of old friends, or memories of old friends I haven't been in touch with for so long, I feel…unsettled."

"Ah. Yes. I know that feeling." He pulled a cigarette from the silver case in his jacket pocket.

"Where exactly did you want to go to scout the mountains anyway?"

"I have heard about this Mount Baldy, which they tell me often has snow and groves of oranges growing below. It might just be perfect."

"Baldy!" Jocelyn smiled to herself. "Of course. But first it's my turn to show you something. Claremont, it has the best view of Baldy for a start. It's also where I went to college, lived in La Maison Française, met my *copines*."

"But of course darling, perfect. The *copines*. Let me guess. Well, J.J. of course. I know all about her. And then isn't one a distinguished scientist?"

"An astrophysicist. That's Gracie. Not too far back we saw the signs for Cal Tech, where she hangs her hat."

"Ah, yes. *Remarquable, chérie.* Then, I'm thinking, some kind of nun, can this be?"

Jocelyn accelerated at the first signs for Claremont several miles ahead. "Yes, exactly so. Sister Eve, if you can believe it. The minister's daughter who fell off the path of righteousness in Paris."

Dru inhaled deeply before releasing smoke into the open air. "But that is perfect, no? What good is Paris if not to go a little bit crazy? And then I think maybe there is one more, but I can't find her story."

"Yes, one more. Melanie."

"Ah, Melanie. A lovely name. Tell me about Melanie."

Jocelyn felt a stitch in her side and waited a long minute before replying. "If only I could."

Chapter 7

Pigeon's words still in her ears, J.J. gripped her small suitcase and walked through the darkened hallway to the room she now claimed as her study. There, in Grandfather's overstuffed armchair cracked with age, she reached for the Melanie files. *It's probably crazy to travel with this treasure,* she told herself. But she might need to check it quickly because of whatever new is coming down. *It's like my Rosetta Stone.*

One folder jammed as she pulled it out—1968. Thinking chronologically, she remembered that the records for '67 were pretty thin. But 1968 had been a mind-blowing year, even—or maybe especially—for Melie. Despite herself, and the need to hit the road, J.J. opened the folder.

Jan. 7, 1968
Rochester

I know this is crazy in a way, but it keeps me going. It's weird how

I'm hating this dark and cold when it used to be what I LIKED, I thought, the sun being so rough on me and all. But now it seems like overall night—when I get up, when I go to bed, and then during the day when I'm inside, or in my "cave," who can tell?

By 8:30, though dark, it's almost midday for these children, most of whom get up so early, like 6, but that's when I crawl in. And immediately I feel, what's the word? Warm maybe. Or light. Or maybe just alive. Toddlers, runny noses, sometimes crying, sometimes hitting each other, often tripping, but there's this rush of...feeling when I see them, hug them, make them laugh. This world, this experience, seems as foreign as any place I've ever been. It makes me wonder, was I ever really this little, this loving, this curious and unafraid? Could I have been as adorable as Melissa with her huge brown eyes and curls, always sweetly pointing at what she wants, coaxing me with a smile? Did my mother ever—well, no use following <u>that</u> line of inquiry. The amazing thing is that this is a revelation about some part of my own past, a deep part of my human experience that I've been cut off from. How strange we lose our own beginnings into unseen caves of memory.

Pascal again. "Joie, joie, pleurs de joie." He of course was talking about a relationship with God, but what in God's creation could be finer than the skin of an infant, the triumphant first words of a toddler, the wonder of a three-year-old discovering a bug? Did he know of this? Silly question. But I do.

Feb. 15, 1968
Rochester

Dear J.J.,

I could tell you about the weather, always a topic here when all else fails, but in truth it gets old after a while. Talking about it I mean. Living with it is rather like a spiritual practice, it's pure abnegation. Here, we are all desert fathers of the tundra (OK, mothers as well, I know my feminist doctrine too). Of course, I exaggerate about the tundra, but some days it feels as if the ground beneath is actually frozen permanently, as well as the sky, and often there is no visible seam in the whiteout to see the difference.

And you, dear J.J., still a creature of the sun and even steamy places, no?

I can't remember who said "the best revenge is denial"—a great French philosopher perhaps, but I think more likely it was Evelyn. Anyway, my antidote to the frozen world is a dazzling kind of warmth, those kids in the day care center! And, though I can't admit it to anyone, I have a special favorite. Little Billy. He's 2½, blond, pale, and shy. But so sweet! Of course I see Hans in him, and watching him is like a revelation. Billy is tentative with the other kids, but so observant, he takes in everything even if he hangs back from participating. Not that he shows any particular talent in music (he even kind of claps off-beat) but he does love drawing. He can make shapes and patterns with crayons, very advanced for his age, and even when in the sandbox he takes a stick and makes pictures of a sort, instead of building "houses" or filling up a dump truck and crashing it somewhere, like most of the other boys (and yes, some girls). But when he's doing his art, he gets completely lost in it, in some world nobody can enter in, and it's often hard to get him to leave, to come along with the others, even for lunch. You see the Hans connection then, the private places even in a child that no one else can ever enter, or share...

Journal—April 5, 1968: Yesterday unspeakable.

Next to those two words was the sketch of a cross, a skull and crossbones, Melanie's only reference to the assassination of Dr. Martin Luther King Jr. Then there were the long, mostly undated fragments regarding the events of May.

Journal—undated: I can't believe it, yet I do. It is like I'm there, more actually there in Paris, than here, in the endless snow, the dark. Flames. Students. Helmeted cops with those shields. Weird. Like outer space, another world. Blood in the streets.

Journal—undated: Wednesday. Strange. My heart races along with them. They're rioting. Against what? Not the war, as is everywhere the case here. But against repression, lack of rights. Against the Administration.

Sorbonne maybe? Crazy! Stupid professors, insane corrupt, hateful professors? Types that take a girl's life and twist it around and nobody cares? ASG? Have they got your number too?

Journal—undated: Friday. Watched again on the news. I am transported. I want to BE there. Blood is not nearly as frightening now as all that snow was then. Boul'Mich. Liberté, Egalité... well. I am marching with you, too. I've never been so inspired, excited by something so political.

Journal—May 22, 1968: Strange how seeing these images makes me feel I am there. The Place de la Sorbonne, millions of people in the streets. I can feel them chanting. A picture of a flic dragging away a student. Of a girl, one of the few actually in these street scenes, in her nice skirt and heels, waving a banner. Must have been from that fancy lycée nearby...nicely dressed, so respectable, all of them. Like me.

Journal—May 28, 1968: OH GOD. I don't believe it. Another picture today taken from a French magazine. Professors and students marching together, holding a banner saying LIBERTÉ. There he was in the center. ASG. Alain Saint-Georges. Smiling.
Le cœur a ses raisons que la raison ne connaît point.

Journal—Saturday, June 22, 1968: Hans says it's frightening, close to anarchy. I asked him what happened to Shostakovich and his recent flirtation with revolution. He said that's different. I said, yeah, it's different. It's here, it's now, it's our time. But I know the problem—it's Europe. Too close to home for Hans, who will never be at home here, really. It's just a place to hide. In his music.

Journal—June 29, 1968: Alain Saint-Georges again. I dreamed they had him, dragged him from the Sorbonne and down Boul'Mich to Saint-Germain. The crowds were singing the Mickey Mouse song! I heard rumors they were taking him to the guillotine. Suddenly I was there right behind him, swinging a long key on a rope.

Joie, joie, pleurs de joie.

Along the margins of some of the pages were also scribbled in heavy ink the initials RFK, R.I.P.

July 1, 1968
Rochester

Dear J.J.,

Here it is summer again, and my heart soars. Not that summer always works out for the best here, or up to all my grand-glorious expectations, but still I feel the blessed sense of the world's renewal, of hope. Perhaps it's because with the muted sun on the lakes and the puffy clouded blue skies, I can actually take what passes for heat here. I see innocence in the giddy green of the grass.

I know such ramblings are just that, a kind of blather compared to all the important observations you make—and the important stuff you write. But anyhow, I just wanted to catch up a little. Thanks for sending me that article you did on folks in Watts, by the way. How horrible all those poor older black people should live in fear when they've done nothing to deserve it! It's hard to make any sense of. But bless you J.J., for being so brave, and a kind of conscience for the rest of us.

I know it seems so trivial in comparison, but my secret music lessons are going so well! I plan to surprise Hans in Sept. for his birthday by giving him a "recital" for a change. It seems so important in a marriage to be able to really communicate, I've come to understand, and to know as much as you can about the world your husband lives in.

The other news isn't so positive— well, not on the first take anyway. It's about little Billy. He's been withdrawn (I mean apart from just being shy) and worse, well, bruised. The director of the nursery school, Carla, has taken all the appropriate steps and talked to the parents. They're very young, from German immigrant parents, no schooling, trying to make a go of a farm in the county, but the land is so poor. Anyway Carla brought up the problems with them, "observations" was the word, and edged into the subject of finding a foster home. At least temporarily, until they can really get on their feet. I wasn't there of course, but she said when she laid it all out there, including the bruises, the law, the need for counseling etc., they were "resigned." Subdued anyhow, and agreed.

J.J., I swear this is the worst thing I've ever done, and please don't judge me harshly. Well I know you won't, which is why I can confess to you. My heart SOARED. I thought instantly, maybe I can have him, at least for a little while, you know? Maybe he could be part of us, just temporarily, and Hans could see the sweetness in him, like the sweetness in the shy blond boy that once was him. I know this is crazy, maybe even magical thinking, but I knew I had to give my heart a chance. I thought carefully how to bring it up to him and got myself quite worked up actually, but decided in the calm of summer and with the long light and all everything looks better. Plus it would be the ideal time to have the child with us.

So last week, after he had a long practice session and was feeling very good about his composing, I did it. He didn't say yes, but then again he didn't say no. He seemed somewhat distracted and said, "Well, if you really want to and you think we could help the child, maybe we could. But we don't have much room, do we? And I couldn't risk having any damage to any of my instruments and such. I'd have to move everything into the recording studio. And it could only work for a short time. But it is just so, right?"

Just thinking about it, I could burst...

Journal—July 4, 1968: Wish Billy were here already. The long weekend, parties and fireworks. He would love it. And I would love the company. Hans working. But he hasn't said no!

Journal—July 10, 1968: Miracle. Hans said OK. "Easier to have that kid in the house than to have you asking every five minutes." I'm telling Carla today that we want to be the foster parents! And Billy was so sweet today, I hugged him extra hard.

Journal—July 12, 1968: Today we start all the formalities. This will include heavy interviews from social workers. Hope Hans is up for all the "intrusions."

Postcard from the Finger Lakes, dated July 25, 1968:

Dear J.J.,

Just to let you know all the wheels are in motion. Billy is living temporarily with an aunt until we're approved. Should be soon. Hans charmed the pants off the social workers, bless him. I've been making the apartment Billy-friendly, got toys 2nd hand through the nursery school & I guess he has clothes. Today I read to him about the cow jumping over the moon. Love, Melie

Aug. 2, 1968
Rochester

Dear J.J.,

I'm heartbroken. Everything is off. Billy's parents have agreed to family therapy and want to start over away from the family farm. They're moving to another part of the state and taking Billy away. I know this is a good thing in the long run, best for Billy etc., but I cannot be so brave for myself. This feels like a death to me, and I can't shake the feeling.

What's the matter with me, chère amie? Words of wisdom?

Melie

Journal—August 15, 1968: Even though I've professed to love it, now I hate this Upstate summer. It's all blue skies and butterflies, a child's book. I can't bear it. It feels HOT, even. I should start back at the school beginning Sept., but the thought of going back there, all that sticky sweetness and NO Billy, I don't, no I can't. Must tell Carla. What is there then? What to get up for? "When one does not love too much, one does not love enough." —Pascal

Aug. 30, 1968
Honeoye Lake

Dear J.J.,

Thanks so much for your note, and no need to apologize for it being short, you being rushed, etc. And especially no need to try to correct my vision of you as somebody on the front lines, despite what you say. I know you write for the travel section when you ought to be a front-page reporter. Still, you manage to work in such great stories, always about important things under the guise of travel, you'll just have to accept my admiration. And yes, after your great pieces on "The Five Countries of California" (and thanks for sending them), I'll keep my fingers crossed about moving into news. Even say a prayer, if you like.

If this is a bit messier than usual it's done in haste and wind. I'm down by this little lake where we like to swim and sail, very close to town, and for once am here by myself. I'm just trying to get myself back on course and am very much trying to take in what you said. Yes, words of wisdom indeed. You're right, I need to be able to be happy on one level for what is happening in that it's probably best for Billy in the long run. If his parents can make it work. I never want to close my eyes and see him in my mind with bruises again. I want to imagine him safe and warm and smiling.

But then the next, hardest, part. What of me? I've decided for now to give up the nursery school and throw myself into the music lessons I've been doing on the sly. If I can make real progress over the next month, then maybe I'll be ready to spring my

*big surprise on Hans for his birthday. I know our being closer is
the key to everything.*

*Thanks, dear J.J., for all your love and support. Keep your
fingers crossed for me, too.*

Love, Melie

J.J. put down the file, surprised that she could find no evidence of correspondence between them for a long time after
the August 15 letter, though she was certain she would have
replied to encourage Melie, despite her own misgivings. In
her mind, she always had a vague, if brief, description from
Melie about the big birthday surprise for Hans, which in no
way echoed the journal entry she later acquired.

Journal—September 30, 1968: *Disaster! Hans promised to take
two hours at least off on his birthday, and he did. I made quiche
and salad and a great German chocolate cake like the one he likes
from home and even sprang for a bottle of champagne, thinking
back to that birthday of mine so long ago. I don't mind the taste
so much anymore, not that we ever have it. After blowing out
the candles, I took him by the hand and said I wanted to give him
his gift, a surprise. I know I was thinking consciously of how he
pulled me into music when he played down in that underground
practice room in Claremont. Oh, God, what a fool to think I could
duplicate something that existed in another world, another time.
My hands too clammy, I know that, so nervous. But I took him
outside and down the street and around the block to the studio
where I've been learning, practicing all this time. I played "Claire
de Lune" for him, so badly that even thinking about it makes me
want to throw up. So much worse than I had done in practice,
because he was there, he was listening.*

*I meant to say—did I say?—how I wanted to be closer to
him, to learn his real language and that is why I wanted to learn
music. When I finished, I didn't understand why he turned red.
Because I was so awful? Because he thought I had no right to
intrude on his world in this way? Because...?*

But when he said I had got to get over this Billy thing and that working in the nursery had made me go all soft and lose my bearings (he didn't even realize I'd stopped working there), when he said, "Melanie, playing me a lullaby is a cheap trick but it won't work. You can't seduce me into having a child. Not now. Just find something else to do with yourself." When he said, "and of course you know as well as I do, it won't be music"... I can't keep writing now, for the tears

After rereading these and several other pages that said mostly the same thing, J.J. sighed and closed the file. The difference in tone between the journals and the letters hit her again. On one level, not really a surprise, she told herself. Weren't her own journals fragments, strands of unfiltered impression, emotions uninhibited by the restraining influence of reflection? Yet reworked, revisited before writing letters or polishing up pieces for publication, her words represented the best unified view of what she really thought at a particular point in time, not two disparate stories. Not like Melie's.

And another thing. Except in reference to something J.J. herself had written, in the letters Melanie never mentioned the cataclysmic events that shook the world around them. The war. The assassinations. Even in the journals, so much was never mentioned at all. The My Lai Massacre. LBJ declaring that he wouldn't run again. The Democratic Convention in Chicago. Astronauts circling the moon. Nixon, for God's sake.

"Time to go," she muttered. Grabbing her bag, turning off the light, and preparing to close the door, she stopped to turn around and retrieve the case with tapes in it, music for the long drive.

Then it hit her. Music. Where was the music in Melanie's life? Of course, she lived in a cloistered world defined by Bach, Beethoven, Shostakovich, and her own bungled Debussy. But music *was* the revolution. Where was the defiance of Jimi Hendrix, or Janice on the cover of *Rolling Stone*, Johnny Cash busting out at Folsom Prison? Where the smoky sounds of Joni Mitchell, the *cri de cœur* of Joan Baez, the sex of Lena Horne? Where the Beatles on their long psychedelic trip with Sgt. Pepper, or Dylan blasting out "Everybody must get stoned"? Or the Grateful Dead doing so at the Fillmore? Where was sultry Etta James delivering "At Last"? Where Linda Ronstadt crooning a "Long, Long Time" to the would-be governor? Where were the Stones themselves?

Backing the car out of the driveway, J.J. knew there was one stop she had to make before heading north.

"Glenview Convalescent Home, an airy contemporary structure built of redwood and tucked beneath venerable oaks with the comfortable feeling of home," J.J. said to herself in the smarmy voice of a salesman reading from a brochure. Still, she did have that familiar rush of anticipation as she approached the graded drive, the very sensation she used to have as a child approaching Gran's house knowing she would soon see Gran. Now of course, she thought, everything is strange, backward, like going down the rabbit hole with Alice. She was living in Gran's house, and Gran was living here, but sometimes the person who lived in Gran's room, in her body, wasn't really Gran at all. *From day to day, I never know. Please God, let her be "home" today,* J.J. said to herself, as if reciting a prayer. *I really need to talk to her. Even if she doesn't exactly know what I'm saying, she will understand about Melie.*

Pushing past the reception desk, she nodded briefly at the nurse in charge, and tried as usual to get to Gran by charging with her head down through the congregation of aged in wheelchairs rolling silent and nodding along polished corridors; past the blasts of sickly, antiseptic smells; and beyond the blaring mindless TV game shows, to Gran's room. Opening the door, seeing Gran's familiar rocker, bed with quilt and pillow shams, knickknacks, pictures, J.J. always found refuge. A sliver of hope.

"Chère grand-mère, c'est moi," she called out the greeting that had become their new ritual. Gran rocked rhythmically. Wearing a soft green dress, her elegant white hair brushed back, an ivory brooch at her throat, she smiled. But her great brown eyes were focused on some distant place. *Where was she?* J.J., sitting next to her stroking her hand for a silent eternity, longed to know. When at last she got the courage to leave, J.J. rose, bending to kiss Gran on the forehead.

Suddenly Gran's eyes focused on J.J. and flashed with life and humor. *"Eh bien, ma petite, bonjour."* For a moment she smiled, acknowledging her granddaughter, then she was gone again. There was no room here for a conversation about Melanie.

⟿

NOBODY HOME. THAT could be the title of my own memoir, J.J. thought as she jammed the keys in the ignition. Gran certainly wasn't there, not today anyhow. Nor her parents, who weren't actually available, either. And how to find anybody else she might want to reach—like Ivan, for instance, who could be anywhere in the universe? Or Gracie, who is at least geographically nearby—even in the same town—but for all practical purposes off in outer space, living in who knows what world? Never hear from her. Or Evelyn, of course, gone to some jungle in an obscure part of Africa. Or Eve's ex, Tom, for that matter. *He was my classmate and friend, too,* and had thought back in the day he'd go to law school; then she'd heard a rumor that he's hanging out somewhere in L.A. as a priest. If true, too weird, but no clue where he really is. *Of course there's my closest friend Jocelyn, my soulmate for God's sake,* who's even farther out of reach in the stratosphere of stardom. *Or maybe just avoiding me again.* But there was always Alice who could be counted on to have her back.

Then back to the beginning, to Melanie. Melanie who died in that fire…?

She remembered the recent call she'd made. On impulse, she'd tried dialing the Harts, and after a long period of ringing, a woman with a slight accent answered. The maid.

"Doctor and Madam are away," she said. "I think they will not be back too soon."

"Right," she said out loud, shifting gears. "M is for Melanie. M is for missing."

Chapter 8

The morning fog blew in cold over the Anderson Valley, parting enough to show a fine blue sky beyond. But J.J. knew enough not to hope. Not for clear sky on the North Coast in summer, not for actually talking to Mama Cass, let alone sighting Moon, not for anything to happen before noon when it was still only ten thirty. She also knew enough not to drive through the night and had prudently found a motel coming up 101, once again bypassing San Francisco with regret.

Still, it was no use to hurry. She needed to keep an eye out for likely places to spot hippies and their threads because that, after all, was the assignment. She marveled at the fog enveloping the grapevines, imagining the fine pinot noir growing inside the grapes like ripe purple wombs. She knew getting the wine right took time, and that despite her growing impatience, it was the same with her stories.

It was still before noon when she reached Mendocino and parked a block from Bread & Beads Café. J.J. decided to wait, watching the fog lift in strands, blowing like unruly hair, and piece by piece revealing strips of summer sky. The shape of something familiar, a battered truck, pulled in just in front of the café and the ursine figure of Moon, beard blustery in the wind, jumped out. J.J. smiled to herself. *It's a date, then*, she thought.

A minute later she was inhaling the wake-up smells of fresh-roasted coffee beans and scanning the dimly lit front room for Moon's bulbous outline. Instead, Pigeon, skinny as the broom he was clutching, stepped in front of her. "In there," he said, nodding to the back room, and she parted the bead curtain.

At first Moon, looking over the page of the *Gazette* clutched in his large paw, did not appear to see her. She approached the wooden table, cleared her throat, and said, "May I?" while sliding into a chair and catching a glimpse of the headline "Police End Investigation..."

"Help yourself, Bones," he replied, still not looking up. "I was expecting you."

"You were?"

He squinted. "God damn, girl, still not enough meat on them bones. Can't you afford a real meal now and again? What is it you do, anyway? Or is it down there in starlet-land it's just the fashion to be a matchstick? You do live down Hollywood way, don't you?"

J.J. was alternately shaking her head yes and no, happy that Moon still hadn't figured out her true profession. "So, I hadn't heard anything for a while, and I tried calling here, but you know...and I'm still trying to find her. Melanie. So why were you expecting me?"

"Well you ain't heard from me because I got nothing to report. Precisely nothing so far. Figured you'd show up any-how, since you're a hard-core curious kind of chick."

J.J. let that pass with a shrug. "Yeah, you know, it's hard to lose track of somebody you're really tight with. Like Melanie."

"Fiddle you mean, but I hear you."

"Yeah, like Fiddle. Actually, how'd she get that name, anyhow?"

"How? Don't you know? She was always fiddling, little country tunes, lullabies, and the like. Name fit right in with our theme."

"Fiddling." J.J. tried not to show her surprise. "Right. Sure. But anyway, you said there was an investigation. Police, sheriffs, you know, fuzz, all over the place. What's going on with that?"

"Like I say, nothing. They called off the dogs, Bones. One day, poof, they was all gone."

"Called it off? Why, for God's sake? There was a fire, the body of a young woman. You told me they were all over the case because they wanted to bust you for good, your whole little commune —"

At that precise moment, Pigeon burst through the beads bearing a tray with eggs, toast, muffins, jam, sausage, juice, oatmeal, jugs of milk, and coffee. While he plopped it down, Moon grabbed a piece of toast for an appetizer. "I already ordered," he said, waving the toast in the air.

"So, as I was saying, they called it off. Good news for our little extended family, don't you see? Hate them pigs snooping around. But as to the who and why, well the biggest frog in this pond that showed himself in this matter was the sheriff, but I suspect he was the lowest link on a chain. It came to a tidy close after some rich So. Cal. folks, staying up in that fancy B&B, come to town. Right soon after you was here. And once they left, the police put out a statement. See, here, you can read it for yourself in the *Gazette*."

J.J. grabbed the paper and read: "'and a forensic investigation has been inconclusive on the matter of the cause of the Hi-Diddle House fire near Little River, named for a communal farm, and on identifying a victim of that fire. With such extensive damage due to burning, no more can be done at this time about the matter,'" said Sheriff Melvin O'Reilly."

What?" J.J. sputtered. "But who, why...?"

"Girl, you're repeating yourself, you know that? Eat, eat. And you know enough to not push old Moon. Out of the goodness of my heart, I'm telling you what I know. Now as I was saying, this rich society-like couple showed up, stayed overnight, then gunned out of here in a big old black Caddie the next day. Who are they you ask? Damned if I know. Not the kind of folks I hang around with, if you get my drift. But I will tell you this, the woman, white as a stroke of sun, looked a dead ringer for Fiddle. In my opinion."

"The Harts," J.J. said to herself as much as to Moon.

"If you say so. I never heard Fiddle utter that name. Hell, we all got aliases, and maybe Fiddle more than most."

J.J. set down her coffee cup and stared at Moon for a minute, letting his last remark sink in.

"As for why? Well now, who the hell knows? And for me and my people, who the hell cares? It's not that we didn't love Fiddle, because we did, if that's who in fact died up in there. But messing around with the remains ain't going to bring her back. And if the pigs just back off and keep out of our business, that's the best news for us. And it's what Fiddle would have wanted, too. Hell, nobody would have been more on board than she would. She hated the pigs."

"Yeah, well I care. I want to know," J.J. shot back indignantly, at the same time processing what Moon had said about Fiddle hating the pigs. "She was—is—my friend, after all, my close friend."

"So fine, little lady. Go for it. Figure it all out. You can thank me for all the info on your way out." Moon shook his head like a shaggy bear. "Just mind you don't trample on our territory while you're about it, though. Having the pigs at a distance is you know, healing, if you get my drift." With that, he threw back his head and bellowed. "But before you go, Bones, would you please finish your breakfast. Damn, girl, you'll blow away in the next breeze."

"Wait, please." J.J. leaned toward Moon as he began to lift himself by pushing hard on the table. It rocked and sloshed her coffee. "I don't mean to sound unappreciative. I mean, thanks for the breakfast, Moon. I'm just a slow eater, but I want to know…" she began shoveling eggs and hash browns down in a bid for time. She was in unfamiliar territory here, trying to get information without tipping her hand as a journalist. "So how are things going for you? Up on the farm. And you mentioned Cat…"

Moon fell back onto the chair, planted himself as firmly as a tree, and warmed to the subject, rubbing his hands. "Well now that you mention it," he grinned. "Business is good on the back forty, especially with the prospects of a harvest without harassment, if you get my drift." J.J. nodded. "As for Cat, well now. She's still my Queen o' Hearts, especially since old Black Jack has split. Not that I exactly got an ace in the hole, but I'm working on it, Bones, working on it. It's complicated, you see."

"Black Jack?" J.J. nearly set her fork down then remembered she needed to keep eating. "Ace in the hole? I'm not sure I follow exactly."

"Sport—I'm talking Sport, that black cat from the city. He took off a good month ago I guess, and Cat, she's been taking more kindly to my courtesies ever since. At least she takes my calls. 'Still my Queen o' Hearts, baby,' that's what I tell her. I wouldn't say I'm back to my rightful status as her Number One Man, but I'm working on it. God damn, yes I am!"

"Could I meet her?" J.J. blurted, elated by the prospect of talking to this woman who had known Melie up to the demise of Hi-Diddle House. "I'd love to just see what she could tell me about Mel—Fiddle, that is."

Moon's shaggy head was swaying no even before she finished. "No can do. I told you, things are complicated. She's not available now, she's…it's complicated."

"How?"

"Well, for openers she's got this kid and—"

"Oh, wow, of course. When we went to find her up by—"

"Cleone," Moon interjected.

"Right. Well when you came out of that house, you said there were baby trappings. But I didn't realize it was hers." J.J. paused to take this in. "Hers and…" She looked up at Moon with the question on her face before she could even reach for the word, "yours?"

Moon narrowed his eyes in anger. "Don't even God damn think about going down that road, you hear?" And with that he rose again and marched noisily toward the bead curtain.

And J.J. knew that the reporter in her had risen blindly and wielded the blunt instrument of her questioning, as it had countless times before. She had stepped on tender, though well-defended, parts of Moon's blustery manhood. She had blown it.

Reeling from her faux pas and the extraordinary news Moon had revealed, J.J., too, headed for the hanging beads on unsteady feet, feeling the fact that she'd spent the last hour inhaling coffee and quantities of food. Pigeon stood in the door frame, a splattered white apron wrapped around his thin frame and a multicolored knit cap perched on his head. A broom still in his hand, he looked like a freeze-frame version of American Gothic, North Coast style.

Across the street the sea twirled and crashed at the bottom of plunging cliffs. On the ridge above, fog-enshrouded redwoods stood magnificent and silent. Turning from them, J.J. saw the unmistakable form of Mama Cass rounding the corner, swathed in brilliant purple and green tie-dye. *Be still my heart*, J.J. thought. Perfect. A great story, but she could hardly risk a conversation with Mama Cass about apparel without blowing her cover as a journalist.

Best to head back toward Boonville, then, where the surrounding woods crawled with "freaks," but far enough away that the folks in Mendocino wouldn't know what she was up to.

A DAY LATER J.J. was content. Her ability to sniff out a decent story when needed hadn't abandoned her. She had come away with a pretty good piece about home-spun, backwoods high fashion centered on an establishment called Billy Coats Gruff. That did leave her one story short, though, and without time to flush another out if she were to make it back to the paper by Monday.

She knew, too, that Alice had pressed her case hard with Purvis, and one angle he wanted was big city market-ing of the backwoods look. She sighed, resigning herself to Plan B—Annie, a.k.a. Mother. She pulled away from Boonville with the conflicted feelings a prospective visit to Annie's always stirred in her.

Another hope was dashed, too. Stopping by the Blue Moon Bar & Far Out Rest Stop, she entered the darkened lobby wanting to find out if Ivan was in the neighborhood. The Blue Moon's proprietor, a faux swami in an incandes-cent blue turban with a star, listened intently, shaking his head. "Sure, I know the dude in question, got no idea where that traveling man might have alighted now."

"Swami Bloomberg from the Bronx," Ivan had described him. J.J. smiled now at the memory. But the encounter passed, a fleeting sideshow. Another question burned more urgently. Why did Melanie's parents come to Mendocino to shut down the investigation of the Hi-Diddle House fire?

Chapter 9

J.J. opened the door of the yellow Datsun parked under a rose-covered trellis on Gran's narrow drive. The car seemed lost beneath layers of dust and bugs. She still felt stiff from the long ride home.

I could use another night's sleep, she thought. The car could use a wash. And she could use a better day than the one ahead. Annie, for one thing. Going to meet her at the Ark in Brentwood for another damn hippie fashion piece. Even before that, dealing with Purvis. What was it all about, anyway?

"Himself has summoned you," Alice had chirped into the phone at seven, awakening her.

"Tell him I've got a great piece in hand, and I'm closing in on the second one," she answered sleepily. Best to skip over the fact that so far this was just an interview, and with her own mother at that. "Tell him I have an interview scheduled and will be in right afterwards, okay?"

"Not okay. Do you think I'm calling from home for my own amusement? The word came down. He wants you this morning. Get your derrière into the newsroom, savvy? I'll be there on the greeting committee."

It was not yet eight a.m., full rush hour, but early still for the newsroom, where the staff tended to drift in closer to nine, or dash in just before the ten o'clock editorial meeting, or phone in any time if they were off somewhere on assignment—just as J.J. had intended to do this morning. Instead, she slipped her dirty car into its parking slot and headed for the back stairs of the *Star* building, where at least she wouldn't run into Himself prematurely. Puffing a little, she pushed beyond the fourth floor to the fifth.

Taking a deep breath, she opened the newsroom door and strode to Purvis's office. The glass door was shut. She knocked loudly.

"Yeah," the familiar voice barked.

"It's J.J.," she said pushing the door and barging inside, "you wanted to see me?" She thrust her story toward him.

They stared at each other for an instant and his hand hung in the air, suspended above the typewriter keys, then grabbed the paper. "J.J.," he said then, bursting into a wide grin. "J.J., dear, sit, sit." Purvis gestured toward the worn couch facing his desk. "We need to talk."

Thrown off stride, J.J. nearly tripped over her black leather boots before dropping gracelessly to the couch. He swiveled his chair to face her.

She noted the ashtray filled with butts and watched while he drew a cigarette from a package of Camels and struck a match. She still pictured him with his flamboyant stogie, but part of the new, reformed Bud Purvis had included renouncing cigars in favor of cigarettes—indoors at least. "So how you doing, dear?" he asked as he drew in his first inhale.

J.J. slanted her head as she watched him, trying to see if a new angle would help. "Doing? Fine I guess. The first piece on hippie threads is what I just gave you, and the second will be in shortly. I've got an interview—"

Purvis waved his hand to cut her off, as his eyes ran over her copy. "No, fine, fine. Yeah, nice job on this goat coat thing." He ripped into a hearty guffaw. At least that part of him hadn't changed. "Those wackos," he waved his cigarette around for emphasis, leaving a trail of smoke.

Then as suddenly, he stopped. "Here's the thing." He was looking straight at her. "You know those stories you were doing periodically, about those chicks you used to hang out with in Paris and whatever happened to their lives. Yadda, yadda, yadda?" J.J. nodded, round eyed. "Well, here's the deal. From time to time you know, we got letters about them from readers, see, mostly positive—I'm sure Alice showed you some of them. But now we haven't run any of those pieces for a while and I'll be damned if I'm not getting more letters, and more peculiar, asking where they are and when we're going to run some more." He shook his head slightly, bemused. "Women, God love 'em. You just never know what B.S. they're going to fall for, do you?"

He laughed as if J.J. were in on the joke. And she laughed back, reassured that the old Bud Purvis was alive and well and living in Pasadena.

"So I am thinking, right, well if that's what the ladies want, then why not have Women give it to them? We need to be respectful of our readers' wishes—or crap, what is it, women's rights—and yadda, yadda, yadda. So what I want to do, J.J., is pull you off regular assignments for a while and have you just work on these stories. A special project. Like a series, you know. Longer profiles getting into all the melodrama. Trauma, triumphs, reflections on a generation, all that B.S. You know the drill. And of course a lowdown on love life and all the juicy stuff." He paused in his soliloquy. "So what do you think, dear?"

J.J. opened her mouth, but there was a long pause before any sounds came out. "Okay, fine," she said at last, trying hard to keep from revealing her shock, not only from the "dear" bit, but from the actual impact of what he was proposing. "Uh. Well, I have tried to follow up on these women, but just sort of on my own. I mean some of them are far away, and without much time or resources —"

He cut her off again. "Oh, yeah, I forgot to mention it, but this is budgeted, too. Even for some travel."

"Well, okay, then. Great. I'll get on it. When do you want me to start?"

"Get your as —" then remembering his new improved self, he rephrased, "get on it now. The sooner the better. Your fans are languishing…" A great guffaw finished the sentence.

"Now? You mean after I finish the piece on the urban marketing of homespun clothes?" J.J. stood at last, her knees a bit wobbly.

"Nah, scratch that shit. One hippie dippy goat coat piece is more than enough. No, I mean get on it *now*."

With that, Purvis turned back to his typewriter, and J.J. left the office, quietly closing the door behind her.

She entered Alice's office without knocking. Alice's pencil-filled bun danced while she spoke into a receiver. "Yes, yes, right… Okay then. Before three o'clock then, or he'll have you for supper, got it?" Then Alice slammed down the phone.

J.J. cleared her throat. "It's me."

"How'd I guess?" Alice still didn't turn to look at her.

"So did you know about this?"

Alice swiveled abruptly, her dark eyes laughing in the corners. "Honestly, J.J., sometimes you surprise me. What the hell do you think I do around here? Who do you suppose runs this place? Here, you best have a look at these."

J.J. glanced at a folder labeled "J.J.'s Women" and stared at what appeared to be several letters.

Leaning back in her desk chair, J.J. put the extracted letters in a neat pile, then started with the one on top.

Dear Editors,

For once you have run an occasional series of something really interesting. I was fascinated to learn about the young woman at Cal Tech, and the one who became a nun, and even the movie star, who seemed like a real person instead of someone out of a Movie Magazine.

What happened to them? Surely there are others. Even your reporter J.J. Rocher seems to be among them, but we don't know her story.

As a housewife of a generation older than these young women, I'd really like to learn more. Their lives seem special, things we would hardly dream of in my time.

Karla Cook, Pasadena

Dear Mrs. Rocher,

I am a 10th grader and my social studies teacher makes us report on the news once a week. Mostly we report on World Events type things, but some of my friends and I love when you write these stories about these cool women. The teachers are always telling us we can do anything (well, most of them) but we don't actually know women like that. When I read these stories, I feel like I do.

Do you have any advice for us?

Sincerely,
Mary Mahone, Sierra Madre School for Girls, Altadena

Dear Mr. Purvis,

I want to congratulate you on running such an encouraging series on the lives of some very accomplished young women. As the father of young daughters, and a person very engaged in local civic affairs (among them as a board member of Pasadena City College) I'm always looking for other local leaders who share an enlightened view, and I assume you are one. I presume, like me, you would like to promote a vision of our city that goes beyond the Rose Parade and Bowl games.

Keep up the good work, and thanks.

Roger Clement, Vice President, Pacific Western Bank

Dear Miss Rocher,

Like me, I see you understand that its not a question if women ought to work, because we do, and we have to. Me personaly, I been working close to 30 years as a LVN, many years night shift, just trying to keep body and soul together.

But you and these friends your writing about in the paper, at first I didn't belive it, kind of like this was some fantasy land report. And I admit, it made me kinda mad. It seemed very snooty with college degrees and going to Paris and all that. Not like real people, not like real work. I mean really a scientist, then this former fancy pants lady who is now a nun in Africa, that blond movie star we see everywhere, and even you a reporter.

But then it kind of worked on me. We keep hearing about empowerment and womens rights and all that, and it came over me, maybe thats it. Not for me, I'm too old. Probly not for my daughters even, because I dont have the means. But maybe this could be real for my grandaughters. Now I like thinking about your stories.

Rita Burnett, Pasadena

After reading all the others, J.J. put her head on her desk and came back to Rita Burnett's letter again and again.

WHEN SHE SAT up, the first order of business was to call Annie and tell her she was *not* coming to Annie's Ark after all, despite phoning repeatedly to set it up. J.J. dialed her mother's number with a slight sense of foreboding. When she'd finally agreed to the story, Annie seemed actually pleased by it. She'd even said, "Well, I guess the old *Pasadena Star* is outside my client zone, God love it, but publicity is still publicity, right? Besides Violette was such a fan of that old rag, I suspect I should do it for her sake." J.J. had made the mental note that at least she had considered Violette's — Gran's — feelings in the matter, even if she hadn't acknowledged that it might be a good thing just to help out her own daughter.

"Annie's Ark, collectibles and delectables," Annie's throaty voice answered, straining a mite too hard to sound chipper.

"Hey," J.J. said breezily, trying to reply in kind, "it's me —"

"Seraphina!" Annie broke in, "wings afire!" evoking the latest annoying name she'd dragged from some mythology or other to bestow upon her daughter.

J.J. swallowed hard and let that go for the moment. "So listen," she began, then paused, trying to find the most diplomatic way to put this. "You know that editor I'm always complaining about —"

"You mean the tough old bird with the pencils in her head —"

"No, that's Alice, and she's pretty cool actually. No I mean Bud Purvis, the managing editor who bounced me out of Travel, remember, just when I was hoping to get bumped up to the front page?" J.J. paused a second, but she heard only her mother's breathing in the receiver. "The guy who bumped me down to the Women's Section."

"Jackass."

"Well he's the one who wanted me to do the story I was coming over to talk to you about, you know, 'urban marketing of homespun.'"

"You mean hippie shit. Selling very well, you know."

"Yeah. Hippie shit. Except now he's changed his mind. Now he doesn't want me to do the story, Mother." J.J. slipped the word in but Annie didn't seem to object.

"Men!" Annie snorted. It was a word that Annie kept reasserting as J.J. spoke, and for once felt she could unburden herself to her mother and have a sympathetic ear. The fact that J.J. was not going to do a story centered on Annie's shop seemed to have slipped away as a concern. What did matter was that J.J. was asserting herself as a strong female archetype over a dominating, oppressive male figurehead. J.J. couldn't get the point across exactly that now the oppressive male figurehead had just handed her the job she wanted to do most.

"Seraphina, darling, you flap those wings. Make fire." The conversation had ended on that high note. Much to her amazement, J.J. felt strangely elated.

In Alice's office again, J.J. began. "Those letters, you never showed them to me."

"I was waiting for the right moment," Alice gave her crooked smile. "This qualifies, I believe."

J.J. shook her head slightly. "So what happened to the negative ones?"

"Very few of them actually. Echoes of Himself." Alice nodded toward Purvis's door. "So nothing new. Hardly keepers. Now, we have work to do. Shall we?"

Together they made a list of next steps. J.J. left with it burning in her hand like a hot ticket. So many people to contact. Cat and that Black Jack fellow, a.k.a. Sport, when she could track them down. Hans, if she could get to him. The Harts, of course. And then the *copines*, first to let them know new stories about their lives were being requested — and then to find out anything they knew about Melanie. Jocelyn first. And Gracie, living somewhere hidden in plain view right there in Pasadena. Then Evelyn. She'd have to get a letter off to Evie right away. And Tom? She added another question mark after his name.

She dialed the Harts, but got the maid again who said they were still away. Then she tried Cal Tech to see if she could get a working number for Gracie. A chirpy-voiced secretary assured her that unless listed in the phone book, all faculty numbers were strictly confidential. J.J. made a face while writing "Go to Cal Tech," in her notebook. She'd have to get over there that very afternoon and make an end run around the administration to find her old *copine*.

Next step: Find the cub reporter who is now Alice's assistant, and ask her to look up all the reviews of Hans's music in the archives and the morgue. Then try to find Hans.

Dialing the long-distance operator for Rochester, J.J. felt suddenly giddy: *Maybe I could even go as far as New York to interview him.* "Some money for travel," Purvis had said. But then she reached the operator at the Eastman School of Music, who transferred her to the Director of Distinguished Fellows, who answered in that officious woman's voice J.J. was coming to know and loathe: "Mr. Bucher is away for the semester on tour to promote his new work while playing with various orchestras. His schedule is available locally, in the cities he is visiting... no, it is not available to me at this time. Besides, it is against university policy to give out personal information about students or faculty."

"*Salope*," J.J. muttered, hanging up in frustration, and assuming the bitchy *femme* at the other end didn't know enough French to understand the insult. "I've already had this conversation today." On her list, instead of crossing off Hans's name, J.J. wrote "Find!"

Drawing in her breath, she then turned to the address book page worn with use and scratch-outs — Jocelyn's — and dialed quickly. That annoyingly New Yorky–sounding Dana person answered, saying: "She's on retreat now, not receiving anyone. But perhaps later..."

"*Merde*," J.J. muttered, slamming the phone back in its cradle, then added "Shit!" for good measure. So Jocelyn, her sometime other half, was refusing to speak to her. The "more positive publicity" argument didn't sway her, nor did the plea "for the sake of her old friend Melanie." Selfish bitch of a big-ass movie star, billboard diva, egomaniac. J.J. began a mental list of depraved characteristics to hang around her friend's sorry neck, but stopped after only a few. The truth was, none of it was true. Something else was going on. Knowing Jocelyn as well as she did, J.J. also knew she'd find out what sooner or later.

One more contact before leaving, she decided, and began dashing out a letter on her typewriter to Evelyn, trying to include what she wanted. First of all, more information about Eve herself, her life in Africa and work in the mission. Then, the all-important questions about Melanie. She decided to hold back, for the moment, about her trip to Mendocino and its frightening implications. She simply stated: "Melanie seems to be missing. Please tell me all that you can about your encounters with her, anything at all that you know and can share. And do understand that I am so committed to finding her for the sake of friendship most of all—way more than to 'write her up.'"

She rummaged in her drawer for stamps, then pushed away, ready at last to "play reporter and expend some shoe leather," as Alice liked to say.

Stopping by her office again, J.J. shouted out, "Thanks again and I'm off."

"Wait, sit," Alice commanded as she wheeled around in her chair. "Basic information required. I was trying to piece together who, exactly, is missing. I went back through the files and read the pieces you already did on your merry band of maidens, but for the life of me, I can't figure it out."

"No," J.J. answered. "You couldn't figure it out because she's the one unwritten—except for that sketch in the overview piece and the letter she wrote. Actually, confession moment: *I* wrote it in her voice. She's been out of contact for a long time. Her name is Melanie. Melanie Hart."

Alice's eyebrows arched in alarm. "I see. So right now, in your own words, tell me: Who is Melanie Hart and why, apart from the obvious having to do with death too soon, mystery, malfeasance, and who knows, possibly murder, should I care that she may have become a heap of ashes in a druggie commune on the North Coast?"

J.J. winced at the description, knowing it well could be true. "Melanie," she began softly, looking straight into Alice's receptive dark eyes, "was the best of us. She cared passionately about the things that matter. She worked really hard, wanted desperately to know things, to do something serious, and to be taken seriously. She thought about things deeply, and seemed to live by the sayings of Pascal. You know his *Pensées*?"

Alice nodded.

"Well, long ago, before I could have told you what that was, she had a social conscience. Probably because her parents are such rich, horrible snots and—"

"I do read the society pages, too," Alice interrupted.

J.J. paused. Before her monologue ended, she had sketched a portrait. A beautiful young woman, fair haired and fair eyed beyond description, fragile appearing, but in fact strong. A young woman whose thoughts and ideas were beginning to range far, to probe the realities of poverty and injustice, but who remained conservative in dress, manner, and demeanor. Melanie of the neat suits and pearls, walking the Paris streets. Melanie the dearest and most loyal friend, who yielded her love and devotion to a man who most likely abused it—and her. A frigid train ride they had undertaken together with Melanie's coat literally freezing to the boxcar while she practiced French verbs so she wouldn't make a mistake when greeting Hans's parents in Strasbourg. The disaster of arriving with blue lips and fuzzy slippers. Melanie and Hans together, shy, blushing newlyweds at Evelyn's wedding bash, celebrating their own secret elopement. Hans's passion for music, and J.J.'s fears for Melie being swept up in it, becoming nothing more than his muse. Melie's abundant letters in those Rochester years. Her descriptions of falling for that little boy Billy, whom she so wished to take in as a foster child, and the crushing disappointment when he moved away. The desperate attempts to please Hans, by trying instead of making their own baby, to learn music for him. Of her failure, his scorn. The diminished contact over recent years, and the surprising fact that Melanie had, a few years back, sent some of her journals to J.J. "for safekeeping." Even more surprising, Ivan's find of more of Melanie's journals and letters in Boonville, and Ivan saying, "It's a sign, J.J. Melanie intended for you to have them. To write her story."

"I don't know. Maybe that's true. Maybe she's reaching out to me now and that I need to do this. I mean 'need to' in some cosmic way that has to do with the Zodiac or such like my mother's always talking about, and which I usually dismiss as crap. But maybe that's right," J.J. said, declining to add how contradictory the letters and journals seemed now. She stopped then, feeling empty.

Alice stared with unguarded warmth. "Wow. Well, okay. You best get to it." Flashing a quarter-moon smile, she turned, saying, "Tootles," and waved J.J. away.

Chapter 10

tepping out of the newsroom, J.J. dropped her letter in the mail slot, then immediately had second thoughts about what she'd said—and hadn't said—to Eve. *God, I have some nerve asking to write about her again, after what happened when the last piece came out.* J.J. cringed at the memory and decided to pull up the story again before leaving for Gracie's side of town.

She retreated to the metal cabinets that stored her files and rummaged until finding the *Pasadena Star* article under her byline from February 1973 with the appalling headline, "From Society Wife to Convent Life, a 'Shady Lady' Takes the Veil." Not her words, of course. It was unimaginable to picture Eve reading it. Then she plopped hard onto her chair to do so herself, again.

For a brief moment in time, the name of Evelyn Greene blazed in lights across the firmament of celebrity like a shooting star, and it was a name on everyone's lips. But the reasons for this blaze of publicity now many years old seem as incongruous, and as far from the reality of this remarkable woman, as her present circumstance seems surprising. Surprising certainly to those who shared her youthful, exuberant days in Paris—and in the name of full disclosure, this reporter was one of them. And surprising, too, to those who knew her as a child, the oldest daughter of Henry Richter, a Lutheran pastor, and his wife Gloria, their pride and joy and a pillar of their church youth community.

In fact "surprise" might be the operative word for the life of the woman who is now called Sister Eve, a Benedictine nun serving in a rural hospital in West Africa. For the word implies curiosity, delight and a willingness to follow whatever turns in the road ahead present themselves. At least that is what the word means to me as it is lived day to day by Evelyn, née Richter, whose married name was Greene, and who, before making a second marriage as a bride of Christ, was called "Shady Lady" by the press.

Those with an eye for scandal may remember the news accounts of 1967, although in those riotous times, such news was likely to be swiftly eclipsed. But that was the year the bright, promising, newly minted lawyer Jay Greene (some called him a JFK knock-off) ran for a vacated congressional seat as the "young, clean-cut, liberal and dynamic Democrat" in a wealthy district of West Los Angeles. Just a few months before the special election, a prominent L.A. art dealer acquired a large nude portrait in a collection from France that looked persuasively like Greene's wife Evelyn.

Indeed, it was she, as she famously told the press herself. "Yes, I had a life before I married my husband, and part of that life was lived in Paris in the company of artists. Why should I deny it?"

The uproar that ensued regarding the pastor's daughter on the loose on the Left Bank was widely reputed to have been the reason the young politician lost his first election bid. However, he had another, successful run the following year despite the scandal. By the year after that, 1969, he and Evelyn filed for divorce. It was assumed at the time that the couple split up because of ongoing revelations—or rumors—about her wild side and bohemian lifestyle in Paris.

But according to Sister Eve herself, that was not the case. "What all that horrid publicity made me realize," she told this reporter, "was that I was not really suited to a life in the limelight, nor certainly to make the kinds of choices and compromises that a career as a political wife demands. Although my life's journey to that point had taken me far from the church of my father and my upbringing, it had not led me on a path that nourishes the spirit and leads one ultimately to make peace with God. I knew then that's what I needed to do."

J.J. stopped reading and rubbed her eyes. It was a motion of dissatisfaction as much as of fatigue, common reactions when rereading her work. This story seemed particularly disjointed. The writing lacked the crisp incisive tone that these signature stories about her friends so deserved. Worse, despite vowing to the public and to herself to reveal the real lives of contemporary women in all their complexity—a middle finger raised to the puffy face of Bud Purvis, which led to her demotion—J.J. could not now read these lines without playing in her head the story not written.

Cute little phrase "bohemian lifestyle." But, really, the true story? The story of Eve running wild on her church scholarship, failing exams, dropping out of the Sorbonne, cavorting with an old count, "the perverted old prick"— Eve's term. The count who considered himself an artist and for whom she had posed nude in his freezing garret on the fashionable Île Saint-Louis in hopes of winning admission to the society ball of the season at Versailles. *Could I have written that piece*, ending with Eve's surprise, but no one else's, that the invitation to the ball had never materialized, but the portrait had?

God, I saw it myself, J.J. said softly, remembering spotting it in the window of that upscale art dealer on the Left Bank, and how she stood there, frozen and astonished at how much it looked like Eve. Later, of course, when Jocelyn heard about it and went to inquire as if she were a potential buyer, the picture had mysteriously vanished, the art dealer telling her vehemently, *"Non, non, mademoiselle…*such a picture does not exist and has never hung in this gallery."

With that, it seemed as if one potential bombshell had quietly vanished from Eve's life. But of course it hadn't. For reasons J.J. never understood, but vowed as a good journalist to investigate one day, the picture exploded on the American art scene just in time to embarrass Jay Greene and squelch his young political ambitions, at least temporarily. And briefly, his comely wife was on view in all her splendor in newspapers and magazines around the country. The most shocking thing about the whole episode, J.J. knew, was not that Mrs. Greene had once been painted in the nude, but that she had refused to deny her past.

"Yes, I had a life before I was married to my husband…" Raised-fist words to the consciousness of the new feminism.

J.J. squirmed in her chair, knowing that the back story in that episode, which she did not write, was only the beginning. From start to finish, her "in-depth" portrait of Evelyn was a study in the sins of omission. Of course she had not mentioned Tom—easy enough to justify leaving him out as an unrequited old love, in other words, not news. And under that wide umbrella, it was also easy enough to shield the reader—and Eve, to say nothing of the others involved— from the public airing of the sad story of Eve's miscarriage and the lost baby from that brief fling in France with him, her old flame. It followed logically to skip mentioning Tom's ignorance of his paternity, or Jay's surprising arrival as a suitor, and his equal ignorance of his wife's pregnancy at the time of their hasty wedding. Their entire circle of family and friends were kept in the dark, too, about the young Greenes' first wedding, that quickie in the American consulate in Nice. But as Eve had put it at the time, "I had to marry somebody, didn't I?"

Betrayal, cowardice, webs of lies, acts of God—the sordid beginnings of the Evelyn and Jay Greene story. *What should I have written of all that?*, J.J. asked herself.

And that wasn't the half of it. Of course with Jay's rising star and the appearance of the nude painting, the celebrity press—that disgusting sensationalist medium that J.J. hated—went crazy. And when the divorce was finalized a couple of years later, another feeding frenzy started at the news that the dishy redheaded bombshell, soon-to-be-ex-wife of Congressman Greene, was becoming a nun. The story that the couple had lost an infant daughter was barely a footnote.

After Jay's loss in the special election, a split had seemed almost inevitable. Gossip columns had buzzed with the rumors. But Eve and Jay vowed to try again. During the regular election cycle, the party decided to try their golden boy once more. And soon thereafter, Evelyn found herself pregnant. This time, she told J.J., she was "deliciously, unambiguously happy."

Of course, I didn't write that either, J.J. acknowledged. How could she? Could she say for all the world to read that one of her closest friends had called at one of the worst moments in her life and had said in a barely audible voice "J.J., come quickly"? And that she had sped through the familiar streets past West L.A. to Santa Monica so fast she had no memory of driving them?

Twisting in her chair, remembering, time collapsed. She was suddenly walking in the doors to the maternity ward of St. John's Hospital, taking in that smell of antiseptics that hovered in the corridors. The tiny baby girl was in an incubator and Eve, she was told, was "resting comfortably." Meaning in hospital parlance that she was knocked out with pain killers after an emergency c-section. J.J. waited patiently by her, just holding her hand until one eye opened with recognition.

Outside, nuns in black habits fluttered by like silent crows, while the nurses in white skulked like ghosts. Then Jay appeared, looking like a ghost himself. "Tell me," she began. The tall, handsome young would-be congressman with that distinctive scar across his face took her hands in his cold ones. His face, bleached with grief, said it all.

Now J.J. remembered most the look on Eve's face when she learned the news. A look that reflected a death inside, a soul death, that was as real as the small, blue body of the dead child. Even without reliving the exact details, J.J. knew that in all her life she had never experienced a thing so profoundly sad as the burial of an infant. It was as if hope, and the ongoing impulse of life itself, had been buried too. And she remembered the tombstone:

Melanie Grace,
Beloved daughter of
Jay and Evelyn Richter Greene
June 2 – June 6, 1968

There had been a lamb in a pasture beneath the engraved words, Eve's one concession to her father. But no reference to Jesus or a loving God. She had been adamant about that.

The real story, J.J. knew, was the one not written: that the main cause of Jay and Evelyn's breakup was that Jay Greene was on the fast track to becoming not a glamorous young congressman, but "a sleaze-bag politician with bags of ill-gotten money where his balls should have been." Evelyn's words. How Bud Purvis would have loved them.

Nor had J.J. revealed how it had been when Jay first left for Washington, and the promises, so dear to Eve's heart, he had made—for a community center in Watts, for expanded outreach programs for health care, for education in Spanish. He also left behind Eve, who said she needed more time to get herself together before moving to the Capitol.

During the "left behind" year, as Eve called it, J.J. recalled fondly how they had often been in touch, sometimes just with quick and cryptic phone calls at the newspaper. Or, when they could, they got together, and J.J. watched the slow, awkward dance of a marriage unraveling. Talk of the community center and the outreach program gave way to descriptions of "glitzy show-stopping fundraisers," and "playing the game." And the first hints of philandering began showing up in the gossip columns.

J.J. could even recall the sound of Eve's voice when she announced that it was over. "I could see where this was going, and I told him so. 'There were always two sides of you, Jay, one a self-centered prick who would do anything to get ahead, and one who was capable of being a genuinely introspective guy, who really wanted to do good. That was the one who I thought showed up in France—though considering what we both did to Tom, now I'm not sure—and that was the one I bet my life on. So did the American people when they elected you. Too bad we both bet wrong. You know it's just a damn shame I didn't buy the nude painting so I could have shown it off myself the second time you ran. Then maybe you would have been out of politics for good and saved everybody a lot of misery.'"

J.J. always knew that any of these stories would have made Purvis salivate, but she had resisted. Now she rested her head in her hands going over the next chapter of Eve's story, her astonishing conversion. In her own mind, J.J. still didn't know why, really, it had happened. All she did know is that after Eve's profound sorrow following the loss of the baby and the split from Jay, she had briefly sought solace in an ashram.

Her piece had summed it up this way:

> Evelyn acknowledged that the experience had awakened a deep longing in her to return to a spiritual life. She knew, too, that although she had turned away from the Lutheran Church of her childhood, she needed to find a tradition closer to her own Christian upbringing than she'd found in the Buddhist-based ashram. "I realized I wanted that profound peace, away from the disappointments and false gods of the secular world, that I had found in the contemplative life in the ashram. Suddenly, the Catholic Church came to me almost like a vision, offering me that way of life and welcoming me with open arms, like the wide-open wings of a mother superior. I could not say no."

B.S., J.J. thought, as she reviewed those words. She had written them because, as she had told Ivan at the time, "that's all I got." Briefly, she had toyed with the idea that part of the allure of the Catholic Church was born of Eve's fascination with the Kennedys. But that seemed inadequate, too. In the end, she knew she'd refrained from writing the truth about Eve's conversion because she hadn't fully understood it herself. That was, of course, before she had Melanie's journals.

Thinking of Melanie snapped J.J. back to the task at hand, and the slight feeling of nausea at just how lame her first run at writing about Eve had been. The initial elation of her unexpected new assignment was beginning to ebb. *I didn't even write half of what I knew last time, so what the hell am I going to write this time? What am I asking of her?*

Pangs of regret for all her sins of omission washed over her, and her thoughts turned to Melanie. *Will I ever find the right words to describe her? Is she, as Moon calls her "Fiddle," the fiddle-player? The angel witch-woman who had the magic? The woman who hated the pigs? The woman who had more aliases than most?*

Or would Melanie mostly remain the reflective, sensitive, inquisitive woman of the letters, who wanted to please her husband by "learning his language," and who fell in love with an artistic little boy? Or would she be eclipsed by the romantic wild child, the daring young woman who was on a hyped-up, drugged-up journey to an unknown destination and, along the way, become a seer?

"Damn," J.J. said as the thought hit her—the search for Melie had broadened. It wasn't merely *where* Melie was; it had become *who* Melie was as well.

Chapter 11

E ve sat on a rattan chair in a common room off a covered verandah. The heat was rising the way wind did back in California before a storm, and the humidity hung so thick over the town, the tin-roofed hospital, and over her own damp skin, it was like a second layer of darkness. The envelope with its bright American flag stamps rested silently on a table in front of her, while the letter from J.J. lay limp in her hand. Sister Beatrice had just handed it to her after returning in her Land Rover from the head mission in the capital, Accra. Sister Bea had laughed in her musical way, knowing that her American friend always relished mail.

"Best to read before rains come in and darkness grows, Sister Eve."

Eve had smiled broadly and then looked with some surprise at the envelope. A letter from J.J., who had not written in ages. And a letter that had arrived in only three weeks to her "bush hospital"—record time. *"Medase, medase,"* she replied, giving thanks to Sister Bea in Twi.

As she rapidly read over J.J.'s letter—and her requests—Eve closed her eyes, lost in memory. Letters always did that, bringing a sensation of connection to people and events now so far from her in space and, increasingly, time. She had been serving in this West African outpost for over eighteen months now. But suddenly she could see J.J., feel her presence. A rush of warmth overcame her. *God knows, I love her dearly*, Eve said to herself, and jumble of memories collided in her mind. J.J. had always been there when needed.

J.J., now the reporter. Something about that had never quite fit, considering her friend's love of poetry, of literature. Not that J.J. lacked curiosity and couldn't be downright nosy, but if she had wanted the sensational scoop that her own sorry life provided, it was hers for the taking. Yet J.J., who knew the inside story more than anyone else, never crossed that line.

Of course before leaving for Africa, Eve hadn't actually seen the piece J.J. wrote, but there had been no scandal fallout that she knew of. J.J. had kept the faith of friendship. Now she wanted more information, reflections of life in a Catholic mission hospital in Berekum to write another story?

But the shocking news was about Melanie. The words "gone missing" hit hard. In a way, Melanie had been missing the last time they'd seen each other, before vanishing altogether. Eve felt her gut tighten as J.J.'s understated fears augmented her own.

What can I possibly say? She bowed her head into the rising wind for an instant, to mouth a brief prayer for insight, the way Father Joseph was always instructing her to do. Then she went for paper and pen, made sure a candle was at hand, and tried to summon her thoughts.

Berekum
July 30, 1974

My dear J.J.,

Your letter got here in only three weeks and I hope mine won't take much longer to get to you.

Before answering your questions about our dear Melanie—because I'm still trying to digest this disturbing news—I guess I'll tell you briefly about my view of the world from here, since you ask. It will rain soon, and the huge banana trees shading the verandah that surrounds the hospital are beginning to sway. It's quite dark for early afternoon, with little light coming through the half-opened shutters, and I have a candle ready for the moment the electricity goes out. But I'll write as long as I can.

You would really laugh, J.J., knowing the glories of my past, to see me literally up with the chickens just before dawn and down with them too, early in the evening. Most nights anyway. But it's the way here, the tropical way, and it's always about light or the lack of it. And I often wonder, did I really come alive in Paris, "the City of Light" (I certainly thought I did at the time), or have I come alive here, rising and falling with the sun, the cries of children, the crowing of the blasted chickens, families making fires to cook for their loved ones (our patients)? The food is pungent, and full of palm oil, peanuts, and peppers, and sur- prisingly delicious.

"Is she demented?" I can see you asking now. Reply: no more than usual.

I am more out of it than usual, though, I do confess. We have a shortwave radio and sometimes get a squawky version of news from the BBC or VOA. Is the friggin' war actually over yet? You see, we really can't tell and at times it seems unbearable to be so far from "reality." Then of course, as Dr. Mensah reminds us whenever he does rounds, this is reality. And the bits of let- ters we get from home hardly fill in the blanks. Both my parents and several of my sibs do an admirable job trying to keep my spirits up with newsy stuff from home. I gather Dad is inching toward retiring as pastor. At which time my parents will fulfill their biblical destiny and actually become poor church mice. I guess I beat them to it! And can you believe it—Mrs. Greene, my ex-mother-in-law (God be praised!) actually sends me official notices of the up-and-coming young congressman's affairs. Oops, make that activities. Then Sister Marie-Claire from the convent sends me convent news and mentioned in a note that she's seen the article you did about me reprinted somewhere. But she didn't send it, and God, J.J., I'm really curious. And I can't imagine (don't dare to) what you'll turn me into next. Nothing remotely saintly, promise!

But to Melanie and your questions about her. I guess I never told you about how she visited me there in the convent a couple of times in 1969. Both times were so unexpected, but so revealing. The first time she mentioned you a lot, how you always kept in touch. So I'm surprised you've not heard from her for so long. But I'm not surprised that she began to wander, given what the marriage to Hans was becoming, and that, like all of us, she needed to find her own place in this world. And oh my God, what was coming down on those small shoulders of hers!

It was, I believe, April when she came, and I'd not been at the convent many months, so it was my novitiate year. The Church itself and the Benedictine Order were in as much turmoil as anyone in those days due to the revolution within, the fallout from Vatican II, and though nuns were no longer required to wear a habit, I chose to—trying to get into the spirit, I suppose. Or just being my usual rebellious self, who knows? Also I kept my own nickname as my religious name, since Eve was made an "irregular" saint, and I do like identifying with the original fallen woman.

Anyway, when the Prioress announced I had a visitor and gave me permission to see her (I was supposed to be mostly silent), I don't know who was more shocked. You can imagine my surprise at seeing Melie, pale as a ghost in a white parka fit for an Eskimo and boots that looked more like mukluks. If possible she turned even whiter seeing me in a black habit.

I asked, and got permission to speak and spend some time with her. I was grateful to the Prioress for letting me be with her, and for letting her stay as long as she liked in one of the cottages on the grounds. They are kind, and wise, those old nuns, and she could probably see how desperate Melie was, how important it was for us to spend those few days together. "Your work is where God calls you to go, my child," the Prioress said. Obviously that's something that stuck with me.

She and I walked long hours on a hillside covered with the hints of new spring—a few blossoms on the bare limbs of trees, a fuzz of newborn grass making its way through the winter mud, buds of brave crocuses pushing up and hoping for sun.

Briefly this is what she told me—well, perhaps you knew, surely you did!—about her attachment to that little boy Billy and her sense of loss after he went back to his parents. That's when she threw herself full speed ahead into the music thing, trying to find a new (desperate, if you ask me) way to connect with Hans. The old Eve would have called him out, loud and clear, as a bastard. But Sister Eve is still struggling with the concept of charity, so how about I call him the "alleged" bastard? Who knows, maybe there was some good motivation in his actions, some desire to do the right thing. Maybe he genuinely thought her mourning for a child she could have at best "borrowed" was unhealthy, as was her attempt to live completely then by connection to his music.

Okay, let's give him the benefit of the doubt, let's say there was some genuine husbandly concern about her state of mind. Who among us who know and love her can't say we've seen worrisome signs at times too? There could be clinical terms for it, sure, but from where I sit now, I try to see other meanings. A mystical gift, for one. Or that spirituality that leads to a touch of madness?

Whatever Hans saw, and whatever his motives, he did the one thing that must have been the ultimate betrayal—he contacted her father. The good Dr. Hart decided what she needed was electroshock therapy, and Hans cooperated by putting her on a bus to some medieval-looking mental hospital in western Pennsylvania. Along the way, she had the sense to change her ticket. Instead of going to the asylum, she headed to me and arrived unannounced in Erie, seeking asylum of a different sort.

Later, when we were walking on the hill, fending off the cold air and taking in the astonishing newness of spring, she asked repeatedly: "So how did you come to choose this path, Evie?" And I remember thinking at the time how she was like those new sprouts of growth. Her demeanor, the other-worldliness in her eyes, how perceptive yet unmoored she seemed. I was going to say in some way she'd snapped, but it's more in the sense of something in her breaking loose. She was in no way broken. I felt she was like those plants, pushing up through the mud, slowly, but would find the sun she needed and be strong and tall in the end. You know how she always quoted Pascal like some kind of sacred writ, well, one of his phrases came to me then, that she was un roseau pensant, you know that, thinking reed. Thinking deeply, bending, but never breaking.

And J.J., when she spoke about that child, and the one she longed to have, I felt for the first time I understood all those icons and images of the Madonna. It was new to me then, this Catholic perspective, and strange, yes, and very painful for reasons of my own losses that you know too well. But Melanie was luminous when she spoke of it, and I felt the holiness too. In that new yet fragile light, with the bells calling us to Vespers, I saw her as translucent, burning like a sacred candle. And for some reason I can't explain, I suddenly told her everything, all the things I'd kept locked inside me for years—Tom, the lost baby, Jay, all of it—that only Gracie and you, until I made confession, knew.

But, J.J., after I finally told all this to her, whom I had hurt so many times and in so many ways, I at last felt the release that must come before forgiveness. She said no words, yet I felt her blessing. By contrast, the confession I had made to the unseen priest in the confessional seemed so hollow, so dry.

Well of course I've gone on too long here about me, when there's so much to say about Melie and now the storm is

The last word was followed by a smudge of ink, while Eve watched the storm at last swallow the candle and turn the African afternoon into night.

Chapter 12

Saturday. Summer. As a girl, savoring those words, she would have turned over to luxuriate in more sleep. But now J.J. sat up suddenly in bed, while her most recent dream—that haunting one with the empty tomb—evaporated into the dawn. A day off merely meant more time to concentrate on her most urgent quest: finding out what had happened to Melie. But now, with more information, the trail had just become more confused. And the need to find the way forward felt more urgent.

At least, thank God, some of the leads were coming through. She rubbed her eyes and went through the mental list: Gracie, who had been on leave for a few months, had now been tracked down, and they'd see each other by summer's end, as soon as Gracie returned to Pasadena. Jocelyn's snarky "keeper" was now willing to make a direct case to the star-in-retreat herself. The maid at the Harts' said they would be back next week. The music critic for the

Star was working on finding out where Hans was performing on tour. Cheered at those bits of progress, she got up, stretched, threw on a robe, and headed for the stairs.

Switching on the hall light, she galloped downstairs, aiming for the kitchen. But a pile of mail in front of the letter slot caught her eye. In the half-dark parlor she swooped it up, then stopped to catch her breath at the envelope in her hand. Stamps with African women wearing bright cloth on their hair, carrying head-loads. Evelyn!

J.J. fingered it a long time and massaged the stamp as if in the magical way of a child she might find a secret passage, as if she might slip in between those proud women and walk in their shadows, unnoticed in the heat, and learn what she needed to know. She put on some water for tea and made toast, then sat at Gran's round kitchen table covered with oil cloth before neatly slitting open the envelope.

By the time she reached the unfinished sentence, "Well of course I've gone on too long about me, when there's so much to say about Melie and now the storm is —," J.J. was exhilarated by the riches of news and frustrated at the abrupt ending. Marveling that it was actually Evelyn who had gotten back to her first, she felt a rising elation thinking: *I've got enough here to get started on a new Evelyn piece.* Then she focused again on the revelations about Melanie.

The journals! She bounded up the stairs to the study, eager to fit what Eve had revealed into her growing chronology. What had Melie said herself about the events that Evie had shared? Pulling the files from that period, she found it puzzling, annoying really, that not only were there gaps of time in her correspondence with Melie, but missing stretches in the journals, too. Late 1968 — after the disastrous birthday "concert" for Hans — through early 1969 were among them. For the period covering the early signs of illness, the first visits to therapists, the crisis surrounding Hans's contact with Melie's father, the "prescription" of electroshock therapy, and the flight to find the cloistered Eve instead, J.J. had no record in Melanie's words.

What she did have was a small satin-covered journal with flowers along the border, now faded, which covered Melie's visit to Evelyn in the convent. She pulled that little book out and handled it gently, as if the delicacy of both form and content might disappear into a cloud of dust if misused. Book in hand, she carried it gingerly back down to the kitchen and settled again at Gran's table.

The first page did not include Melie's arrival at the convent, nor her initial meeting with Evelyn, but carried on with a narrative clearly already begun.

Journal—April 22, 1969: *Interesting to see the hyacinth pushing up through the recently frozen ground. They are such intoxicating flowers—that smell when they bloom—it's hard to place them here in a monastery when I always associate them with that poem by Baudelaire that J.J. used to recite. "L'Invitation au Voyage." The title is kind of perfect for where I am now, a voyager. Eve, too. I asked her if she knew that poem and she nodded her head vigorously. We were walking on that hill behind the little cottage where they're letting us stay, looking for daffodils.*

"Tell me about Billy," she suddenly said. It was hard at first because I think I had buried the words under everything else, but I did. Strangely, she began to cry.

Journal—April 23, 1969: *I think after vespers you're supposed to be quiet and pray. But last night, after we were each lying in our little cots, we began to talk again. Eve asked me again about Billy, this time why I thought he had mattered so much to me. I had to admit that in addition to my falling in love with his sweetness, part of it was that through him I saw a young Hans, almost a way somehow to reach and connect with the man I had married. I told her I knew that was probably crazy (even though that's a scary word for me now), and certainly immature, I mean the idea of becoming closer with a man through the* connection with the small child he was, especially a child neither one is actually even related to.

But Eve said no, it made a lot of sense really. Then she said she needed to pray and we'd talk again after breakfast. But I'm sure she was crying, silently, as I went to sleep.

Journal—April 24, 1969: Eve went out quietly for early morning prayer with the thought of not waking me. She came back with a mug of tea! Very sweet. Even though outside it clouded over and looked like rain, we started walking again, as though we were on some path or destination together, and it didn't require even deciding about. Then the morning sort of unfolded in a burst of sun, and so did the conversation, as if preordained. Babies again, our losses. I could open my heart to her, tell her everything, and sometimes she'd just stop still and look at me with those green eyes peeking out from under that hood thing. And I could see from her eyes the one thing she believed about me is that I am not crazy. She even said she thought I had holy gifts. I felt the way I do sometimes when I read Pascal and I know he is speaking right to me—lifted up, whole.

But now I know she was crying last night, because it all just leaked out of her, like rain. Of course, she said, I wanted to have a child to share in that mystical intimacy with Hans. Everyone wants that union with their mate—well not everyone, but you know—people want to connect with the past they can't see and the future they can outline through the ties of blood and family and genes. Through love. We were by then walking on wet grass, weaving around crocuses popping up, and I was focused on her feet, on those strange thick-soled sandals, and remembering her high heels, when she stopped again. The headpiece had blown off of her so she stood bare-headed, her wild red hair escaping everywhere and she just looked at me with her eyes about to spill over. She looked like a painting. "Oh, Melie," she said, "nobody understood, nobody until you came along, what it was like when my baby girl died. Melanie Grace. You never said if you liked the name. But I felt as if my hopes for a life with Jay were taken away with her life, because we had to connect *through real flesh and blood, create our own family, make that together, or we could never overcome all the lies." She said she believed it couldn't happen again, that she couldn't even think about another baby, and for a while, much of that year really, tried to make Jay's career, his ambitions to do great and noble things, enough for her too. But then she said she had to face that that was never going to happen, that Jay was going to be a sleazy politician like any other, trading on charm and good looks—and a rich family.*

It was like a stab wound when she said, "I had to face it. Losing my baby again was punishment for all the lies, what I had done to Tom. By not telling. What I had done to Jay. By not telling him, either. God was punishing me, even though I didn't believe in God, and I was furious. I even screamed. Damn it, I would have loved that child, been the best mother this side of the Virgin Mary."

Then she said she knew she had to find another way to live.

J.J. read that entry again. *So out of character for the devil-may-care Evelyn I ran off to Paris with in another life,* J.J. thought. But there was a logic to it, and Melie so clearly understood it. For Eve, there was the underlying logic of the Christian faith that she'd had been immersed in throughout childhood. In these revelations of guilt and despair and crisis lay plausible explanations beyond any J.J. had come up with for why Eve would turn away from the world. What exactly were the things were that Melie so connected to in Eve's story? Two came to mind: the loss of a child and the doomed love for a man were sorrows they shared. And to the still puzzling question as to why Eve had become a Catholic nun, the answers were there, too, jumping up from the pages of Melie's faded journal from 1969.

Journal—April 25, 1969: My last day here. Tomorrow morning early I head to the bus station again. But it has all been worth it. This is the asylum I needed. No electrodes, just Eve who is now gifted with the healer's touch. More souls in communion, hers and mine. She said I could return if I need, she's sure the Prioress will let me. So I now have security in the world again, a place to turn to. It's the real money in the bank (ha! Father, tricked you). I felt I got everything about what had brought her there, except I still didn't quite understand how she found herself in that Catholic world, which was in no way hers. So I asked, earlier today, and she just went to a cupboard and pulled out an old envelope. She said she wasn't supposed to have any personal effects from her former life around during this novitiate stage, but she'd snuck this one in. Same old Evelyn.

She handed me this fraying old newspaper article. It was about Tom, saying how the football great with all the prospects in the world was not turning pro, but rather studying to be a priest. The reporter asked him if it was not hard to give up "the world of riches, of fame, of women?," and he answered that so far riches and fame were theoretical, and that as for women, he had lost the love of his life and had no desire to find a second-hand replacement.

When I gave Evelyn back the article, she said, "I decided I wanted to be in the same place with him now, spiritually, working out our destinies together as individuals in a kind of family, even though the family never existed in the world, even though he'll never know any of this."

That revelation still had the power to "send the breath from the angels," J.J. thought, remembering Gran's old phrase. It was a lot to absorb. Evelyn, in entering her second marriage as a bride of Christ, was actually in some mystical way uniting with Tom through a life of denial and good works. And just as he never knew about the existence of their child together, he wouldn't know about this union either.

Tom, J.J. thought, wondering again where he was and what priestly name he might have acquired. And how he'd carry out his role in this invisible alliance if he knew.

There was another thing, too. In reading this journal, J.J. had come face to face with the fact that Melie succeeded in putting together all the puzzling, missing pieces in Eve's story that she, J.J., with her investigative skills, hadn't been able to. And for all that the luminous, "holy" (to use Eve's word) Melanie had to say, precious little of it had been about herself. She had just landed at Eve's nunnery, found herself welcomed for a few days' stay in a hospitality hut, and walked in the budding spring landscape with an amazing ability to pry open Eve's inner life, which Melie then poured into her journal. Of her own broken heart, of Hans, doctors, her family's meddling, of proposed horrific cures, of madness, or accusations of it, of running away from one asylum and landing in another, there was barely a mention. Nor did she say, as she wrote rather breezily of heading to the bus station, where she thought she was going.

Then, after two other uninformative entries, several pages appeared to be ripped out of the journal.

Chapter 13

E ve took the cloth from her hair and used it to wipe her forehead before stepping from the Land Rover. Back at the mission hospital after the messy trip to quell an outbreak of dysentery and all the other miserable facts of life with "her people," she was exhausted, muddy, and troubled. Her basic training as a nurse wasn't nearly enough for the task at hand. *I need to talk to Dr. Mensah about all this*, she told herself.

Parking the Land Rover on the driest ground she could find, beneath a banana tree, she plotted the best path through the mud to reach the verandah. Then glancing up, she saw the lights flickering inside the hospital. Maybe there would be enough hot water for a good scrub, and if the electricity held, she'd finish that letter to J.J. Reviewing those unexpected and most surprising visits from Melanie all those years ago had made her introspective and a shade melancholy. Especially with the news that Melanie was missing. "Where did you go, girl?" she mumbled under her breath.

June 29, 1974
Berekum

Dear J.J.,

Forgive the hiatus between letters. I intended to finish writing as soon as I had the next break with enough sunlight to write. But this is rainy season, so the storms light up often and would you believe it, it's cool and damp now. Then, best-laid intentions and all that, there was an outbreak close to the Ivory Coast border. I was the driver as well as chief medic for this one, and I won't go into the roads, breakdowns, waiting for petrol games, and many other bush adventures we endured before getting to the trouble spot. Three weeks of treating dysentery, the perennial flowering of malaria, river blindness, and a nasty tapeworm, and I'm back, eager to resume my life of relative comfort here.

Darn, J.J., but I do feel I let you down with the last bit. Please forgive me. You can see that in matters of humility and self-effacement, the supposed essentials of my trade, I am still woefully deficient.

Melanie. After that first trip to the convent in Erie in spring of '69, she made another surprise visit later in August. When I say she came back, it's true but not quite—because the person who came in August seemed like someone else altogether from the girl who had arrived like a snow angel, all white in ethereal spring.

For my part, again I didn't know she was coming, and it was a bit more awkward. The Prioress had been very indulgent the first time, but by August I was more settled into my routine, my devotions, and for the most part the discipline of silence. I actually don't know when Melie arrived and how long she had to wait, but they allowed me a visit on Sunday, after noon Mass. The first thing about Melie that time was the most obvious, her get-up. That's the best word I can find for it. She had something fringy on her legs, resembling cowboy chaps, and a knitted cotton vest over a T-shirt with an image of Jimi Hendrix on it. Her hair was long and flowing free, and if you can believe it, she was a glowing pinkish color, as if she'd been cavorting in the sun. I don't need to tell you how un-Melanie all this was. And then there was, how shall I put this? Her obliviousness. I mean she was sitting on this little hard-backed chair in a waiting room when I walked in, and she looked up at me with eyes so wide they might have been dilated, smiled, linked her arm in mine, and began talking in a monologue that was basically one way, nonstop. No hello, no explanation of how or why she had gotten there, no awareness at all that it might be difficult for me to see anybody just then. She just began talking as if we'd been interrupted in a long conversation only a minute before. And when we went out along those paths we'd walked before, now burning in the August heat, she seemed oblivious to that too. And you well know how she'd always shrunk from the sun.

I wish I had her exact words to relay to you, because they sounded so unlike her, too. But for the most part, the best I can do is to recount what she had to say. Basically she had just come from Woodstock, "a crazy, sacred mess of music" she called it, with no explanation of where she had been since I'd seen her last nor why she had gone to Woodstock. Names of musicians kept pouring out of her—Janice Joplin, Bob Dylan, Creedence Clearwater Revival, the Grateful Dead—and strange references to holy rain, holy mud, holy smokes. At the time my contact with the outside world, including the news, was very restricted, so frankly I didn't know what in holy hell she was talking about. I just knew that she was jazzed, floating, high on this transformative lovefest of music. I asked her about how she made that leap, from muse of the blond wonder boy and the rarified world of classical to this—well I have to call it as I see it—excitingly pagan rollick and frolic in the mud. But she never really answered my question, or any question actually. In some way it was as if I didn't exist, that she was talking to herself in an uncharacteristically high, fast voice. Or maybe she was talking to me in some generic sense—she kept mentioning with a kind of rapture that there had been nuns there too, in habits.

And of course the music wasn't all. I don't know what you know about this whole escapade, but she went on and on about a certain John C. Calhoun (can you believe that name?) and how he, also, was a "lost star of the North" who had ended up at Woodstock by magnetic pull and no particular forethought, *just like her. The draw was music. I remember having this vision of John C. as the strong, quiet, deep type—also like her, really, or how she had always been before she got "fringy." Unlike her, though, he actually played music—the clarinet. He came from Chicago, and Woodstock was a detour ("fate," Melie called it) on his way to the South. Going to do God's work, civil rights that is, rather like your Guy...*

Chapter 14

Fumbling with the door key while carrying a disorganized pile of debris from the car, J.J. glanced down at an envelope stuck in the mail slot. African women dancing on stamps! Her heart soared. An interview with the Harts tomorrow, and more news from Eve now.

Slumping onto the porch swing next to one of Gran's enormous potted plants, she began reading.

Dark had settled over the house. Shadows from the full leaves of summer that kept it cool also blocked the sun as it began to slant westward. J.J. finally finished all of Eve's letter. She could barely digest the details. Life in a damp rainforest doing unimaginable and heroic work. Then, the impact of Eve's description of a frenetic, eccentric Melanie in some kind of altered state followed by the surprisingly painful reference, so casually made, to Guy, now commingled in Eve's mind with the mysterious John C. Calhoun who went South to do battle for racial justice. Her letter had filled in much of the puzzle of that long-ago summer.

J.J. pushed the old-fashioned light button to illuminate the stairs and vanquish the shadows, before returning to the desk with the Melanie files and journals again.

She set Eve's letter next to Melie's papers from the same summer, putting them in chronological order. After the initial journal entries from Melie's first trip to the convent in April 1969, there was nothing until Woodstock, and not much of that.

Journal—August 13, 1969: Sure it's the right decision. Bus ride long, but hell I can do buses. Oh, do I do buses. My means of transportation, my escape vehicle like those far-out landers on the moon. Moon dust. I'll be kicking some up soon, hoofing it to the scene at the end of this line. Moon. Soon. Hoof. Croooon. Ha!

Journal—August 16, 1969: Oh my. That was a long one. More buses in my future I guess. Hippie girl buses all painted in sunflowers. To keep me warm. Lucky I came early though. I didn't have to suck too much dust on the road. Tomorrow they may have to walk 20 miles. Now I've got my patch of grass and the sun do shine. Somebody said that. Luckily I brought my umbrella, just to keep the sun off. Even so I feel the heat and everything dancing in front of my eyes. Twirling. So many people, all young, babies even, but I can't think about that. Colors, like rainbow, skirts, shirts, skin too. And noise. Calls and shouts or was that gospel? Motorcycles—don't like them. Sound equipment squeaks and buzz saws building stuff. Sleep now. Should have brought a tent.

Journal—August 17, 1969: When I fell asleep on my piece of grass, there were plenty of spaces around here. Then I woke up, in a sort of tent and inside one wave of a sea, all people. The tent, or canvas, kind of strung up over me on some poles, made me safe. J.C. meant for it to just make me safe from the sun. But

I needed protection from the wave. "Hey, lady," he said when he poked his head inside. "You OK, now? You looked like you were going to fry." J.C. just moved into this spot next to me with his motorbike so he brought a lot of stuff and had the extra canvas, just in case, he said. He's got short curly hair with a red headband and he wears glasses, just like me. He's shy like me and came here for the music, not the scene. Like me, likes books... Asked me if I'm a musician. I said "yes, but only in spirit." He said "cool" and pulled out a clarinet.

Journal—August 18, 1969: Can't talk about the music last night, it's too loud in my head. Everything too loud in my head. J.C. bigger than the sun. Or is that the night? I think I did some things, but I'm always too close to my dreams. So did I or didn't I? Smoke too. I think I went to the moon.

Journal—August 22, 1969: J.C. my hero, like a knight on the black horse. I think I didn't used to like motorbikes, but when he carried me away on his, I felt like a girl in a fairy tale rescued to safety. First the tent to keep off the sun, then the rains, oh god the rains. When we left it was a world of mud and all those human waves only riptides, flowing slowly like this, like that, stuck at the feet. The wave was too much, the people, J.C. could see that, could see I would drown. Took me away. But I remember Richie Havens, so cool, so good. Like J.C. but old. When he sang "Motherless Child" I felt my insides turn around. Then J.C. started singing that Bert Sommer's song "Jennifer," about a woman you'd handle with care. Said it was his favorite. Then the rivers started flowing from my eyes. It all came to me, from me, even the mud. There was something of me in that song. Maybe more than in Hans's symphony even. Did I tell J.C. about the symphony? Just tears and I can't remember.

Puzzled, J.J. realized these were the only journal pages from August. Why? The only other thing she had from Melanie for that period was a postcard showing farmlands and a barn with a caption: *Bethel. Life in rural New York,* written, she noted, on the same day as the last journal entry.

Aug. 22, 1969

Dear J.J.

It's been 2 days now since it's over and I've had a hot shower, but was worth the rain & mud & all to hear such music. Not felt this way since walking in fields of stars in Paris, with Pascal. Among the greats I was a musician at last. No, I was music, not just its inspiration. New refrains. So long piano lessons. No need. New friend.

Love, Melie

Now she appeared to be a muse of another kind, for a clarinet-playing Pied Piper named J.C. J.J. observed again, with more scrutiny this time, the way the signature curved along the side of the message, leaving room for the row of hearts and flowers and musical notes along the border. Like a little girl, J.J. thought. Or a motherless child. And she had not mentioned J.C. even by initial. Nor Hans, of course, except to allude to the symphony he was writing using her as his muse.

Determined to get a grip on these colliding images, J.J. drew out a new sheet of paper. Chronology '68–'69 she wrote across the top. Under '68 she made a note saying, "muse, Hans's symphony." For '69 she added, "Woodstock, muse for J.C."

Then she returned to Eve's letter, the part in which Eve asked the questions about where Hans was in all this and what turn the relationship between him and Melanie had taken over that summer. On the first read-through, J.J. had stopped cold at the mention of Guy. Now on second and third, she stopped cold there as well.

Chapter 15

J.J. pulled into the circular drive of the Harts' faux plantation-style house in the shadow of the graceful Colorado Street Bridge that crossed the arroyo near the Rose Bowl. Suicide Bridge, some called it.

Pushing that thought from her mind, she straightened the skirt of her gray cotton suit, smoothed her pastel pink blouse, and rubbed the toes of her low-heeled gray pumps against the back of her legs to wipe off any extraneous dust. On the one hand, it was good to have a reporter's notebook in hand again and a small tape recorder in her bag. At least now she didn't have to skulk around about who she was. On the other hand, images of these people, the Harts, skittered across her memory from college days when they descended—or condescended, as Eve would say—upon Melie and her band of friends. J.J. remembered the Harts well. Cold, superior, often cutting in their remarks, and way too well dressed. Especially Mrs. Hart.

As for Dr. Hart, he'd rather hung in the background like a gray cloud.

Reaching for the brass knocker, J.J. felt her gut tighten. She was prepared to think the worst—close to original sin for a journalist.

The knocker reverberated in her hand, and the door opened wide. The maid silently ushered J.J. past a formal living room to a sunlit enclosed porch, or lanai, as they called it these days. "Just a moment, Dr. and Missus will be right with you," the maid said and left, her black uniform disappearing into the darkened rooms behind her. Sitting in a comfortable wicker chair, J.J. wondered. Was the setting, the calculated wait, designed to put her at ease, or to intimidate?

Claire Hart entered the light-filled room. Her white-blonde hair was as remembered, pulled back in a perfect chignon, and the casual summer dress was her signature celery color, Espadrille shoes on rope heels to match. J.J. lifted herself awkwardly to take the hand Claire extended and to look into those bottomless blue eyes. She felt she was seeing Melanie, only older. Older too than Claire Hart the last time they'd met. Despite the exquisite care she took of herself, makeup couldn't conceal all the shadows on her face. The effects, perhaps, of sorrow?

"J.J., how delightful to see you." Her tone was well-polished warmth. "It's been too long. Sit, please and just make yourself comfortable. Adele will bring some tea."

J.J. sat, running through the options of how to play this. Old friend? Casual interviewer to garner a few facts for local paper? Investigative journalist? "Yes, it has been a long time, and I appreciate your agreeing to see me. I was hoping, too, I might be able to see Dr. Hart. Will he be able to join us?"

"Oh yes. He'll be along soon." Mrs. Hart paused while Adele placed a large tray with tea and a plate of cookies on the low table in front of J.J. The tea afforded another moment of delay before figuring out how to jump in. She laid her notebook on the table next to the teacup for a moment and decided on a wide-open beginning.

"As you know, Mrs. Hart, I've been working on the local paper, the *Pasadena Star*, for a number of years—"

"Oh yes, we do know and are always so proud to read your columns. To think that one of Melanie's close friends has become so prominent!"

"Well, thank you, but I'm hardly...still making my way in the profession, I guess. But I have been working on a little project, using the group of us who went to France together as the basis for individual profiles, a kind of study of what paths we've taken in the decade since, and I wanted to follow—"

Claire Hart interrupted again. "Oh yes, and marvelous stories they are too. And my, that Jocelyn, isn't she something? As glittering a star as any from the Golden Age I'd say. Simply a wonder."

"Yes," J.J. answered, hoping that the Jocelyn genie would go back in the bottle before it came all the way out and took over the room. "But I'm here because I need some more information on Melanie. I've, well, I've rather lost touch with her..."

"Yes, yes," Mrs. Hart replied in a low voice and a look in her eyes that made her appear to have left the room. "Well sometimes she is hard, you know, to keep up with. She moved East, don't you know?"

"Yes, to Rochester when she married Hans. We used to correspond rather regularly, but then, I don't know, I seem to have lost track and wanted to fill in some gaps from you."

"Ah, Hans," Mrs. Hart replied. "Brilliant young man, so gifted in music, don't you think?"

J.J. picked up her notebook and began writing down what Claire Hart said, while remembering the cracks from a dozen years before about the "pale little Belgian" and how quaint it was to have a classical musician in the house.

"Yes," J.J. replied. "A brilliant musician. Have you heard from him recently?"

While talking, J.J. also pulled out her tape recorder and announced, "I'd just like to have this on for backup and to make sure I'm accurate, if you don't mind."

Claire Hart seemed to pay no attention. "I guess it's been some time since we heard from him, but," she brightened and turned her smile on J.J., "he seems to have done quite well for himself with that symphony he wrote. Based on Melanie, don't you know? Whatever that means. But my, the reviews have been quite excellent, haven't they? Even all the way out here."

"So what about Melanie? When were you last been in touch with her?"

"That's what we were hoping to learn from you, J.J.," a man's voice intervened. She looked up, startled to realize that Charles Hart had slipped in the room and stood in the corner opposite his wife, a stealthy presence in a gray suit.

"Dr. Hart," J.J. nodded and started to rise, but he waved her back into her chair. "We don't do press," he said, filling the room like a dark cloud. "Never. Except of course for charity purposes."

J.J.'s interior file cabinet suddenly flipped through all the society clips she remembered of them, many shown to her by Melanie. "Well," she responded, "in that regard I guess I wear two hats. Press, but also friend. As you know, she was — is — my dear friend." J.J. swallowed, trying not to let her fears about the fire at the Hi-Diddle intervene now. "I'd just like very much to get in touch with her."

J.J. observed both Harts carefully to see their reactions. Claire stared at the window vacantly, trying to mask a wave of sadness, while Charles's eyes bore down at her, turning the color of stainless steel.

"Yes. Well, so would we. You must realize—and please understand that this conversation is strictly off the record as you say, and any attempt to breach that accord would be a game, if not a career, changer, I'm sure you grasp my meaning—so if you must know, we don't know where she is..." He paused long enough to see if J.J. registered the threat. If so, she gave no sign of it. "Thank God she survived the year of living on her own in Paris without going off the rails—I was *very* opposed to that uproarious caper you all pulled, and for the record, whoever put that idea into her head is really the one responsible for this mess. Radicals, dissidents, drinking, free love, to say nothing of those crazy French intellectuals," he paused to give into a moment's shudder. "Some girls, I suppose, are sophisticated or strong willed enough to survive such an assault without permanent damage, but Melanie was fragile, easily influenced... and if you have to know, she never really came back to us. Not as the agreeable child we had raised, not as a member of this family. We should never have agreed to that French non-sense, wouldn't have either, but it seemed the only way at the time to get her away from that Moonlight Sonata lover boy whose parents speak German for God's sake—"

"Well, they did end up getting married, you know," his wife interrupted.

"Yes, Claire, I know they did. Without the courtesy of even informing us of course, without so much—"

"Well you did tell them you never wanted to see him again, dear, and her either if she was still attached to him."

"For God's sake, Claire, this is hardly the time to get into all that ancient history." Charles rolled his right hand into a fist and tapped it rhythmically into his left palm. "The point is that, surprisingly, even that ill-conceived match seemed to be going well enough, but after a few years she really did begin to go off the rails, seriously. Got into all this political ballyhoo, ran off to music festivals, mixed with radicals and all that sort, and left the poor old boy rather out in the cold I gather, and well, despite all our efforts, she just cut us off. We've not heard from her for—"

"But he did do rather well for himself after all, don't you know?" Claire cut in.

"Who?" Charles snapped.

"Why, Hans. Our son-in-law. He's turning out to be quite prominent in music circles, Charles. I've read it in all the papers."

Her husband waved her away with his unfisted hand. "So that's why we agreed to see you. Since you snoop for a living, we thought maybe you had some information you could share with us."

"Well," J.J. answered, setting her pen down while she looked up into Charles Hart's eyes, seeing if she could penetrate them, "that's why I'm conducting interviews with everyone I can who knew...knows her. I'm trying to find out where she is. I haven't actually seen her for years, but she did keep in touch with me through those Rochester days, and then just sporadically after that. A postcard here or there."

"You let us know when you find her, won't you?" Claire's vacant blue eyes seemed filled now with something, maybe the remnants of life. "We'd just like her to come home." A strand of perfect blonde hair fell away willfully from the chignon as her lip quivered silently.

"If I find her, I'll certainly be in touch," J.J. answered, then turned to Charles who still stood in the center of the light-filled lanai like a statue in a park. "But I'd like to ask you what you were doing in Mendocino lately. Or rather why, as I was informed, you went up to halt an investigation into remains supposedly found in that unfortunate fire last fall on the Hi-Diddle property off the road from Little River?"

"My God you are a snoop, aren't you? The worst sort," Charles said, his steely face turned white as he at last dropped into a cushioned wicker chair. "If you got that far then you must know that, well, there were *rumors* that someone resembling Melanie was found in that god-forsaken rat hole, and then when the thing burned down, *rumors* went around that a body was," he halted a moment to inhale, "was found. Or the remains of one. A young woman they said." He looked up at J.J. now. "Well in our position, we have to be very careful of rumors. They can be ruinous, you know, and we simply needed to put an end to them. Whoever that...unfortunate soul was, it was not our Melanie."

"Oh, no, not Melanie," Claire added.

J.J. gave a nod of recognition to the unfortunate maid, Adele, who held the door for her as she left the house, shaking slightly, to go down the steps bordered by plantation-style columns. Adele was the one person there she felt she could understand and connect to, in lieu of Melie. Poor Melie.

Gunning the car in reverse, J.J. felt her head swimming. This time it wasn't from the presentiment of head-ache, but with facts, which were collecting in her mind. The Harts didn't have a clue where their daughter was and hadn't actually seen her for years, although J.J. had not been able to pry out of them how long it had been exactly. She didn't know, either, how long it had been since Melie had actually communicated with them directly. They had been extremely skillful about evading what they wished to evade. But one thing was clear: they meant to control Melie's story. "Rumors" obviously would be anything that contradicted their version of who "our Melanie" was. And how in the hell had they heard rumors anyway that had con-nected Melie to Hi-Diddle House and the fire?

"Shit," J.J. said to herself. Instead of finding coopera-tion, she'd stepped into a new front in an escalating war on the truth.

Switching on the radio for distraction, she heard a sonorous voice announce breaking news: "President Richard M. Nixon has just resigned."

Chapter 16

J.J. held the receiver in her hand, ready to call Alice. After a night of sleeping badly—"monkey mind," Annie would say—it was still early, and dawn light was just lifting from the spreading avocado tree. The jays were still making a racket from the branches, too. "Damn birds," she muttered. She began dialing, trying to push away the disturbing thoughts that had crept up on her after meeting with the Harts.

"So Alice," she began, overdoing the chipper tone a bit, "I know you—well *he*—wants me to get going on the pieces about "les girls" as you call them, so I was thinking about hiding out here to start on the Sister Eve piece this morning. No distractions. I'll show up after lunch. What do you think?" She jumped into her monologue before Alice could say more than a brisk hello.

"You're becoming so sensible lately, I hardly know what to make of it. Yes, time to feed the beast, ever hungry for copy. See you then. Tootles." Alice hung up.

J.J. went to the den and plopped down hard in front of the typewriter. Forty-five minutes later, she was still trying to figure her way into the Eve in Africa story. Eve the dishy redhead, former celebrity, ex-wife of a congressman. Sister Eve a habit-wearing nun, healing the sick and impoverished in some jungle hell-hole. Then again, was it a hell-hole, really? Eve's descriptions sounded lyrical, exotic. And was she actually wearing a habit these days? J.J. didn't know and began a long list of "verify" questions. Still, she couldn't find her lede.

Agitated, images of Annie doing a little "monkey mind" jig kept popping into J.J.'s head. She let her thoughts drift, imagining an unannounced visit to her mother's house, always half invisible in the shifting light of the deep canyon of oak and sycamore. She could see herself banging the knocker on the front door, waiting to be let in. That's what it always felt like calling at that replacement house for the one that burned. Waiting to be let in, then not sure she wanted to go there, into the garage sale ambience of its weird and jarring collections.

"Stepping inside is like tripping with the Stones singing 'Paint It Black' with Ravi Shankar background notes," she'd once complained to Jocelyn.

But Jocelyn had countered that it wasn't really the décor that bothered her. "So many conflicting memories, so many emotional split ends," Jocelyn said, referring to the days when J.J. had lived there off and on after college, shuffling meaningless romances in and out, and the many times with Guy when… J.J. shut it down right there.

But she couldn't shut out Alice, whose voice began ringing in her ears. What was it she'd said to Alice anyway? She couldn't remember the subject of her rant about Annie just then. But she could remember Alice's even, insistent, maddeningly wise tone. "You know, J.J., at some point we can't go on blaming our mothers for our lives."

IT WAS LATE morning when J.J. pulled into the oval drive of the Glenview Convalescent Hospital. *Please God, let her be "home," let her know that it's me, let her be happy to see me. Let something go right before I show up empty-handed at my desk.*

Inside the hospital foyer, decorated with the depressing faux homey look of a funeral parlor, she slipped in quickly, as always, and made a beeline to Gran's room. But at the end of the polished linoleum corridor, a nurse stepped up. "Oh, Miss Rocher," the woman called out. "Please, I need to speak to you."

J.J. stopped in her tracks.

"It's not advisable that you go in your grand-mum's room just now."

J.J. stared, not moving.

"Yes. Well, yesterday she had an episode—a seizure we believed. We thought it best if she went to the hospital to be checked out. Your mother came. She accompanied Grand-mum to the hospital and stayed there the night. Grand-mum just came back to us this morning, but she's sleeping now. Sleep's the best medicine for her just now." The nurse smiled. *Treacle*, J.J. thought, *the color of my car.*

"Hospital? Episode? So how is she? Is she going to be okay? Can she—"

The nurse interrupted. "Grand-mum recovered quite nicely, and the doctors tell us there aren't likely to be any changes in her from this episode that they can determine. We're taking what precautions we can against other problems in the future."

J.J. nodded and spun abruptly on the shiny linoleum, heading for the door.

Closing her eyes a moment, she slid back behind the wheel. The only piece of this news that she could take in at the moment was that Gran had been in trouble and she hadn't known. *Why the hell didn't Mother tell me?* She felt anger against her mother rising again. But being pissed at Annie for not calling in the middle of the night to say Gran was having trouble wasn't really a punishable offense, and she knew it.

Better leave it alone, she told herself, *before I have to hear Alice telling me what I already know.* That at least Annie was there for Gran. *That may be my problem — I just wanted it to be me.*

The Datsun knew its own way to the *Star* building.

———

J.J. SLIPPED TO her desk shortly after one, eager to get to work. Everyone was preoccupied by the fallout of Nixon's resignation and the new President Ford. Happy for the distraction, she found her way out of misery and into her story at last.

> The air is heavy with heat, the scent of hibiscus, wild flowering vines, and the colorful trill of tropical birds, when Sister Eve (Evelyn Richter Greene) first slips her feet into rubber-soled sandals. She throws open the shutters on a dawn still wet with night rain and glances down at the verandah. It is already filling with the ailing and their families, some crouching over small burners cooking breakfast, waiting for the hospital doors to open at 8:00.

She paused before beginning on the second 'graph — a brief review of the high points of the "shady lady's" life before taking the veil. If that was the operative term. And did she wear those rubber-soled sandals? J.J. added that to her "verify" list.

Then she noticed the note on her desk from Annie: "Didn't want to disturb you in the middle of the night, but

Violette had what they think was a seizure last night and was rushed to the hospital. They gave her some drugs and she came through fine and she returned to Glenview this morning. I went and spent the night by her side. She looked up at me, called out your name, and smiled. All is OK for the moment. Call when you can. And be well, Seraphina."

Before she could finish dialing Annie's number, Alice came to her desk. J.J. paused, uncertain, as Alice smiled, glasses down on her nose. "Hard at it, I see." Then, noticing the note in J.J.'s hand said: "The receptionist put your mother through to me when you were out. I told her I knew you'd be very relieved that she'd been with Gran. It seemed pretty thoughtful of her, not wanting to wake you in the middle of the night, no?"

J.J. nodded, hoping the sensation of burning cheeks didn't actually show.

"So, how's it going?" Alice continued.

"Ah, great, all things considered," J.J. smiled back, not saying that so far she had written exactly one paragraph.

"Well, this just in," Alice put a piece of paper on the desk. "From my assistant."

Alice vanished, and J.J. read the press release: "Hans Bucher, rising young composer on leave from the Eastman School of Music in Rochester, N.Y., will be performing with the Pasadena Orchestra and Youth Symphony at the Pasadena Civic Auditorium on August 29. For tickets and information, call…" J.J. hurriedly read the rest and copied the phone number, making a mental note to call right after calling Annie. Then she finished a draft of the Evelyn story.

It was late afternoon when the phone rang, 5:07, she noted—and too damn late to call the box office.

"Pick up on line 3, J.J. A Mrs. Hart for you."

J.J. took a deep breath, then punched the line.

"J.J., this is Claire Hart speaking."

"Yes. A pleasure to hear from you. How—"

"Perhaps you've heard, Hans will be performing on the 29th at the Civic Auditorium. Well, I'm sure your paper will be covering it. Should be quite an event, don't you know?"

"Yes."

"Well, Charles and I have season tickets, but he's away for a couple of weeks. Medical convention. Of course, we'd be going to the reception afterwards, and I thought that perhaps you'd like to go along with me."

J.J. barely remembered the rest of the conversation. Her heart raced as she hung up.

Chapter 17

J.J. lifted the knocker.

Claire Hart opened the door. Regal in a satin mid-calf dress—"barely mint" J.J. guessed the fashion writers would call it—Claire gestured graciously before saying: "Come in. So good of you to join me. You look wonderful, dear."

"Thank you," J.J. replied, making note of the word "dear." The very word Bud Purvis had used when making his surprising offer. She also took in Claire's perfect chignon, her triple strand of pearls with earrings to match, and shoes the same color as the dress. So like Melanie might have been. In the fading light Claire looked much younger than she had the last time, almost as J.J. remembered her from those college years. But now with the hard edges worn off. Make a note of that when the notebook comes out, she told herself.

"Do sit for a moment, we have plenty of time," Claire said, leading her to the formal living room. "Adele's off now. May I get you something to drink?"

"Tea would be lovely, or juice if that's too much trouble."

"No wine, then? I do remember when Melanie came back from that Paris trip she did love her wine. Very French, don't you know?"

"Yes," J.J. smiled. "Very. But not for me just now, thank you. I'm working—that is, I'm going to write up a little something about the program. Best be alert."

"Tea, then. I'll just be a minute." Claire Hart beamed in a way that J.J. couldn't remember seeing.

Pulling out her notebook to jot down a few notes, she looked carefully around the room, taking in as much as she could. Suddenly, a flash of blond hair caught her eye and she watched as a slim young woman dashed down the hall, a figure so like Melie that she skipped a breath before calling out.

"Hey, hello."

The figure stopped and turned around, slowly entering the room, a mirror image of Melie as she'd been at twenty-one or twenty-two. Except this young woman wore a black turtleneck and black trousers and had exaggerated black make-up ringing her eyes. Her lips were almost colorless.

"You must be...well, you look so much like Melanie, for a moment I thought you..."

The young woman sneered, sat down on the wooden stair into the living room, and stared at J.J.

J.J. stood. "I'm an old friend of Melie's. You must be her sister. Anyway, I'm—"

"I know who you are. J.J. The reporter." She refused J.J.'s outstretched hand.

"Yes. Well as you probably know your mother kindly invited me to use your father's ticket for—"

"Yeah, I know. I only hang around here when the old man's gone."

J.J. nodded. "We're going to see your brother-in-law, Hans, perform."

"That prick."

"Really? What's wrong with Hans?"

Melanie's sister rolled her eyes. "Oh my God. Nothing much. Only he's a selfish, pompous bastard who stole my sister's name for some stupid composition and would have happily let her rot in some loony bin, with our dear father's help of course, if she hadn't been smart enough to escape."

"Wow. I see," J.J. answered. "Do you know where she escaped to? Where she is?"

The girl looked straight at J.J. through the black rings of her eyes, the blue ice color of Melanie's on a winter day. "You're the girl genius reporter. I thought that's what you were supposed to figure out."

J.J. sat back down. Claire turned the corner just at that moment, carrying a tray with tea.

"Oh, I see you've met Natalie," she smiled again at J.J. "She's a drama student, aren't you dear? A very first-rate program right here at Pasadena City College. Many of the students even perform in the Rose Parade, don't you know?"

Natalie quickly stood, rolling her eyes again. "Yeah, we met. Well, I've gotta split now. See you later." She bolted down the hall.

⟿

THE STATELY STONE Civic Center with the ornate blue décor over the windows always reminded J.J. of something exotic, like a scene from *A Thousand and One Nights* or *Scheherazade*. As a child, stepping inside the painted, vaulted corridors had always made her think she was entering a sultan's palace. When Gran used to bring her there.

She drew in her breath. Everything Natalie had said reinforced the view she already had of Hans—the one Evelyn in her more saintly frame of mind had tried to refrain from expressing. By the time she and Claire had been shown to their seats, she was eager to be embraced by the darkness that would come when the music started.

But Hans would not appear until the second half. She strained to scrutinize him, unprepared for that first glimpse: the graceful figure in the black and white regalia of formal tails; the white-blonde hair falling in an appealing shock over his forehead. Where does the evil lurk? she wondered.

Following an effusive introduction, Hans turned to bow toward the audience, and J.J. gazed into the spotlight. She could see clearly but read nothing. He is what he always was, she told herself, a blank.

Then that familiar, accented English. "I am happy to be able to perform for you the prelude and first movement of my new symphonic work entitled *Symphony in G for Melanie.*" He lifted his baton.

J.J. closed her eyes to listen. With flutes and tambourines and the sweet strain of violin, Hans' trademark, she allowed herself to be transported to another place. She could see Melanie, a child dancing in a meadow, her flaxen hair flying in the wind, wildflowers bending to her to be picked. With the violin playing Melanie's voice, it was the unfettered sound of a child's laugh.

Then the first movement. The full orchestra came in, but the refrain of a carefree, laughing girl still rippled through. J.J. followed her until her sound ripened and she moved into a harmonic duet with her lover. The dance became their pas de deux, the rapture and retreat, the call and response with flute and violin, until the tension built, drums pounded their rhythms, cymbals crashed on cue, and the first love-making took place with a dizzying crescendo.

Grateful for the dark, J.J. felt her pulse quicken as her breath came fast. The passion, the adoration, this is not what she had expected from the cool, politely formal Hans. Nor the intense moment of first love, which played over that description from Melie's journal that had left such an indelible impression. It had been her twenty-first birthday. He had toasted her, said her name *Mel-an-ee* in his peculiar way, called her an angel, and played for her on a guitar the thin sketch of what he called "Song for Melanie."

Afterwards, after they had made love, she had written: "…I don't even know the words for my feelings. It must be happiness. But so strange, too, I don't know, like bitter chocolate, with a taste of sadness."

J.J. had sketched in the rest for herself. Melanie bleeding and unfulfilled, sad that imagined ecstasy had not been hers. That was Melanie's truth. Now she had heard Hans's.

The lights came on, the audience stood to cheer the young composer, and J.J. stood, too, looking for clues to the feelings of Claire Hart. But her tight smile was unyielding. Was she reacting to the passionate version of her daughter that had just reverberated through the music hall, or to the swell of approval that washed over Hans, her son-in-law?

Leaving the concert hall, J.J. led Claire Hart to the head of the receiving line in the ornate reception room, then quietly moved toward the end. "No, no, family should be right up at the beginning," she said, gently guiding Claire by the elbow. "Press always comes in at the end," she lied, "and as you know I'm going to write up a little description of this." Claire nodded, ready to bask in the reflected glory Hans would bestow, and J.J. slipped away. Nursing a glass of champagne, she relished a chance to think. Best to have my own moment, she thought, alone with Hans at the end.

Stepping in front of him at last, J.J. remembered to have her best reporter's armor on, steeled for whatever came—lack of recognition, hostility, anger—anything.

Finally seeing, Hans burst into a wide smile and grabbed her free hand. "Oh my God, J.J., it's you! How wonderful. I never imagined…"

She smiled back, flustered for a moment. "Of course. I live here. I couldn't miss it. Anyway, I wear two hats—reporter for the local paper—perhaps you know? And, of course, friend."

His hand still clutched hers.

"Hans, I know your schedule is very tight, well nearly impossible to follow actually, because I've tried. But I'd really like to talk to you. Is there any chance — "

"Yes, of course. We're in luck. Tomorrow's Sunday and I have the day off, before we go on to Portland."

"Perfect. Tell me where, and — "

He interrupted her again. "Afternoon, all right? I'm having dinner with the Harts in the evening, and have some, well, some other plans before. But maybe three o'clock? How about at Huntington Hotel on Oak Knoll, you remember?"

"Of course," she answered, surprised at his choice. The site of Evelyn and Jay's infamous wedding party, where he and Melanie had secretly celebrated their own.

"Outside by the pool, is it okay?" Hans looked at her intently, as if searching for something. "But just one hat, okay? Friend only please."

J.J. nodded. "Of course."

DRIVING BACK TO the Hart's house, Claire seemed somewhere else. Useless, J.J. realized, to attempt any conversation. Maybe Claire was now lost in the idea of Hans coming to dinner. Still, it was a rare chance to speak to Claire by herself. I've got to break the spell and get through to her, J.J. told herself. I need some answers.

Luckily, Claire's good manners automatically turned on and did the trick. "Would you care to come in for a drink of something?" she asked.

"Oh, yes, I really would, thank you," J.J. accepted, relieved.

Following Claire, J.J. once again found herself in the formal sitting room, when Claire asked, "A bit of port or brandy, dear, or sherry perhaps if you like it at this hour? Or do you still prefer tea?"

"Oh, port would be lovely," J.J. answered, spying it in a decanter on a side table, and hoping Claire would sit down to join her and focus a little, rather that wander into hostess, tea-making mode again.

She poured two small crystal liqueur glasses, then sat on the sofa next to J.J., looking at the darkened window.

"So, Mrs. Hart," J.J. began, "what did you think? I mean, was it what you had expected?"

Looking directly at J.J. for once, Claire mustered a faint, vapid smile. "Oh marvelous, wasn't it? I mean, well, the music, and then he is quite the star isn't he? And the applause, well…"

"Yes," J.J. agreed, wanting to ask Claire if she knew when Hans had last seen Melanie, but deciding that might wait until after tomorrow night. "I'm sure you'll hear all about it, and so many things, when you have dinner together."

Claire, her eyes dreamy, answered, "Oh my, yes."

"Well, I hope we can talk about it sometime afterwards. You know, maybe share notes. But I have something else I'd like to ask you, about a different topic."

Claire looked at J.J. again, head cocked as if surprised. She set her port on the glass-covered antique coffee table.

"You know when I was here last time, I asked Dr. Hart about how you and he happened to go to Mendocino, and he said you'd heard rumors about a commune and a fire and the body of a young girl. But where did you hear these rumors? I mean nobody has written about such things, and best I know only a few local people up there heard about it. So, Mrs. Hart, how did you know?"

The composure on Claire's well made-up face fractured, and suddenly, as if released by internal combustion, a few hairs strayed from their tight chignon. Claire picked up a cocktail napkin and wound it around her fingers. "Well now, let me think. It's all a bit of a muddle just now, perhaps Charles—"

At that moment, both of them jumped at the sharp ring of the telephone in the study off the hall. "Ah, please excuse me for a minute," Claire rose on her pale green satin heels and hurried toward the sound.

"Damn," J.J. said quietly to herself, resting her forehead in her palms as she watched the moment slip away. But, feeling another presence in the room, she opened them again and looked up to see Natalie slumping on the stair just as she had earlier in the evening.

"So, you want to know about the 'rumor'? You think *she'll* tell you anything? Hell, she's so loopy, who knows what she even remembers. But, so, I can tell you about the rumor. So one day they get this phone call from this freak up the coast. Says he has some important information about their missing daughter, but they need to get up there. So *vaboom*, they're up and outta here the next day. Went in the old man's Caddie, the black one. So they go up to Mendocino, and the freak meets them. Said he was like a bear."

"Moon," J.J. said.

"What?"

"Nothing. Please, go on."

"So this big hairy dude tells them about this commune and how a girl that must be their daughter had been living there, but how there was this fire and a girl's body was found and that's probably their daughter, and now the sheriff's office is getting all over it and it's going to be a big mess. A big story."

"So what did this hairy dude want from them? Why did he call?"

Natalie smirked. "Duh. He wanted from them what everybody wants from them. Dough. They're, like, loaded, my parents, in case you didn't know. He scared the shit out of them with the scandal this would cause, the shame of it. Their daughter, to be found dead in such a creepy place? Never! Personally, after all the grief my sister's caused me,

I mean she left me to cope with this mess myself, but I have to say I think this is the coolest thing ever. Not that she died, I mean, but that that's where she went after all this time."

"So this dude, he just wanted money from them? How was that going to stop the story?"

"Right. See, this was a two-part pay-off. First a visit to the sheriff—the messenger was hairy dude himself, right?— to get him to lay off the investigation, making it worth his while of course. Then hairy dude keeps a cut for himself, after the parents are assured the investigation isn't happening. Just a business deal, you see?"

"I see," J.J. nodded, her head spinning.

But Claire entered the room again, a spring in her gait. "Oh, how lovely you two are chatting. That was Charles, your father, Natalie, just wanting to know how the evening had gone, don't you know?"

"I'd say it was quite amazing," J.J. offered, standing up to go.

In a moment, she was crunching across the gravel drive again, having left a silent Natalie slumped on the stair and a radiant Claire waving her farewells. J.J. nearly broke into a trot to get to her car. For the third time that night, she longed to be wrapped in darkness, free to concentrate on the images exploding in her brain, and another question now eating at her: How did Moon know about the Harts and where to get in touch with them?

Then, turning the key in the ignition, it hit her like an explosion. "Duh," she said out loud in her best imitation of Natalie. "*I* told him. *I* was the one who said 'Fiddle' was 'Melanie Hart,' who told him about Pasadena. My God, I've become my own leak, my own worst enemy."

Chapter 18

Nursing a lemonade. J.J. sat at a table back from the pool's edge. The large straw sunhat she'd grabbed from Gran's hat rack was probably a hundred years old. So old that it had come into fashion again, as Annie would say. But it worked with the peasant Mexican skirt that Annie had donated last year, which, along with the rope and canvas sandals, were as close as J.J. was likely to get to high summer fashion. And the hat, more than the umbrella overhead, provided protection from the brutal September sun and was even better for hiding. She tried concentrating on the vacationing kids splashing in the pool. Anything to erase the images of the fateful wedding party—the grand ballroom, the Chinese gardens, the poolside terrace itself—images this old hotel threw so vividly back at her.

Hans slipped in like a shadow, and he reached down to give her a peck on the cheek before she saw him. "J.J.," he said, grasping her hands, "I'm so very happy you could meet me today."

She looked up to see him, but he was a white blur in the sunlight, just the way Melanie had so often been.

"What may I get you to drink?" he continued.

"Well, maybe a G&T," J.J. answered, remembering she'd promised to come as friend only, not reporter. "It's my widest, friendliest hat," she smiled, "and I think it's gin and tonic weather, don't you?" She paused. "But I guess Melie would have ordered champagne on a day like today."

Hans nodded. Sitting now, and shaded, he came into her line of vision with the rose-colored tint of the very fair who have been in the sun. He had a healthy, even handsome, cast to him, she had to admit. But his eyes brooded with melancholy.

"The music, your work, it was, well, I was very moved," J.J. began. "I'm only sorry I didn't get to hear the rest of it."

"Yes, a pity because—well, I mean the full symphony, it tells the whole story. In some performances on this tour, Vancouver and Chicago and so on, we do the complete work."

"Right." J.J. nodded, pausing while a waiter took Hans's order. "But what do you mean the whole story?" she continued, immediately regretting that she'd slipped into inquisition mode so quickly.

"Ah, classic, tragic love story," he answered, his accent rising as if for emphasis. "Love glimpsed in the perfect form of a young, beautiful, pure woman. Love recognized. Love consummated."

"That took us through the first movement," J.J. broke in.

"Yes. But then the storms start, slowly at first, almost like summer rain so you don't recognize them. But they grow, crash, destroy, and in the end, when they pass and the sun returns, it's all gone. Or she's all gone. As if only a vision." Hans reached for his glass of wine and sipped slowly, his eyes on someplace too distant for J.J. to follow.

"The storms," she finally said, "what caused them?"

"Oh," he looked directly at her now, "they were the manifestation of grief. Brought on, I'm sure, by her intense desire for a baby. Did she ever tell you about that boy she wanted to adopt?"

J.J. nodded.

"Well then you probably know, because she did feel so close to you, J.J., how much she wanted to get pregnant. How hard it was for her. I mean all the terrible procedures we went through…"

J.J. shifted the straw hat on her head, trying to turn speechlessness into sympathy. The gin and tonic glass began sweating, rivulets of water running onto her hands.

"So, you know, when it all failed so badly, when she accepted that, well, she couldn't…" His pale blue eyes reflected the pool and the sky, as, it seemed to J.J., he looked through her more than at her. "I guess it's natural that the depression came. I mean, it could have come anyway, at least that's what all those doctors said. God J.J., there were so many of them, so many treatments, so many hours of 'talking it through' you know, and for me, too."

"Actually I didn't know. By the end there, I mean the end of the Rochester years, our correspondence had sort of fallen off." J.J. tried searching out Hans's eyes again, but they had turned away. The list of accusations and questions was spilling into her head, but she sipped her drink slowly, trying hard not to move too fast.

Hans looked back at her, giving a tight smile. "So she disappeared from you in a way just as she did from me."

"Disappeared?"

"Yah. One day she just wasn't there. The first time it was just a few days, you know, then she came back. No explanations. Then it happened more, the length of the times got longer. When she came back, it was just as if she'd never left. I was really worried, but she wouldn't talk. I tried to get her back to the doctors, but no, no, she just refused. One time her father called when she was on one of her 'voyages,' and he was so alarmed by what I told him, he said he wanted her to go right away to a specialist he knew of at the Menninger Clinic. That time, when she returned, I told her about her father, about what he suggested. I mean, I tried to put it in the best light, but she went what I guess you'd call crazy. It was a mistake, I know. I never should have told her."

Impulsively, J.J. reached out and put her hand over his. For a hot afternoon, it was uncommonly cool. "Actually, when did she come back for the last time, Hans?"

"After she announced she was checking herself into an asylum—I admit I was out of my mind when she said that—she was gone for a couple of months and then she came back for a few weeks. After that she took off again and never really came home, except once, a little over two years ago. That would have been in '72. She didn't stay though, and I hardly recognized her. She looked… I suspected drugs, and her clothes were, how do you call it? Revolutionary, maybe. She said, 'I'm just coming to collect some of my shit.' Can you imagine? One of the things she took was our wedding picture, one taken in there, actually," he gestured toward the grand ballroom. "I never saw her again." He paused, looked away. "I always feel guilty now for being so involved in my music. Perhaps if…"

J.J. shifted uncomfortably, trying to contain a whirlpool of conflicting feelings. Moving as Hans was in presenting himself as the aggrieved Good Husband, a part of J.J. wanted to rise up and confront the bastard. Or "alleged bastard," as Eve would have put it. What about the years of neglect, his cold shoulder to the idea of taking in Billy, his appalling reaction to Melie's attempt to please him by performing that birthday song? And what was all this crap about trying so hard to conceive a baby? What about his role as co-conspirator with the diabolical Dr. Hart to ship

Melie off to an asylum? Didn't he know she'd read Melanie's journals?

Another voice rose in J.J.'s head as if to answer her. Of course Hans didn't know what was in the journals. What did he actually know about how Melie had laid out the story? On impulse she decided to punch back by asking, "So what about John C. Calhoun?" but caught herself before the end of the question. "So what about…music? When did she become interested in learning herself?"

"Ah, well, let's see. I guess she began taking piano lessons—that was a secret, a gift to me—about the first or second year we were in Rochester. Of course, it was normal I suppose, we were living in a world of music, surrounded by it. You know, all through the summer it came in the windows of our little apartment. She really liked that." He smiled a private smile. "And even though it wasn't her training, she had a talent. A feel for it. I told her so many times."

Hans looked away, over the roof of the hotel, into some horizon J.J. couldn't imagine. "You know, I think in the end that's what drew her away. Music. It was like the Pied Piper took her away from her sorrow. I think when she left, she went to find music. Concerts, festivals, that kind of thing, but music of her own choosing, not what was already around at the Eastman School."

You mean like Woodstock? J.J. wanted to say. But she continued to hold back. "It's quite an overwhelming story, Hans. It must be hard for you, then, returning to this place where—"

"No, actually, it isn't. It's, how do you say, deliberate. I've come here to visit all 'our places.' This morning I went to the college. I wanted to find La Maison Française, but—"

"I know," J.J. interrupted, feeling suddenly sympathetic again.

"Anyway," he went on, looking at J.J. directly, "this whole tour. The symphony, the places we were, the places she might have been, it's a kind of a farewell trip through my memories. I need to make peace with it now, with the fact she is really gone."

"Gone," J.J. repeated, not saying what was running through her head. *So what do you make of the rumor that your wife's body was found in a burned-out commune on the North Coast?* "Actually, where do you think she is, Hans?"

The blue of his eyes pierced her now. "I don't think she is...anywhere. At least not in this world. Where did she go? I don't know, but my feeling is probably South. I imagine that music made her follow those tunes of social justice, civil rights, that sort of calling. I imagine she went there, and in the crowds and violence and noise, she just got lost. It was too hot for her there. She disappeared."

J.J. looked back at him as directly as she could bear, noticing he had not actually said the word "dead." But of course that is what he meant. So they had both reached the same devastating conclusion, although their roads to it were completely contrary. For Hans, she understood that he had to come to terms with Melanie being lost forever. In all ways that mattered, she was dead to him. But for herself, it was the opposite. As piece by piece she built a story based on facts, increasingly she feared her evidence: the fire, the body, the complete vanishing of Melanie from anyone's sight for so long, including her own. And unlike Hans, she came to this conclusion very much wanting Melanie to be alive.

They both knew it was time to leave and rose together. "J.J.," Hans was saying as he stood and gallantly pulled out her chair, "thank you for being so good a friend to her. It meant so much, especially because things were, what is the word, so strained with her family." He put his hand on J.J.'s back as if to guide her through the hotel grounds and lobby and all the painful memories she did not want to revisit.

They paused at the majestic reception desk, while he searched her face for a minute. "Thanks, too, from me. For wearing the 'friend's hat,' and not the other one."

J.J. swallowed, muttered, "of course," then hesitated before asking: "Hans, is there a recording of the symphony yet? I'd like to hear the whole thing."

"Ah, yes, there is. I'll have the publicity people send you the L.P. album." He stood for a moment outside the wide revolving doors, summoned a valet to find his car, and smiled. It was a smile J.J. couldn't read except to know it was tinged with sorrow. Then he stepped into the sunlight, which swallowed him.

A HOT SEPTEMBER day. So hot the asphalt turned soft and smog blanked out any view of the world and Alice remarked, "It's the California equivalent of a blizzard."

"Whatever," J.J. answered. Just then, as if summoned to break the tedium, a delivery boy dropped a package on J.J.'s desk. "Hurray," she shouted while hastily ripping it open. There, spilling out, as Hans promised, was the recording from his publicist. Still for a moment, J.J. just stared at the album. *Symphony in G for Melanie* by Hans Bucher, the cover in gold and silver shimmery tones suggesting a young woman's form through the filtered light of a forest, the hint of a lake. It worked its magic. She continuing to stare.

"Look, Alice," J.J. ran to her, holding up the record like a prize. "The whole symphony just arrived. I'm going home to listen to it."

Alice, who had already heard J.J.'s recitation of the rendezvous with Hans, studied the cover briefly. "It's close to the end of a long day's work. I'd really like to hear that, too. Would you mind if I came along and we listened together?"

A half hour later, they settled into Gran's darkened living room, the shades drawn against the heat just as if Gran had pulled them herself. J.J. had found some presentable enough orange juice and the cool glasses made puddles on

Gran's silver-ringed coasters. J.J. placed her collection of records sloppily on the floor, then delicately put the vinyl with Hans's symphony on the turntable.

When the first strains of the prelude began, she sank to the floor herself and lay prone to listen. The familiar sweetness of the first movement washed over her, and she gave way to the rest. The summer rains, as Hans had described them, of the second. The bits, unfinished, of a lullaby. A piano. The rising of a huge storm, its clash in a crescendo of fury. Drums, cymbals, bass. Discordance and devastation after the storm, the ravished landscape. Strange percussion, strings, flute. The return to the sweet refrain of the beginning, tinged with grief and loss. The violin.

Alice broke the silence. "A nod to Debussy with a prelude, hints of Mendelssohn, then a Shostakovich finish."

J.J. sat up. "I didn't know you were such a classical music buff."

"There's much you don't know, as it happens."

"So tell me what I should know about this."

Alice inhaled. "Well, he is brilliant. This is dazzling. And if you wanted his real story, this is it. The music doesn't lie."

"I agree. He really loved her. The loss of her is almost unbearable."

"Correct."

"I can accept his feelings are real. But that still doesn't make all the B.S. he told me the other day real. It doesn't mean I have to buy his version of events."

"No. But that's just the point. He's putting forth his version, just as you are. That's what we all do. That's how we get from day to day."

"Well, but 'my version' as you call, it is not what I'm making up. It's based on what Melie said, what her journals and letters told me. The facts."

"So it is. But that's Melanie's truth. She has her version just like everybody else. Her facts."

Chapter 19

"Time to review the bidding," Alice said, swinging her chair around to face J.J., who had just been summoned to her office. Alice looked particularly disheveled, J.J. noted, with wild strands of gray hair sticking like flying buttresses out from the central edifice of her bun. "First of all, Himself liked the writing on the Saint Eve story well enough, but grumbled about the lack of the 'juicy stuff.' I reminded him we are, after all, dealing with a nun here, assuring him that the stories to come would be remarkably different."

"Thanks," J.J. replied. "I know you're stepping in to keep him off my back for a while. I appreciate it."

"Least I can do," Alice's mouth twisted into a wry smile. "He seems to think we won't have readership without sex and sensation. I did remind him, though, that some stories of powerful young women with spiritual callings have staying power. Joan of Arc, for instance, has had a pretty good run."

J.J. gave a wide smile, deciding to keep it under wraps that Alice, too, deserved a recommendation for sainthood.

"But beyond that, you've got yourself one helluva mess to deal with—in fact, it's hard to remember when I've seen one as bad as this, so giving you some space to sort it out would seem to be called for."

"Helluva mess," J.J. repeated.

"Well, a missing friend who may or may not be alive, who is by turns the studious, deep, bright daughter of local society family; the wife-muse to a brilliant young European musician; an innocent runaway who turns up and turns on at a legendary rock concert, cavorts with a savvy, young clarinet-playing activist from Chicago; then drops out of sight, which stands to reason because she likely burned in a fire in the North Coast woods. Did I get that right? Meanwhile, the investigating officer in said alleged crime has most likely been bought off, while the young woman's family is almost certainly guilty of bribery and interfering with justice. Which doesn't even get to that shaggy Big Foot character who could go to the Big House along with the others for extortion, to say nothing of drug charges, if anybody is interested in such. Oh yes, then there's the aggrieved husband, abandoned, suffering, and a sublime musician, who is also the spinner of fantastical tales about the relationship with his departed wife. Unless her accounts are even more fantastical—a possibility you don't even want to entertain, I know, but ultimately you must. So I'd say this is the veritable definition of a helluva mess, wouldn't you?"

J.J. nodded, adding a weak "Yes."

"It's also a helluva story, J.J. One that rarely comes along. And even better, now that the investigation is off and nobody else is on the scent of this, it's yours to pursue, if you want to. So, you have two things to decide: What do you want to do with this, and what can you do with this?"

"Let's start with the second part. What can I do at this point anyway, even if I want the whole big front-page-flash-bulb-popping thing?"

"Smart girl. That's the right question. And I'll jump in uninvited to answer. What you *can* do right now is precious little. We're a small, local paper hundreds of miles from the scene. You need backup, support, and connections to take on an investigation of this order. Oh, yeah, you also need the law, which would mean leapfrogging over the authority of the sheriff, a move about as fraught with problems as I can imagine. Not to say that it can't be done, but as soon as you move on any of these fronts, you lose control of the story, savvy?"

"Savvy. So got any suggestions?" J.J. covered her eyes with her hands to listen more intently.

"What you need is a very reliable source on the ground up there, somebody tuned into the scene who will be able to tell you when there's a shift—and there will be—and a thread in this tangle of contradictions that can reasonably be pursued. Know anybody?"

"As it happens, yes. One of my oldest friends."

Alice pushed some of the attacking strands of hair back, allowing a small burst of relief to cross her face. "Good. Get in touch with her. In fact, get on up there, fill her in, set up some line of communication."

"Him. My friend is a him."

"Fine. How are you coming along with the other contacts?"

"Well, you know Evelyn has already come through, and I've met the Harts and Hans of course. So far Gracie and Jocelyn, the closest to hand, haven't responded, but I'm working on it."

"Okay. Just get your friend up there in God's country in place. And meanwhile, keep those profiles rolling." Alice gestured toward Purvis's office.

—⟩

J.J. SAT FIDGETING on a lumpy couch in the "reception" of the Blue Moon Bar & Far Out Rest Stop. She'd decided to meet Ivan in Boonville so as not to tip her hand that she was poking around again in Mendocino. Swami Bloomberg, sans turban, had greeted her briefly and inquired if she wanted a room.

"I do," she answered tersely.

"How many nights?"

"That depends. I'm waiting for my friend. You know Ivan, right?" J.J. stopped there.

"Oh, so you're that chick," he answered. "Right. Expect he'll show up any time." To J.J.'s relief, he then disappeared. She didn't feel like talking to strangers.

When she heard the roar of a distant engine approaching, she breathed evenly, in and out. Ivan's motorcycle. "Harley-Davidson Sportster Ironhead, very groovy," he'd once informed her. It was the most reassuring sound she'd heard for days.

In a moment, Ivan was next to her, giving her a ferocious hug. "So, got your message, J.J. My buddy here sent me the smoke signals."

J.J. realized Ivan meant the Swami, her contact point for Ivan, and further realized she had no idea what the Swami's real name was, as was the case with so many other people these days.

"Good to see you, kiddo," Ivan was saying. "So, shall we repair to the bar and you can tell me what's up."

In a moment they were huddled in a dark corner which they shared with a couple of stray cats. J.J. nursed a cold beer, while Ivan lit his pipe, looking at her expectantly.

"Well, I'm on assignment," she began. "Orders from my editor — Alice, with the pencils — to find you."

"Really? Well, I'm flattered. And somewhat amused."

"Look, this whole thing has escalated…" And she continued until Ivan was filled in on what she knew.

"No shit," he exhaled slowly, letting J.J.'s story settle along with the smoke.

"Bottom line, I need somebody close to the ground up here. Somebody who can tell when there's a shift in the situation and will let me know. I'm not really in a place right now to launch into a big investigation, but when the smoke clears," she smiled at herself, "and we can see the way enough to act, then…"

"I hear you." Ivan smiled back, his dark hair longer than she remembered and curling slightly behind his ears. "In fact, I already sort of knew this. Had a vision. I'm already on it."

"No shit," she echoed back. "Really? So what do you know?"

"For one thing, that Moon dude has been out of sight. Maybe on the lam. If not, will be soon. And that girl, Cat, she hadn't been seen for some time, but she's visible again."

"Wow. Interesting. Maybe I could find her."

"Maybe. But what we have to do first is get to Sheriff O'Reilly. Because his ass is getting kicked out of here soon."

"No kidding? How do you know—well never mind. What do you mean we have to get to him first?"

"I misspoke. *You* need to get to him. Ask him straight up about the visit from the Harts."

"You crazy?" J.J. twisted the napkin around her fingers and drained the rest of her beer. "He's not going to tell me anything. Assuming I could get to him. Remember I can't even play the press card yet. So I'm just some outsider drifting through checking out a rumor?"

Ivan handed her the pipe and a match. "Exactly. That bit's even partly true, and no, no, of course he's not going to tell you anything, at least not in words. But his body language, his vibes. It's all about reading the signs, J.J. Therein you catch the conscience of the king, dig it?"

With a couple of puffs, J.J. began to relax, and soon she retreated upstairs with Ivan where they lay on twin beds in a musty room laughing about how the circle turns. It was like another night they'd spent in a cheap hotel in a red-light district in Paris about a thousand years before. The night when he'd delivered Guy's gift of Chinese love poems to her several months late.

BY MIDMORNING J.J. was on the back of Ivan's Harley, hair whipping into strands like the enveloping fog. Fog in September when it should be clear. Going cold turkey to knock on O'Reilly's door was madness. Yet Ivan seemed so sure.

Then she gave herself over to the windy road, the majestic redwoods, the barely visible road leading to Fort Bragg, a town large enough to have an outpost of the county sheriff's office. Mendocino didn't rate one. The bike stopped and brought her back to the present. Reality. A nondescript station, a dusty patrol car parked out front.

Ivan hopped off, adjusting his leather jacket. "Okay, go for it. You know what to say. Bereaved friend who's heard rumors, yadda, yadda, yadda."

J.J. smiled wanly, pushed her hair from her face, and headed for the door. In a minute she returned. "Rookie at the desk told me the sheriff is out right now. But get this, he's in a meeting at Bread & Beads Café."

"Right on," said Ivan. "We can use some breakfast anyway."

In minutes, they were swinging off the bike again and entering the café. Pigeon settled them in the front room. After scrutinizing Ivan, he slammed some silverware and menus on the table, sighing. "You come for all the fun?" He nodded to the room behind the swaying glass beads. "I didn't see your name on the party list." He smiled crookedly, amused at his own wit.

"No. I'm just back in town for... so what is all the fun?"

"My lips are sealed." He slinked away.

Soon after he returned with coffee and toast, J.J. heard the deep voice of Mama Cass rising above a medley of others. The beads parted and a tall, lean man in a uniform held them for a young dark-haired woman with a long skirt, high boots, and a gingham jacket. Cat. Just like the vision she'd had in Moon's truck. A baby with dark tight curls nestled on her hip, a baby who was part black. J.J. set down her cup, staring in amazement. Of course. Cat's boyfriend, Sport, a.k.a. Black Jack. It was all falling into place.

"Well if it isn't!" Mama Cass boomed, spotting J.J. "What brings you to town this time? No, I get it. You just can't keep away from our nourishing victuals." She shook with laughter and waddled away.

"I was just—" J.J. began, but Moon saw her, too, and interrupted. His hair flew more than the last time she'd seen him, and his eyes looked wild, even menacing. She was glad to be in company. He rushed to envelope her in his bear hug.

"Damn, Bones, good to see you, girl. Good to see you chowing down here at Mama's too. Still need more meat on them bones." He guffawed.

"Well, I—"

He broke in again. "Damn, girl, should have told us you was coming. As you can see, we've been having ourselves a little party here. This here's our very own keeper of the peace, Sheriff Melvin O'Reilly, and my good lady, Cat." He reached out as if to put his hand on her, but she stepped back.

Melvin O'Reilly nodded, then waited for Cat to pass before heading to the door. Moon followed, then J.J. rose. In a moment they were all on the wooden stoop of the café, the sea shimmering beyond the hill across the street. Cat stood apart, holding the baby tight, while O'Reilly walked toward his cruiser.

"Yup," Moon continued, "we've just been having a little party of peace and reconciliation, ain't that so, Cat? All's well that ends well, if you get my drift?"

Cat looked away. O'Reilly pulled up, got out, opened the door, and the young woman and baby got in the back-seat.

"Yup," Moon boomed out, "just one big happy family."

J.J. scrutinized Cat as O'Reilly revved the motor. Suddenly she saw Cat look back, studying her. Then Cat shook her head back and forth and made a gesture for J.J. to see. She moved her finger and slid it like a knife across her throat.

When the car pulled away, J.J. turned again to Moon, who was now staring at her strangely. "So, Bones," he said, the menace in his eyes unmistakable, "just can't stop snooping around here, can you? Dangerous habit, you know."

"No, I just came up to visit my friend," J.J. answered, grateful that Ivan had joined them and stood right behind her. Doubly grateful that he wasn't wearing any feathers in his hair nor peace signs, but a leather jacket. And that his macho Harley was right by the curb.

"No shit," Moon turned, apparently taking in Ivan for the first time. "So this your old man?"

J.J. nodded. "Yeah, we're real tight."

"Well, I'll be God damned." His eyes narrowed as he studied the pair. "So a little friendly advice for you, Bones. Get over it. Fiddle, she's gone and she ain't never coming back. Time to move on, Bones. Time for everybody to move on."

He turned quickly on his heel and walked across the street, hair flying wild in the wind, toward the sea.

Chapter 20

This was the last trip until she returned as a reporter, J.J. reminded herself. With that thought, she'd been pulled by the strong temptation to hide in San Francisco instead of returning to Pasadena. The Grateful Dead were playing at Winterland, and she could feel them calling her. She jammed in the tape and played *American Beauty* over and over—and kept dodging traffic, driving home, her head spinning.

Once there, to calm herself, she turned on a low lamp and lit a candle smelling of woods and wild herbs that Annie had given to her. "To lead you to your soul's beginning" Annie had explained. Then, sipping herbal tea, she propped up against the mahogany back of Gran's sleigh bed, where she had taken to sleeping lately, and closed her lids. The image of Cat, eyes wide open, giving that throat-cutting gesture, and the suddenly menacing Moon haunted her. Compulsively, she pulled out her Melanie files to scour

for any allusions to Cat. Loose pages, some torn from the
Woodstock trip, slipped from a folder.

*Strange how I can see so clearly. See women, some my friends.
Wondering about the oldest ones, Maison Française habituées,
J.J.'s territory. I mean, the wondering then writing about it is
hers. I see Gracie, swirling like a kaleidoscope, star-shaped, colors of the sun. This will be where she goes—to the stars and sun.*

*Jocelyn. Can't actually see her at all, just a misty outline
of her face. She's wearing veils and veils. Blue, green, violet, all
those cool colors. She'll only be vapor until she removes the covering from her face. But she's afraid. She needs to let down the
ropes of her long hair and climb out of her own window. I did
that once. For Hans. So he could take my virginity. I did everything for Hans. But she can do it for herself.*

Eve. More spinning.

At the bottom of the page, J.J. studied the curly, circular lines drawn in ink. An illustration of Melie's mind during
whatever trip she was on? The following three pages were
blank, then the narrative continued.

*Eve. The Madonna. Now she's even wearing the costume. She
too is mourning her child. Only she lost two of them, both
infants. Didn't live to grow up and be worshipped—like their
father wants to be still. Or I should say one father, the sleaze-
bag she married. That's what she called him. Pretty boy Jay still
makes all the papers. But poor Tom, now deep into the father-
hood of the church, he never knew about the other one. Poor
Father Tom. Where is he now? What a weirdness, both of them
in these Mary and Joseph clothes not knowing about the other.
Tom not knowing anything. Does that make him a true innocent? I used to be one. But now my head hurts from too much
inside it.*

J.J. turned to another page. All were undated, unnumbered.

Babies. Motherhood. The thing all young women our age seem to do, but not us, not the used-to-be girls of la Maison Française. Not us, the barren travelers, refugees from a year in Paris and years of wandering in the wilderness like Christ himself ever since. Sound like my own father. Whoa though, I'm seeing colors I know he never even imagined. Dancing through some mighty flames.

Babies. Well, Evie did have some, even though she lost them. Jocelyn, if she ever got close, she must have had abortions. Just lovers and lovers I think, but no domestic drama. Can't see that. Wheee.

And Gracie. It's not the physics and all the brain power thing that's in her way. It's the thing with men. After she tore herself from Tom, who never knew she was in love with him, she was only, what's the word? Scar tissue. She should try this stuff sometime. She'd like it and see the stars close up like she's supposed to. Of all of us, she's the one who would be a real mother.

Oh god. Heat and light.

Yeah. And me? Lost Billy, who was in the spiritual sense mine, the way a mother really loves and bonds with a child. Lost him. And Hans, though he pretended otherwise, wanting no baby of our own. Not really. He said he tried, but I think he was faking it. Lost Hans. Lost hope. Funny, it all seems long ago. Now all is just swirling colors, music. J.C. and love in a tent. He is so—it was never like that with Hans, so head to feet, so shimmery. Ecstasy. Shhh, don't tell Pascal. A baby. J.C. and I, maybe...

J.C. running like me, though more to something than from something. And he wants the high of feeling free. Like we are here, just music, mud, this little tent, no past or future as important as this, love in the present tense. "My Golden Gypsy," he calls me. Me, like everybody else, I call him J.C., short for John C. Calhoun. Don't know his real name. Don't want to know.

The writing stopped there. J.J. turned another blank page, aware that in her strung-out state Melanie had neglected to speculate on her, J.J., and the prospects of motherhood. Apparently later, in a different frame of mind,

Melie had caught the oversight herself. On the last loose page, she found her own name at the top.

> J.J. Little Mother of a Hundred Girls. Now I'm sober as a stone and my head has quit hurting, though it rains like the days of the Flood. Outside this tent, where I'm hiding out with J.C.'s flashlight (all this stuff is his), I can just see the pairs marching two by two to the Ark. Trudging through the mud. So weird, but I've been wanting to send a postcard to J.J. All these years and I send postcards to her of my adventures. She writes to me, too. A GOOD friend. As I was kind of meditating there on being married with children and how none of my old friends did that, I finally came around to her. She took another path. In a way, she's a mother to the rest of us, a hovering protective spirit, trying to find and keep our histories. A mother with a scrapbook. Trying to prop us up, help us get wherever we're going. In a way, giving birth to us through her stories. Inventing us. I guess that's what mothers do really. Mine tried, but she had only one mold to fit me in, and not enough imagination to shape another. Imagination, that's it. If anything, maybe J.J.'s got too much. Maybe she comes by it naturally, too, if her own mom—who always wants to be called Annie, not Mom—is any indication. From what J.J. says, she's like a piece of fiction, with all those travels, strange collections, and very out-there ideas. So totally the opposite of my scaredy-cat, uptight society mother, so different from J.J.'s own Gran with her alluring French charm, her warmth, her big heart. Lucky for J.J. she had true-blue backup.

At the end of this entry was another drawing, one with wobbly hearts cut through with arrows resting on fields of cheerful flowers. The psychedelic images had disappeared into the imagery of a child.

Each of these revelations was like a fire cracker going off before her eyes, and then inside her head, which was holding too much. And too little. Of course there were no hints of Cat. There were no records of anything from the

Hi-Diddle period. "Magical thinking," she chided herself. Then blowing out the candle, and turning off the light, she wished at that moment she'd had what Melie was smoking so she, too, could collapse into a repose of multicolored bliss.

By morning, J.J. knew she had blacked out more than slept in the normal sense. She longed to find solace and calm in Gran's reassuring presence once again before going in to face the newsroom, her life, and the "helluva mess" of her present situation.

WITHIN A HALF hour J.J. was ducking her head in the antiseptic corridor leading to Gran's room. Mercifully, today there were no annoying nurses to waylay her. Even more mercifully, when she opened Gran's door after a swift knock, she found Gran elegantly dressed and sitting in her favorite wicker chair.

Her eyes opened wide with delight at seeing J.J. "Ah *ma petite*, I told them you were coming and I am ready. So there you are. Isn't it lovely?"

J.J. sat next to her, rubbing Gran's smooth hands in her own while they chatted. Gran seemed convinced they were sitting in her rose garden and the scent was transporting. J.J. could only agree, smiling, and glad herself to be in that happy place.

Then Gran suddenly asked, "So how is she then, *chérie*?"

"Who, *grand-mère*?"

"But your sister."

"My sister?"

Now Gran's tone seemed a little annoyed, but her eyes were warm. "Yes, of course. Your twin sister. The blonde one."

"I don't know, Gran, but I'm going to find out." And she rose with a clear plan in her head at last.

Chapter 21

The sun cut without pity through the huge glass window. Jocelyn, who had sunk deep into the comforts of the orange couch for the night, tried resisting the blaze by covering her eyes with a discarded sweater. She had even fumbled around on the glass table for earplugs, trying to block out sound, too. But a persistent ringing penetrated all her defenses. Defeated, she finally sat up. The doorbell. She was expecting nobody. "Officially in hiding," she had informed Dana and gave strict orders not to be disturbed. She stood at last, shaking her disheveled head, and moved to the door, squinting out the peephole.

"Divine's Delivery," a man in a brown uniform kept shouting. She opened. The small landing was overwhelmed with roses, dozens of them, long-stemmed, fragrant, red, white, *and* blue. She signed the Divine Florist's receipt and laughed to herself while beginning to haul in the vases.

Then, with blotches of red, white, and blue in jarring

juxtaposition around the magenta, orange, and yellow room, she sank down on the couch again to read the note.

Dru's voice began speaking the words. "Darlink, I send these in homage to the new sweetheart of all America. You vill capture hearts everywhere, as you have mine. Harding so happy too. The blue ones to celebrate your vonderful eyes, the Pacific of course, and even who knows, the new patriotism? A bientôt, chérie, Dru."

She smiled at this last, the touch of French that was their secret code, and at the kindness, and craziness, of the gesture. It was so like him. Then rereading the note, she frowned. Harding? Publicity was at work already? And the new patriotism? Oh, please, let's not go down that road. Well, she was off-duty now. Best not to think about any of it.

But the noise seemed to persist, and she realized it was the phone ringing. She stumbled to the kitchen to grab it. "Hey Jocelyn sweetheart," Dana's voice crackled in those sharp New York tones through the receiver, and Jocelyn instinctively pulled it slightly away from her ear for volume control. She could picture her unruly-haired agent with oversized glasses fidgeting at her desk because she had so much energy, sitting still "gets on my nerves," she claimed. Dana was the only person, apart from her mother, whose calls Jocelyn was taking at the moment. "So listen, I know you don't want to be disturbed, but there is someone who wants very much to get through—"

"If it's Harding, tell him no. Maybe in a thousand years."

"Ouf, touchy touchy this morning, aren't we? No darling, it's not Harding. He knows you're incognito at the moment and the man's not suicidal—"

"So who is it?"

"Well I got this call from the *Star* newspaper. That reporter there, J.J. something, who did a piece a while back. She claims to be a friend of yours, says she wants to see you... wait, here's my note. She says she needs to talk to you. She's trying to find out about somebody named Melanie."

Jocelyn closed her ears. Just now she couldn't think about J.J., let alone Melanie. It was easier to shut her eyes, to drift back to yesterday. Had it been only yesterday?

BENEATH THE CLIFF the waves curled alabaster under a rising moon. A slender figure shadowed a window open to the sea. The face of a woman cast in unworldly light stared out. An oval, classic face, some said. Her face. Beautiful but mystifying, framed by wisps of blonde hair. In that light it was impossible, she knew, to tell the color of the eyes as they swept the horizon, eyes full of sorrow or grief perhaps—or was it hope? For a long moment, an expression like light passed across cheekbones, brow, nose, and slightly tremulous lips. It could have meant anything. In that instant, the face—her face—might have been twenty-two, or one hundred. Then all went dark.

"Damn," she muttered as she turned, tripping slightly over a long, patterned corduroy bathrobe, vintage 1944. But her voice was lost in the uproar of shouts, "Cut!" followed by "Hot damn, we did it!" "Far out," and "Kiss my ass baby, but we're gooood!" As the cameras wheeled back and the soundmen untangled wires, the bright overhead lights snapped back on, and Jocelyn realized she felt hot.

Then Dru jumped down from the director's chair, gray disheveled hair sticking out from under his cap, and ran toward her. His signature black turtleneck and black pants fit him as snuggly as they had twenty-five years ago. Only the body beneath had changed. "Perfection, darling—that last shot. I always knew you had it in you," and he slipped his arm tight across her shoulder. "Now we really must celebrate. We have finished our masterpiece."

Pacific Blue: The Louis Dubois Story, based on the

bestselling novel, was a masterpiece. That was the word the critics used, but "Blockbuster," "Nominations," "Oscars," "Best Picture"—those were the value words in Hollywood.

She heard her own voice. "Yeah, great. Thanks Dru. But actually, I'm sort of…lightheaded right now. I think I'll just go home," and gently removed his arm from her shoulder.

"But darling," he tried to slide his arm around her again, "this is your moment. By God, you were Edna. Please come. Everyone wants to toast you."

"Thanks, but no. Not now, Dru." Beads of sweat breaking out across the makeup sealing her forehead, she offered a pale smile then sank onto a chintz-covered armchair to watch the noisy dismantling of the heavy equipment.

"Okay, darling. Okay. Until next time then." Dru patted her on the head with a kind of paternal tenderness. They both knew "not now" meant "it's over." They'd been there before and as usual, the affair had lasted as long as the film, an intense, carnal involvement that seemed an essential piece of her total surrender to the part. Directors, producers, screenplay writers, actors, even a cameraman once, she sighed, knowing she took inspiration where she found it. But whenever she worked with Dru Jablonski, she gave herself completely to him. Letting go of Dru this early, as soon as the shooting ended, was unusual, because normally the attachment lasted through the difficult period of winding down the project, of waiting for reviews, publicity, the trailers, or maybe even the frenzy of initial interviews after release. Perhaps when all that started, they would be together again.

But "release," that was a word dancing in her head as she'd sat, still and unobtrusive, on the set. Usually release came easily in its own time, because for her there never was any emotional attachment beyond the camaraderie of the film "family," and the affairs ended naturally, like candlewicks snuffing themselves out at the end of long, melted tapers.

But this time was different, just as the whole film had been different. The heat, the lightheadedness, the sensation of being empty had overcome her in the last scene. Dru had been right—she had pulled something off. She had reached a new height in her acting. She had truly become Edna in a way she'd never become another character. But the film had also brought her to another new place, and this one was personal.

A shadow had been cast over her all through the filming, and now she wanted to let it take shape. She'd wanted to be not Jocelyn playing Edna, but Jocelyn herself sitting on the set. The set from the '40s with its deco coffee pot and ruffled curtains and rounded radio from which swing and the voices of FDR and Bing Crosby and Frank Sinatra once soothed frightened Americans, and Harry Truman gave 'em hell through crackling static.

She wanted to sink into some other, personal reality where the main characters were her mother Madge and herself, a small child, as they lived in a little yellow house—so like that set—on a promontory overlooking the sea. Of course, when they had looked toward the Pacific with longing, it was not with the certain knowledge of the lost hero-husband Louis that Edna had, but with a wistful, unspoken *un*certainty. Jocelyn the small child, just like the grown woman, wished to know her father. She assumed from all the possibilities that he had been the tall, blond Navy flier who never returned from the war. She assumed her mother mourned him as she did, and that mourning had made it impossible ever to speak his name. This belief had been the most comforting version of her own story she could come up with.

She closed her eyes with the image of herself as a baby in the arms of her smiling mother, long dark hair framing her face. It was a photograph on the wall above the orange sofa. She imagined a small version of it inside a folding leather cover—like the one Louis Dubois had—in her father's breast pocket as he flew west over the endless Pacific.

She also remembered how often she'd questioned her mother, and how Madge responded with a vague smile and no concrete information. "I honestly don't know who... you were a grand surprise." Then she would inevitably add, "the best." So it always ended. Jocelyn with her adoring mother, who attached with equal passion to motherhood, cleanliness, good health, and free love.

Back in those days in the little yellow house, Jocelyn had made up her own mind. The flyer. She had always wanted some tangible item—that photo, a note, a ring maybe, or a cross—something to verify what she was certain she knew. But that thing had never materialized. So she made *Pacific Blue*, a French-American war romance, with a real hero to love, as an homage to her missing father.

She hadn't known it at the beginning, but now at the end, sitting in the dark, she knew why she had said good-bye so precipitously to Dru, to the cast, to the partying. Wanting to sink deeper into this mood of reverie and revelation, she had decided to go home alone. Watching the sun play over the city below, where the lights dazzled as brightly as the stars above, she knew that was where she needed to be.

Sitting on the couch in the cacophonous living room, she also knew she couldn't bear an intrusion from J.J., or even worse, questions about Melanie. Melanie! She had already heard the charge that *Pacific Blue* with its patriotic undertones was political. But this was not political—Gloria Steinem had it wrong. This was as personal as it got.

Chapter 22

The phone rang again, and Jocelyn slammed down the receiver with an abrupt: "Tell her not *now*, Dana…I'm resting for God's sake."

J.J. What a pain she could be sometimes. Ever since that awful article had been published, they hadn't spoken. J.J. did leave messages trying to apologize for the "shitty headline." She had no control over headlines, but the damage had been done.

"Superstar a Virgin Still."

Really? The "shitty headline" had been pulled from a discussion deep in the story drawn from a conversation like dozens they had had over the years.

J.J.: You know when we were young there was so much pressure—and ridiculous effort on the part of adults who felt in charge of us—to remain virgins—

JOCELYN: Except for my mother.

J.J.: So true! And so, I've always wondered, was it rebellion against her notions of "free love" that made you hold out so long?

JOCELYN (smiling enigmatically): So long? I consider myself a virgin still.

Of course J.J. understood perfectly what she meant, because they always understood each other. Still the ridiculous—and ridiculed—headline stuck in the public's view.

The problem wasn't so much things that were factually wrong, nor the tone, which was almost flattering, but still the story stuck in her craw. J.J. always in search of "the truth," remained blind to any version but her own, and when she put it on public display, that hurt most. That and the other thing J.J. did so easily, so unaware—betrayal.

J.J. probably still didn't know how it felt to be left behind when she went off, head over heels, after the man of the moment. Of course, she *did* love them. Guy, especially. Jocelyn still felt the sting of the fight they'd had over him, when after running off with "that frizzy activist" as J.J. had called the woman Guy eventually married, he had showed up in J.J.'s life again. When Jocelyn had pointed out that it was stupid, along with immoral, to take up with a married man, even if he was separated, J.J. had been so vile, saying: "What do you know about immoral? At least I don't just go down with any passing pair of pants."

"But I don't love them," Jocelyn remembered saying, while not saying the obvious: that J.J. did. Yet J.J., so blinded by her passions—including her quixotic quest for "the truth"—could never see, let alone understand, what the betrayal of abandonment felt like. What good, Jocelyn asked herself, was a roommate who barely entered the room for weeks at a time? A friend who became totally unavailable when the man she claimed to love came along?

As for men, Jocelyn knew it was hard to count now how many there had been, and how little overall they had meant. The haunting, the obsessions, the pain of relationships. Early on she'd resisted men physically; those she feared loving deeply and then losing herself in, she'd gotten over a long time ago. Submitting her body and keeping her feelings in reserve was so much easier. Virginity? It was a question of emotions, a question of the heart—a place perhaps in her darkest, quiet moments, she still longed to visit. Better to be busy and not think about it. "A virgin still?"

She retreated to the downstairs bedroom. Drapes were drawn across the glass doors facing the city and the great round bed, still covered in a red satin spread—another nod to Madge's peculiar sense of décor—looked inviting. With Madge's airy paintings of her as an angelic blonde child in fields of flowers on the wall, this room had always been a special sanctuary. Instead of finding romantic bliss there— Madge's peculiar maternal intent—she had found oblivion, a state of numb repose that mostly led to dreamless sleep. Seeking that now, she dove into the inviting red satin and pulled the oversized pillows over her head.

Annoyingly, J.J. came to her instead—the times she had come to this house when, as college girls, they had laughed themselves into a stupor on the round bed in Madge's great amorous "set." Drifting off, she wished she could remember what the jokes had been. She was not to be blessed with a dreamless sleep.

J.J. STOOD ON the step pounding on the door. The pounding was soundless as Jocelyn looked through the peephole and watched J.J.'s mouth open and shut as if she were singing silently, or was a fish in deep water. Her long dark hair swept around in that drifty way it would in swift currents. Slowly, so as not to let a flood of water in, Jocelyn opened the door, surprised to see J.J. there in a bright green sweater and skirt. Brown, dry scrub covered the hills just behind, and her hair fell lank and still about her shoulders. A perfect Los Angeles day, more suitable for fire than for flood. The word "burning" fell out of J.J.'s mouth, and Jocelyn knew they had been there before. Even in dream state, she knew the very house she was standing in had only been rebuilt two years ago, after the last great fire. But God, it was hot. It was August. She knew by the way the light bent. Then J.J. was saying "fire" before slipping into the house.

They both pushed hard to shut the door. Perhaps it was wind, or perhaps water again. Jocelyn couldn't tell. Then they stood together in silence in front of the glass doors facing the city, watching the smoke rise from its heart. The gray ball grew larger and larger, holding bits of flame, as if rising from a furnace. Soon it was a wave blowing toward them, about to break over and engulf them. Time to run, scream, escape, but she could do nothing, only stand her ground. Then J.J. disappeared.

Jocelyn opened her eyes abruptly in the still semidark of her room. The sweat around her hair and face seemed to have crossed over from another time and place. August 1965. It all came to her now in precise detail. Watts in flames, and J.J. arriving on her doorstep in semi-shock, wearing bright green. They stood together behind the glass watching, the glass kept shut to hold back the acrid smell of fire, the smell a tripwire to panic since the fall of 1961 when both their homes had been consumed. But to J.J., who had just come from the edges of the catastrophe, the smells were more specific—burning rubber, plaster, wood, wire, glass, cars. She couldn't bring herself to say people. And then there were the sounds: explosions from fireballs, gunshots, shattering glass, the screams of sirens, bells, fire engines, human voices yelling, cursing, calling out to each other in the black void that soon swallowed up their identity.

To Jocelyn, who had just finished her year touring the state as Miss Calbrew, the Beauty Queen of Beer (who didn't drink, but that was a publicity twist she was saving for the future), the very existence of Watts had come as a surprise. Suddenly she felt the restlessness again that bordered on mania; it was a thing that plagued her life.

Remembering Paris, she felt how it was to walk its endless streets, her only purpose to outpace her anxiety. She also knew that the other place where she found calm was to lose herself deep in thinking, in books. That seemed a better bet than to try roaming the Hollywood Hills. So she enrolled in summer school at UCLA and signed up for two courses in philosophy.

Then that August came, and J.J. bringing the unhappy, burning, real world into her own realm of make-believe. Even now, nearly a decade later, she could feel the shivers of cold shoot through her as if she were watching smoke from the window. *Watts.* A new vocabulary word. Its definition included other words: ghetto, racism, Black Power, riots, police brutality, fury, urban war, and of course, fire. It would have been possible—preferable, from that deep, meditative place inside that brought calm—to close the blinds across the glass and remain safe in her sanctuary in the hills. But J.J. had forced her to look, and there was no going back. She could still feel that resentment, too.

Immobile on the round bed, Jocelyn felt the sweat begin to dissipate. Eyes wide open, she stared methodically at the playbills and photos and movie posters on the wall, as if on a forced march through her own life. From Paris to Miss Calbrew to her early theater days playing Joan of Arc, to her sassy first movie, *Good Time Girls*, to… her eyes stopped at the poster of *The Jade Empress*, the noir film set in L.A. where she'd played a "sexy detective broad" in a wide-brimmed hat. It was after that film they'd asked her to sing before the troops and to appear at the "Honor America Day" on the Fourth of July in Washington. There, from that stage, she'd encountered Melanie. If remembering J.J.'s

kick to her conscience merely annoyed her, it was the memory of Melanie that haunted her still.

Chapter 23

Even after slamming the phone down, the obnoxious voice kept ringing in J.J.'s ear. "Not now, not now," it mocked her.

Well, ask Her Majesty when? she wanted to shout back, knowing how snotty and childish she sounded.

A hot Sunday in September and the roses in Gran's garden beckoned her. They needed water, and attention, as did Gran herself. To say nothing of Annie, who said—and it was true—that J.J. hadn't been over to visit in "a wicked long time." In her motherly way, she promised to whip up a terrific meal based on the latest soy products. Then, she added, as if this were the real *pièce de résistance*, "have I got a great surprise for you!" J.J. knew from long years of experience, this meant that Dad had moved back in again. Another doomed reconciliation and a heap of soy beans. *How can I resist?* she asked herself.

To stall a bit longer before facing the day, she started a

fresh pot of coffee, looked over the new postcard from Ivan, with the menacing, toothless logger in front of a stand of redwoods, and flipped it over to reread his message: "This dude reminds me of your guy Moon, who has not been seen in weeks. Nor the chick with the kid, either. And to my surprise, officers of the peace all in place as before. All quiet on the Northern Front, Eyes & Ears Ivan"

J.J. poured her coffee in a Thermos, screwed the cup back on, and headed to the back porch, telling herself that she'd get through the day with the least stress and worry if she had a plan—though she knew she needed to feed the beast soon, as Alice kept saying, and without Jocelyn, she hadn't got another story lined up. "Roses first," she announced with perky resolution.

Instead, she turned and ran back upstairs to the den.

Rummaging through the desk, she pulled the file labeled "Melanie, '70" and sat back in the reclining desk chair. After extracting what she was looking for, J.J. held it and stared for a long time.

The glossy postcard still looked new. Red, white, and blue bunting curled along the edges, and bold print announced "Honor America Day, National Mall, July 4, 1970" over a background of exploding fireworks. "Pray for America with Rev. Billy Graham. Stand with America and Presidents Truman, Johnson & Nixon." In small print it listed the celebrities who would be present: Bob Hope, of course, and Vince Lombardi, Pat Boone, the Lennon Sisters, Jocelyn..."

J.J.'s eyes stopped there, turning the card over. Before reading Melanie's ever-correct handwriting, she wanted to visualize her. What would she have looked like at that moment, standing in the throngs and heat of that July day, 1970, in Washington, D.C.? J.J. tried to imagine. Would she have been in the crazy fringes and colors that Evelyn had described when she last saw her? Or would she have been in the fuzzy white of the previous visit? Or maybe something political, like an upside-down flag shirt, or a black one with peace signs and "Stop the War" emblazoned on it. In truth, J.J. couldn't conjure Melanie there, couldn't even remember what she was wearing when they'd seen each other briefly for the last time. White space, J.J. thought. *I can't bring Melanie out of the perpetual light around her which blinds me from any real vision of her.*

She turned then to all she had for certain, Melanie's words:

Dear J.J.,

Who would have thought I'd be here for this, the great patriotic bash with all the flag-wavers, and You Know Who among them. Intro by Bob Hope. She put on quite a great show, and sang along with Pat Boone, if you can imagine. I only came to bear witness. I'm sure she didn't know I was there. Still solidarity, no? One way or another.

Love always, Melie

Chapter 24

*B*arely awake from a troubled sleep, Jocelyn pushed into the kitchen, reached in the refrigerator to find the orange juice she always kept stocked, and stared at the phone. Then she grabbed it and dialed Dana. "Okay, now, I'll call her now," she said without giving her agent a chance to interrupt. "J.J., the one who called from the *Star.* But I need her number."

Jocelyn held the phone in one hand, and gulped from the glass in the other while trying to control the anxiety in her breathing.

"J.J. here," the throaty voice on the other end answered.

"Hey, it's me," Jocelyn replied softly.

A pause followed, then: "Oh my God. Right. How are you?"

"Okay. Fine. I guess we need to talk…about Melanie."

"Yes. Yes we do."

"Well, it sounds noisy there. I mean all those typewriters and… shall we meet?"

"Name the time and place, and I'm there," J.J. answered, adding, "I'm glad you called."

~~

IT WAS EARLY evening when J.J. found a parking space on Sunset Boulevard near Musso & Frank's, the family restaurant Madge and Burt, sometimes accompanied by Jocelyn and herself, used to dine in every night. She blinked stepping in from the light to the dark of the bar to find Jocelyn at a corner table, her blonde hair falling over her face, leaning forward, as if reading. She did not look up.

J.J. hesitated a minute before trying to break the ice. "Well, I guess I'm the one making the dramatic entry for a change."

Jocelyn looked at her old friend for a moment, then offered a faint smile. Neither extended a hand, and J.J. sat abruptly on the chair across from the banquette.

"I, well," J.J. began, but was interrupted by Jocelyn.

"Thanks for coming all this way," she said.

"It's the least I can do for Melie." Taking notice of Jocelyn's juice, she summoned the waiter. "I'll take a gin and tonic, please. I'm drinking for both of us."

Jocelyn smiled again, twisted her napkin around the juice glass and stared at it, as though it contained the secrets of the monologue she was about to commence.

"So the last time I saw her was at that big July Fourth thing in 1970. 'Honor America Day' sponsored by Bob Hope. He asked me personally because I'd done a couple of shows with him earlier to entertain the troops. Did you know?" Jocelyn looked up.

J.J. saw her friend's eyes change color, green to gold, as they always had. *A tiger*, she thought. "Yes, I knew. How'd you get into that, anyway?"

"My people—well mostly Harding, my main publicity guy—thought it would be good for my image."

"Yeah?" J.J. controlled her impulse to interrogate.

"Yeah, well," Jocelyn looked back at the glass. "I mean, there was a niche there to fill, the hot Hollywood babe who wasn't a dissenter."

"You mean like the un-Fonda?"

"Exactly. I mean we were filming *Walk on the Woman Side* and he thought, you know, we could reach a larger audience of women, housewives and all, if I had a more mainstream image. So I did the USO shows and that went well, and then Bob Hope called…and I went to Washington."

J.J. took a long swig of her drink, swallowing her impulse to ask what in the hell that had been like. "And you saw Melie at that event?" she asked, remembering Melie's postcard saying the opposite.

"Yes, I saw her. She came because I was there. I know it. She must have seen the ads for it on TV. But I definitely saw her. She was right there in front—wearing all black, can you imagine—and holding a sign. It said in big letters, *Pourquoi me tuez-vous?* And all around the edges were images from the war, some drawings, some photos. Huts being burned, children bombed and bleeding…"

"Why do you kill me?" J.J. translated. "Words of Christ?"

"No," Jocelyn answered quietly, "Pascal. But echoing Christ. That was what she was getting at, that I had crossed over to the other side. That by supporting this 'God Bless America' event, by supporting the troops, I was also contributing to the killing."

"Do you think she was right?"

Jocelyn stared straight at J.J. then, her eyes shifting from green to gray. "Yes. Of course she was right. That's why I couldn't acknowledge her. It was too…"

"Why didn't you ever tell me any of this?"

"Dear God," she replied, tears spilling down her cheeks, "I couldn't. The image of her standing there silently with that sign has haunted me ever since, made me see what my life had become—a lie hiding inside a publicity poster. A fake woman hiding inside the persona of an invented one. She was saying to me with her presence, 'Jocelyn, you've sold out. Where is the real you?' How could I tell you? I was so ashamed."

⟶

HOURS AFTER J.J. drove the two of them back up the hill to Jocelyn's house, when the chill came in with deep nightfall, they moved from the balcony to the orange couch, where the conversation went on unbroken.

They shared all they knew about Melanie, then lapsed into silence. Jocelyn finally spoke: "This is an amazing story—a mystery, J.J. From what I saw, and what some of the others have said, we know Melie became very political. An activist, really. And all those strange encounters you had with her family, no wonder she split. Then the commune thing, the drugs, the husband! Hans, good attentive husband? Complete jerk? Eccentric, talented composer? All of the above? And, God, where is she? I want to think she's alive somewhere."

J.J. sighed, not wanting to admit her own gut feeling—that Melanie had perished in that fire. There was nothing more to say, really, so she decided to shift the conversation back to Jocelyn.

"There is another thing we need to talk about. My editor wants follow-up stories on all the *demoiselles*. Like what have they all been doing for the last ten years. Can I ask some things about you?" she said softly.

Chapter 25

ctober had blown in, taking the smog with it. J.J. paused for a minute to inhale near the window overlooking Colorado Boulevard. She imagined she could smell the blue of the sky even before seeing it. The sounds of traffic below, the honking horns, the sirens, seemed a refrain, harmonizing now with the phones, clacking typewriters, the call of voices back and forth in the newsroom. *My sounds*, she said to herself, *my city*, and strangely felt like humming. Easing into her chair, she flung her canvas bag on the desk to pull out the notes from her extraordinary interview with Jocelyn.

"Well, don't we look like the cat who swallowed the canary?"

"Alice!" J.J. looked up to see her editor looking down with a wry smile. She smiled back. "To what do I owe the pleasure of your company?"

"I am but a messenger. Himself requests an audience." Alice jerked her head toward Purvis's door.

J.J. watched as Alice turned and walked away, her old-fashioned pencil-style skirt reaching well past her calves. Mindful of her own long tunic over bell-bottomed pants, a new look she'd decided to wear to the office on days without meeting the public, she smoothed down the top over her round hips before knocking on the boss's door.

"Yeah, come on in, it's open," Purvis barked out as she pushed the handle. He waved her in, a cigarette in one hand and the phone in the other, while his eyes wandered over her torso. *He's probably looking over my outfit, giving it a thumbs down,* she decided. But at least the "new improved" Bud Purvis knew enough not to say anything, whereas the old one would probably have made a crack about the beauty of short skirts and showing her legs — previously a favorite topic.

"Sit, sit, dear," he said at last, putting out the stub of his smoke. "I've got to hand it to you, dear, despite my fears about that nun story and religious sh — stuff, we've gotten a helluva lot of letters from broads of all ages who claimed to be 'moved and inspired' by your Sister whatever-the-hell her name is."

"Eve," J.J. broke in. "Sister Eve."

"Yeah. So the female readership is going crazy for all this, just as anticipated, and who would've guessed it, but some men are even writing in, too. Okay, priests and bishops and such, but we can stretch the point and still call them men can't we? So what the hell, J.J., we're breaking new ground here, getting not only the ladies but those church boys in skirts to sign on. Hard to beat that!" He grinned openly.

"Well, great, then." J.J. grinned back.

"Have a look," he said, thrusting a pile of letters into her hand. "And keep it up. So when's the next one coming in?"

"I'm working on it now," J.J. answered, standing, and thinking to herself: *If you liked the nun story, fat boy, you're going to die and go to heaven over what I've got for you next. An exclusive with Jocelyn, full of what you crave most, juicy details.*

Humming under her breath that new Joni Mitchell song, "Free Man in Paris," she carried the letters back to her desk to revel in the remarks of her happy readers.

It was early afternoon when J.J. realized she'd not even taken a lunch break and had spent the morning drinking black coffee. An apple core nested in the pile of litter swallowing her desk. Still, she couldn't bring herself to quit the interview she'd just finished transcribing, and she heard Jocelyn's voice even as she read the printed words. She could even picture the new headline: "Superstar a Virgin No More."

J.J.: You've projected so many images on the screen from medieval warrior-woman in "Joan of Arc," to a mysterious, scheming "noir" sleuth in "The Jade Empress," to tough and sexy hard-core feminist in "Walk on the Woman Side," but now perhaps you've done something very different. For your forthcoming film, "Pacific Blue: The Louis Dubois Story," the buzz is that you project traditional values of faithfulness and patriotism. Can you comment on this?

JOCELYN: Well, of course, I am an actress, so the characters I play differ a lot from one to the other. But, even though I understand the natural tendency for the public to confuse the role with the person, I am none of those characters. I am merely myself.

J.J.: So the hype about the new film and its emphasis on the fidelity and virtue of the long-suffering heroine, Edna, isn't really a personal statement about you, then?

JOCELYN: No, not at all. I actually like a variety of men and have enjoyed the company of many over the years.

J.J.: Just for the record, when you say you've enjoyed their company, you are speaking of having many lovers, many affairs, yes?

JOCELYN: Of course, and in that article you ran a couple of years ago about me, you got it quite wrong about calling me a virgin, you know. I was speaking only metaphorically—about a kind of inexperience with life-altering love. I still believe in that, look forward to it, so in that way I am a traditional girl. But traditional in another way, too, because I did follow the advice my mother always gave me, and as you well know, she was a firm believer in promiscuity.

Following that revelation, Jocelyn went on to name a few well-known names in her list of liaisons—the stuff gossip columnists' dreams are made of.

Then with the tape turned off, she had said: "You know, J.J., the studio is going to go crazy when they read this, and Harding, my publicist, who cooked up this whole 'wholesome girl patriot' campaign, is going to soil himself."

"Yeah, I'll bet," J.J. had replied. "So do you really want to go through with it? Is this going to ruin things?"

"No, not in the least. It'll stir things up for sure, and they'll all buzz like mad hornets for a while. But in the end, it will only create more publicity, and that will be good for the film. Besides, there is another good reason for putting all this out there—it happens to be true."

When J.J. turned on the tape again, she switched to another topic, the one that interested her the most.

J.J.: So patriotism is another theme that is linked to your new film. Can you discuss its importance for our readers?

JOCELYN: Certainly. As you know, the story takes place during World War II, a time of great heroism and pride in America, so naturally, the characters, including the French hero, Louis Dubois, reflect long-standing Western values. But I think that patriotism exists in abundance in our own times, too, and is expressed in many ways.

J.J. Could you give some examples?

JOCELYN: Certainly the soldiers and others who support our war effort in Vietnam now are putting their lives on the line and are patriots in the traditional sense. But others, who question the damage we are doing in the war, and our reasons for fighting it—like Jane Fonda, for example—are also patriots because they love our country and want us to live our highest values.

J.J.: It's well known that you have done a lot to support the troops with USO performances and appearing with Bob Hope in that big Honor America rally in Washington. Doesn't that suggest that your sympathies are with the pro-war side in this great debate?

JOCELYN: Not at all. My sympathies are with all parties who care deeply for our country and where we are going, and I believe that if we are sending young men to fight and die in a war, we all owe them support. But my sympathies? Frankly, they were probably best summed up at that rally by a young woman who came as a witness to the horror of this conflict. She came in silent vigil, standing in front of the stage, wearing all black. She is somebody I know—someone we both know—from a long time ago. She carried a sign, showing pictures of burning villages and wounded children and bodies piled in ditches. The sign had a quote in French that simply said, "Why are you killing me?" It came from her favorite philosopher, Pascal, but also invoked the wounds of Christ. My sympathies? They are with her and the message of her sign.

Chapter 26

The phone rang. Before she could reply, J.J. looked up to see a slim figure in black approaching, and exhaled in surprise. It seemed an apparition right out of Jocelyn's description of Melanie at the rally in Washington. J.J. took a moment to collect herself, taking in the badly dyed black hair and kohl-rimmed eyes of Melanie's sister.

"Natalie!" she said, not attempting to hide her surprise. "Please, sit down."

Natalie perched nervously on the edge of an old chair next to J.J.'s desk. "I can't stay," she announced, pulling out a cigarette and lighting it with jerky movements. "I've got rehearsal."

J.J. merely nodded in sympathy, knowing it was a moment to keep her powder dry, as Alice had often advised, until the time was ripe to unleash the rapid fire of her inquisition-style questions.

"So," Natalie finally said, exhaling smoke, "I brought

you some things—stuff of Melie's I'd sort of stashed in my room. I had rescued them from under her bed actually, when the parents... well, this stuff was locked up in here all the time, but you get the picture." She put a box on the edge of J.J.'s messy desk.

"Thank you," J.J. said quietly, not taking her eyes off Natalie's. "What kind of stuff, if I may ask?"

"Um. Well, you'll see. But it was just things she collected—some of it you'll recognize, seeing as how you wrote it."

"Right." J.J. nodded again. "Out of curiosity, why did you decide to bring it to me instead of keeping it yourself?"

"Well, I bounce around a lot, where I stay, I mean. And it had been in my old room at home, but some weird kind of shit is going to come down over there I think, and I wasn't sure it was safe in the old pad anymore, even locked. Probably better off with you. You'll see..." Natalie stood abruptly.

J.J. stood too. "I'm really grateful, Natalie. How could I get in touch with you now if I had some questions?"

"Look, I've got to go," she replied, and bolted toward the reception area.

Two hours passed while J.J. carefully fingered the treasures Natalie had brought her, until the dying October light fell in stripes across her desk. Then she arranged the contents in different stacks. There were school papers, certificates of academic achievement, and pictures going back as far as junior high. There were letters, some in the childish hand of her younger sister, some from a long-gone and doting grandmother, some from other girlhood friends, and several from her college years. There were photos documenting birthday parties, Christmas, skiing trips, a beloved kitten. The ones from her parents included only newsy notes, were or about society doings, with clippings inside. From the Paris year, there was a collection of love letters from Hans. And from the years following, a few letters from Grace and

Evelyn, one announcement of a film opening with a brief note from Jocelyn, and to J.J.'s surprise, an extensive pile of letters, postcards, and a few clips from herself. "Melie, my God, you saved everything I ever sent," J.J. said to herself.

But, she noted, a lot was not saved either. Not one negative or scolding word from her family, although J.J. knew plenty of those existed. Not a word from or about Hans after Paris. Not a hint of medical records or a mention of doctors or asylums. Nothing on Woodstock or other adventures. And of course, nothing in her own words. If the letters she had sent and the journals she had kept were Melanie's call to the world, then this box contained its response. But one carefully edited, so that all darkness was expelled and only the light remained.

The sun had vanished from the window completely by the time J.J. stood and twisted her aching back to get the knots out. She had carefully put rubber bands around the various stacks. Amazing material to add to the Melanie files. She decided to bring it home tomorrow in new folders. For the moment though, she held two pieces in her hand that she meant to take with her now, as if touching them would help her absorb their meaning.

One was a black and white photo where Melanie, overexposed so that most of her was blotted out except for her face, stood smiling widely in front of a tent. Next to her, with his arm around her, stood a good-looking young black man with an Afro held in place by a red bandana. On the back was written, "J.C. & me."

The photo rested on top of a letter, the one item J.J. had not worked up the courage to open yet. It was postmarked December 14, 1970, had a post office box in Birmingham, Alabama, as its return address, sent originally to Melanie's old apartment in Rochester, and finally forwarded to her parents' home in Pasadena. It was clearly written in Guy's hand.

Gathering her bag, jacket, and purse, J.J. knew it was time to shut down and visit Gran. "I hope she needs to see me half as much as I need to see her," J.J. said to herself.

⌒

IT WAS AFTER seven thirty by the time J.J. arrived at Glenview Convalescent, long past dinner time for the residents.

"Grand-mum would be in the lounge watching TV with the others," the receptionist informed J.J.

J.J. nodded and made her way to the big room where inviting sofas and armchairs, a faux fire in the fireplace, and cheery pastoral prints on the walls were all intended to project a cheesy coziness. But atmosphere could do nothing to change the basic reality of a room filled with aged, disabled, and often demented people who were passing their last days — or years — there in miserable decline.

"God's waiting room," Alice had once caustically remarked after accompanying J.J. on a visit to Gran. And J.J. could only agree, again feeling the sting of guilt for putting Gran in such a place. It was hard enough just to find Gran in the awful company of her peers. Now J.J. stood warily at the edge of the room, scanning it to find her. As her eyes adjusted, she spotted her grandmother, white hair swept back elegantly as ever, sitting in a wheelchair. Gran seemed animated and alert, focused on the TV game show. As soon as Gran noticed her, she burst into a huge grin.

"Oh, good, you've come to get me out of here," Gran laughed as if they were in on a conspiracy.

"About time," another old lady called out. "Frenchie thinks she's so smart, she calls out all the answers to the questions. Ruins the show for the rest of us."

Laughing out loud, J.J. wheeled Gran away, sorry to be taking her only as far as her own room and not really springing her as she deserved. But Gran laughed too, and her eyes danced with happiness once she and J.J. were safely inside her room.

"So, is that true? Do you know all the answers and shout them out at the game shows?"

"Well," Gran said, looking mischievous, "not all of them. But really, you know, some of these ladies are, what shall I say, so *stupide, n'est-ce pas?*"

J.J. relaxed. After all the day's turmoil, it lifted her spirits to have a real visit with Gran, and a blessing to have her "home." And she vowed to herself she had to find a way to bring Gran home, in the real sense, soon.

As J.J. helped her transfer from the wheelchair to her favorite armchair, Gran continued to chatter, mostly about other residents or attendants, who were unfamiliar to J.J. Glancing at the photos on the nearby bureau, she found new subjects to introduce.

"You know, Gran, the garden has been really great this year, although I think it misses you. The avocados were really good, well you do know, because I brought some to you, and now the lemons and oranges are coming and the roses are still blooming and—"

"*Oui, chérie, je sais…*" Gran smiled sweetly.

"Oh, sorry. I guess I've already told you all this."

"*Non, ma petite, c'est ta mère qui m'a tout dit.*"

"My mother? Annie told you about the garden?"

"Oh yes. She brought so many pictures, up there, see?"

Gran pointed to a stack of prints which J.J. reached to pick up, puzzled. Perhaps Annie had come by while she'd been away, perhaps she'd tried to call. J.J. felt a sharp pang as she began looking through the photos of the colorful blooms with Gran, knowing she had been pretty neglectful of Annie. Sometimes there were messages at work. Had she remembered to call back?

"*Voilà,*" Gran pronounced, pulling out a picture of both

her parents, embracing for the camera. "As you know, your father has come home again. It's better this way, *non*?"

J.J. nodded, not admitting to Gran how little she knew, really. She had guessed her parents were "working things out" once again. But it seemed such a tired mantra from her childhood, she had not really bothered to find out.

"So Gran," J.J. said, wanting to change the direction of the conversation again. "You know a while ago you asked me how my 'sister' was, and I have a lot of news about that." She launched into a long description of her visit to Jocelyn, her latest movie, the interview with her and the article she herself had just completed. "I'll bring you a copy first thing when it comes out. It's pretty sensational, actually," J.J. promised. "And Gran, you seem so much better now. Maybe you'd like to see her new movie, too. It has a French hero. It takes place during World War II."

"Oh yes," Gran said, nodding in agreement. "I always like going to the theater. But tell me, *ma petite*, how is that sister of yours? The blonde one."

J.J. hesitated, inhaling. Perhaps Gran's "good spell" was fading now. "Well, I've just been telling you all about her, Gran, remember?"

"Oh, but you didn't say anything about the baby. Has she had that baby yet?"

Chapter 27

J.J. dashed up the stairs to the office, hoping to slip in unnoticed. Monday morning 10:05, and she was late. Opening the door, she stood for a moment, dazed. Phones were ringing off the hook, her colleagues stood talking animatedly. "There she is," the receptionist called out, and a flashbulb went off in her face.

"George, what are you doing?" she snapped back at a staff photographer.

"Hey, girl, just orders from the top," he grinned at her.

Confused, she stumbled toward Alice's office. "What the hell's happening?" she blurted to Alice's turned back.

"Just celebrating our own star. Aren't we having fun?" Alice replied without looking up.

"Having fun?"

Alice swiveled to face her, glasses dangling on a chain around her neck, lipstick slightly askew. "Well, some of us certainly are." She nodded toward Purvis's office. "As you may remember, since I presume you saw the layout, your piece on Jocelyn went out yesterday, top spread in the Sunday edition with fetching photos—which, if you'd bothered to answer your phone at home you'd know—and it's been nonstop ever since. 'Hot' and 'incendiary' are only a couple of the adjectives the TV critics are using. Big papers and chains, like the *L.A. Times*, the *Washington Post*—you may have heard of them—are calling us for reprint rights. TV stations are calling for contact info so they can get to her for their own juicy interviews... get the picture?"

J.J. blinked. "Really?"

"Well, you can believe it or not. Suit yourself." Alice grinned and gestured to the chaos in the newsroom.

"So what's up with George taking my picture?"

"Himself is running a short bio on you. You're now a story in your own right."

Within minutes, J.J. was sitting in the office with her boss, who in an altered state had reverted to the Old Bud Purvis. "Hello, sweetheart," he grinned, as he grabbed the ringing phone with one hand and waved a cigar around with the other. Finally, slamming the phone into its cradle, he blurted out: "Jesus H. Ke-rist, J.J., it's a sensation. Dylan and Brando, what's his name, that sexy mayor from New York, and every big shot in Hollywood. Who did that girl not go down with? I always knew you could do this, J.J., I always knew you had it in you." He grinned like the Cheshire Cat, smoke slowly encircling his face.

"Well, I..." she began, but he cut her off.

"Look, dear, we've got a little problem, though. These big boys from the networks, not to mention the Hollywood tabloids and several big city papers, have been calling nonstop, asking for reprint rights and sniffing around. What they really want of course is access, so they can do their own story and completely undercut us. Truth is, nothing's stopping them, but they can't seem to find out how to get to

Jocelyn. She's behind a complete wall of silence, I'm gathering. True? Tell me this is true."

"Yeah. True. Tell you what, I'd readily make available the contact for her press person, who's going to be spitting nails about this interview and no way, no how, can they get past that barricade. She's a piece of work." J.J. grinned now too, imagining Dana breathing fire on them all.

"What do you mean 'spitting nails'? Aren't those Hollywood types always happy with publicity, especially publicity that gets as much attention as this is getting?"

"Not always. In this case, they were trying for a completely different image—loyal girlfriend, good patriot—the Virtuous Jocelyn, for the upcoming film. She kind of blew that wide open with this interview, wouldn't you say?"

"That's for damn sure."

"But look, don't worry about anybody moving in on this story. Even if they could get through to her on this, which they can't, she promised me an exclusive, and that's what I got. Trust me on this."

"Oh, I do trust you, sweetheart, I do. Always have."

J.J. decided to just let that pass, while Purvis was already moving on.

"So, what's next, dear? What have you got to top this one?" Before she could even conjure a reply, he answered himself. "Of course! Since we're running a short profile on you, the *Star* Reporter of the Month, a new feature—what'd you think? —the next piece should be yours. 'J.J. Tells All.'"

"Me? Look, I really don't think, I mean, you really don't want to take the edge off this sensation, do you?"

She dashed back into Alice's office and slammed the door.

"God. This is a zoo, and I need some quiet to think, you know?"

Alice turned in her chair and fixed her amused eyes on J.J. "Ah, yes. Quite a tempest you've unleashed here."

"Yeah, well, a thousand thanks for your part in this, too. But seriously, what's got me going is what he wants next—a piece about me." J.J.'s voice transmitted a plaintive anxiety. She hoped for sympathy.

Alice only gave her half-crooked smile. "No he's quite serious. And you know, Melanie isn't the only one missing from the profiles of the *demoiselles*. Personally, I can't wait."

DOWNSTAIRS IN A dimly lit coffee shop on Colorado Boulevard, J.J. retreated to a quiet corner with her reporter's notebook. She wrote "J.J." on the outside cover as she usually did, but could not bring herself to write in the subject of her inquiry.

"Tells All," she scribbled on the inside page, quickly filled with doodles. Tells all. About what? *About my non-life? My days chasing other people's stories and writing them up for no glory and little pay? My ditzy mother and arrested-development father?*

"Her birth took place in an atmosphere of a lost and found, where the mother plucked the child from a bed of ostrich feathers and tribal circumcision wear, and thus was miraculously found. The father, however, remains lost in its maze to this day," she wrote, then hastily crossed it out, knowing how Alice would chastise her churlishness.

"Love Life." She underlined this twice, then lifted her pen in the air. The only truth to tell about that would be to leave a blank page. What is there to say? A parody of Jocelyn's story, where she named a few anonymous names of forgettable dates in between deadlines and meaningless gropings in, yes, oh God the cliché of it, cars...and in non-descript apartments or at her parents' cluttered house in Mandeville Canyon where she house-sat when they were traveling.

"My truest and deepest connection is to my grandmother," she wrote before crossing it out with a single line.

"Not because it's pathetic," she told herself. "Because it's personal."

And almost true.

The pen lingered in the air again.

"My truest and deepest connection," she wrote emphatically, "is to a dead man who was married to someone other than me."

Since finally opening the letter from Guy to Melanie found in the batch Natalie had dropped off, J.J. had carried it with her like a talisman. Pushing aside her coffee, she slowly withdrew it from her bag to read again.

My dear Melanie,

Thanks again for your last note, and I am sorry, truly, our paths have not crossed down here. But it is a comfort to know they have crossed in the greater sense, and that we are working for the same goals, however distant achieving them sometimes feels. Still, despite all the suffering, bloodshed, and violence, and despite the terrible losses (yes, losing MLK still hurts on a daily basis), slowly, slowly we inch forward. Yes, since you asked, I'm still doing community work in Birmingham—I think its ties to King give me strength no matter what comes down—and yes, I'll be here for a while more, but not too long I fear. After my years of struggle with the draft, I think they are finally going to get me soon—to make an example of the Peace Corps, peacenik, troublemaking crowd for which I am sort of a poster boy. For complicated reasons of conscience I won't bore you with, I've decided to go. So unless you get down here fairly soon again, I'll most likely miss you.

As for the question of your friend, no, I haven't run into anybody of that description. But I will put out an alert through my networks and see what I can find out. John C. Calhoun? At least the guy has a sense of humor! If I hear something, I'll certainly let you know, but you're right to be concerned. As you know too well, in addition to the well-publicized assaults, lynchings, burnings, and the rest that make the news, the quiet campaign of

*terror against "our kind" and especially "black agitators" goes on
regularly and without much notice.*

*But let's hope I find some good news—"La Vie en Rose," as
J.J. always says. Speaking of her, how is she anyway? As you
may know, I've not had any communication with her for some
months now (her idea, not mine). I don't think I'm revealing too
much to say that the impasse is my fault completely. I could
never push for the finalization of the divorce because my wife
(who was at the time pregnant, but terminated the baby) was,
and remains, so against it. If the draft board hadn't won their
fight against me, I would do it now, but... Anyway, my feelings
for J.J. are undiminished.*

*Was it Apollinaire who wrote that line that I always love:
"Et comme l'Espérance est violente"?*

Oh yes, among her many gifts to me, French poetry.

*Take care, Melanie, and write me back at this address when
you receive this letter and I hope to have news for you.*

Always,

Your friend Guy

Trembling slightly, she remembered her dream after the
first time she read the letter. She was in a cemetery with
the two coffins, this time lying on the ground in front of
her. Instead of being empty, they both contained bodies.
She approached them from above, like a hovering spirit,
and leaned down to peer into each one to see the faces of
the dead. But before she could see, a great light blinded her,
and she woke up.

Setting her pen down at last next to the cup of cold coffee, she said out aloud. "Yes of course. I *will* write my untold
story. Just try and stop me."

Chapter 28

J.J. leaned back in Grandfather's old leather chair, files spread all over the desk. But the only thing that riveted her now was the small postcard with the picture of a nondescript tropical beach which she had touched so often it shone. Of course, she knew its brief message by heart, but read it one more time, like a diver taking a final spring at the end of the board before leaping into deep water.

> *J.J. dearest. I cannot say just where I am, except in Vietnam. All is well with me, except I have much to tell you. Your gift, an awakening to things French, keeps me going. Where some park a Bible, I have a copy of* Les Fleurs du Mal *and so want to send you "Une Invitation au Voyage." All in good time. Be well chère amie.*
>
> *Guy*

The card had arrived in February 1971. Two months later, she received the news from his parents that Guy was missing in action.

A Reporter's Story
By. J.J. Rocher

The news came in April 1971 that my old and dear friend, Guy Halbert, was missing in action in Vietnam. A well-known Civil Rights activist and Peace Corps volunteer, he had for many years battled his draft board, which, he claimed, wanted to make clear that his kind of work would not in any way exempt him from his "duty." Suddenly, just before Christmas 1970, he was finally drafted and swiftly sent to Vietnam. He had been there barely four months when he disappeared.

By way of full disclosure, I will say that we had once been romantically involved. However, we had gone our separate ways and he had married another woman in 1965. I heard from his family, who kept in touch with me over the years and agonized about his fate. They informed me that he and his wife had separated before he went overseas. I also knew that the Halberts' anguish grew with time, as did mine, over the uncertainty of what had happened to him. The next year they requested that I, in my capacity as a journalist, do what I could to find out. It was, I remember, February 1972, just when Angela Davis was released from prison. I knew how much he would have appreciated that. Because of my respect for his family's wishes, and for him, I decided to try.

I requested an assignment from my paper, but my editor deemed that a war zone was no place for a female reporter, so denied my request and turned down my application for press credentials. However, I was determined, and the following year I had accumulated enough time off to take a leave of absence. With my own money, a folder full of clips, relevant information about Guy provided by his family, and a passport, I left for Saigon in June 1973. My hope was to get on-the-spot credentials as a stringer.

Luckily, during that period after the Paris Peace Agreement was signed in January and the remainder of U.S. forces withdrew, it was easy to do. Also, the nature of my quest was more defined, if more harrowing. Guy's name did not appear on the POW list provided by the North Vietnamese and Provisional Revolutionary Government (the Viet Cong), nor was there any word of him when the official exchange of prisoners ended in March.

My first act after arriving was to find a ride to town and head for Givral's Café on the main square, a hangout, I was told, for journalists. Sure enough, within minutes, I had made the acquaintance of Zak Thornton, a fortyish photographer from Georgia, who worked for A.P. I told him what I wanted to do—a profile on a friend who went missing late in the game. I needed to get to the last place he was known to be. That was near Ben Cat, on Highway 13, north of Saigon. "Also," I told Zak, "I need press credentials—but I am a journalist, for real." He took me to the A.P. office, and I was quickly an official stringer.

Zak called the place I wanted to visit a "godforsaken mess," but also said he'd like to do a photo shoot of the area. I agreed, and within a couple of days we had picked up Tommy Tran, a wiry and indispensable translator/ guide, who at 53 was a tough nut. Together we stood at dawn, a peculiar threesome, outside the Continental Palace Hotel looking for transport. That turned out to be a taxi so old it must have been on life support. It was necessary, Tommy told us, to go early because during the day the road was patrolled by the South Vietnamese, but at night it belonged to the Viet Cong.

The cab ride, nearly two hours, was bone rattling and noisy. Like most Americans, no doubt, I imagined the "godforsaken mess" that Zak wanted to investigate to be an unruly jungle, or a forbidding delta, or a hilly landscape harboring lethal tunnels. I was not prepared for the low, open scrub, the madly scrambled traffic of military vehicles, smoke-spewing trucks and cabs, bicycles and sometimes water buffalo all sharing the same pitted road. I was not prepared for the oppressive low-hanging sky, the pathetic, dusty clumps of trees.

When at last Tommy said, "Okay, we arrive," we found the perimeters of the helicopter base (Hueys) and went beyond that to the district chief's office. Outside, the heat and swirling red dust weighted us down. We went there because the district chief, a South Vietnamese major, was the person most likely to know what happened to Guy's patrol. He greeted us with curt civility and asked in English what we wanted.

I pulled out my folder, explained that I was trying to see the exact spot where this American soldier had disappeared two years before, and showed him what I had: the name Fire Base Louise and the coordinates of where Guy's patrol was hit. He frowned, grunted. "Can't go there now," he announced. "V.C. territory. Not secure. Only few farmers now." He waved, turned his back, but oddly seemed to point to something.

"Ha! O.K." Tommy said, when we stood outside again. "He say officially we can't go. We go unofficially, O.K ?" And he gave a big grin, as he herded us back into the cab. "Now we find P.F. post."

Bouncing overland again, Zak explained: "P.F.s are like local militia, little outposts with a few hooches inside some kind of barbed wire and no heavy weapons, maybe just a .50 machine gun on top of a mortar."

And as we saw a settlement just like what Zak described, he leaned out the window and began shooting pictures.

Soon enough we reached the P.F. post, and Tommy jumped down to engage with a grizzle-faced platoon leader. Tommy told us the platoon leader, a sergeant, knew where F.B. Louise was and that it probably would be safe enough to get there now, but it would have to be by motorbike.

Within a half hour, I was on a bike with Tommy, Zak with our sergeant, and hanging on for dear life on a rutted, dusty track off the highway.

Minutes later, we slowed. "Ha!" Tommy said. "Fire Base Louise"— or what remained of it. Piles of rotting sandbags, old artillery casings, rusting barbed wire, looking out on an empty savannah with bare patches of red earth and clumps of low scrub. I could have stayed a decade in Vietnam trying to find meaning in this war, but I don't think I would ever learn more than what was offered by that desolate patch of earth. Tommy and Zak walked with me to the perimeter of the firebase, and Zak aimed his camera in the direction of the distant tree line.

"This is it, what your map say. Ha! But we stay here. Not safe beyond camp. Mines maybe. No good." He nodded with his chin.

I heard him, but I didn't. I knew the tree line was where Guy had gone on patrol for the last time. I knew that he had gone just into it and the V.C. snipers had got him. I knew it because now I could see it, could feel him. Then I stepped a few feet beyond the base onto the useless, withered, treacherous earth and knew what I had to do.

Guy's family had sent a small packet of treasures with me "to pass along" when I found out where Guy might be. There was a cassette tape from his teenage sister with songs she had been singing in her high school band, a note with a small prayer book from his mother, and a bronze star from his father that he had been awarded during World War II. It was wrapped in a box with a small tag attached that said simply, "Be safe, son." Guy and his father had argued bitterly about the Vietnam War, but when at long last Guy had gone to fight, his father finally felt he could "be proud." He had told me himself.

I knelt down in the choking patch of earth and began digging a small grave with my hands in the red dirt to bury these last offerings from Guy's loved ones. I felt him there with me and, for the moment, did not weep.

I turned back just as the sky thickened and knew the afternoon rain would drop upon us soon. It was then I saw the sergeant looking at me, and felt suddenly foolish. Hundreds, thousands of people had died anonymously in his country. Whole villages had disappeared. I imagined he wondered at this strange American woman who had come all the way around the world to find just one of her countrymen. Then he began to speak. Through Tommy's voice, this is what he said:

"Is a good thing to find your own man. Bury him how you can. So many ghosts of people not buried come here, walk around sad. At night can hear them calling. Cannot stay between land of living and land of dead. Is better to bury. Then find peace."

J.J. pushed back the typewriter and leaned into grandfather's chair, amazed at how quickly the words had rushed from her once she had finally dared to let them come. After rereading what she had written, she hunched forward once more to add the last thing she meant to include: her byline.

J.J. Rocher is a long-time staff writer for the Pasadena Star who in 1973 worked as a stringer for several publications after a few weeks in Vietnam. Her publications included three photo-essays for A.P. in collaboration with award-winning photographer Zak Thornton, and a profile of Guy Halbert that first appeared in the Modesto Bee and News-Herald in August, 1973.

⌐

IT WASN'T LATE when J.J. finished the piece, and for once she felt quite good about a first draft. So good, she broke a general rule she tried to stick to and popped open a bottle of wine. Normally, it was best to avoid drinking on "school nights" so she wouldn't have a buzz in the morning. But tonight she felt the warm presence of Zak, and knew he'd approve when she said "to hell with it" out loud, and poured herself a healthy glass of Cabernet Sauvignon. She could hear the pleasure in his soft Georgia drawl, too, as she imagined him saying "Here's to you, darlin'," after reading the byline with the credits they both deserved. She thought back to those short weeks in Saigon together after the trip to Ben Cat and the toasts they'd shared at the rooftop bar—the Journalist's Bar some called it—at the old Rex Hotel.

She remembered the old world, shabby grandeur of it, the small black and white tile floor and twisted, narrow stairs leading to the rooftop. Its well-aged bar, its dark French shutters flung open at night, with neon lights, horns and the traffic of the city beating steadily in the streets below. She remembered the beautiful young girls with silk black hair who sat at the bar, smiling provocatively at the worn expat faces—some of them journalists. She felt again the sense of unreality. As if the war, which was far from over, didn't exist. As if the short and easy affair she'd fallen into with Zak would go on and on. Sitting there on top of the Rex, she felt as if she'd known him forever. She'd talked openly about herself: about her parents and Gran, her job, her yearning to go somewhere—in her writing, in her life. She'd spoken of her friends, her worries about Melanie, and Bud Purvis. More than any of her descriptions, that one had made Zak laugh.

"Darlin,' I can just see that big old fat boy now. With the likes of you on his tail, his days are numbered, but he just doesn't know it yet!" Then he ordered another round of drinks.

What she hadn't told Zak was about her real feelings for Guy. Nor did she mention that among the things buried in the makeshift grave she'd dug was the book of Chinese love poems he had sent her so long ago, and the annotated copy of Rimbaud's *Le Bateau Ivre* that they had read together on the sagging porch of La Maison Française, when she'd lived there. But somehow, Zak knew.

On their last night together, as the stars closed in over the Rex, he took her fingers gently and said, "So tell me darlin,' how bad is it still? I mean, you think you're going to get over him now, seeing him as properly buried as can be, or is that ghost going to wander between you and the living down all the corridors of the days and nights to come?"

Only after rereading her piece did the real story—the one she hadn't shared with Zak, the one she hadn't written—begin to unwind in her head. Guy. She could see him so clearly that first time he came back to L.A. from the South, from his first separation from his wife. She could hear him—that voice on the phone that caught her at Annie's house—"I need to see you J.J. Can I come over?"

Soon he knocked. She saw his hands for once still as they pressed against the door frame. She wanted them on her. Then the taste of him was in her mouth, his rough cheek against hers, and the long, hard, strong body pushing her to say *yes, yes, yes*. She took him by the hand, down the darkened corridor, dropping her clothes all the way to Annie's room, and fell onto the soft, full mattress, the pile of pillows. Guy, naked, perched over her, leaning on his long, muscled arms, gazing into her face in the half light, then found her body, first with his hands, then with his tongue, then with his long, searching cock, pushing into her again and again and again until she laughed. Or cried. Or screamed. Soon it was dark. And soon they began again, and so it went all night, tangled in sleep, tangled in love, tangled in each other until the light came soft again. That time they were together two days.

Well, I can hardly write that, can I? Nor about the next time. Nor the next two years, whenever he could get away to L.A. The days and nights spent together at Annie's house. *Days we had only enough time for a grapple in the car, like a couple of teenagers.* The highs and lows at LAX, as he came, then went. The lies to get off work early, come in late, the excuses. *And the parts I can't bear to think about.*

The absences and the work he did for those long stretches in the mysterious South, with its marches and bombings and blood, another country. And the wife, with her dumpy little body and Earth Mother get-ups and her passion—their shared passion—for great causes. Was she smart behind those granny glasses? Did she make him laugh? Did she bring any poetry, any beauty, into his life?

"It's not love," Guy always said. "It's a partnership of commitment."

So when had he gone back to her anyway?

Then there was the other thing. The thing Jocelyn, damn her, had said aloud. Was making love with your first and true love, who happened to be married to someone else, really adultery? Or was it Guy who had been cheating on her all those years of his "partnership of commitment"?

Dark had settled in, but J.J. couldn't sleep. She switched on the TV and found one old movie starting. *Casablanca.* Of course.

⟶

RESTLESS BY DAWN, she grabbed her typed draft, a traveling mug of coffee, and drove to work early. She strode into the office and knocked on Alice's door.

Alice looked up, surprised. "Well, look what the cat dragged in at dawn? Are we feeling better after all the excitement yesterday?"

"Jesus, Alice. You are always here. Do you ever go home?"

"When the mood strikes. So what do you have for me?" She smiled, peering over the top of her glasses.

"What I've got is the 'J.J. Tells All' piece, as per request. Here's the thing though. I want you to edit it, make it right, but when you're done, I want it to go to him as a fait accompli. I want you to tell him that it goes out as is, or it doesn't go. He can't touch a word of it—and trust me, there's much he's not going to like—but he takes it or leaves it."

"My, my. I see." Alice raised her eyebrows.

"No, wait," J.J. said. "Don't tell him anything. I'm going to tell him myself."

J.J. snatched the story from Alice's desk and marched toward Bud Purvis's office. He was just arriving.

"Well, top o' the morning, J.J. dear. What a pleasant surprise to see you first thing." He unlocked the door and gestured for her to enter. "Please, sit, dear."

She followed him in and leaned against the door. "No, I'd rather stand."

"So what can I do for you?"

"For openers, you can look this over." She thrust the piece at him. "It's not edited yet, but Alice will take care of that. Once those changes are made, though, my conditions for this piece are that there won't be any other changes."

Purvis sat up sharply, startled, then glanced at the story.

"You should start with the bottom, the byline. There you will notice the other publications who accepted my war stories, when of course this newspaper would not. I fully expect those credits to run, however. And, if those terms aren't acceptable to you, I'm sure they will be to other papers. I am getting lots of offers, as you may imagine."

He flushed, then turned slightly pale. It had not occurred to him, evidently, that she wouldn't stick around forever, taking his guff. Nor that now that she had become his personal superstar, others might want to snatch her away.

Before he could speak, she turned on her heel and left.

Chapter 29

*D*ear Gracie,

Where have you disappeared to? Need to see you urgently regarding Melanie. Also want to see you for you yourself, too, of course. Plus the paper now wants more profiles! Tried getting your number from the "front desk," but it's a no go. Please call ASAP. It's been too long.

J.J.

GRACIE STARED HARD at the message. Now that she was officially a postdoc and no longer a grad student, she felt slightly annoyed that the Cal Tech admin staff still shielded her from direct contact with "strangers." Yet her first response had been "thank God."

Thank God, Gracie thought, *because the message gives me time to sort out what to say. So complicated you are, J.J. My good friend. My old friend, who could be so clueless. Like encouraging me to come to Paris with the others, so sure it would be easy. As if I'd fit in.* Now, so determined, so ferocious, going for "the story," J.J. was still so blind to the obvious. Okay, she couldn't foresee how painful that Paris year would be. *But neither could I. And the truth is, my truth — it forced me to do what I needed to do. Thanks to you, chérie.* And the first profile of Gracie, J.J. really did nail that one. *The real reason I've been keeping out of sight? My story, for once, not yours.* And now the urgent question about Melanie. What to do? What to say?

Gracie leaned on the bureau top overlooking her small California garden — geraniums, lemons, birds-of-paradise all blooming haphazardly together. A grapevine, now heavy with plump grapes, hung in shaggy splendor over a little arbor in the corner, a reminder of home.

A moment later, her head lifted as she reached for the desk phone to dial J.J.'s home number. After several rings with no answer, she tried the *Star*. Waiting for the receptionist to find J.J., Gracie tried to form a script in her mind as to how that conversation would go.

Sorry to have been out of touch, but I've been on the mountain again... meaning of course the big observatory on Mount Palomar.

Or, *So what's the news you have about Melanie? The last time I saw her...*

Or simply, *Congratulations on the new stories. I guess the one about Jocelyn really kicked up a storm...*

"Your party is not in," the receptionist broke in, "would you like to leave a message?"

"Okay," Gracie replied. Tit for tat.

GRACIE CAUGHT THE first glimpse of J.J. entering the coffee shop from the sunlight, rich reds and golden tones dancing in her shoulder-length brown hair, dark bell-bottom pants on her long legs over stylish boots, with an

Indian-looking multicolored blouse and large silver earrings dangling in fashionable loops. Glamorous as ever. Gracie caught herself stiffening, studying every detail of her friend's look as she had always done. As if preparing for a big exam. But J.J. was as out of place at Cal Tech as Gracie had been in Paris. The revelation made Gracie smile. And she tried to breathe slowly just as Fleur had been teaching her to do.

She nervously fingered her coffee cup, hoping this had been the right place to meet. She could hardly bring a reporter into the lab, even though the easiest part of J.J.'s multiple requests had been about work.

"Hey," J.J. said softly, as she stood looking awkward, flickering a smile.

Gracie realized the next move was up to her. "Hey," she smiled back. *"Assieds-toi,"* she said, gesturing to a chair, surprised at how easily she'd slipped into French.

J.J. folded herself gracefully into the low seat, hesitating a moment before speaking. "It's been a long time, Gracie. Too long. I guess we've both been busy."

Gracie lifted her gray-eyed gaze directly at her friend while nodding. *Absolved.* That's what J.J. had done, absolved her with that generous phrase, taking on part of the blame for the silence, wiping the slate clean.

"Gosh," J.J. continued, flinging her dark hair back across her shoulder, "we have so much to catch up on... I hope you're okay with filling me in on all this," she swept her arm out to indicate the campus. "I mean, the first story was just a sketch, really, and now your public is clamoring for more."

Gracie nodded, silent.

"Where to begin?" J.J. finally asked.

"I guess where we left off with that first piece. You put in the quotes about Feynman." As she spoke, Gracie remembered the conversation they'd had on the phone when J.J. was doing the story, right after she'd gotten her PhD. Over the years, they'd sat on the porch of Gran's house, or gotten together in cafés or restaurants in town. But never here, never in her territory. By design.

"Yeah. I loved that, loved your story. But we just covered the basics, you know, about how you'd made the incredible switch from French major to being accepted into grad school here, and barely scratched the surface of your interaction with Feynman."

Gracie, smiled, remembering. There was so much left unsaid. It was time, Gracie thought. "Look, let's walk a little. I'll take you on a tour."

As they started out the door, Gracie made a right turn. "We'll start with the Olive Walk," she said, not bothering to explain.

"Right," J.J. agreed. "About that first article, I always meant to apologize for the headline. I mean, really: 'From French to Astrophysics—Girl Genius against the Odds.' Sorry about that cheesy title, but we don't get to write our own, you know."

"Cheesy?" Gracie replied. "I thought it hit the nail on the head. Especially evoking the word 'odd.' *Against the odds.* After we walk around, you'll see what I mean."

They turned beneath the shady arcade of olive trees, planted in the '30s, Gracie said, to go along with the graceful Mediterranean-style architecture. "I've always found my solace here," she remarked.

"You could be in Provence," J.J. added.

"Exactly. Well, except for those modern buildings along there. Student dorms. Not for me, of course."

J.J. paused, waiting for an explanation.

"Guys only," she began. "I was always the odd man out here. Not a man, of course, but then at first neither an undergrad nor a grad student either. Those were the days when I went to the famous Feynman physics lectures in Bridge Physics Lab. Over there. I got to audit them while I was taking all the makeup classes I needed at the junior college, and those lectures were so tough, so brilliant, I'd come away with my head spinning. But bit by bit, I'd try to work out what he was getting at, and in the end I'd get it, at least part of what he said. That was my breakthrough. So, I'd pace here, thinking." She put her arm under J.J.'s elbow as if to pull her along, aware that once more she was lost in her tall friend's shadow.

"The perfect ending to that story you already know," Gracie continued, 'the beautiful moment when I was before the admissions committee trying to get admitted as a grad student despite my very bizarre history, and they asked 'What reputable person known to us might recommend you?' and I replied: 'Ask Richard Feynman.' And so they did. And so I'm here."

They approached a graceful Spanish-style building surrounded by trees and flowers. "How's this for inspiration?" Gracie asked. "The Athenaeum. It's the faculty club. Come on, we can peek inside."

J.J. took in the rich furniture, the arched ceilings with Moorish designs, creating a sensation of awe.

"I like this place, especially because they delayed their first faculty dinner for three months until Einstein arrived. Nineteen thirty-one. So if we turn around from here and go back to the other end of campus, the walk is littered with ghosts of luminaries, Nobel laureates, momentous leaps in science. In the last building at the other end, for example, Richter fiddled around with his earthquake scale."

"Let's go back and you take me to the places along the way that are the most significant for you," J.J. said, trying to figure out a way to anchor the next story.

"Right," Gracie agreed, and J.J. followed slightly behind, noticing how little Gracie had changed. Still short with a too-big head. Her midcalf denim skirt was an unflattering length on her slightly bowed, awkward legs, her shiny curls still unstylish and unruly. Yet J.J. sensed an assurance in her, a self-acceptance. *That* was different. Something she'd need to probe—gently of course—to grasp fully how her most brilliant friend had evolved.

"Let me take you to another favorite spot," Gracie said, "but make a note of that building. That's Millikan, where the astronomy story begins. Well, in the Kellogg Radiation Lab, actually. Ever hear of Willy Fowler?"

J.J. shook her head.

"I thought not. I'll explain. One day about my second year here I read his famous paper, 'Synthesis of the Elements in Stars.' I was in love. Pretty soon I started studying with him—a nice, Midwestern kind of guy, good sense of humor—and what he was working on cracked open my mind. He believed, then proved, that all the elements of the universe were created inside stars. He said, 'All of us are truly and literally a little bit of stardust.' So the center of my universe shifted, too. I moved from the Bridge to the Kellogg Lab, from Feynman and his atoms and molecules to the exploding nuclei of astrophysics with Fowler, and I began getting time in with the telescopes. Can you imagine being on the mountain at night and looking deep into the secrets of existence, at cold gas and dust and the interstellar material that the stars and planets are made of?"

"No, really I can't," J.J. answered, hearing the awe in her own voice. "I guess I have to rely on you to see it for me."

They entered a small wrought-iron gate that opened into an idyllic garden. October warmth soaked onto grass like a green carpet spread between beds of still-blooming roses and golden chrysanthemums. "Dabney Gardens," Gracie said. "It was always a refuge when things got rough."

"Did it get rough often?" J.J. asked, pulling out her notebook and beginning to write furiously.

"Yes. More often than not." And without further prodding, Gracie wove the story of her life here, from those early days in physics in the exhilarating light and terrifying shadow of Feynman, to cracking heads with other students over impossible math problems—sometimes covering more than twenty blackboards—to the surprising reputation she earned with students and faculty alike for being able to write clearly. "The advantages of my helter-skelter undergraduate life came through at last. Other guys even offered to pay me to help them with their papers. Would you believe it?"

J.J. smiled. "So you're a writer, too. Are you publishing physics papers?"

"Yes and no. In the academic way, no matter how much of the work I do, my name appears near the end of the list of authors. It's a seniority thing. The head of the lab, or at least the project, is first author. And the papers aren't exactly in straight physics. Astrophysics."

After a long silence, J.J. asked: "So, of all these special places of yours here, which is your true home? Here in Dabney Gardens, in Bridge, where Feynman gave you your chance, in the lab with Fowler? Or maybe up on the mountain staring at the secrets of the heavens through a lens?"

Gracie sat still, her head resting in her hands, as if puzzling hard over a difficult question.

Then she looked up. "All of the above in their different ways, but then none of them. There's another place I haven't shown you. I guess I will. But first, remember when we were talking about the word 'odd' and I said after you walked around here you'd see what I mean. So what do you notice?"

"Well," J.J. answered cautiously, "first it strikes me as so beautiful, so peaceful in that California-Spanish kind of way. I mean, it could be a monastery somewhere in the South of France or Spain. I guess it's such a contrast to the space-age, cutting-edge 'out-there' work done here. That strikes me as odd."

"Agreed. Anything else?"

"Is this a test, Gracie?" J.J. laughed.

"Okay, point taken. But seriously, notice anything missing?"

"You mean like girls, women? It's a bastion of brainy boys and brilliant men."

"Exactly. And that's a huge problem. They only just let in women undergrads a couple of years ago. There are only two women on the faculty. And the guys have the social skills of Neanderthals." Gracie pulled herself up from the bench and began walking again.

J.J. followed. "So what is that like for you? I mean is it terrible being a woman alone in this, what, frat house of supernova male intelligence?"

Gracie stopped and turned to face her friend. "No, J.J., that's the thing. It isn't. Even though some of it was horrid. Some women here are ridiculed, pushed aside, or treated like porn stars by these socially deficient nerds. Some of the faculty, who also come from the Planet of the Apes when it comes to accepting women, are equally determined to keep science 'unpolluted by the weaker sex.' They say this kind of stuff openly. Can you imagine?"

J.J. nodded again.

"But for me, the worst was being overlooked, or plain ignored. As if I didn't exist. Being short, I was used to it. And in Paris, because of my size, my looks, it happened all the time. So I learned to deal with it. And here, in a weird way, I fit in. The boys and I, we understand each other, and they never hassle me like the other girls, if you know what I mean. From the moment that Feynman and I had that conversation after his lecture, I understood. If I could have the likes of him behind me, I could make it. He seemed to access and respect my mind. It was uncanny, so like the encounter I had long ago at the Sorbonne with that horrid Professeur Saint-Georges, who crushed me because all he saw was my mind. I was the only girl he didn't try to seduce. And I remember how undone Melanie was because he *did* try to seduce her, couldn't see her mind. But it's one of the things I've come to terms with here. I know now I'm not a girl like the others. And I'm fine with that."

They stopped in front of another building and climbed the steps going up to the front door. "You wanted to know my real place of the heart here. It's Fairchild Library."

"The library," J.J. repeated, trying to parse its meaning.

"Yeah, the library," Gracie answered. "I met someone here." She paused for a moment, hesitating, then started back down the steps. "Come on now. It's time I took you home. We can talk about Melanie there." She paused once more to look up at J.J., her eyes searching her friend's face. "I hope you don't have to write everything."

AFTER A FIFTEEN-MINUTE walk along tree-lined streets, Gracie led J.J. up the drive of a large brown-shingled house with an inviting front porch. Ivy crept along the sides, and well-manicured roses bloomed below leaded-pane glass windows. The wide green lawn looked too perfect to ruin with footsteps.

Gracie bypassed the front door, and then a side door, which J.J. assumed led to the kitchen, and went around behind the house to a wooden fence. Then she lifted the latch on the gate and let J.J. pass through. J.J. gasped.

"This is unbelievable," she said, taking in the small brown cottage, and the more unruly garden surrounding it: a climbing rose, a lemon tree still heavy with fruit, geraniums in red and pink, even a few golden poppies, birds-of-paradise, and a climbing grapevine.

"Yeah. I was lucky to find this. Since there wasn't any housing for women, the Dean of Admissions took pity on me and went through the school network. The house belongs to a professor of engineering. Come on in."

Gracie unlocked the dark wooden door and led J.J. into a cozy, light-filled room with a soft sofa, a big armchair, and a large coffee table strewn with glasses, books, and papers. "Sorry it's such a mess. I actually wasn't preparing for company."

"Are you kidding? This is enchanting. And mess? You have seen my 'den' at Gran's house when I'm in the midst of something, haven't you?" J.J. glanced around and saw a small kitchen off to the side. The table held the remnants of two breakfasts.

"That chair's comfortable," Gracie said, flopping on the couch.

J.J. sat, a reporter's notebook in hand, staring at the garden dancing in sunlight. She waited for Gracie to speak.

"So you know when I was telling you about that paper of Willy Fowler's I read on the origin of the stars? Well it would be easy to say that was my first awakening to the subject. But actually it wasn't. Long before that, Melanie took me there with her obsession over Pascal. Remember how she was always quoting him?"

J.J. nodded.

"'*Le silence éternel de ces espaces infinis m'effraie.*' Stuff like that. We used to have lengthy conversations about such topics and whether when he said "the infinite space of the eternal stars frightens me," we agreed. Actually, for me, many seeds were planted long ago, including in Paris. I just didn't understand what it all meant until my years here."

J.J. shifted in her seat. "So did you keep up with Melanie much, afterwards, I mean?"

"Not so much directly, at least at first. Those years with Hans when she was in Rochester, I knew about all that from you, J.J. Then she seemed to become mobile, something of a vagabond. I'd get postcards from her, sometimes from music festivals, sometimes from the South where she appeared to be working for civil rights. I say 'appeared to be' because she never said straight up. What she'd write would be a vignette, a quote, something indirect, and never connected to the last thing I'd heard. She never said, for example, where Hans was."

"Did you ever talk to her?"

"Once in a blue moon. Occasionally she'd sweep through Pasadena, as you know. I'm not sure if she saw her family or avoided them, but when she was nearby she'd call. I've seen her two, maybe three, times in all these years."

"So when was the last time?"

"Well, you know. That time close to a year and a half ago after she'd been to your house."

"My house?"

"Yeah. Your Gran's house. Of course you weren't there, but Gran was, and Melie was so distraught that she told Gran everything and felt so comforted by her kindness. Well, who wouldn't have been distraught?"

Gracie looked down. "I feel bad that I didn't follow up with her, J.J., I really do. But I knew you would, and I did do the best I could. It's just that…"

J.J. met her gaze and held it. "I don't know what you're talking about. Almost a year and a half ago? I would have been in Vietnam. Gran never—well, Gran doesn't remember things."

Gracie shook her head slowly before saying, "Oh my God," then swallowed hard. "Melie went to find you first. And of course that's when she met Gran—I assumed Gran would tell you everything when you came home. Melie was a few months' pregnant, you see, and absolutely beside herself about not wanting anything to do with her family ever again. I don't honestly know what went on with them, because by the time she got here she was focused on wanting to escape 'forever'—and to find somewhere to have her child born 'naturally in an atmosphere of love.'"

"Oh, no. I see," J.J. muttered. "The Hi-Diddle."

"What?"

"Go on. I'll explain later."

"She stayed here a couple of nights, slept on the couch. I offered the bed, but she said no, she'd be fine. What she really wanted was to find a good midwife."

"And a community of peace and love?"

"That, too," Gracie continued. "Nothing could have been more out of my element, as you can imagine, than helping her with this. But I do have my ways with research. After a day or two I came up with a name, a woman with good references I have to say, and Melie picked up the phone over there and called. That was it. The next morning she was on a bus."

"A bus?"

"A bus up the coast. I offered to get time off to drive her, offered money, offered for her to stay on here even. But she insisted. I also begged her to let me know how and where she was. She promised. And to let you know everything."

"Did you ever hear?"

"Not a word."

"For God's sake, Gracie, why didn't you call me?" Anguish overpowered the anger in J.J.'s voice.

Gracie's head slumped in her hands. "I swear, I thought you knew. I thought you'd let *me* know when you learned something. I even called that number once, but it was disconnected. Then time passed, and I never heard from you, and then, you know, it was…awkward…"

J.J. turned as the sound of the opening door broke into Gracie's thought.

Chapter 30

J.J. flopped on the bed in what Gran always called the "sleeping porch," the upstairs room fitted with permanent screens, but no glass windows, to let the air in. The fresh air regimen had been favored, she knew, by Grandfather, though eventually he had agreed to sturdy canvas that could be pulled over the windows to regulate just how much weather he really wanted. J.J. guessed he slept there a lot and never used the canvas unless rain was driving in. But it was only a guess. Nobody had ever told her much about him.

Now, on the same old bed, she sighed. It was mild for November, mild enough to sleep in that peculiar room, though she had carefully drawn the screen covers, which would still let in enough longed-for fresh air. God knows, she was exhausted. The piece on Gracie had been turned in to Alice for a quick run-through—she imagined the words "Amazing Grace, Superstar" in the headline—and relaxed.

Rubbing her eyes, she wanted now to think of anything but the lives of her old *copines* and reached for the story of *Sybil*. Annie had gushed over it and thrust into her hands, declaring it an absolute "must-read—everyone in the store is talking about it, though it came out last year." But J.J. couldn't find her way into the thread of "The Classic True Story of a Woman Possessed by Sixteen Personalities." *Good God, Mother,* she thought crossly, *isn't one personality enough?* Soon, after her eyes had drifted across a few pages, the book slipped from her hands. Another story had begun unwinding in her head.

THE TURN OF the handle and the slight creak of the door at Gracie's little cottage. The long moment of silence as the petite young woman with short cropped hair and delicate features walked through, and they all stared at each other, surprised. The longer moment of comprehension—was that before or after Gracie had introduced them?—as J.J. took in what she was seeing, and the young woman absorbed the fact that a stranger was in what had been a very private place.

"Fleur," Gracie had said evenly, "please meet my old friend and college housemate, J.J." She then added, in case the situation wasn't quite clear, "Fleur is a research assistant at Fairchild Library."

Fleur flushed slightly and crossed over, hand extended. As J.J. rose to greet her, Fleur smiled. A winning, wide-open smile that showed her perfect white teeth.

J.J. swallowed a gasp, warmly shook Fleur's hand, and uttered "Hi," feeling as though she were time traveling. In Fleur she glimpsed the reincarnation of another woman from long ago. Camille. Camille, the spirited, gay, charming housemate of Gracie's in Paris. The young woman who gently deflected the endless barbs and hostility of Madame, the aging, bitter professor of cuisine who had made her fashionable apartment into a *pension* for students. Camille, who surreptitiously helped Gracie maneuver the minefield of utensils and strange food at Madame's table, who escorted Gracie evenings arm in arm, in the French manner, into the neighborhood for a cigarette and a nightcap. Camille, who no doubt enjoyed the love of women, and who knew? Maybe men too.

"It's a pleasure," J.J. added, before sinking into her chair again.

"J.J.'s the journalist friend I've told you about," Gracie broke in. "She's going to do another profile about members of our old gang for the *Star*. But she's also trying to find out about Melanie."

Fleur's small face turned serious. "Right," she said. "Wow. Yes. Well, look, I just popped home for a bite on my lunch hour, and since it is that time of day, why don't I make some quick lunch for us?" The smile flashed again.

"Thanks, Fleur. You're a dear. As I was telling J.J., when we dashed out this morning we really weren't expecting company."

That scene, and others which she didn't write, played over and over in J.J.'s head as she mined it for its many meanings. Gracie, who in those early years had been like a battered child washing up over and over again on the shoals of love. The ridiculous Canadian adolescent who fell in love with her on the student boat to Europe. Her painful years of devotion and longing for Evelyn's one-time amour, Tom. Tom, who cared for, and loved Gracie—like a sister. The humiliation of being recognized as a genius, yet never seduced as a woman. Then, finally, the acceptance of who she was, "not a girl like the others," she had said. And now this. Life with a pretty young woman. With Camille...

As these turns in Gracie's life settled into J.J.'s mind, so did another revelation. The reason she and Gracie had seen so little of each other, that Gracie had not called, was

of course because of her secret life. Things were changing—
even in the uber-masculine sphere of world-class science,
where few women had been allowed in, and where Gracie
had made her place. But they were changing slowly. Gracie
and Fleur had made their place, too, but quietly, out of sight.
J.J. could only guess from the hints she'd been given what
tortures Gracie had endured to finally reach her idyllic spot
in a cottage with a garden and her love. They both knew
J.J. would never betray this, although nothing of the sort
had been spoken between them.

J.J. also understood that the ground Gracie stood on
was precarious, built over fault lines that could rip any time,
or vanish like starlight into unseen dark forces.

Closing her eyes now against the reading light, J.J.
tried consciously to put herself back in the sun-filled sitting
room with Gracie and Fleur. She strained to hear Fleur's
gentle voice as she described her encounter with Melanie
from a year ago. From Fleur's telling, she could easily see
Melie there, across from them in the large chair, her small
frame given ballast from her rounded, growing center. Her
hidden child.

"Tell me, what did she seem like to you, Fleur? You'd
never met her before."

"She was somebody really grounded, focused on the
future, I'd say, and what she was going to do about it. Those
descriptions you've given from some of her other friends,
they don't sound like they're describing the same person." Fleur spoke softly, but with confidence. She looked
directly at J.J., revealing smoky hazel eyes. "Honest.
Compassionate." J.J. had written in her notebook.

"True," Gracie broke in. "The stuff you've been telling
us—Melie going to rock shows, doing drugs, demonstrat-
ing—I don't know, they sound unbelievable."

"She seemed to me like somebody who had been through
a hard time, of course she didn't say what exactly," Fleur

continued, "but she definitely didn't seem spacey, like you were saying, and certainly not like somebody who was using drugs. She really wanted to do what was right for her baby and be in a safe place."

"Even though I urged her to find a real doctor," Gracie broke in, "and not go down this midwife route, she was very clear-headed about what she wanted, and why. So of course I helped her."

Then Melie's voice broke in, and J.J. could picture her curled in the soft beige chair, her hands folded gently across her rounded belly. *Sorry you weren't home, J.J., though Gran and I had such a good chat. I'm sure she told you all about it. Only you know, really, the places I've been, but now I've got to figure out where I'm going from here. Gracie has been such a dear. From what I've learned, midwifery is the most caring and positive way to bring life this into the world. Of course, you know why I have so little faith in doctors. And Gracie has helped me find this terrific woman to see me through. Katerina McNealy...*

"Right." J.J. said aloud, as if she could speak directly to her friend, whose white blonde hair framed her face in that light as though it were a halo. "That would be Cat."

Turning on the light as if to finish the day's revelations with Gracie and Fleur, other images began tumbling through her mind.

Hans, that swimming pool at the hotel shimmering behind, speaking earnestly about the medical treatments they were undergoing. To become pregnant. Then calling out "Mel-an-ie" in that way he always said the name, before turning to finish his thought. "I think she's left again, J.J. I'm afraid for her."

The thundering face of Dr. Hart, unable to control its shades of anger, repeating the name, *Melanie,* over and over, like a hammer hitting a nail. Mrs. Hart, a celery stick behind him, saying, "Yes dear. But of course you did refuse to speak to her..."

Melie stepping out of a bus, disheveled and confused in tie-dye threads, arriving at the convent to find Eve. Eve's voice, "Seriously out there, you know? Drugs? Legit or not, I couldn't say. Probably both."

Guy's handwriting, scrawled and distorted on a giant postcard, "Haven't heard of nor found a trace of your friend. But best not come hunting here. Too dangerous..."

Jocelyn standing in front of the Capitol in Washington, about to lead the multitudes in song, suddenly silent, her mouth half open. In front of her Melanie, dressed in a pert suit and heels, as if about to walk to the Sorbonne, waving an enormous sign: "Stop the Madness." Cops in riot gear closing in from the sides.

The large round face of Mama, vibrating in tune with her rollicking derrière, "Yup, a fire all right. Somebody died, you know? They found the body of a young woman."

A huge poster hanging from a building advertising a rock concert. Melie in a Granny dress, and a tall skinny dude with an Afro, a bandana around it, his arm over her shoulders. J.C.

Mama's face giving way to Cat's, drawing a finger across her throat as she steps into the squad car, baby on her hip.

The bushy, weird face of Moon, shouting into the wind, "She's gone and she ain't never comin' back. Get over it."

Catching herself, J.J. sat upright on the bed, uncertain whether the voices she had just heard were real or imagined. *What am I doing, talking like this? As if by conjuring these images —Melie's voice —somehow I can bring her back. As for where she really is, what happened to her, I've got nothing. Not a single fact, just a chorus of contradictions based on fragments, distant sightings, rumors. I need to face it, like Moon was telling me. Melie is gone and she ain't coming back. Melie is dead. The only story I can honestly write is her obituary.*

Chapter 31

"A new medication, with unintended side benefits," the nurse chirped as J.J. pushed past her down a corridor to the small room filled with Gran's scent—rose dusting powder. Inhaling, her anxieties began to waver. In the stuffed armchair covered in needlepoint doilies, Gran sat alert and upright, her hair newly coiffed, a mischievous look moving across her face. "*Bonjour ma petite*, so glad you're here at last." Gran grinned. "We have so much to plan."

"Do we indeed?" J.J. grinned back. "Shall I wheel you into the garden so we can discuss it?"

"But, *chérie*, I am not *une invalide*, you know. Just take my arm." Gran stepped out of the armchair easily.

Strolling slowly along the well-tended brick path with her grandmother attached to her as if they were one peculiar organism, J.J. continued the conversation. "So, what are these plans we are making, *grand-mère*?"

"But for Thanksgiving of course. It's coming right up as you know, and I was wondering, *ma chère fille*, did I ever teach you to make the pies?"

At once J.J. was back in the kitchen of Gracie's Madame, the terrifying professor of cuisine in Paris, with the hilarious, rheumy-eyed, sharp-tongued maid Marie looking on. The pies were the sole triumph of that ill-begotten Franco-American Thanksgiving feast. But even old scold Madame had had to admit their superiority, finding a "French hand" at work on the perfect crusts.

"*Grand-mère,*" J.J. paused and looked at her grandmother in mock horror. "But of course you taught me, and my pies are superb. Even in the fussiest kitchens of Paris. Surely you don't doubt me!"

"Ah, but no, of course not. They must be then, if I taught you properly." Gran's eyes crinkled shut with pleasure, a small smile resting on her lips. Sunshine, the last of the roses, a joke with her granddaughter. Gran always sought "the roots of happiness," as she said, a fact J.J. admired—and envied.

By afternoon's end, plans were firmly in place. Gran had the menu locked in, while J.J. was making the guest list in her mind. Annie and her father, of course. Alice. Gracie and Fleur. Ivan, if she could find him. Maybe Jocelyn could come. And then, the guest of honor, Gran. Home at last.

"I'll get everything ready for your homecoming," J.J. promised, "and I'll pick you up in a few days—in time for my birthday." It was a marvel how the new medicine with its unintended benefits—lifting Gran's spirits—had given Gran the gift of herself back. And maybe also the unintended gift of the best birthday she could imagine. "Oh Gran," J.J. said, surprised at the quaver in her voice, "it will be so wonderful to have you back."

Once again at the *Star*, J.J. knocked crisply on Alice's door, calling out, "Anybody home?" She let herself in to see Alice swivel on her chair. "So, what are your plans for Thanksgiving?"

~~>

RETURNING TO HER desk, J.J. glanced out the office window, imagining the upcoming feast and reliving the visit with Gran. So much to think about. Only a week ago, she'd met Gracie and Fleur. Soon it would be her birthday, a dismal prospect now sweetened by the promise of Gran coming home.

The phone rang, jolting her. She picked up with a curt "J.J. here," only to be met by silence. "Anybody there?" she asked at last.

"So," the voice on the other end finally began. "Um, this is Natalie. There's something you need to know. They're going to bury Melanie—not that they even know if she really died or have a body or anything. But you know, I guess they just want to write her ending themselves."

J.J. couldn't remember later what, if anything, she had replied. Only Natalie's words. "All Saints Church at ten a.m. on Saturday, December 21. Merry Christmas. It's something like: 'A memorial service for our beloved daughter who disappeared on a yachting trip in the Gulf of Mexico last summer.' Can you believe this shit? But then I'm sure you can read all about it in your paper."

J.J. only nodded into the receiver. "Of course I'll be there," she answered, then on impulse added, "We'll be there," unsure of just what she meant.

~~>

THANKSGIVING MORNING. J.J. watched with pleasure as Gran emerged from the downstairs bedroom they had created out of the former breakfast room. Wearing an old kimono—once all the rage, J.J. guessed—Gran burst forth in a bloom of silk peonies, orange and pink, her hair a crown of white.

"Gran," J.J. cried out, "what a vision you are. The flowers match the garden — those orange chrysanthemums and the last of the pink roses. We have a lot to be thankful for, don't we?" The cheer in her voice was a ploy to keep from thinking about what was to come in December — Melanie's "burial" and what would follow.

She glanced at the perfect pies, constructed the day before, sitting on a shelf over the ledge. Then watched, amused, at how quickly Gran went into supervisor role, as she directed J.J. on how to set the large mahogany dining table with lace and linen, polished silver, where to place the Havilland just so, and how best to arrange flowers fresh cut from the garden.

"Gran," she called out in early afternoon, "it's time to get gussied up. People will be here." And she helped her grandmother into a favorite mauve dress, adding pearls and an ivory brooch. In attending to her, a sense of wonder flooded J.J. — the house would fill again with gaiety and guests, as it had in her childhood. The smells of pumpkin and cinnamon and savory dressing and roasting turkey always evoked that past for her. Today they would rise again, in this place that was her only true home. *But the cast of characters has changed,* she thought. *They now belong to me.*

Before seeing Annie's long Madras fabric skirt, J.J. heard the call of "Saraswati, darling, we are here." She nearly answered, "Whatever happened to Seraphina?" but decided to let it go.

"Hey Mom, Annie, whatever, welcome!" She meant to give her mother a hug, but instead found her hands filled with platters Annie thrust at her. "As I told you, I was all prepared to do a tofu turkey dish instead of the usual wasteful slaughtered bird that only encourages carnivorous behavior, but you know your father, such a traditionalist."

"So where is he, anyway?"

"He's busy bringing in said slaughtered beast, stuffed, roasted, the whole bit," Annie sighed. "But I did make quite a lovely arrangement of what I call tasty tofu tidbits. They'll do very nicely for appetizers or as a substitute for those with an inkling of a conscience who want a healthy vegan alternative."

J.J. placed the trays on the kitchen table and glanced sideways at her mother, who, despite her long dark hair, looked strikingly like Gran at that moment, if slightly more rotund. Same height, several inches shorter than her own five feet nine. Same mouth, same large dark eyes, but so completely different in personality.

A loud thump at the door, and she rushed to open for her father.

"Ah, my darling daughter, make way for the feast I have prepared," he boomed.

She laughed, calling out, "Dad!" and watched as he bent agilely to open the oven door. Tall, silver-haired with a neatly trimmed gray mustache; she noted again that, despite his weaknesses, he was a dashing man. The fact he was in so many ways a rogue she vowed not to think about today.

"Smells wonderful," she said, imagining the perfectly browned turkey beneath its foil wraps.

"Nothing short of a masterpiece," he shot back, laughing.

"Right," J.J. replied, grateful for Dad's prowess as a chef, which in those times when she'd not been with Gran, had been such a blessing in her childhood. At least in those times when he was around.

The front doorbell began to ring. Alice arrived first, carrying bags leaking the aroma of freshly baked bread. "You know me, I can barely boil water for tea," she announced, "but I do know how to bake."

J.J. hugged her, noting that the usual pencils in her hair had been replaced by what looked like chopsticks encrusted in rhinestones. "Very posh," she said. "The coiffeur."

Alice gave her crooked smile.

Then J.J. spotted Gracie and Fleur, each carrying a dish as they walked up the path. "So great you could come. Can I help?" J.J. asked.

"No, no, we've got it," Gracie answered. "The least I can do is carry, since I can't cook. Thank God for Fleur and her many talents. Creamed onions, green bean casserole, all sorts of wonders."

Fleur blushed, while J.J. took a dish to carry.

Shutting the door behind her guests, J.J. paused to look at the dressed-up table, hear the sounds of laughter and chatter, inhale the smells of the dinner to come. The house, filled with festivity, became alive again—with both her parents and Gran at the center of it. J.J. offered up a silent prayer of thanksgiving. But also, with Gracie and Fleur there, Jocelyn soon to arrive, and maybe Ivan, it was also a replay of that Parisian Thanksgiving of long ago. A partial replay. Without Madame, thank the Lord. Without Evelyn. Without Melanie... *Don't go there*, she told herself.

All were seated at the table to watch Dad enjoy his starring role at the head wielding a silver carving knife over the browned bird when the doorbell rang. J.J. jumped up to greet Jocelyn and Dru.

"Sorry we're late," Jocelyn apologized, and thrust an immense box of French chocolates into J.J.'s hands before removing the scarf she'd carefully wound around her neck and head. "Coming in from the west side, the traffic was awful."

"Yes, darling, so sorry," Dru added, handing her the beret which covered his erratic gray hair. She noted his trademark black turtleneck was now beneath a chic velvet smoking jacket. He reached to peck J.J. on both cheeks. "I'll carry these in for you," he offered, as he hugged an immense vase of yellow roses, and headed to the sideboard in the dining room.

Once J.J. had frowned at their off-again-on-again Hollywood affair of convenience, on again now because they were working intensely on publicity. But as Dru set his vase down near the arrangement of fall flowers and fruits that had arrived the day before from Zak, sending his love from Atlanta, J.J. understood too well the attraction of a companion, workmate, and good soul who stepped into the void passion had left hollow.

Gran, who had insisted on French wine, had also insisted on place cards, so there "will be no confusions, *chérie*," motioned for the pair to sit opposite her. Dru lifted his glass to toast first Gran, "To *charmante* Violette," then Dad, who had cooked the turkey. "Such an admirable dish at this, the most remarkable of American holidays," he concluded. With his silver hair, wiry frame, and theatrical charm, J.J. was struck by how much he and Dad had in common. They were, after all, almost contemporaries.

Before finishing her thought, or her dinner, the phone interrupted. She ran to the hall to answer it.

"Ivan," she called out delighted, "where are you?"

"Sorry to interrupt, kiddo, and sorry I couldn't make it," the deep voice resonated through a crackling line. "But something has come up here. It's Cat and the baby and—" his voice faded in and out. But she heard the crucial words: "You need to get up here, *tout de suite*."

PULLING OUT OF the pass toward I-5, J.J. was grateful few cars were on the road at this hour on Thanksgiving Day. So much to be thankful for. Including the great luck that, just as she hung up, Jocelyn was entering the kitchen from the dining room.

"Looking for the loo," she said half laughing, "pretty sure I remember where it is." Then noticing J.J.'s stricken look, asked, "Is everything okay?"

J.J. rushed through a version of Ivan's call and Cat's request, and the necessity of leaving right away, adding, "but I'm really worried about leaving Gran now that I've finally brought her home. My parents aren't…"

"No worries," Jocelyn broke in. "Gran and I go way back, as you know. She bailed me out more than once. I'm still officially in hiding while Dru and I work through the rollout for *Pacific Blue*. This house is perfect. We can stay here, and we'll take great care of Gran. Dru has already completely charmed her with his French ways, too…"

Remembering the conversation, and grateful she didn't have to involve Annie and Dad just now, J.J. shifted in her seat and stepped on the gas. She thought about the party she had so abruptly left and imagined Gran commanding Dad to make the whipped cream, as she took charge of serving the pies. Then jammed *American Beauty* into the tape deck, listening for "Ripple," and hoping the Dead would fill the place that had recently been swimming with strange visions of Melanie. She tried not to think of what was waiting for her at the Blue Moon Bar & Far Out Rest Stop, at the end of an awful drive. Heavy rain was predicted.

Chapter 32

Ivan waited in the darkened corner of the lounge where they had met before. It was close to two a.m. when J.J. arrived, her arms outstretched beneath a plastic raincoat trying to shake off the water before entering.

"You look like a bat," he glanced up, giving a slight smile.

"If you mean from hell, that would be me," J.J. answered, stomping her feet. "That's what it is out there, hell. The wet version."

Ivan stood and grabbed her, giving a strong hug. "I know, just glad you made it. Hate to drive the roads in a storm like this."

J.J. sat down hard, but remained on the edge of her seat. "Thanks for waiting up. So where is she?"

"Asleep, not surprisingly. You know me, J.J., if you're the bat, then I'm the owl. This is my time. I'm afraid the bar is closed, but I've got coffee in this Thermos. And my old faithful, of course." He pointed to his pipe. "May I share?"

J.J. shook her head no. "I'm exhausted, but wired, you know? Your voice kept cutting out on the phone, so I don't really know what's going on. Fill me in."

Ivan inhaled, released the smoke from his pipe, then answered. "It's complicated, and Cat will have to tell you herself. But this is what you need to know for now. After vanishing for a long time, Moon has resurfaced. Cat feels that she and the baby are in danger. She needs your help."

J.J. looked intently at Ivan, but her brain was too tired to figure out what, exactly, he meant. What was it that she could possibly do for Cat?

"Best to get some rest, J.J., and you'll be in better shape in the morning." He put a reassuring hand on her shoulder, while she noted his latest headgear, a striped knit wool cap, perfect for a woodsman. "Oh, and good news. Thanksgiving not being exactly a big destination holiday for the old Blue Moon, they had plenty of vacancies. Tonight we don't have to share a room, unlike another rainy occasion I can think of."

Tired as she was, J.J. smiled at the memory of that rainy night they'd spent in a bordello in Paris. It was a long time ago. She picked up her wet pack and headed up the stairs.

A HOWLING SOUND made J.J. start and sit up. She tried to push the deep sleep from her eyelids as she oriented herself. The iron bed frame, the darkened window, strange, slightly faded psychedelic posters covering old chintz wallpaper. She glanced at the clock. Nearly eight. The howling, she understood, was not rain, but wind. She needed to come to quickly and get downstairs. She needed, at last, to meet Cat.

Guarded winter light filtered through the corner window in the lounge. J.J. paused for a minute on the bottom stair while she took in the picture of Cat, bathed in it. Cat wearing a gingham, flowing skirt over boots, her dark hair falling gently on her shoulders. So like the first vision J.J. had had of her in that dream. But now, sharing the light in a tall wooden high chair was the curly-headed baby she had met a few months ago. She was amazed at how much the tot had grown.

J.J. approached the table, and Cat looked up from the child for the first time. Offering her hand, J.J. said, "So glad to meet you properly at last."

Cat rose halfway from the chair and took her hand gently. "Why yes. I'm Katerina. They call me Cat."

"I feel as if I know you already." J.J. slipped into the chair across the table, not mentioning her surprise at the sound of Cat's voice: low, gentle, full of Southern notes.

"We're right happy to be with you face to face now, aren't we, baby?" She looked at the boy who was busy picking up pieces of pancakes and fruit with both hands and stuffing them in his mouth.

"Nmmm," the child grinned.

"I really would like some coffee, and maybe a little something else. May I get something for you, too?" J.J. asked, biding for time. She knew the corner she was sitting in was as delicate as the web of light filtering through the wind. She didn't want to destroy it by entering Cat's world in the wrong way.

"Why, no, Miss J.J., but thank you kindly. We've eaten." She gestured to the mess on the baby's tray and a smattering of half-eaten plates on the table. "But we do need your help with other matters…"

The pause lingered between them, then J.J. responded. "I'd be glad to help you if I can. But, of course, I hope you can help me, too. As you know, I've been looking into the disappearance of my good friend, Melanie Hart. I believe you know her, too, as Fiddle?"

"Oh, why of course I do. You see, then, we're both here for the same reason."

"You sent a message to me because of Melanie? You know where she is, Cat?"

"Why yes, and no, Miss J.J."

J.J. felt her heart race and couldn't help herself from breaking in. "Is she alive, Cat? Did she die in that fire at the Hi-Diddle?"

"I don't rightly know, Miss J.J. It's possible, but as I live and breathe, I don't think she did."

J.J. could only nod and wait.

Cat continued. "Let me tell you the story. Some many months ago, I got a call from somebody down south, some scientist lady. She said she was calling for a friend who needed a good midwife and a place to be after her baby came. A place that could take care of the both of them, you know. The call came through to the clinic over there in Fort Bragg, where in a building behind, kind of under the table, they got a little birthing room for those who want to bring on life in nature's way, without the interference of modern medicine. I'm one of two midwives attending there. Now, I'm here to tell you, I don't have no proper license, certainly nothing the state of California would allow. But I swear, Miss J.J., I am qualified. My own ma, who learned from my gran before her, taught me. They was both known as the best midwives in three counties back home in Carolina."

"I believe you," J.J. said softly.

"So when this young lady arrives on that Greyhound down in Fort Bragg, I did take care of her, yes I did. Pale as an angel she was. A real woman of the spirit. We took her right in up there at Hi-Diddle, gave her comfort and saw her through. Then when it was her time, she came on down to the clinic, and it all went smooth as silk."

"Mmm, mmm," the child started banging a spoon.

"It sure did, didn't it sugar?" Cat continued, holding a cup of milk to help him drink. "Then they came on back, the two of them, and they folded in just easy as pie. Everybody helping out, everybody loved them both."

The questions tumbled in J.J.'s mind as she tried to swallow them. "All of you? Was Moon among the happy band?" she asked before stopping.

"Moon?" a dark cloud appeared to cross Cat's face. "That freak? That living fool? No, by that time, he daren't step his big old boot inside there. He was up by the farm, up to all his usual mischief."

"So you weren't his 'lady'? He told me you and he were, you know, together."

"No ma'am. I was not, never was, his. He just wished it so, him being a lying, sneaking fool. We got on peaceable enough though, living all together up in the forest, until Sport comes along. Sport and I, we got on real good together, and that's when all the troubles began. Old Moon starts acting like a damn fool. Even though he was one of the originals of Hi-Diddle, a founding father you could say, after he starts carrying on and making trouble, we take a vote. Very democratic. Everybody agrees he was not living by the creed of peace and love. He's got to stay up there on the farm."

"And he accepted that?"

"No way, Miss J.J. No way. It got so bad he finally burnt the place down. Oh, yes, Miss J.J. that's what he did. Me and Sport was forced to flee, with everybody scattering every which way. That's what happened to the Hi-Diddle, ma'am. And that's the truth."

"But why would he do that? It's insane to burn your own place down," J.J. said.

"He'd like to kill me, that's why. When he finds me with this little old rascal in my arms, he becomes a crazy man, thinking, you know, all that about Sport and me. Then one day, he comes into Hi-Diddle all a-blazing just when he thinks for sure I'm there. Afterward, so darn cocky, so sure of himself, he starts the rumor that a young woman died in the fire, so convinced—hoping anyways—it was me. Since everything happened so fast, maybe it was true that somebody did die. Maybe Fiddle... Well, we all did scatter to the winds best we could. To this day, nobody knows really. Spent the next weeks trying to keep clear of that old crazy man, and when I feared him getting close, I went to the law for protection—the day you saw me. Another mistake..."

The baby, restless, began to fuss, reaching his arms out to Cat. "Okay, sugar, I know. You need a new diaper and a good nap." Unlatching the tray, she put it aside and picked up the squirmy little boy, who rewarded her with an enormous smile. "I'll just settle this child down and be back in a few minutes, Miss J.J. Hear?"

BY THE TIME Cat reappeared, J.J. felt windswept, a shipwreck of raw emotion, and so far from being professional, pretending to be professional was no use. Ready to burst with questions and filled with confusion, she knew at least enough to not reveal her state by asking anything. She simply put her notebook away, gave Cat a weak smile, and gestured for her to sit.

"Please do go on," she said.

"Like I was saying, Miss J.J., Fiddle—we call her that right away, because she could play some, you see—she comes to us needing space and time. And music, too. She knows a lot of music and can play right on along when anybody starts strumming the guitar or the banjo, or the pipe I play. She could join right in. She's kind of a quiet type, but can get into the storytelling when the mood is right, the fire lit and night coming on and all, and lord, the things she can talk about, Miss J.J. She's seen and done so many things, way more than most in a lifetime, and she can go on about God and philosophy and travels and justice and injustice in the world, oh my. She can speak French, too. Do you know that?"

J.J. looked steadily into Cat's large round eyes and nodded.

"But then the spirit comes over her from time to time, too, and it passes through like a dark shadow. Sport, he says it's like the voodoo spirit down there in Louisiana, where his people come from, but I don't know, Miss J.J., I always think maybe it be something else. Fiddle, she never says where she comes from, who her people are."

"The spirit like a dark shadow," J.J. repeated, letting the words hang between them.

"Yes, ma'am. And a few times when those visits come, she would take herself away. Truth to tell, nobody knows where, exactly, she goes. But when she feels ready, usually in just a few days, she comes back. She always comes back."

"These spirits, did they seem to come on from using drugs, anything like that?"

"Why no. She says, you know, some time back, that she would try a bit of this and that, but it never set right. She wanted to be pure as gold for her baby."

"Her baby. Of course. What's happened to her baby?"

"You mean when she takes off like she does now and again? Well everybody at the Hi-Diddle loves babies. But Fiddle and me, we're real tight you know. Mostly when she's going off, she brings him to me."

J.J. leaned forward, trying to keep her voice from rising too much. "So where is he now?"

"Why, upstairs asleep. That's what I need to tell you."

"You mean that boy is not your baby?" J.J. forced herself to remain seated.

"Why no, Miss J.J. You're thinking just like Moon, that the child is mine by Sport. But we never did get pregnant, I mean to say that little one is Fiddle's child. She calls him Jazz, a song she says, to remind her of his daddy.

"So now, just like before, I take him in and love him and wait for her to come back. When that fire comes, the baby, he's safe with me, away from Hi-Diddle. But it's many months now, and still no sign of her. I feel in my bones this time maybe she ain't coming back. She would know how to find me here, or near the clinic in Fort Bragg, or any of the places where I've been laying low."

"But if Melanie—Fiddle—was so devoted to her boy, why would she just leave him, go off like that?" J.J. broke in, not hiding her anguish.

"Why, Miss J.J., because she is devoted, you see, because she loves him so much, she gives him up when that darkness passes over her so no harm can come to the child. And then, when it passes again, she picks him up in her loving arms. But this time, I swear, I don't know where she can be. And I'm afraid, you see, that maybe this time the darkness never did pass at all.

"That's why I need your help, Miss J.J. I need to get back to Carolina now. My ma is doing poorly and I got to get away from Moon and all this hate. And I can't take the sweet little fellow with me, because he ain't mine. I'm hoping you can help me locate some of Fiddle's kin, so baby Jazz here can grow up with his own people, where he belongs."

Chapter 33

anctuary. Kin. The words replayed over and over in
J.J.'s head, like a mantra. They were the words that
had led her to quickly agree to what, from a rational
and professional point of view, was surely madness. Cat and
baby Jazz needed sanctuary—distance and a safe house,
bluntly put—from a newly threatening Moon. Cat and Jazz
also needed kin, that is to say a family to claim and commit
to the baby so that Cat could resume her life and Jazz could
properly begin his.

With winds and storms pummeling the Blue Moon
Bar & Far Out Rest Stop, it had seemed like a no-brainer.
She had a house, a big one, nearly empty. When she'd left
it so abruptly, it was filled for the first time in years with
friends and family, and a table groaning under the weight
of the Thanksgiving feast. *It was alive*, J.J. told herself, and
that felt right. It was also far from Moon, and such kin as
Melanie had were close at hand. Cat and Ivan had agreed:

Cat would bring Jazz within a few days to Pasadena. Only when J.J. got home did she realize the enormity of what she'd agreed to do. And, in so short a time, with enormous help from Annie and Dad, the house had been made ready.

One thing she hadn't considered was how Cat and the baby would actually get there. Then two days ago, Ivan had called. "Cat and Jazz are coming by Greyhound, kiddo. It was the cheapest way for her to bring all the shit she needs for the baby, plus fairly comfortable. And safe. Though with the Moon dude lurking, nothing is for sure. That's why I'm sticking close by both of them, and will ride alongside just to make sure he doesn't show up…"

Now J.J. stood at the edge of the bus station parking lot in the drizzling rain. A gust created from the giant bus pulling into its slot caused a melancholy whirlwind of trash, sending paper bags and old cups scudding into the gray air. From the edges of her vision she took in the drunks and their heaps of miserable possessions as they huddled in the driest corner under the eaves of the station. The Greyhound station, a place, J.J. admitted to herself, that she'd never paid attention to. Some kind of reporter.

The big doors of the bus opened with a whoosh. She strained to see Cat's dark hair in the crowd streaming off the bus, to hear Ivan gunning the Harley up close in his role as vigilante. He roared next to her, unstrapped his helmet, and gave a thumbs-up with his gloved hand. Swallowing back the sour taste of anxiety rising in her throat, she felt, for a moment, reassured.

~

"SEE HERE," ANNIE was explaining to Cat, "I just painted over this old chest of drawers but with a rubber pad on top, I think it will work fine as a changing table. You'll just have to watch him carefully though, as I see that he's is a fine wiggly little fellow."

"That he is, ma'am," Cat answered, as she deftly lifted the child up to begin changing him.

J.J. watched from the threshold of the room, feeling again a rising gratitude to her parents, and to Ivan, for being there. She was glad for the hubbub, for the many helping hands and voices.

I don't know squat about babies, she thought, *and wouldn't know the first thing about how to make a mother and child feel at home. But thank God Annie does.* Annie, who had haunted resale shops to find a crib, high chair, and car seat, and out-fitted the new nursery in a duck motif—even covered the windows with ducky curtains.

Backing quietly away from the nursery, J.J. reflected on the changes in her household. Gran had had another "spell" and was back in Glenview Convalescent, where Jocelyn and Dru had taken her with much fanfare. Her room there was still filled with flowers, expensive bed jackets, boxes of chocolates, and large, signed glamour shots of Jocelyn that they had brought along with her.

J.J. tried to imagine what Gran would think when she returned. Gran *will* return, J.J. vowed, to this house now outfitted to suit a baby, tended by a gentle young woman in clothes out of another time and place, who played harmonica and sang like a dream. To Annie and Dad, who had practically moved in and hovered, dewy eyed, over a small dusky-hued boy. She smiled in wonder. *Her parents*, who seemed positively giddy at the prospect of playing *grandparents*. At that very minute Dad was out in the workshop trying his hand at making a rocking horse with Grandfather's ancient tools.

Sneaking downstairs to gather her thoughts, J.J. ran into Dad who'd burst through the kitchen door whistling. "Oh there you are, my favorite journalist," he smiled, ruffling her hair.

J.J. winced, remembering this old exchange between them, how he used to fill in the blank with "favorite little girl," or later "favorite movie star," while she'd reply with her favorite ice cream flavor. "You're my best rocky road," she'd giggle, "my best caramel fudge."

"Listen, I really can't get very far with that old saw. I'm going to have to come back with a better one, so our little guy can get in some good rocking time. But he does have some things to keep him going, you know—blocks, a teddy bear, some nice chewable books, according to your mother." He winked, then went on. "I'm going to have to tear her away from here. Thank goodness she has a job, you know, or she'd never leave. Anyway, I think these two need a little time on their own to settle in, don't you?" Then he ruffled her hair again and looked at her knowingly, leaving little doubt about who he thought needed a bit of settling in time.

A minute later J.J. heard Ivan's Harley taking off up the street, then Dad's Ford convertible, its top up this time of year. A sudden wave of loneliness washed over her, a feeling she never experienced when she was simply by herself. The loneliness of being with people who were strangers. Nothing could be stranger to her at that moment than a baby. Even if he were a living link to Melanie, she felt inadequate, knowing so little about how to relate to him. It was a shortcoming, a failure on her part as a woman.

Just now, she wished not to be reminded of her failures. She wished the whole baby situation would just go away. Then remorse swept over her, and she closed her eyes. "For God's sake, forgive me, Melie," she muttered like a silent prayer. Knowing, too, that of all people, Melanie would understand.

"There is nothing lonelier in the world than to be in the company of one who doesn't know you are there," Melie had written in her journal during the Rochester days. "I am more alone in a room with Hans when we are inhabiting separate worlds than I ever am in the splendid solitude of my own making."

"Miss J.J., that baby boy has gone down like a lamb in his little old room. I guess he sure does like those duckies your mama fixed up for him. Mighty sweet of her." Cat, who had entered silently, sank like a graceful flower on a long stem onto a kitchen chair, wrapping her skirt around toes covered in rainbow-colored socks, knees pulled beneath her chin.

As J.J. half turned to take in the apparition who was now her new housemate, she felt the girl's composure. Cat had been through hell in the Hi-Diddle House, in the fire, with Moon, with Sport in a relationship that had come and gone, and now as a de facto single mother on the lam—not even taking into account what in her past life had driven her from Carolina to the California coast. Yet she radiated a kind of serenity. *I'm the only one*, J.J. thought, *who's tied up in knots about this. The only one who can't see how this could possibly work...*

"Care for some tea?" she asked. Cat nodded yes. J.J. reached for the kettle as a way to buy time. There was so much she needed to ask, but she knew enough to stifle the reporter inside. It was the moment to approach this situation in a different way, as a different kind of person. She just needed to discover how, and who.

"So, Cat," she finally started, handing her a mug of steaming hibiscus flower brew that Annie had left. "I know there are so many things for you to sort out, and I have to say I'm amazed at how well you've managed in this crazy situation, and I want to help, but need to know how."

Cat looked up, her large eyes searching J.J.'s face. "Why, thank you, Miss J.J. But you're already doing so much."

"A safe place to stay was one thing," and J.J. gestured around with a faint smile, "easy enough with the generous space of my gran's house. But the other thing is to find Jazz's family, somebody who can take him in and care for him and commit to making sure he grows up well."

"Right," Cat agreed.

"First though, we have to take into consideration the fact that the boy does have a father—if he's alive, and if we can find him."

"Yes, ma'am. That's right."

"Any thoughts on where we might find Mr. John C. Calhoun? What his real name might be, for a start?"

"You got me there, Miss. J.J. Fiddle, she never did call him by any name other than that. A mighty strange thing, too, for some black fellow with a big old Afro taking on the name of a deader 'n a doornail Southern coot, as racist as the night is long. In my opinion."

"I do agree with you, but think it was intentional, you know. I expect he was being ironic, that is just making a point by doing something contrary, if that makes any sense."

"I expect," Cat frowned.

"So if Fiddle never told you anything more about him or his whereabouts, I believe we're rather stuck, Cat. From her papers, I know he came from Chicago originally, that he played the clarinet and loved jazz and justice, and that he was headed south. I expect she found him there at least once—"

"Well our little Jazz, he's fair proof of that," Cat smiled.

"True. But I don't have any idea how often or where she met up with him down there, do you? Seems like from one letter I read, she went looking for him in Alabama, but didn't find him. Do you think he's even still alive?"

Cat sat upright, planting her feet on the floor. "No, Miss J.J., I do not. Fiddle never did say directly, but from everything I gleaned from her, she brought this child into the world without his daddy."

J.J. paused for a minute to absorb this. "I was afraid of that. If I had a name, just something to go on, I'd be blanketing Chicago to find who his people are. He may have grandparents there just aching to welcome him with open arms. Even if their son had cut all ties. But without a name, a clue…"

"Well, as for grandparents, uncles, aunts, all of it, he's got that here on his mama's side, doesn't he?"

"Yes, and no," J.J. replied. "It's complicated, something we need to look into. You'll see."

Cat took this in by nodding thoughtfully, running her tongue across the rim of the teacup. Then she was on her feet heading for the sink as quietly as when she'd entered the room. "I'll just see to clearing all this up, Miss J.J. Never you mind." She paused for a moment, spying a large bowl of fruit, one that Annie, bless her, had left full.

"Why there are some mighty nice-looking oranges here, Miss J.J. I have a mind to make a cake with them, if that would be all right with you. Our little fellow Jazz passed his first birthday a couple weeks back, but we weren't in a place where we could rightly celebrate. Now I do believe we are. May I?" She smiled marvelously.

"Of course. A great idea," J.J. answered, realizing how that girl was working. *She's going to make me feel at ease here despite myself.*

———

TWO DAYS PAST the birthday party, when Annie and Dad relished his four-tooth grin, his laugh, his budding words, his near steps as he clung to a kitchen chair, Jazz ventured out toward Dad, holding onto his fingers. At the party, Jazz had stepped into the chaos of torn wrapping paper, crumbs of orange cake on the floor, the lingering light of one burning candle, and grinned. J.J. sank into a web of surprise at all the transformations. Mostly surprised at how, she, too, was coming to relish it.

Annie had also commented on it. "You know, Saraswati, even goddesses swoon under certain domestic conditions with an adorable baby in the center. It's just been hard for you to get there, being an only child and all, no fault of your own of course. Nor your father's if he'd had his way. Oh my, he'd have happily fathered a tribe to fill this house — sticking around for it, now that's a question for another day. But no, when I saw the perfection of you, that was enough for me. Stop right there, my inner divine light flashed to me."

Annie's speech was still in J.J.'s ears as she wheeled the Datsun into its tight spot in the parking lot behind the *Star*. An artful parsing of the truth, she acknowledged, leaving out the bit about Annie not really liking the midnight feedings–changing diapers routine; not admitting how her passion for exotic travel and collecting "weird third-world junk," as Ivan put it, overran her tepid maternal instincts. But never mind, "the perfection of you" bit was a nice touch. J.J. slammed the door and ran up the back stairs to the newsroom.

"Come on in, the water's fine," Alice shouted out, as she swiveled to watch J.J. enter through the beveled glass door.

"Hey, just checking in," J.J. smiled. "Presume you got the Gracie piece okay."

"Indeed. Sit," Alice motioned to the chair opposite her desk.

"Well?"

"Oh, it's a fine piece, no question. A remarkable story, in its way. Girl from poor agricultural family — wait, make that motherless girl — scrambles to get into Cal Tech as grad student with flimsy credentials, wows the likes of Feynman, wins over the committee, works her way into major astronomy lab, does astounding work, blows away all the big boys. Yeah, remarkable in its way."

J.J. knew from Alice's tone, from her overarching eyebrows, that more was to come. "But…?" she finally asked.

"But you know, and I know, that's probably half the story. Am I right?"

"Well, in a manner of speaking. But you know, too, that I can hardly write the story of Fleur, can I?"

"Hardly," Alice agreed. "But here's the thing, J.J. You've been given amazing latitude here, more than most reporters ever get. And you've been given a pass along that dangerous boundary between objective reporting and telling personal stories. You've been allowed to be in the lives of these profile subjects in ways that are, in general, and for good reason, taboo. In this case I'm aware of the story not told, but I guess I want to know what else haven't you said? What are you withholding, even from yourself?"

"I don't—"

Alice stopped her before she could even formulate a sentence. "This is not a debate I want to engage in, and I'm certainly not interested in any defense. This is a question—a hard news question—I'm asking you to answer for yourself. If you walk too far into the territory of the stories you're reporting, at some point you cease being a reporter. You become just a storyteller. You have to answer for yourself if that's what you want."

Alice turned then. The conversation was over.

At least between them. But it raged on, as Alice intended, in J.J.'s head. And she was grateful. Even more so after a meeting with Bud Purvis.

"Sit down, sit down, J.J." he had invited her courteously. "Well, well, what can I say? The raves keep coming in." His smile was so obsequious that J.J. wished for a moment a cigar were hanging out of his mouth, that he had a coughing fit of laughter over some crude, sexist joke.

"That physicist gal, amazing really. That piece, another brilliant bit of reporting by the way, goes out right after Christmas. Don't want it to get lost in all the Christmas hoo-haw, do we?"

"I guess not," J.J. answered.

"I suspect we'll be getting some calls from those science bigwigs on the other side of town come New Year's, don't you?" His grin was almost as salacious as in the old days, when he'd fantasized about tits and ass.

Right, fat boy, she thought to herself. *I delivered Hollywood stars and now maybe celestial-sized super scientists with Nobel Prizes attached. Your ratings and your readership have shot up like the stars themselves, and whatever I might do to prostitute the reporting, as long as the numbers keep going up, you'd be happy.*

Driving home, J.J. could feel the sting—the truth—of Alice's admonition, and breathed hard wondering about Alice's reaction if she knew what awaited at Gran's house: a main witness of the Hi-Diddle story and Melanie's orphaned baby boy, her new housemates.

Chapter 34

J.J. walked alone under the narrow, winding passageway leading into the sanctuary. Above, the sky, a perfect blue after the rains, filtered down its winter light upon her, and she wanted to believe in it now more than ever. The Gothic structure had thrilled her as a child, when Gran brought her here for Christmas pageants, and the passageway made her believe she was about to enter a strange, medieval world. Now that world was going to be transformed again as she entered All Saints to bury Melanie according to the scripture of Charles Hart. She inhaled and stepped inside, ready to embrace Evelyn, Gracie, and Jocelyn, ready to join them as they sat in judgment.

"The Lord works in mysterious ways, doesn't She?" Eve winked. J.J. slid into the pew to hug her, noting the simple blue skirt and white tunic and the small cross hanging from her neck. The glorious red hair that had once been shorn to accommodate a wimple was long and wild once more, sticking out at will from beneath a barrette at the nape of the neck.

"The devil works in mysterious ways, too, I hear." Eve winked again. "They're playing Hans's version of her, aren't they?"

J.J. tilted her head to hear. "Of course. It's part of the first movement of the Melanie symphony. My God, seeing you, it makes this all worth it," she whispered over the music.

Breathing the mingled smells of pine boughs and candle wax, the residue of incense, J.J. took in the altar set off by red poinsettias, ribbons, huge sprays of red and white flowers, the crêche in the corner ready for a Christmas pageant. Then closed her eyes against all she couldn't bear. She opened them again to Gracie, who had slid in next to Eve, followed by Fleur.

"Oh my God," Gracie said, loud enough to be heard over the organ, "if I may be allowed to say that."

J.J. felt dizzy, as if about to be swept away in a riptide of emotions. The unexpected joy of sitting next to Eve and Gracie together, and Jocelyn to soon join them, slamming against the revulsion of what was taking place. The grotesquerie of the Harts "putting Melanie to rest" in this High Church sanctuary of her own childhood, so far from where Melie had gone, what she had become.

Yet eyes closed, a single candle lingered in sight, and she felt Melanie hovering there, finger to her lips, saying "Don't worry, J.J. All's well."

She watched then as if from a distant plane, as though Melanie had pulled her there. She nodded at Jocelyn and Dru, who had slipped into the end of the pew, next to Ivan, who was back to wearing a feather in his hair, and gave Jocelyn a thumbs-up. Next the Harts filed into the reserved seats in front. A sad-faced Dr. Hart, with Claire, like a '40s mannequin, dressed in a black suit, a black hat with veil covering her unknowable face, clinging to his arm. Other dark suits followed, an older brother J.J. vaguely remembered being mentioned as a banker; cousins, aunts and uncles, all looking wan and expensive, a tottering dowager wearing at least half the family jewels. Then Natalie. Unlike the rest of the family garbed in the expected mournful dark, Natalie, whose usual black looked suitably funereal, appeared in a startling white wool dress that fell to her boots. Her hair was tucked inside a matching white beret, and the only remains of the Natalie J.J. had seen before were in the kohl-rimmed eyes and exaggerated eyebrows.

J.J. startled. *My God*, she thought. *Natalie exists not as Melanie's double, but as her negative.* Only after exposing Natalie through some magical process did she appear, either dark to mirror Melanie's light, or now white to dispatch Melanie's black.

J.J. felt the church fill and swell behind her, but did not turn to look. Somewhere in its throngs, she knew, were Cat and Jazz, who had been brought by Annie and Dad. The *demoiselles* all had work to do this day, serious work. Not the business of "putting away and moving beyond the grief," as one of the bereavement pamphlets counseled, and certainly not that of accepting a buried Melanie according to this deranged spectacle. But to sit in judgment, to decide who among Jazz's kin was worthy of knowing him, of taking him into their lives.

The music, so incongruous on an organ, shifted from the second movement to pieces from the third of Hans's opus for Melanie, and J.J. shifted in her seat.

Then a sudden stillness, followed by a robed priest, acolytes, a parade of incense and banners, the carried cross, and the sung anthem, "I am the Resurrection and the life, saith the Lord." Psalms, scripture readings, intonations, blessings, the words of St. John, "In my Father's house are many mansions." Lace and vestments stitched in gold, readings all from the St. James version of the Bible, as High Church as possible in this parish given to folk and jazz masses, protests and peace vigils. And, J.J. knew, the last thing Melanie would have wanted.

Finally, the priest stood for the homily, but instead of entering the pulpit, bowed to the family asking who would like to say a few words of remembrance. Charles Hart rose first and lifted his pallid face and red-rimmed eyes toward the church. "We come to mourn our dear and beloved Melanie," he began, "who left us suddenly by the terrible misfortune of a boating accident, but who as a devoted, devout, and loving daughter and wife, blesses our gathering today as we pray to send her spirit to heaven..."

J.J., contrary to what she expected, felt the stricken man's real grief, but could listen no more. Not to the stifling banker brother, nor the stream of suits in expensive ties or designer heels, who followed. All she took in was Claire, fixed and mute as a statue, and Natalie, true to form slouched in the back of the family section, trying to be invisible.

When the last lines of "The Lord's Prayer" were finally uttered, J.J. steeled herself to stand and to enter the next room of this nightmare—the reception in the church hall. *My father's house has many mansions indeed*, she thought. But instead of ending the service, the priest nodded to Natalie, saying, "Now Melanie's sister Natalie would like to close the service with a special tribute."

Natalie rose like a specter from the last family pew and, heading toward the altar steps, tucked strands of boot-polish blackened hair back under her beret. "Right. As we all know who love Melanie, music was, um, is a huge part of her life, way more than being the subject of some well-known symphony. What most people probably don't know is that she played—plays—some instruments and secretly sings and always loved the music and the, um, spirit she found at Woodstock. So I would like to sing a song that she would most appreciate hearing at this time."

J.J. tensed, feeling the packed church inhale.

Then, like a choir girl in white, Natalie opened her mouth in a perfect angelic "O," and a sweet soprano voice caught the air before the impact of the song hit.

> Live your loving life,
> Live it all the best you can
> And if you pay no attention darling
> To what you might ever hear from your man.
> I think you're just like a servant
> And try to keep it all to yourself.
> Don't you know it makes the world go round,
> You gotta go and honey share everywhere else.
> Come on, come on, come on!

The raucous, wild words of Janice Joplin sounded sweet as a whole church chorus in Natalie's pure a cappella soprano. *Janice, our generational soul sister*, thought J.J., as she remembered the shocking news of her death only four years before. Accidental, by way of living too hard, loving too much, and oh, yes, drug overdose. Or was that a boating accident?

> As good as you've been, babe,
> So good I wanna be here,
> Oh, good as you've been to this whole wide world,
> As good as you've been, babe,
> So good I wanna be here.
> Ah, the way you love your mother,
> The way you love your sister, your brother.
> The way you love your aunt, your uncle,
> Anybody now, everybody now.

The anthem finished, the final prayer, and J.J. led her little band into the aisle to leave with the rest of the stunned mourners. It struck her that in the song's list of those loved ones, there had been nothing about "your father." Nor of course, had it mentioned "your son," the very person at the heart of Melanie's last chapter of life. And perhaps, her leaving of it.

"Come on, come on, come on," J.J. sang silently to herself as she headed out of the sanctuary. The first thing she intended was to find Natalie, to thank her. But as she watched the family form into the obligatory receiving line, Natalie was nowhere to be seen.

J.J. TURNED TO make eye contact with those in the line behind her; with Evelyn, who winked again, this time in solidarity; then Gracie, who looked back clear eyed and unblinking; and Fleur, who nodded in understanding and gently held onto Gracie's elbow; next Jocelyn, flanked by Dru and followed by Ivan with the feather. Jocelyn, who wore a large, stylish hat and dark glasses, trying to be as anonymous as possible, gave a small thumbs-up with a fashionably gloved hand. J.J. took special care to smile at Cat, who nestled between Evelyn and Gracie, as if for protection. Jazz snuggled against her, happily chewing on a teething biscuit. J.J. turned to pass through the line, as if a gauntlet, knowing the troops behind her were in order. They all knew what they had to do.

She first met Charles Hart, and was unsettled to look into his sad red eyes. "Dr. Hart," she said nodding, "we are all deeply sorry." He took her hand in a surprisingly strong grasp and nodded back.

Similarly, she greeted the banker brother, a phalanx of aunts, uncles, and cousins, trying to look each of them in the eye, trying to imagine who among them could know and love Jazz. She looked behind to watch Cat, shiny black hair falling about her shoulders, long calico skirt flowing beneath a homespun blouse, move as if in a dream. She noted how Cat lifted Jazz a tiny bit toward each person she met, as if making a silent introduction, if not an offering of kinship.

At last, on the far end of the line stood Claire Hart, the bejeweled matriarch planted staunchly next to her. J.J. mumbled her name and condolences to the imposing older woman, then turned her attention to Claire. Only when she stood directly in front of her could J.J. actually see through the veil to observe Claire's face. Only then could she see that Claire Hart had become a wax impression of herself in the fashion of Madame Tussaud's.

"I'm so very sorry, Mrs. Hart," J.J. said, extending her hand. But Claire did not reach back, and greeted her by only a faint smile and a weak "yes." If a certain death was being acknowledged here today, J.J. understood, it was that of Melanie's mother.

Cat had just passed the matriarch, who visibly took a step back while regarding the pair—the sleek-haired young woman in peasant clothing and the curly-haired, half-black baby. Turning to Claire, she whispered in a voice loud enough for half the receiving line to hear, "First, they start bringing home these Oriental half-breeds from overseas, and now these little home-grown mix-and-match pickaninnies, what next!"

For a brief moment, a flash of life came forth from under Claire Hart's death mask. No sooner had her own grandson moved past her than she whispered back to the matriarch: "Yes, quite a scandal isn't it? Imagine what people will say. I'm just so glad my girls…" she paused, then let the sentence fall unfinished.

Chapter 35

J.J. stepped into the yellow Datsun and gunned away from All Saints as quickly as possible, riding the wake of Ivan's Harley, trying to get home before the other *demoiselles* arrived. Pulling into the drive behind the house, she waved to Dad on the back lawn, rolling a ball to little Jazz, who would take a tottering step toward it, then fall down laughing. Cat clapped on the sidelines.

Wonderful smells from the kitchen greeted her, and J.J. knew her parents had been at work. "Your father made his winter beef stew," Annie sang out to her without turning around, "so of course I'm contributing the healthy alternative. Vegetarian chili, fresh cornbread."

"Thanks," J.J. said, taking in the kitchen table with bowls, plates, and cutlery laid out for self-service, the green salad and fruit bowls temptingly filled.

"Beverages in the fridge," Annie continued. "Chief

Runnamucka has already helped himself. He's in the living room."

J.J. waved at Ivan, who sat cross-legged on the floor nursing a beer. The doorbell rang. Jocelyn entered first, sans hat, her hair pulled back neatly in a twist. "Dru dropped me off and says good luck with this and can he have first movie rights. He's back at the hotel." Gracie and Fleur followed.

"Come, gather around the table and fix yourself a plate. Fuel to keep us going," J.J. called out, opening the door to Eve. Arms around her, J.J. declared, "My God, this is unbelievable, all of it, but having you here…"

"Crazy, isn't it? I mean the timing, but it really was preordained. I truly am here to do more advanced medical training, to become a proper nurse practitioner." Eve passed a coat and an orange and black African cloth she'd worn as a scarf to J.J.'s outstretched hands. Her red hair, having slipped the noose of the hair clasp, hung free to her shoulders.

~

WITH THE SMALL gathering sprawled on Gran's Oriental rug, J.J. felt the house breathing again, expanding with life. She knew the moment had come. "It's hard to state how overwhelmed I feel," she began. "First with gratitude to have you all around me, because swear to God, I couldn't face the loss of Melanie—and that performance today—alone. I mean those *people*. Like Cat said—and she'll join us as soon as she gets Jazz down to sleep—of course they should know about the baby. They're his kin."

Jocelyn, stretching her full six feet onto the floor, propped herself up on an elbow. "I've seen this script before. Any ideas about the father?"

"The famously elusive J.C. Calhoun? I tried every avenue to figure out his real name, but couldn't get anywhere. The only one who might have been able to help, who might have seen him—seen her—in the South was...Guy." J.J. stopped there.

The room remained silent for a minute, and Ivan, who sat on the outer fringes of the others, began passing his pipe.

"'Holy shit,' isn't that what they call it?" Eve reached for the pipe. "And that name. J.C. Calhoun, like giving the finger to the Man. He must be quite a guy."

"Must have been," Gracie broke in. "You probably know that I was the last one of us to see Melie. She tried to see J.J., but only saw Gran, because J.J. was away, in Vietnam. Instead, Melie came to see me—us, because Fleur was there—before going up the coast. Melie was a few months' pregnant and needed help. I asked about the father, and she wouldn't say much, except that he was a great guy. She pulled out this picture of the two of them, but clearly didn't want to talk about him. I got the feeling there was some tragedy, that maybe he'd died down there in the South."

"So we're stuck where we were," J.J. added. "A no-name, probably deceased father and those conniving, lying Harts."

"Yeah, they are conniving—and manipulative. They want to make their own version of Melanie and preserve her there. But," Jocelyn looked around at her friends with her famous chameleon eyes, "are they so different from us? I mean, we're all hurting from this loss, trying to preserve her as best we can in our own ways. In my case, needing to make amends for so many things, but especially needing to say sorry for turning away from her at that war rally when she stood before me waving the truth in my face. I so feel like thanking her for making me see myself through all the disguises. But we all have our own memories, experiences, versions of Melanie, and the need to reconcile them. Don't you think, J.J.?"

J.J. said nothing and took the pipe from Eve.

"So where do we go with this?" Gracie asked, sitting up straight and reaching for a glass of wine. "We don't even have proof, really, that Melie is dead. We do know she's disappeared and that, at first glance, her entire family are losers—hopeless prospects for Jazz. A couple of the cousins look to be the right age and in circumstances—like married—to take on a baby. But would they, even if they knew? And if so, what would they be like to him? Maybe they'd treat him like another family retainer. And what if Melie comes back one day and…?"

"She's not coming back," J.J. broke in. "I understand Cat thinks otherwise, but I just know it in my bones. If nothing else, the proof is that she would have come back already if she were going to. She wouldn't be the kind of mother to abandon her baby."

"Wrong," Eve nearly shouted. "Look," she sat up to face her friends, "you'll excuse me for pulling rank here, but don't forget that Sister Eve was also, however briefly, a mother. The only one among us. And I'm here to say the feeling, the pull, toward that baby—you have no idea. If Melie sometimes felt controlled by demons, depression, drugs even, that might in some way harm that child, then out of that pure, fierce maternal love, would she leave him in the hands of someone better able to care for him? Would she 'abandon' him, as you say, J.J., even at the cost of enormous grief on her part in doing so? She would."

The air seemed to leave the room as J.J. recoiled slightly, receiving another rebuke.

"Okay. Let's leave aside what we can't know and look at what we do," J.J. answered, reverting to the comfort of facts. "There is this baby and a young woman who has cared for him like a mother, but she needs to leave California now and go back to her own people. The baby is not hers, and she can hardly take him out of state, let alone across the country, legally anyway. Then there's the matter of… Well, the mountains of Carolina with a half-black child. I thought that the baby's own relatives should be the ones to step in, step up. But today we all had a good close look at them to decide if so, who among them? What do we think?"

"I think," Eve started, but stopped when Cat swept into the room.

"Sorry, but I had to get Jazz settled. I'm so glad y'all are here because this is a frightful mess. I had thought, well kinfolks, at least where I come from, they're where a person belongs when there's need, or troubles. But seeing those... those cold strange folks today, I swear, I could not turn this sweet little child to a one of them." She paused, sinking effortlessly on the floor in the center of the circle. "I felt that all through today, but then at the end when those wicked women scorned their own flesh and blood because of his color... I could expect to find such attitudes at home, but here in California, from these hifalutin' rich people, I swear I did not think to find such ignorance."

The room fell silent as the last rays of sun slid off Gran's horsehair sofa onto the floor, and Ivan quietly refilled his pipe.

"Christ help us," Eve spoke up. "Of course. Cat's right."

"What shall we do then?" J.J. posed the question on everyone's lips.

Ivan, sitting behind Cat, spoke up for the first time. "It seems to me, if you're all just still enough to listen, Melanie will guide you. If you think about it, she has always left a trail, a way to know and see her life through all its changes and mysteries. Just last year that packet of letters, with a note on it 'for J.J.' was found up in Boonville. A random happening? I don't think so."

"No, no, you're quite right, Ivan," Eve broke in. "I saw that quality when she first came to visit in the convent. She could enter another realm—in the old days they called people with gifts like that either saints or devils and burned them alive—but Melie, she could go there."

"Well, she was a Pisces," Ivan added.

"Please," J.J. put up a hand as if to stop him and closed her eyes.

"Whatever. Still, she might very well have left us clues, J.J.," Eve continued, "especially you, since she kept sending you her things, dropping crumbs about where she was, where she was going. So maybe there will be some way to know what she would want now."

Jocelyn sat upright. "Fair enough. You've got a point, both of you. But how do we divine now what Melie would want to do? Not by some hokey séance with candles I presume, or by making her horoscope."

"No, we don't have to," Ivan agreed, "although those might help, but—"

Cat rose with no sound, her long skirt falling around her like a queenly robe. Towering over the others, she brushed her silky hair back from her forehead and faced them. "Here's what y'all need to do. I do believe that Fiddle would want y'all to take him. At least one of you, to care for and love him, but the lot of you to draw around him, like a real family would. Because in the ways that matter, you are kin to him."

Silence, natural as the coming nightfall, claimed the room, as the group on the carpet heard Cat's indisputable voice of authority. They felt the need to move, and got up, wanting a break. Some drifted into the kitchen or hallway or lingered in the powder room, while Annie went from room to room turning on the lights. Only J.J. remained in the living room, where she sat on the horsehair sofa rubbing her temples.

One of y'all. She kept repeating Cat's words to herself. She remembered Melie's observation, too, about how, unlike the rest of young women of their generation, the past-thirty *demoiselles* seemed to have no gift for marriage, much less motherhood, although Eve had given it a try. But her losses were tragic. And now, contrary to anything that made sense in this world, she was a nun. As for Jocelyn—the thought of the superstar turning her hand to things domestic, things *maternal*… She laughed gently. Then Gracie. Clearly all that was not in the cards for Gracie, while she herself… The very idea was overwhelming. She had no idea why. Of course Melie, who had at least brought a child into the world long enough to hold him a little, Melie had left them all, baby included, to their own devices. And they were supposed to figure out what to do according to her wishes? *Like hell*, J.J. thought, *and I'm the one she sent her collections to*. The one whose name was on the packet of letters.

J.J. barely noticed when one by one the others started to reassemble. Annie followed Cat into the room. "Anybody care for any more refreshments?" she asked.

Suddenly Jocelyn filled the room. Stretching on the floor again, hair escaped from the funereal bun, shoes kicked off, she began a monologue, one arm flung over her eyes, the other waving in the air to accompany her seemingly stream-of-consciousness thoughts. "I can do this. I can do this. Madge did it when I was young, and we lived in a little yellow house in a promontory overlooking the sea. It was magical, pure, the essence of how childhood should be before the world and its corruption, the temptations and the pull of lights—all of it—sets in. I could be that mother, like it was implied I would be in *Pacific Blue*, maybe I was in training without even knowing, maybe Dru—"

"Wait a minute, Jocelyn. I think you better hear me first."

Jocelyn sat up to see Gracie, short as she was, looming over her as she stood in the center of the room. "I think your offer is generous, sincere, but since you're, since we're all in a state of shock, it's probably not well thought out. But I have a different offer—which is that Fleur and I take the baby. We are, as you know, a couple, even if not one that the world would recognize, but since we are together and mean to stay together in love if not in law, I think we qualify. The one thing we are missing, and we've talked about it a lot, is that we both long to have children. You may think that odd, but I come from a big Italian family, which in a way is a definition of life. I've always wanted," Gracie stopped, tears starting at the edges of her shining gray eyes, "and it would make Papa so happy, too, a little boy…"

Fleur came up to stand next to Gracie and slipped an arm about her waist.

"I know that I'm lacking in many of the qualities required. I always knew growing up I was not like Mama, much as I loved her, that I couldn't be like her. But Fleur, she…she has the gift. So we'd like, we'd love, to take Jazz for our own."

J.J. let out her breath, uttering, "Oh my God," as she remembered the puzzling way Gracie had closed the letter a couple of years ago when asked to address current *demoiselles de la Maison Française.*

"Liberté, Egalité, Maternité," she had written.

"I see now. It's all true," J.J. said more to herself than the others.

Cat, who had been standing at the edge of the room, stepped in, lifting her magnificent skirt. "I can tell y'all this. Fiddle, she'll be mighty pleased."

Chapter 36

J.J. lay in darkness, hoping that sleep would find her. She tried to shut down the events of the day. But they kept coming at her. Literal shots in the dark.

First Annie calling out, "I really don't understand you sometimes, Saraswati," as she slammed kitchen doors shut and threw cooking utensils brought from her house into cardboard boxes. "Knowledge, music, divine winds for God's sake, you may be all up on these. But you still have to pay some heed to family, to your own flesh and blood. If nothing else, think of your poor father—you did hear the one about 'honor thy father' didn't you? Can you imagine how he's going to take this? Not that your Grace and her little Ophelia don't mean well, but honestly…"

Stupefied, she watched her mother dart in annoyance, swishing her long nouveau gypsy skirt as she shut the kitchen door hard behind her, calling out, "After all we've done for you, too."

LIGHT IN THE room. A big fire jumps in a stone fireplace and takes command behind a cat on its hearth, three dogs curled on a faded rug. A rough-hewn table, a clutch of wildflowers in a pottery vase perched on top, fills one end of the room. Across from the fireplace, a rocking chair in front of shelves. Above the shelves, on the wall, a sampler: "Hi-Diddle House, All Welcome Here," stitched in a center bordered with flowers and redwood branches. Figures, too shadowy to make out, move in and out of doors. Fire crackles, a cat stretches. A dog rolls over. Music—a distant flute, the strings of a violin, a sweet soprano voice.

A woman in long white skirts settles in the chair and begins to rock, holding a baby. Her face—Melanie's face—becomes visible. Like posing for a closeup in front of a camera. She smiles, blonde hair falling down her back in the shape of wings, blue eyes dancing. She holds the baby upright and Jazz begins gurgling.

More music, louder and louder. Figures drift in, a troupe of medieval players with pointy hats and shoes, belted tunics over leggings. They beat on a sheepskin drum, a tambourine, blow on a fife. Others enter. The room swirls with dancers. Now Melanie, dancing among them, gestures to baby Jazz nestled into a little cot near the fireplace. Voices and laughter, but no understandable words, except for Melanie, who picks up a fiddle and strokes it with a bow. It points to the mantle above the fireplace and a large framed black and white picture with huge crowds of mostly black people, police, and dogs. In the center of a street a familiar figure, Martin Luther King, leads the dancers, who become marchers through danger, into fire. His face fades then is clear again. J.C. Calhoun, a headband around his Afro.

A young woman in gingham skirts begins rocking the chair, long black hair swimming down her back, her arms reaching out. Melanie approaches, stops. She holds the baby tight to her chest, kisses him hard on the forehead, then passes him to the waiting hands. Cat's voice says, "Come on, sweet boy, I got you."

Melanie's face, tears streaking down from eyes now dancing with sorrow. A small explosion of light, like a flash going off. Melanie is gone.

Only a puff of white light remains where Melanie was, the kind that blinds you for a moment, then stays in your sight so long afterwards, you think it may never leave.

J.J. opened her eyes to find Melanie's tears escaping them.

Chapter 37

J.J. sat on the corner of her desk, out of the melee of the annual Christmas party. Making merry with a bunch of colleagues buzzed on cheap champagne and eggnog, all the while avoiding Bud Purvis's new annoying obsequiousness and steering clear of Alice, was more than she could handle. But George found her out soon and passed a glass to her while readying his camera for a barrage of shots. "Please, no, I've had too much already this season," she said, pushing the glass away, hoping he would get that she also meant she'd had too much of the *Star*'s star routine.

No sooner had the dread words passed through her mind than Bud, more idiotic than menacing in a flimsy Santa hat, spotted her too, and offered up a toast. "To the *Star*'s star reporter," he grinned. Soon all her tipsy colleagues were surrounding her, lifting plastic glasses in noisy cheers, while plates with cake and cookies piled up and spilled on her desk. "It's all a team thing, you know. Here's to the real stars." She saluted no one in particular, then backed away, pretending to admire the plastic Christmas tree with flashing lights reflected in the window, mirroring the winking lights on plastic wreaths with fake snow on the streetlamps below.

Just when it seemed possible to slip away unnoticed, she felt a hand on her elbow. "Step on in," Alice whispered, guiding J.J. to her office. As Alice shut the beveled glass door, she regarded J.J. with wry amusement. J.J. breathed easier. "Lordy, I do wonder how your friend Jocelyn puts up with this all the time. You must just be exhausted from your brief stint at Wonder Womanhood. Luckily, as we know in this biz, this too will be brief."

J.J. laughed, wanting to reach out and hug Alice, but not daring to. Guilt, she knew, was even more constraining than adulation. And she did feel guilty for not telling Alice — who had always been her champion — the truth. But letting Alice in on it was a complication she couldn't even think about just now. Harboring Cat, a key witness in whatever breaking news story was going to come down in Mendocino soon; keeping her dead friend's baby in her home, a baby whose legal status she increasingly worried about; setting herself and her friends up as judge and jury to decide not to inform the Harts, the known living relatives, of the existence of said baby; conspiring to have the baby entrusted to Grace Battaglia and her legally invisible partner, Fleur van Ness, who had no claim to him whatsoever; and the untidy journalistic/ethical twist to all the rest — the fact that she, J.J., had written or was about to write about all the characters in question. *What would Alice say?* she'd asked herself a hundred times. *I think I know. Don't want to know.*

"...I took the liberty," Alice was saying, as J.J. snapped back into focus, "of bringing all these in here. Thought, you know, leaving mail and messages on the desk, now that you're 'Miss *Star*'s star,' might be, shall we say tempting?

Journalists are snoops by definition. You may have heard that rumor." Her mouth cocked at an angle to her askew glasses as she handed the pile to J.J. "Oh yes, do read Laura's piece, which I assume you haven't seen. Sent her as a reporter to Melanie Hart's 'funeral.' I figured you certainly weren't up for going notebook in hand. But she seems to have captured it. Tell me what you think."

J.J. nodded. "Thanks. For all of it. I'll have a look."

Alice leaned back against her desk, buttoning her Christmas sweater with reindeer that she wore every year. As if reading J.J.'s thoughts she said, "Wearing this bit of haute couture is my stab at ritual. It's nearly as ancient as I am."

J.J. smiled. "It wouldn't be Christmas without it. Have you got plans, Alice?"

"Going to my niece and her husband's place and will do my annual diplomatic two-step to make nice to my dreadful sister. You?"

"As soon as I leave your office, I make a bee-line to Glenview Convalescent and spring Gran once again. She seems to be doing extremely well at the moment, and I mean to keep her home as long as possible."

Alice lit up at the news. "Brava for Gran, for you. I imagine a family Christmas rather like that wonderful Thanksgiving. Please say hello to your parents for me, and to Gran of course. No, better yet, I'll pop over and give them greetings myself."

"Right," J.J. answered, hoping her wince didn't show. "Great. Just give a ring first to make sure, you know, she's…"

"Of course," Alice broke in. Then she reached over to give the longed-for hug to J.J., who mumbled "thanks," and turned to flee the office, hoping nobody would see her red eyes.

⌒

J.J. HAD TAKEN care to clean up the car and to make space for Gran's belongings, which now piled up in the backseat and filled the trunk. With her hair freshly done and wearing a smart mauve winter coat, Gran looked regal, elegant. J.J. reached over to take her hand before pulling out.

"You know Gran, you are such a fashion plate, and you look so glamorous today, you really put me to shame."

"Well, *ma petite*, that skirt is rather dowdy, and your hair could use a good fix, but I've always told you, you have good bones. Lots of, what shall we say, *potential*? If you want to use it." Her eyes danced with mischief.

J.J. laughed. "God, *grand-maman*, you are a tonic. The best possible Christmas present. I'm so happy to have you back." She presumed Gran would not know she meant that in two ways, but given how very sharp she was now, even that was possible.

As they pulled out of the parking lot, J.J. decided she had best prepare Gran for what was awaiting them at home. She had mentioned it before, but it was best to double down.

"You know that we have guests. That young woman, called Cat, I told you about, and the baby."

"Yes, yes. You told me about it, *chérie*."

"Well, did I tell you that the baby is not Cat's, but actually belongs to Melanie, my dear friend who was buried this week, well not buried really, because nobody's verified that she's dead, but her family thinks so, and they had this dreadful service at All Saints—remember how we used to go there at Christmas?"

Gran nodded, *"Oui, chérie."*

"Melanie, she's the one who came to see me when she was pregnant while I was away and I guess you talked to her."

Gran nodded again, *"Oui, oui."*

Then the story, all of it—Cat and Jazz, Ivan as vigilante, the funeral, the music, Natalie's surprising finish, the terrible Hart relatives, the gathering of *les demoiselles*, their judgment after Cat's pronouncement, the decision that Gracie and Fleur should become guardians—all she wanted but could not say to Alice, poured out of J.J.

By the time they had pulled up to the house, J.J. felt spent and foolish for loading so much onto poor Gran. But Gran reached over and took her hand again, showing that she was herself, that she could handle anything.

"C'est beaucoup, ma pauvre petite, but you have always been strong. You and your dear friends, they are strong too, *tu sais?* You will manage this all for the best." She smiled. "Come now, the best thing is to go inside and let's get ready for a nice Christmas. Do you know that old song by Bing Crosby, 'I'll Be Home for Christmas'? Well for me, *chérie*, it's not 'only in my dreams.'"

J.J. laughed, then reached across Gran to open the door. "There's something else you need to know, *grand-maman*, I rather doubt Mother and Dad will be coming. They seem to be very angry about, well I'm not sure, but it has something to do with the business about the baby."

"Oh, là-là," Gran answered. "But yes, they are coming. We have talked many times in the last few days. Of course they have been unhappy because they think that the father of Gracie will now become the grandfather of this little Jazz, but you just must tell them from your own heart that, of course, a lucky child can have many grandparents, *n'est-ce pas?* You just need to give a little call, that is all. *Tu vois?* Now let us go in and see what we must do for Christmas."

⌒

J.J. FELT THE post-Christmas chill and a slight wind as she pulled closed the heavy oak door of the house. On the covered porch, Gran's huge pots of succulents were thriving after all the rain. Ivan sat poised on the steps, leather jacket zipped and helmet in hand. The Harley, also washed by the rains, glistened on the driveway in the December sun. J.J. walked down to meet him and gave him a long, silent embrace.

"Thanks, *mon ami*, for everything."

"*Au contraire*, it's I who should thank you. I can't remember a Christmas like that, ever. Your mother and dad doing all those wonders in the kitchen, Gran holding court like a queen. My God, J.J., but she is witty when she's in form, isn't she? That imaginary dinner between Nixon with his cottage cheese and catsup and de Gaulle complaining that the Camembert was not ripe and the *pigeons farcis* were overcooked and… so, what can I say, kiddo? It's been real."

"You left a bit out about this holiday, *mon vieux*. The household is becoming a live one with Cat and Jazz in it now — thanks to you getting them here in good shape."

"About that," Ivan wrinkled his brow. "It's huge that they're here and I know they'll be safe until you can get things worked out with Gracie and Fleur. How, exactly, I don't know, but with the combined brain power in this neighborhood, I know you'll make it happen."

"I hope you're right. At this point I don't have a clue."

"But look, J.J., I think the next time we meet, it'll be up north. I threw the I Ching this morning and it verified what I've been feeling ever since I left. Something big is coming down and soon."

J.J. let the I Ching remark pass to focus on the larger message. "So how will we be in touch, then? Same old system?"

"It works, doesn't it? After all this family tradition thing, I decided to stop by the Berkeley Lab on the way back, say hello to my old man. It's been a while. But very soon I'll be back with the Hupa. My people. So much work to do on the reservation."

"So, just call Swami Bloomberg if I need to get in touch?"

"Right on. My roots up there are all underground. They spread far. Take care, kiddo. And trust me, we're going to meet up again soon."

J.J. watched as the Harley slid down the driveway, then gunned up the street, shattering the illusion that any quiet old neighborhood could hide in the past.

She turned around to see Cat, who had come to the door to wave good-bye, too. "My knight in shining armor," she sighed. "Such a nice fella. Has he got a girl somewhere?"

J.J. closed the door behind them and looked at Cat's round eyes, surprisingly innocent looking considering all they had seen. "No," she said, pausing while considering what to say about the time she understood that she had not been the only one in love with Guy. "I'm pretty sure his interests, romantically speaking, don't run to girls."

Cat thought for a moment. "Still, a right nice fellow in my book."

They stepped into the living room where Jazz was sitting in the middle of the Oriental carpet surrounded by a pile of toys. He held a little toy truck that went from his mouth to the floor then back. He shrieked happily.

"Come sit down with me, Cat," J.J. gestured to the horsehair sofa. A Christmas tree blinked its lights in the window, while holiday debris—boxes, folded wrapping paper, a huge basket with fruit, cheese, and chocolates sent by Zak, a tin of homemade molasses candy from Cat's grandma—filled table tops and corners. "Now that the holidays and all the rest of it are over, we really need to brainstorm. I'm truly happy— and still surprised—by the idea of Jazz living with Gracie and Fleur, and I think everybody else is too, including you."

"Right you are, Miss J.J."

"But I don't know how to make this work, actually. I mean legally and all. Since you've been in the baby business, so to speak, what do you think?"

"Funny you should ask that, Miss J.J., because the fact is that my work, being not strictly in the open, always remained in what you might call the shadow of the law. On the right side of God's law, to be sure, if you reckon that trying to do best by the children you help onto this planet is what really matters in God's eyes, but as for the other, I don't rightly know. But there is something I've been needing to talk to you about."

J.J.'s eyes widened attentively.

"Yes. Well on the day of the funeral, as you know, your ma and pa brought me to the church and we were hanging toward the back. But during all those testimonials, Jazz started to get fretful and I could see that he was winding up for a big old storm, so I took him outside, and from around the corner comes this priest. He sees us, and before you know it, he swoops Jazz up in the air in his big arms and Jazz, he turns from crying to laughing in a little bitty minute. Then we get to talking even while he's swooping Jazz about in the air. Big, handsome fellow, in my opinion. Kind of thought it a pity he's a priest. Father Yves is his name. Said he knew Miss Melanie. Said he knew all of y'all."

J.J. stared straight at her. "Oh my God. Tom." She had finally found his name a few weeks earlier. Father Yves, as Tom was known to the Claretian brothers. The law connection was there too. He called himself after the patron saint of lawyers, good lawyers, the description said, ones who defended the poor. She'd left a message with his order, but had had no reply. "Go on," she urged Cat.

"He said he'd just come to pay his respects, but he couldn't stay until the end. I figured maybe he didn't want to mingle with those cold-hearted Harts, but he just laughed when I suggested it. Said, no, he was used to sinners of all kinds, that was not troubling to him. Said though that someone did trouble him, someone he'd not imagined seeing 'until the end of time,' was how he put it. A nun. The only one came to mind was Sister Eve, but I didn't ask."

"Oh my God," J.J. uttered again.

"Anyhow, he was real kindly and I felt easy talking to him. So I guess I kind of confessed. Told him about Jazz, about the Harts, about everything. He just nodded like it was an everyday kind of thing. Then he said, 'I'm a priest, but I'm also a lawyer and I do all kinds of work with what you might call troubles that aren't precisely in the daylight. If you need any help, call me.' And he handed back a smiley old baby and a piece of paper with his number on it."

Chapter 38

J.J. pulled her coat tight against the drizzle, then paused as she entered the sanctuary of All Saints. The hunched figure in the bleeding light of the back pew was unmistakable and unchanged. Wide shouldered, muscular, a thick neck upholding a head graced with generous wavy hair. In a moment, she slipped in beside him, and he turned to pull her to his broad chest now encased in a black priest's tunic beneath a white collar.

"Tom!" she said with genuine pleasure. "Or Father Yves, I should say."

"Oh, please, Tom for God's sake."

"Tom then. I can't remember when I last saw you, but I have to say, you look absolutely the same."

"Well, there has been a change of costume," he grinned. "And you look completely unchanged, too, although I have seen you since you've seen me. At least twice. Once at a certain wedding, then here just before Christmas. I seem to have a habit of sneaking out of church services I don't like."

"So I heard. You didn't care for this one either?"

"Not so much. But then I do understand it—why they did it. Understanding, compassion, they're part of my job description."

"Not mine, I'm afraid. Mine goes more along the lines of slash and burn, expose the guts to reach the glory."

"Well, that must be tough for you, J.J., since your sensibilities go so much the other way."

She turned her glance down, not responding to his surprising remark, and focused on the massive hands resting peacefully on his lap. "Look," she finally said, "I know you met Cat here during the service and she told you her—our—situation. I already knew that you are also a lawyer—sleuthing in a way is my line of work. I found out where you were a few months ago and sent a message. Did you ever get it? And now Cat says you might be able to help with this baby. True?"

"True indeed. Here's the thing, my work really centers on poverty and justice and there are lots of people in my flock, if you allow me such a priestly term. Folks who have problems similar to the ones Cat described, starting with being undocumented from birth. We help them all the time. I've got a network, inside and outside the church to be sure, and I've been in touch already. As for hearing from you, yes, I confess I did. I didn't respond right away because, well, for a lot of reasons. But I did intend to, please believe that. It is wonderful to see you after so long a time."

"Okay, Father, I believe you." J.J. watched Tom wince at the name. "I even believe you would have reached out right here at All Saints had it not been for a certain nun. Am I right?"

Tom gave a wide, embracing smile. "Totally."

"And now here you are, a lawyer who's willing to help us. It's amazing. What do we have to do?"

"Well, there are a couple of things we have to get straight first. One, that there really is no birth certificate. What do you know about that?"

"Cat was the midwife in an under-the-radar clinic in Mendocino County. Actually, the whole situation—Melanie's whereabouts, the Hi-Diddle House commune, the birth—it was all under the radar. The formalities of a birth certificate, doing things according to the law, weren't part of the scene. So no, there's no birth certificate."

"Just checking. And good. It may uncomplicate things. But there also is the matter of next of kin. Cat explained the 'trial by jury' thing you sweet *demoiselles* pulled off in regards to Melanie's family."

"You disapprove?"

"God no. I can't see any of them being suitable either. But it's the baby's father who worries me. Clearly this wasn't Hans's work."

"Clearly not," J.J. smiled.

"What happened to Hans is a story for another moment. For now, what do you know about the father of this child?"

"Only that they met at Woodstock, and he was like her Pied Piper. He seduced her away with his music, and then she rode away on his steed—a motorcycle. I have a lot of her letters and papers. He went by the name of John C. Calhoun, if you can believe that, and met her there as he was leaving his hometown, Chicago, and heading south to do political work. I've tried really hard to find his actual name, so I could track him down, or his family, but have gotten nowhere. And Gracie, who was the last among us to see Melanie, had the impression from what she said that J.C. was dead."

"Gracie," Tom lit up as he said the name. "I saw the piece you wrote that just came out about her. Amazing story."

"That's not the half of it," J.J. answered. "But I guess you know some of that too."

"Right. And she and her lady friend now want to adopt this child."

"Yes. Do you think it's possible?"

Tom pursed his lips. "In a word, yes. Obviously, it's complicated. But if you're willing to, ah, brush aside certain technicalities to achieve the best outcome, yes. The best path is to have the young lady Cat declare herself the mother—having no birth certificate helps—claim she is indigent and unable to care for the child, and at the same time state that she has found a relative who will adopt. This bypasses a lot of the legal mess she'd be in otherwise. And she has to establish residency in L.A. County for upwards of a year. Much easier if the adoption stays within the same county."

"Gracie a relative? Of Cat's?"

"Works for me. Distant cousin? In these cases, below the radar as you put it, a biracial child and a well-qualified, willing mother, they're not going to ask too many questions. Also in her favor… But look, it's so chilly in here. Let's go to the coffee shop across the street and let me buy you a coffee and lunch."

J.J. LOST TRACK of time and was startled to realize it was close to three when she checked her watch. "Wow," she said, pushing away a coffee cup that had gone cold. "I was supposed to show up at the paper around two. Yet even after all this talk, it feels as if we've barely caught up on each other's lives."

"That's because we are among the blessed and have rich ones," Tom replied. "But I need to run too."

"So I'll share what you've told me with Gracie and Cat, and we'll get as much of the paperwork going as we can."

"Perfect," Tom said. "I'll be in touch soon to see how things are coming along. Only one piece of this still bothers me a bit, and that is, much as we don't know what happened to Melanie, we also don't know about the fate of J.C. I'd hate for this poor man to actually be alive, well, able and willing to take his own son, but not even know of his existence."

J.J. felt as though she'd been slapped by a rush of cold air. *The things you do not know about your own life, poor Tom*, she thought. "Well, I do have a picture, if you think that might help in any way."

Tom stood to help her put on her coat. "That would be great. This network I'm part of reaches far, in fact all the way into the South."

"I know we'll be in touch again soon, and I can't thank you enough for your help. But, Tom, of all the things we've caught up on, a big one has been left unspoken. Eve. Perhaps you know she's been working in a medical mission in Africa. But she's back now for a long stay in order to get some more advanced training. Call her. You owe it to both of you."

She thrust a piece of paper with a number on it into his hand before pushing the door open into the wind.

Chapter 39

J.J. rested her head against the steering wheel. The main street of Mendocino loomed eerie and abandoned as black storm clouds shifted east over the coastal mountains and fog moved in with strangling silence. As though the ghosts of the dead dropped in quietly to cut off the living. She looked from the rock cliffs and the drop-off to the magnificent cove below, but fog had already erased the view. Across the street, Bread & Beads Café was shuttered. "CLOSED FOR SEASONAL REPAIRS" said a sign, hastily scrawled with a marker, which hung on the door.

In her head, she replayed Ivan's voice crackling more than usual over the phone line. "It took longer than expected, but it's coming down, kiddo. Get yourself up there ASAP. Sorry I can't make it." To Ivan's list of what, exactly, was coming down—Federal crackdown and raids on drug dealing, stepped up manhunt for Moon and his co-conspirator

Sheriff O'Reilly, who had just gone missing, and a reopened investigation into the fire at Hi-Diddle. J.J. added for herself the obvious: Examination of the remains found in the fire. Possible allegations of arson, of attempted murder, if Cat's charges stuck. Or actual murder if...

A piercing siren shattered the unnatural silence, and an official car, its red lights flashing, slammed to a halt in front of the café. Two uniformed men jumped out and pounded on the door. "Federal Bureau of Investigation," one yelled, "Open up." He drew a gun. The door opened a crack, and the men barged their way in. Within minutes, they came out again, and shoved a scraggly Pigeon, handcuffed, his head hidden under a puffy knit cap, into the car.

J.J. watched, heart pounding, as the car, siren off but lights still blinking, roared back up the street. Then a movement caught her eye and she saw the large shadow of a figure pass behind the still open door. "Mama Cass," J.J. yelled, and bounded across the street to insert herself before the door was definitively shut.

"Mama Cass, let me in!" she yelled again, sticking her boot in the door, while a heavy weight shoved against the other side.

"Can't you read, woman, we're closed!" the familiar voice called out.

"Not quite, you aren't. I'm coming in," J.J. shouted back.

A pair of eyes scanned her through the crack. "You! What the fuck do you want?"

"To talk." J.J. increased her toehold on the opening, and Mama Cass relaxed her resistance.

"Who the hell are you, anyway?" she asked as J.J. pushed her way into the darkened café.

"Like I told you the first time we met," J.J. stood facing her directly, "I'm a friend of the woman who went missing up at Hi-Diddle, whose ashes were found there, according to what you told me. That's Melanie Hart to me, Fiddle to folks around here. Also," J.J. paused, "I'm a reporter."

"Oh, shit," Mama Cass shook her long, stringy hair. "They do say when it rains, it pours, don't they? So why the hell do you think I'm going to talk to you now? You can see for yourself, woman, I got troubles enough."

"You're going to talk to me now because it's the best way for you to get your story out, whatever it is. Because I can, as you well know, keep my mouth shut for a long period of time—like you told me to when I first came up here. Because I like to get it right. Even though I've been working on this story ever since I first came around, you haven't seen a word in the press about this, have you? Think about it. And also, because I'm fair. You know and I know this thing is about to blow apart big time, and the press is going to go nuts. So far nobody else knows, and I've controlled it completely. If I can keep it that way, the story that comes out will do the best justice that can be done to everybody involved. Including you. Now, is there somewhere we can talk?"

Mama Cass jerked her head to indicate the space behind the strung beads. "It's warmer in there," she said. And J.J. followed her impressively swaying derrière once again.

Seated at the familiar table with the oilcloth covering, J.J. gratefully took a mug of hot tea from Mama, who plopped onto a chair across from her.

"So what is it you want to know?" she finally asked.

"Let's start with Pigeon and work back from there," J.J. answered. "What was that all about?"

"Hmph. Pigeon, my ass! He should have been called Squirrel, or Weasel maybe. That would have been more like it. That two-faced little piece of shit. After all I done for him, right here in my own establishment, selling me out like that." Mama's words came out as fiery as ever, but her face looked drawn, melancholy.

"Like what?" J.J. began scribbling fast in her notebook. "Selling you out to whom? For what?"

"Why, he was a regular mouthpiece, he was, to that no-good O'Reilly and all his boys."

"Glad you brought him up. So, what's the story with O'Reilly? Where is he?"

"Damned if I know, or care. But it's been two, three days now maybe and he just never showed up for work. What folks are really buzzing about is a big local charter fishing boat that went down off the Lost Coast. Speculation is, he was on that boat." She shook her head and pressed her lips together. "They got no idea what shit he was up to, and where he might be—and now Pigeon trying to drag me into the mess by telling the feds every little thing that was coming down around here."

"Actually, what was coming down around here, Mama?"

Mama drew a shawl with fringes tight across her expansive chest and gave a kind of shudder. "Well, my business partners and I, we had a little franchise here to, you know, move local products to a wider market."

"The local products being weed and other such pharmaceuticals, and the market being black?" J.J. left her pen poised in the air.

"Well, you could put it that way, yes."

"And your business partners?"

"Well primarily that worthless turd, Moon, on the supply side, and a small network of, shall we say other enlightened café and tavern owners up and down the coast, on the demand side."

"Right. So what's happened to Moon, anyway?"

Mama's eyes rekindled, as if someone had just raked the coals in a dying fire. "I swear to God, I don't know. Since the day he vanished, I haven't heard a word. I can tell you this, though. I was partners with him only about the business already mentioned. But seems that worthless turd was into way, way more than that. Extortion, theft, arson, kidnapping, murder, thunder and lightning, the rumors that swirl around about him! And I will also tell you this, woman," she turned her burning glance full bore on J.J., "ain't no way I'm going to share the rap with him for all that shit. No way."

"I hear you," J.J. said, writing furiously.

"In fact," Mama shifted forward in her chair toward J.J., "if I could get my hands on him, I might have a murder rap for myself."

J.J. wrote without looking up, then asked. "So what was Pigeon's piece in all this? He was ratting you out to Sheriff O'Reilly, but clearly the sheriff had no interest in putting anybody away."

"Hell no. What O'Reilly wanted was his own cut of whatever was coming down. And of course, the two-faced weasel got his cut, too, from O'Reilly."

"So why did you wait until now to call attention to the two-faced weasel's crimes and misdemeanors?"

Mama Cass pulled herself upright in a gesture of indignation. "You may have noticed, Missy Reporter Woman, that the *federales*, FBI, DEA, the big boys have now moved in. Hello! The ante has been upped. It was time for Mama Cass to figure out a new strategy here, if I wish to pass the rest of my born days peacefully in my own little establishment, not rotting away in some hell-hole provided for by the federal government. You know what the good book says, "There is a time to rebel, and a time to stop rebelling. A time to cooperate."

J.J. put down her pen and looked straight at Mama Cass. "So that's what the good book says, meaning... Let me see if I've got this right. You're cooperating with the feds—names, places, dates, contacts, etc.—in exchange for...immunity? So far so good? And just to show your genuine intentions, you offered up Pigeon—Weasel—first.

Kind of like an appetizer. Their own informer, but one with a sideline they were uniformed about—that is, he was getting kickbacks from the sheriff's own illegal deal. Have I got that right?"

"Why, Missy Reporter Woman, you do have a way with words, don't you?" For the first time, Mama cracked a wide smile, showing a considerable gap between her two front teeth.

J.J. grinned back. "Well, Mama, it seems you, too, believe in justice. Of a sort."

"Hell yes. As you can see, I'm a solid citizen, you could say, from way back." She closed over the gap in her front teeth, smirking, pleased at her own joke. "What I don't believe in, though, is spreading lies like varmints through the press. Nor, come to think of it, do I like even spreading the truth through the press, if that truth involves my name. See, I'm rather shy when it comes to matters of publicity."

J.J. could only smile to herself. If Mama Cass was about to trade secrets for federal immunity, she could hardly be named anyway. "I take your point. And since you're good at making deals, let's make one between us. As long as I have a good and accurate source of information, I don't believe your name has to ever come up. Do you?"

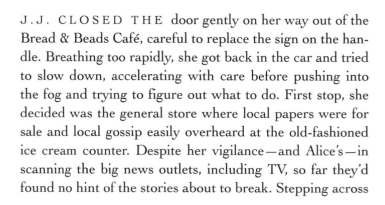

J.J. CLOSED THE door gently on her way out of the Bread & Beads Café, careful to replace the sign on the handle. Breathing too rapidly, she got back in the car and tried to slow down, accelerating with care before pushing into the fog and trying to figure out what to do. First stop, she decided was the general store where local papers were for sale and local gossip easily overheard at the old-fashioned ice cream counter. Despite her vigilance—and Alice's—in scanning the big news outlets, including TV, so far they'd found no hint of the stories about to break. Stepping across the old boardwalk and through the high wooden doors, J.J. felt, as she often did in this town, that she had entered a different century. The smells of freshly ground coffee, just-baked bread, and the sassafras used in ice cream sodas hit her all at once. She paused by the newspaper rack to scoop up all the local rags. Just like Mama said, they all screamed with the headlines of the charter boat that crashed off rugged cliffs in a high sea. Then J.J. looked up at the bulletin board. Staring straight at her was a wild-haired and sinister-looking Moon, with the words "WANTED BY THE FBI" written in large print across the poster.

She took her papers to the counter, ordered a coffee, and tried to lean in unobtrusively on a conversation between a bearded guy in bib overalls and a young woman in jeans, boots, and a woodsman's plaid jacket. The weather, the infernal fog, and "you know that Melvin O'Reilly's body is one they've found in that boat, don't you?" Others who strolled past repeated the same news. *What is it about shipwrecks and convenient endings for inconvenient stories?* she asked herself, then wandered the aisles to pick up a few snacks and other overheard conversations before going to the register.

A woman with stringy gray hair, a cigarette propped in the corner of her mouth, took her time ringing up the purchases. "So, anything new around here I should know about?" J.J. asked casually.

"You from out of town?" the woman shot back without looking up.

"Yeah. I come here from time to time, though, you know, to take a break from the city."

"Uh huh. Well you come at a bad time, what with the rain and all the fog. Heard about the fishing boat wreck I suppose. Come back in May. Much better weather. New you say? The only other new thing for sure is that prices keep going up. You do come back then, you best bring your groceries with you."

"What about that guy?" J.J. nodded to the picture of Moon. "Is he a local?"

"Moon? Yeah, he used to come in regular. Disappeared months ago. Weird dude. Good riddance, I say. Now if we could just get rid of the FBI and the goddamned DEA too, while we're at it. Nothing worse than the feds poking around." She handed J.J. her bag, dropping cigarette ash on the counter.

J.J. took the bag and stepped out to wander by foot through several blocks. Everywhere she turned, another FBI poster, limp in the fog, turned up too, Moon's eyes seeming to follow her every step.

Shaky and cold, and needing a place of refuge, she climbed into her car, to lean back in the seat. *God I wish I had a bit of famous coastal weed right now*, she thought. *Where's Ivan when I need him?* This was one town in the state where nobody would notice. But now she'd come out as a reporter, she could hardly go shopping.

Uncertain where to go next, J.J. pulled out her box of cassette tapes to listen to some music while she gathered her thoughts. One by one she thumbed through the box, smiling at an album by the Mamas and the Papas, considering the Stones, Aerosmith, Joan Baez, Jefferson Airplane, Joni Mitchell, and then paused at the old '69 album *I Got Dem Ol' Kozmic Blues Again, Mama*. Janis Joplin. Suddenly J.J. was back at All Saints, Natalie delivering her own stunning eulogy to Melanie. Slipping in the tape, she shut her eyes.

Pushing so hard the dream/I keep tryin' to make it right. The refrain kept repeating in her head, until Jocelyn's voice intruded. "Are the Harts so different from us? We're all hurting from this loss, trying to preserve Melanie as best we can in our own ways."

No, that's not right!, she wanted to shout back. *Maybe they're trying to preserve her the way they wanted her to be by*

conveniently changing her story's ending, but not me. I'm only try-
ing to find the truth.

With a renewed sense of purpose, she switched on the engine and headed south of town to the turnoff and the road where the charred bones of Hi-Diddle resided in the forest. Halfway up the distance to the property, the way forward was impassible from the recent rains. She pulled the car over and climbed out to walk. Ferns along the edges of the road marked how it turned; the fog and dim winter sun, quickly fading, swallowed other visual signposts. J.J. was startled to find herself suddenly stopped by yellow police tape. "DANGER. CRIME SCENE. DO NOT ENTER."

She stood, silent, staring at the blackened boards of the house, at the life that had already started to sprout in its fertile remains. Vines wrapping around its planks; seedlings sprouting in the needles where the living room had once been; squirrels and birds industriously scampering and nesting along the falling eaves. When she could see no more, she turned to find her way back to the car, feeling the path along the edge of the ferns by instinct, feeling calmed by the renewal of life pushing up from the charred remains. Feeling that she had been in Melanie's presence.

J.J. DROVE AWAY from the ruins of the Hi-Diddle House just as she had the first time so many months ago. Taking the same rough track back to the paved road, she followed her headlights in the darkness. With the same sense of relief, she pulled into the overlook she had found then, and turned off the engine to collect her breath. The sea pounded below, she knew, but she could only visualize it in memory as night enveloped her. Then, closing her eyes to see better, she rested her head on the steering wheel.

MELANIE STEPPED OUT from a darkened room into the light of the living room. The Hi-Diddle sign hung crookedly by the bookshelf, and she stepped over Jocelyn, sprawled on the rug near the fire. Her hair fell in yellow waves down her back onto a shimmery sequined vest, identical to Janis Joplin's on the record cover flung on the floor. The record went spinning round and round, but made no sound. Like Hans, standing in a half-lit corner, silently sawing his violin.

At a wooden plank table by a flickering candle next to Fleur, Eve fingered the gold cross on her neck as it caught the light. They were working at copying words on small cards, chatting and laughing. But the words could not be heard. Melanie strolled over to them and picked up the book that lay open between them. "West African Cookery."

Her eyes shimmied back and forth, the way they always had done. "Le cœur a ses raisons que la raison ne connaît point," *she said.*

Soon she was standing next to Hans, who spoke to her with animation while never letting up on his violin. She crossed the room again and went to the bookshelf. A large picture hanging above the mantle came into focus. J.C. Calhoun, a headband on his wild hair, marching in the streets of Mississippi.

"What do you think, Cat?" Melanie called out. But Cat did not appear.

Then Melanie crossed the room to stand in front of a rocking chair. The figure in the chair, who had been rocking slowly, began to rock faster. Coming into the light, Gracie's face broke into a deep, satisfied smile. She held something in a blanket in her arms as she rocked.

Melanie turned around to face Hans. "You were right, Hans. We were not the best choice for Billy. It's better he be with the ones who can truly care for him."

Frozen in place and mute, Hans kept playing the violin, even though it had disappeared.

Chapter 40

Gracie rocked on the covered front porch swing surrounded by Gran's huge succulent-filled planters.
Jazz climbed up then hopped off the swing to return
to the rattan rug and push his cars and trucks. "Twuck,
twuck," he showed her with delight. Then he took her hand,
"Gay Cee," he commanded and led her again up and down
the cement steps.

*Wow, she thought, this is hard. Harder than I imagined, but
good. Better than I imagined, too. So tireless he is, so endless his
needs, so boundless his curiosity.* It had gone well enough, this
first run taking care of him by herself. Before Fleur had
always been there, Cat nearby. But it was time, Fleur said,
and she agreed, and Cat had errands. So here she was, alone
with her boy. The very words made her smile.

Even if the smile faded thinking of Papa's recent visit
to the cottage. "If your Mama only live long enough," his
face had clouded over, "maybe then a different life, a *normale*

life for you. But..." he had opened his strong wine-stained hands to the heavens, a gesture of despair. It was then, for the first time, that Gracie understood his true feelings about her relationship with Fleur. It wasn't outrage or condemnation so much as profound puzzlement. It was not *normale* for a good Italian girl, daughter of a winemaker and his Madonna-worshipping wife to live with her head in the stars and share her home (he could not bring himself to think what else) with a woman. Certainly not *normale* to adopt a child that didn't belong to either of them. A half-black child.

"No. Is nice kid, okay. But is not your kid. Is not my kid. Grandpapa? Is better in *famiglia* no?"

Gracie had nearly collapsed with those words. After Papa had closed the gate, she sat for what seemed like a year by the window overlooking the little Eden of a garden she shared with Fleur. *What could I have been thinking?* Wanting a family—even if not a big, Italian one—and to give Papa a grandson, was at the heart of it. *I have to question if adopting Jazz is the right thing. I have to question everything.* Then Fleur had come to embrace her, to tell her that "adopting this little boy is the right thing in itself, and it's right for the two of us."

Gracie had heard the words, had wanted to believe them. But despite her efforts, becoming *normale* seemed a hopeless quest.

Then, wanting to look to friends for support and advice, she was bewildered as to where to turn. If anything, life at Cal Tech was a laboratory for the abnormal. But was it worse than the lives of her old friends? Eve, the oft-loved, once-married, briefly-a-mother turned nun who worked in an African mission? Jocelyn, the movie star who attached and unattached to men, according to J.J.'s articles, with astonishing speed? J.J. herself? Thinking of her as a new sort of matriarch, presiding over this household with her charming but sometimes not-quite-there Gran; Cat the

Mountain Girl and her little charge Jazz; her eccentric and frequently feuding parents; and now with Gracie herself and Fleur often in residence, Gracie had to laugh. Interesting, yes. Conventional, *normale*, hardly.

She sat on the cement steps to watch Jazz, who was now amusing himself by running and falling down on the grass. Again she studied his face to find Melanie, his real mother, in him, but didn't see her. It was Melanie, Gracie realized, that she longed to talk to most. Not just because, improbably, they now shared a son, but because of all the *demoiselles*, Melanie seemed to have had the greatest range of human experience, even if much of it was still mysterious. Melanie for sure would have had something to say about Papa and the heartache of his rejection. Nobody knew more about rejection from family than Melanie. Nobody knew more about a lot of things...

"Gay Cee," Jazz ran toward her holding the petals from a newly blooming camellia.

"Thank you, Jazz," she said, taking the petals and impulsively hugging him. "Good boy." Watching him as he was at that moment, trying to imagine his future, she was terrified. Besides her crazy brothers and cousins, what did she know about boys? True, most of her colleagues were just boys, if social skills and maturity were criteria for manhood, and she herself had been called "one of the boys" a thousand times. But how would she guide him to be a different kind of boy? A man?

Staring at his little face intently watching a bug, she felt that surprising surge of love once again and a sense of joy at his curiosity. It took three honks of the horn to snap her out of her reverie.

"Gracie," J.J. was calling out of the car window. "What a great surprise."

Gracie stood up and waved at her. "Didn't know when you were coming back."

In a moment, the two were sitting on the cement steps together, watching Jazz play. J.J. closed her eyes and inhaled deeply. "Such a blessing to have a bit of sun again, to see the scarlet camellias in bloom. It's such a long drive. Was such an intense trip." Then she knew enough to drop it. There was plenty of time ahead to share all the news breaking to the north. "How are things here?"

"Fine, great," Gracie said, looking down at her hands. "Gran's good. She was out back enjoying the garden for a while. Now I think she may be in the living room, dozing on that scratchy old sofa probably."

"So you're flying solo today. How's that going?"

"Great," Gracie answered brightly. "Well, maybe great with a few caveats. Okay, let's scratch great. Would you believe terrified?"

"Actually, I think if you stuck with 'great,' I'd suggest a psychiatrist. 'Terrified' is better. More realistic. Sane."

Gracie looked up at J.J. "You're probably right. I've spent much of my life being terrified, worried I'd fail, but I don't know, somehow things have turned out."

J.J. nodded. "Sure you want to do this?"

"Oddly, yes. I think I knew at some deep level when Melanie came to visit, pregnant, that there was a longing in the middle of me that I didn't imagine I'd ever fulfill. And then, Fleur feeling the same way just reinforced it. Of course, I didn't foresee *this* happening…" Gracie gestured to Jazz.

"Nobody could have foreseen this, any of it. But, as I hope you know, you and Fleur are not alone in this. A lot of people are standing with you."

"I do know, and I'm grateful. And it's coming from some unexpected places," she paused, deciding not to mention the expectations that were falling short—Papa. "Speaking of support, I asked Tom to come over in a little bit. Hope that's okay, but I couldn't ask you first. He's going over some of the adoption forms with me and Cat."

"No problem," J.J. started to reply, but was cut short by Jazz who had taken a tumble and began crying.

Gracie rushed to swoop him up. "Oh, lord," she shouted over his wailing. "I think he needs a diaper change."

~~⟶

GRAN SAT BEMUSED, watching, under the avocado tree while J.J. took a turn throwing a big rubber ball to Jazz. "You look very *naturelle, ma petite*, perhaps you have a hidden gift?"

"Me? No, *chère grand-maman*, none. It's all improvising. Like Gracie, I'm somewhat terrified," she shouted back. Then she sat next to Gran under the tree and let Jazz run after the ball on his short legs, leap on it, and fall onto the grass with shrieks of laughter.

Gran took a sip of her tea, looking regal with the light behind her. "Terrified? *Pas possible.*" And she reached for J.J.'s hand. "Children are such a delight, *ma petite*. I do not give up hope that you will discover this one day at last."

"I thought those three needed to talk, don't you?" she said, steering the conversation to safer ground. "I mean Father Yves, our old friend Tom from so long ago, is a priest of course, but he's also a lawyer and he's come to help Cat and Gracie with all the legal work for the adoption. You understand that Cat needs to go home to her people and that Gracie is going to adopt the baby, don't you?"

Gran seemed far away again, so J.J. was uncertain what she knew and what she didn't.

"Yes, yes, *chérie*, you have explained it all. Many times." Gran suddenly looked at her granddaughter with piercing clarity. "So, tell me, *petit chou*, this Father Yves, was he at one time friendly with Gracie?"

"Well, yes, they were, as you say, friendly. Close friends, but…"

"So I thought," Gran smiled again. "He greeted her with, how do you say, *beaucoup d'enthousiasme.*"

"Oh, you saw that did you?" J.J. said, reviewing the *enthousiasme* in her own mind. Tom swooping Gracie into the air, planting a big kiss on her cheek. "Oh, doll, you are just the same. What a tonic to see you." Then rushing to the boy to do the same, making him laugh.

"A pity he is a priest, *non?*" Gran said, her eyes now alive with mischief.

"Oh Gran, you don't know the half of it," J.J. began, and was in a moment spilling out the long-ago story of a love triangle in Gran's native Provence. "But of course, this had no fairy-tale ending," she said, deciding to stop before revealing some of the more painful details: Eve's pregnancy, her betrayal of Tom at Jay Greene's urging, Gracie's heartbreak.

"But of course," Gran picked up where J.J. left off, "this ended not well for all of them. These stories never do. But then, with time, they turn positive again. That is the part, *chérie*, you can never see when you are young."

In a moment, Cat and Gracie, Tom between them, came to greet Gran under the tree. Jazz raced toward them, and once again Tom swooped the boy up in his arms, stretching his black clerical shirt against a muscular back.

"I'm going up to do the bath now, with Cat's supervision," Gracie said. "Wish me luck."

"You'll do great, doll. Just like you always do." Tom winked and handed her Jazz.

"I'll do my best. And Tom, do it, okay? Just call her."

J.J. watched the three retreat for the bathtub before turning back to Tom, and giving him a quizzical look.

"She was telling me what you told me—to call Eve. I could give you a million reasons why I shouldn't, some of them fairly obvious. But the main one is pretty simple: fear. Remember that line by T.S. Eliot about 'disturbing the dust on a bowl of rose-leaves.'"

"Yes, I know it well. 'Burnt Norton,' one of my favorites. But then I'm sure you know this line, too. Book of John, 'There is no fear in love, but perfect love casteth out fear.'"

They looked at each other in surprise, each thinking what the other thought: how ironic that he should be quoting poetry, while she quoted the Bible.

"Life is amazing, isn't it, J.J.?"

Then Tom turned to Gran, saying, "I hope you don't mind me calling you Gran? May I sit with you a moment?"

Chapter 41

Monday, March 2. J.J. noted the date on her desk calendar as she pushed old memos, scraps of paper, notes left unanswered into the trash. Two weeks to go before Jocelyn's big night: the premier of *Pacific Blue* at Grauman's Chinese Theatre. She sat for a moment, head in hands. *I ought to be used to it by now, how sometimes switching gears so often, so fast, gives me a headache.* She would be there to cover the story—a big one to be sure—even more than to be there simply as a friend. *There's so much to think about, I'm feeling nauseous, panicky. Good God, I don't even know what to wear.*

Desperate, she dialed Annie's Ark, feeling impatient to get beyond the chirpy greeting. "Annie—Mom," she said swallowing hard. "Look, I've got a huge Hollywood question, and a favor to ask of you…" Before she could inquire what priceless rag Annie might come up with, her mother exclaimed, "Ah, my darling daughter, the vintage film star look, perfect!"

"Shall we, my dear?" Alice broke in as J.J. rang off with Annie. "Let us look over the potential story list and see where we stand. Or shall we say, open the envelope and see that the winner is…"

"God, Alice, please. I have a bad enough headache already."

In a moment, they were in Alice's office where she sat on her desk swinging one down-at-the-heel black pump. "So, what do we know?"

"We know plenty," J.J. said, relieved to be back on the surer footing of solid facts and evidence—the realm of journalism—than in the doubt-filled mists threatening to overtake her.

"Here's how I see it. Mama Cass is off the table as a subject, at least as long as she holds up her end of the bargain and continues to be my best inside source. But I think we've got five stories. One: O'Reilly, when they bring him in— miraculously resurrected from the latest shipwreck cover story—and his beautiful tale of law enforcement corruption and complicity. Two: Moon, when they catch him, and his drug empire, with his sideline good works in arson, intimidation, intent to murder, and perhaps murder. Three: The Harts and the morality tale of bribery and manipulation— the local angle." She smiled at Alice.

Alice looked back, eyebrows twitching. "You really want to go there? Family friends, in a manner of speaking?"

"Is it, or is it not, part of the story? Helluva story, as you said, don't you think?"

"It is indeed. May I take it that our little heart-to-heart about remembering your duties as a reporter actually sank in?"

"I'm ignoring that. Story four: The Hi-Diddle, what did and did not go on in the self-proclaimed love nest of peace. Five: The body. What the bones reveal when they reinvestigate and have the coroner's report. What happened to Melanie, at last."

Alice sat, motionless for a minute. "It's stunning, really, J.J. Huge. So many ways we could run with this. Five in a row I'm thinking, if they're all wrapped at the same time. Of course, we'll have to get photogs and graphics all over this, consult with Himself. But tell me, how close are you to writing these, what kind of backup do you need?"

"I've done a lot already. Once they net the big fish, it will all come down very quickly. I think another reporter to help with some of the mop-up, fact check, be a gofer."

"Laura?" Alice asked.

"Fine."

"Soon, we think?"

"Ivan has been saying soon for some weeks, and now that Mama Cass is in the bag, she's got a finger on every pulse. All the rumblings verify what Cat was saying when she was terrorized by Moon and took flight. The rumblings are—and when Mama rumbles, you hear it—that although Moon and his erstwhile accomplice, the good sheriff, fled North, possibly heading toward Canada, the interstate alerts may have closed those routes and forced them back closer to home territory. There are plenty of places for the likes of Moon to hide out in those back mountains, but the more he doubles back, the tighter the snare closes. It could be any day now."

"So, time to line up a photographer, graphics, alert Laura?" Alice's foot began swinging faster.

"Yeah. It's time."

"Okey-dokey. Can do. But when I have my little chat with them, they have to understand their role in this scoop of the decade depends on being able to keep the lid on. It's amazing nobody else has a clue about this yet, and we need to keep it that way. The one I really worry about is Himself. When he gets a whiff of how big the *Star* is about to become, I'm afraid he may wet himself."

J.J. laughed at the thought. "God, Alice, you are like the proverbial good wine, better with every passing day."

"Well, like that wine, once you let it out, you can't put it back in the bottle. But, you, my dear, can rest assured that what you've done in a short year will bring enough kudos to this pissant little paper that the Bloviator-in-Chief will go to his grave positive that he was indeed a great newspaperman. He'll be a blowhard to the end, but a happy one."

J.J. laughed until her eyes teared. "You know I was only an instrument in your hands." She paused to wipe her eyes. "Seriously, Alice, it's all because of you. Thanks… I mean that."

"Okay, my turn to be serious. I seriously hope that coming to the end of all this will mean you can put it to rest and finally get some peace."

"What are you saying?"

"That you discover the truth about what happened to Melanie and can finally write the last story—her story—and get on with…whatever it is."

Chapter 42

J.J. lay in the sleeping porch, wide awake. Past its medley of noises—country tunes, harmonica music, blaring radio, Gran's TV news, and the rich harmonic array of a small child, from gleeful shouts to whimpers to sobbing—the household was, at last, breathing as one in sleep. Except for J.J. It was a mild enough spring night to open some of the awnings and let in a fresh, perfumed breeze and an angle of pure light sliced by the avocado branches outside as they caught the full moon. All had gone well with Alice, the outline of the stories, the plan to move now. J.J. liked the comfort of being back on sure ground, of finally being ready to hit the "go" button at any moment.

So, she told herself: *I should be able to sleep.* Unable to be persuaded, she switched on the light and reached for the nearest thing at hand. *Sybil.* The gift from Annie about the woman with sixteen personalities that she'd left untouched since dropping it as she'd fallen asleep. She picked it up in desperation, hoping it would put her to sleep again. Instead, she read until dawn, skeptical, intrigued, disturbed.

THE PHONE RANG before she got through her first cup of coffee. "J.J.? I hope I didn't wake you. I just finished with morning prayers and am dashing here and there, but wanted to get a hold of you right away."

J.J. smiled, relaxed to hear Tom's deep, reassuring voice. *He must be a marvelous priest,* she thought, even if, as Gran said, it was "a pity."

"No, no, I'm up. Great to hear your voice."

"Listen, I'm calling because, as I told you I would, I sent out feelers to some of my contacts in the civil rights move-ment — God's underground — in the South about this fellow J.C. Calhoun. Something came back and I wanted to show you."

"Holy shit," she blurted. "Sorry for the language. It's the company I've been keeping of late."

Tom gave a deep laugh. "Listen, I'll put up some of my characters, see yours, and double you any day. I was won-dering, I have some business in at the San Gabriel Mission later in the afternoon and thought I might swing by. If you'll be there."

Seeing Tom later in the day was the best plan she could think of. And a great excuse not to go in to the paper at all, since she had nothing to do there but wait. And the appeal-ing prospect of avoiding Bud Purvis, whose hyped-up pres-ence these days gave her hives.

"I'll be here. After three, then?" she heard herself say-ing, already sketching another audacious story in her mind. This one strictly off the record.

EVE SAT ON the covered porch behind Gran's shingled house, the breeze catching her hair, which was now unrestrained by any kind of clasp and flew in red waves. J.J. picked up her iced tea glass and saluted her friend, taking in her simple cotton skirt, white blouse, and navy sweater, the cross made from African cloth, the sandals on her slender feet. "Well, I've got to say it, you sure don't look like any nun I can think of. You look—what's that word Gran used? Saucy! That's it. You look saucy."

Eve was staring out at the back garden and the lawn where Fleur, who was with Jazz today, rolled a big rubber ball to his commands. "You think? Well at least you didn't say sexy, *quelle horreur*. Guess I've cured myself of that. Along with all those other sins, like, let's see, anger, greed, envy, vanity, selfishness, oh, I could go on. But I wouldn't want to be obnoxious, either, would I?" She turned her full wicked smile at J.J.

"No, you sure wouldn't. You haven't changed a bit, have you?"

"Probably not. But I do try. From time to time."

J.J. had intended to get together with Eve to tell her about Tom—Father Yves. That he was in L.A.; that he'd come to the service for Melanie and left, shaken, when he saw her; that he was a remarkable man. A graduate of Loyola Law School, and a priest in the Claretian Order, which specialized in working with the poor, especially Mexicans; that he spoke Spanish and had been arrested for protesting in the antiwar movement; that he obviously loved kids, had stepped up to help Cat and Gracie with the adoption complications, and more; that he promised, just as Dad had done, to be there as a man to help father the fatherless child. J.J. also meant to tell Eve the last thing she wanted to hear—that Tom, of all people, needed to know the truth of the child she had carried and lost. On her mental list she had not included that he was still a gorgeous hunk. In their lives now, it was beside the point. Or Eve would figure it out for herself.

"So, Eve, tell me," J.J. said, suddenly uncomfortable with the conversation she had laid out in her mind, "what is this course you intend to do?"

"When I go back to my hospital, I want to have better skills, J.J. I want to be able to do more. The need is so great…" J.J. listened while she spoke about the lives of the Africans she lived among and outlined the nurse practitioner course she was starting at UCLA. Then, without J.J. steering it, the conversation changed course. "But enough of all this. What I want to know is, what happens for *you* now? Where do you go with your writing after you finish all your profiles of us?"

"God, I wish I knew. You have no idea what is about to come down. Well, no one does." Suddenly, like a dam breaking, J.J. flooded the air with the tale of Moon and the sheriff, of the charges against them, and their imminent arrests; then moved on to an update of Mama Cass and her tender relations with, as Mama called them, the *federales*. The stories poured out, and J.J., outlining the five pieces that would roll in like a storm smashing the coast from the Pacific, realized this was what she had really wanted to talk to Eve about. Spilling her guts to her old friend, she asked for guidance on what to do. Spiritual guidance, though she could not bring herself to use such a word. Nor could she bring herself to mention the dreams, the visions, the voice of Melanie that had been haunting her.

Eve just looked at her, round-eyed. "Wow," she said quietly.

"So tell me what you think, really? What I mean is, am I doing the right thing?"

"Well, for yourself and your career, like your editor Alice said, this is certainly the big one. Your prospects will skyrocket, even more than they already have with the notoriety boost the profiles have given you—Jocelyn being the big-gie, of course. For doing your bit for justice, you'll help put away the heavies like Moon and the big bad sheriff. And life in the commune, a general public service story I should say—and a great read. Personally, I can't wait. So far, I'd say 'Girl Reporter Does Her Bit for Truth, Justice, and the American Way.'"

"Okay so far. And then?" J.J. asked.

"I'll bet you're worrying about the Harts though, true? Is it fair going after them? I'm sure it's a legit story, like your editor said. But do you want to do it—go after them for fall-ing on the dark side while trying to write the story of their daughter the way they want it? Because you're more or less doing the same thing with your reporting. That's a call of conscience, J.J., and I can't make it for you. What do you think?"

"I think," J.J. drew herself upright into the chair, "it's an entirely different thing. I'm only trying to find out the truth—the facts—and I'll go where they take me."

"Really?" Eve flashed a smile. "Okay. I'm guessing the second thing that's bothering you is the Melanie story. Do you think the bones, whatever they reveal, will tell you what you really want to know? An inquest may settle the question about her end, as you expect, but it won't tell you about the true face of our missing friend who seemed to have so many of them. I'm going to let you in on a little church secret. We're loaded with bones: holy ones, sacred ones, mysteri-ous ones, relics of every kind, most more imaginary than real. The bones, or their powdery remains, don't actually speak, and they certainly don't show us the way. At best, like any mysterious object we venerate, like the end point of any pilgrimage, they give us permission to go to the next step, to the next layer of truth. And you may be sure it is many layered and not contained in any bejeweled reliquary, or any single decree of an inquest."

A scream caused them both to turn toward the lawn where an unhappy Jazz had fallen on a stepping stone and scraped his knee. Suddenly J.J. remembered to check her watch. Almost time for Tom to arrive and she'd said nothing she had intended to say about him.

"Look," she jumped up, waving to Fleur who was gathering up Jazz, "why don't you go upstairs for a few minutes and chat with Fleur while I see to Gran?" J.J. jumped off the porch steps before Eve had time to reply.

EVE HAD BARELY gone inside when Tom arrived, bounding up the driveway a few minutes early. Gran, who had just come out from her rest, was sitting beneath the avocado tree. J.J., standing behind her, put her hands on the shawl across Gran's shoulders. She felt Gran sit up straight as she saw Tom, who eagerly took her hands in his. "Well, this is a sight for sore eyes. Generations of beauties under the shade of a mighty old tree."

J.J. leaned in, surprised to see Gran blush. "I see where J.J. gets her charms, Gran," he continued. "If it's all right with you, I'm going to pull up that other chair there and sit awhile so we can have a good chat. After your granddaughter and I go over there in the sunlight so I can show her something."

In a moment, standing by the birdbath, Tom extracted a paper from his battered briefcase. "Truth is, I just wanted to share this out of Gran's earshot," he said.

"What have you got?" J.J. whispered.

"Some of our brothers down there are quite, shall we say, *involved*, and I had them search their records, archives, for anything about a John C. Calhoun. Found out some things. For one, he's evidently quite a jazzman. And, they just sent me this." He straightened out a black and white photo of a man with an Afro sporting a headband, holding a gun, and crouched in front of a bank building, his face caught front on by the camera. It was J.C.

"You've heard of the Mississippi Seven perhaps? A group of black revolutionaries who broke from the path of Dr. King and followed the way of violence? This picture was taken moments before they blasted into the bank, robbed it, yelling 'Money to the People,' and killed a teller. Your J.C. here — Melanie's J.C., I guess I should say — is the one they think pulled the trigger."

J.J. stared at the picture, speechless. Tom patted her hair gently. "He was shot, but escaped. They believe he's from Chicago. Still trying to identify his real name. A lot to think over, isn't it? I'm going to go sit a moment with Gran, while you take this in."

J.J. felt the ground slip beneath her, felt as if she had been twirling on the grass with Jazz and needed to find a way to right herself again. Then she heard footsteps and his squeals and knew in a moment he and Fleur would be there again. He and Fleur and...

In a flash she was behind Tom, her hands now on his broad shoulders. It was not the way she meant for this encounter to go, but she hadn't played her role, hadn't prepared either of them. "Look, Tom, I know I should have told you, I meant to say, well it's too late now. There's someone here you should see and... Eve?" she called out the name, as a warning, and the door pushed open, the wind catching long strands of red hair.

Chapter 43

The image of the open door—Eve stepping into the wind, into a surprise encounter with her past—stuck in J.J.'s vision all the way through the long, traffic-filled ride to Hollywood. At the last minute, she'd averted her eyes and hurried away from Eve and Tom, embarrassed at her own meddling. Had they faced each other awkwardly? Had Tom swept Eve into his open embrace? J.J. had no idea, but worry at what she had wrought now wove into her mounting anxiety about what lay ahead. Not the least, Tom's startling revelation about J.C. Calhoun. It was, at last, all coming down. The knot in her stomach grew and she was relieved to have Jocelyn's Hollywood story to do as a distraction from what was about to break open hundreds of miles to the north.

"Oh damn," J.J. swore as she opened and closed the limo door again, trying to free the fringe on her dress, "this is ridiculous."

"Really?" Jocelyn asked, turning her silky, upswept hairdo around to look at her friend in the seat behind. "I think it's perfect, honestly. My look is retro '40s, to fit the style of the film, and you go back to the '20s, the nouvelle flapper newspaper gal."

"J.J. darling," Dru turned to J.J. now as he patted Jocelyn's shoulder, "her gown is an homage to Katharine Hepburn, Lauren Bacall, Ava Gardner—the classy dames of the classic period. But of course, she is already a celebrity herself. And now interest in *Pacific Blue* has been, how do you say, over the moon. No film opening has created more excitement. I was worried, but Jocelyn was right. Controversy is a very big seller, no?"

J.J. nodded.

"And it's true, you are a big cheese now too? Jocelyn says you get many offers from big papers, am I right?"

"Right," J.J. answered, not daring to say more.

Once delivered from the limo, J.J. discreetly took the reporter's notebook from her sequined bag and began to scribble the obligatory notes about place, noting the famous cement walkway with the stars' signatures, hand-, or footprints, Jocelyn's soon to be among them. "Check date," she wrote. Then she followed the red carpet into the auditorium, "an ornate Chinese lacquer box," she wrote, found her assigned seat in the press section, and waved to George who was snapping pictures for the *Star* from the sidelines.

After the last applause and bow from Jocelyn, J.J. made her way through the crowds to the street, past the line that snaked around the block, and snagged a cab to take her back up the hill.

IT WAS PAST eleven thirty when she slipped the Datsun into a parking space and rang security to let her into the *Star* building. An old fellow with a pack of jangling keys on his belt ambled to the door. He looked at her with puzzlement, then asked, "What did you want, Missy?"

"I want to get in my office at the *Star*. I have some late work to do."

"You work for the paper?" he asked skeptically.

J.J. had forgotten how she looked, how strange she must appear. "Yes, yes. I'm a reporter. I've just been in Hollywood covering the opening of a big new movie, starring Jocelyn, you know her?"

The old man's face lit up. "You saw her? In person?"

"Yes," she answered fumbling in her bag for a flyer from Grauman's Chinese Theatre showing a gorgeous shot of Jocelyn. "See here, you can keep this. But now I've got to get in to write the story. A big story." She smiled as he opened the door wide for her.

Once inside the office's main door, she locked it, headed for her desk and switched on the small lamp. *Adrenalin is a reporter's best friend*, she thought, pulling the cover off her typewriter.

Sweeping down the red carpet at Grauman's Chinese Theatre last night on the arms of two dashing men, suave director Dru Jablonski and heart-stoppingly handsome co-star Kostas Moreau, Jocelyn stole the crowd and the night. While the blond beauty in her striking gold satin '40s-style gown paid tribute to the period of her new film, *Pacific Blue: The Louis Dubois Story*, as well as to the glamorous stars of that era, the thoroughly modern actress also embodies a new patriotism that sometimes includes protest...

J.J.'s fingers flew across the keys as she wove these threads into what she thought was a colorful, bold, and highly original portrait, pausing now and then to study her notes. "Work in smthg about the place," she had reminded herself. "Stuff for sidebar on J's biggest films." "Hollywood gossip about what she'll do next?"

J.J. had no idea what time it was when she fell asleep; she only knew that, feet numb and cold beneath the chair, she woke up to realize her head had been lying on the story she'd ripped from the typewriter. Straightening her aching back, she glanced at the clock: 6:18. *My God, I've been here all night.* She stood slowly, remembering that she was still in that ridiculous dress, and that she hadn't been home all night. Then she heard noises and understood she wasn't alone.

Shoes in hand, she tiptoed in the direction of the sounds, stopping in her tracks a few feet from Bud Purvis's office to inhale the unmistakable odor of cigar smoke. Feeling foolish, disheveled, and suddenly exhausted, J.J. backed away, hoping to sneak away. But he spotted her.

"Sweetheart!" he called out loudly while holding a hand over the receiver of the phone. "What are you...and why are you dressed like that? Been to the circus or something?" He guffawed loudly. A sound J.J. realized, she'd not heard for a long time.

"No, I'm just a working reporter, remember? I came in to do my story on the big Hollywood opening, Jocelyn and all that. So it can go out first thing. Hang on, I'll go get it."

She returned with the wrinkled piece in her hand, catching her reflection in the window. *I do look like a working girl, a girl working the streets*, she thought. Then entering his smoke-filled lair, she slammed the story on his desk.

"Sorry," he said, trying to wave away the smoke, while covering the receiver again. "Came in early to, you know, do some deals. Business calls. Acquisitions, baby, we're going for the big time. And don't worry, sweetheart," he was whispering now, "you're in too. Got big plans for you." He winked.

J.J. just nodded and turned quickly so he wouldn't see her laugh. She could hardly admit to herself, let alone him, that it was actually refreshing to see the real Bud Purvis again. What was it Gran always said about a leopard changing its spots?

Passing the receptionist's desk, she saw the phone light up. Who the hell is calling in at this hour, she wondered, and on impulse punched the button.

"This is the *Pasadena Star*," she answered.

"Kiddo, is that you? I tried calling you at home, think I managed to wake up everybody and set off quite an uproar there, but nobody seemed to know where you were. So, I took a flier that I could at least leave a message for you at work, figuring nobody would really be there at this hour."

"Yeah, it's me. And I just happened to pass the phone, took a flier myself, and answered. So what's up?"

"Plenty. The feds picked up O'Reilly at the Canadian border and they're bringing him back down to California. Moon seems to have gotten away, but the net is closing in. O'Reilly's arraignment should be in a few days, in Ukiah. I'll be there. With a couple of my elders. They'll be in full regalia, perhaps doing some chanting and prayers for justice."

"So it begins," J.J. said quietly. "You've been a great friend. Thanks. See you there."

She hung up, standing still for a moment by the desk, head buzzing as if she had been drinking. *Got to get on the road*, she told herself. But first she had to make some calls. After hanging up with Mama Cass, she meant to dial Alice, but Alice walked in the door before she got the chance.

In a moment they were in Alice's office with a big map spread over her desk. "I see how this could play out," Alice began. "So we need to have our battle plan, then we need to hit the road. Like I said, I checked the wires just now and the fact that Sheriff O'Reilly, 'long assumed dead in a fishing accident,' has been picked up by the feds while trying to cross into Vancouver has been noted. The local papers and TV stations from Ukiah to Santa Rosa will be on this today.

The big boys will follow quickly. What we've got on them, of course, is the big picture. If we waste time, we'll lose our advantage."

"We need to get our asses up there. That's what Mama just told me," J.J. broke in.

Alice gave her that look. "Right you are. But you, Miss *Star*'s star, look like hell. I'm getting on the road myself with Laura and George. You go home and get some sleep and follow when you're rested. You can't do anybody any good the shape you're in. That's an order."

Chapter 44

van had been right. It was a zoo at the house when she arrived. Gran rattling pans in the kitchen where the radio was blaring; Jazz crying inconsolably, cranky no doubt from being awakened too early; Cat in a rough woven tunic trying to comfort him by crooning "Hey diddle diddle, the cat and the fiddle," but Jazz wasn't having any. "Mama, mama," he cried intermittently while tugging on Cat's long hair. J.J. approached to give him a pat, but he turned his face into Cat's shoulder, crying "Mama" once more.

Did he mean Cat? J.J. wondered. Or was he calling out for Gracie, or Fleur? Or did some small part of him still remember and long for Melanie? She shook her head as if to make that conundrum disappear. "Hey, everybody," she called out, "I had to work all night to get that Hollywood story done. I'm exhausted so going to sleep now."

As she turned to go upstairs, Gran suddenly took notice

and set down her pan. "Ah, it's you *ma petite*, and where did you get such a beautiful dress?"

～⟩

THE CLOCK SAID 1:17 when J.J. cracked one eye open. Light filtering past the edges of the window shades on the sleeping porch told her it was p.m., not a.m. Afternoon. She sat upright trying to grasp quickly where she was.

In the kitchen Annie sang while a giggling Jazz stood on Dad's shoes as he tried to negotiate a two-step. "Saraswati!" Annie cried out. "There you are. Well, it's all a wonder, isn't it?" she grinned as she slid the late edition of the *Star* across the table. "I'm guessing the dress fit the bill to perfection, no? Of course, the glory all goes to the Queen of the Night and not the mere chronicler, so no picture of you. But never mind. Hollywood will buzz with this one, I have to tell you, and the fact that you, my very own little girl, wrote it will be known far and wide. Annie's Ark will be the hottest place in town by week's end, mark my words."

J.J. felt as she frequently did in her mother's presence, dumbstruck. "Yeah, right, well great," she managed to reply.

"You look…" Annie started to say, as if actually noticing J.J. for the first time.

"Tired, maybe?" J.J. filled in. Then raising her volume over the squeals of Dad and Jazz waltzing, "I was up all night. First at the event, then at the office, writing the story. Is there some coffee around by any chance?"

"I can brew up some," Annie shouted back. "But you better go outside. A gentleman to see you. If he's still alive after Mother finishes flirting and charming him to death."

～⟩

J.J. STEPPED OUT into the full light of afternoon to see Gran, resplendent in a lavender dress and brooch shaped like a *fleur de lys* smiling at an elegantly tailored man with swept-back silver hair. Dru.

As she approached, Gran called out, *"Ah, ma petite,"* and Dru rose, turning toward J.J. and took her hand to kiss it. "It was a long night for all of us, J.J., and I did not want to wake you. Your charming grandmother has been keeping me company, telling me the most amusing stories."

"I can only imagine." J.J. smiled. "But you came to see me? You read the piece...?"

"Ah, no, I confess not yet. But yes, I did come to see you. May we talk somewhere?"

They settled in the shaded living room, the light filtering around half-closed damask drapes. Dru sat upright on an antique chair, his long legs crossed, a cigarette and gold-tipped holder in hand.

"So," he said, inhaling slowly. "I have come to see you, dear J.J., because I cannot leave her like this. Well, I will leave her of course, that is always understood, and this time it is I who has left, yes, already, so soon I know. But it is only because, I must confess to you, I really do love her.

"I always know after each time we work together we will part, because I am too old for her, and she must have her life—her freedom, yes?—and normally she gives the sign. But this time I must do it first because I think I can only be a danger to her now."

"A danger?" J.J. set down her coffee cup.

"Yes. I will explain. She is in a terrible crisis."

"What?" J.J. burst in. "But last night, the movie, the coverage, it was all a triumph."

"A crisis, I tell you, brought on by the very success of last night. Of course one cannot see because she is a great actress. Always playing the role, but she is suffering a great depression. The more successful, the worse. 'It is all false, phony,' she says to me. 'It means nothing, all lights and glitter and no meaning.' She says she wants to leave films, go on the stage, do something small, something real. She mentioned doing the story of Melanie."

"You're kidding."

"No, my dear J.J., I am not kidding. But you see why I must leave her quickly. I cannot help her do what she wants to do now. I will only be in the way. And partly I blame myself for this idea, for taking her last fall to Pasadena and showing her the old Pasadena Playhouse. Perhaps you know of it? Ever since then, she has talked romantically about 'real theater, real life, no phony lights' and such. No, I cannot help her with this crisis. But you, you can. You are the only one she can really trust. And you are the only one I trust to be by her side."

"Me?" J.J. looked directly at Dru, whose head was now encircled by smoke. "I can comfort her as a friend, of course. But help? At least you're a director. I know nothing about the stage."

"Of course, of course." Dru waved his cigarette holder in a circular gesture. "But this is something different, something profound, I don't know, maybe something, how do you say, existential? I think you can help her because maybe you, too, are in the same place. Well, Jocelyn believes it anyway. Last night she says to me, 'J.J. is just like me. She is becoming a superstar journalist, but it is the wrong path for her. She should be a poet.'"

Chapter 45

S he passed the sign for Thousand Oaks and decided to
clear her head with music. Fumbling through the box of
cassettes with old favorites, she picked one at random.
Surrealistic Pillow by Jefferson Airplane. Wriggling into her
seat, now uncomfortably cracked along the back, she let the
pure notes of Grace Slick and "White Rabbit" wash over her.

Thinking of Alice ten feet tall made her smile. And feel
relieved that Alice, who was a giant in her world, would
already be on the ground in Ukiah when she got there.

At last the coast, and the breath of the sea, and songs
to distract her from what lay ahead. Ventura and the flat
stretch of beach so close she could almost feel the waves.
The Stones. Dylan. Carpinteria. Santa Barbara. Breakers
rolling in over white sands, tiled roof villas overhanging the
hills, already turning brown. The Moody Blues. Heading
north toward Pismo Beach. That spacey new album she'd
bought last year, Pink Floyd, *The Dark Side of the Moon*.

SHE PULLED INTO Pismo Beach and found the road overlooking undulating dunes leading to a sweep of beach. She knew she would sit there as the sun died for the day, taking its fiery orange light into the sea. Because it was too late in the day to go the distance, she would find a little place for the night, perhaps near the cottage she remembered from childhood and the long-ago days when she had come here with Mother—before she became Annie—and Dad, and even Gran, who never cared for the sand. She would get up before dawn and arrive in Ukiah in the morning.

Meanwhile, she would sit by the Pacific, the place she had always been most at home in the world, and get herself together. Watching the light play on the lip of the waves, the gulls swoop and surge along the foam of tide, she inhaled, trying to find strength. Like last summer, when she'd pulled over and stared down at the pounding surf of Mendocino, minutes before she'd seen the Hi-Diddle House for the first time.

So many months, and she still didn't know how to write the story of Melanie. Now she was about to find out.

The sky was folding dark over the last trace of pale light, and the foam of the waves broke silver into the edge of night. It was time to go. *One more song*, she decided, and slipped her favorite Joni Mitchell into the tape deck to hear "Both Sides Now."

Suddenly, another torrent broke through, one that was swirling at her foundations. The hurried, angry conversation she'd had with Jocelyn on the phone right after Dru left.

"How dare you tell Dru, that like you, I'm going in the wrong direction with my life?" she'd yelled at her best friend.

"Just like with dream work, I can't tell you what to think. All I can say is, ask the question and answer it yourself," Jocelyn replied.

"And what the hell do you mean, you want to tell Melanie's story?"

"I don't want to tell Melanie's story. I want *you* to. It's made for the theater, J.J., so you write it. I want to produce it, direct it. Make it happen."

⤳

SAFELY BEHIND THE closed door of the Victorian B&B in Ukiah where she'd been staying for days, two editions of the *Star* sat on the cluttered desk where J.J. huddled over a small portable typewriter. She stretched for a moment, then let her eyes turn to the papers again, for inspiration.

The first headline in bold type screamed: "Lost. Found. Lost Again. Sheriff Gets 15 Years in Federal Pen. Date April 20, 1975. Dateline, Eureka. Byline, Alice Riddel, with Laura Smith." "Yes!" J.J. said aloud. Alice had nailed it. The writing, crisp, incisive, devastating, was old school, like Alice. It let an artful buildup of the facts from the trial in the federal courthouse—corruption, drug running across state lines, taking bribes, extortion, among others—make the case against Melvin O'Reilly.

The second story, dated five days later, "Smoke, Mirrors and Fire: The Lost Commune of Hi-Diddle House," was her own. Although it contained enough free love, drugs, and racial mixing to titillate readers who wanted to be scandalized, J.J. was proud that the shock value was actually low. After all the time spent poking through rubble, collecting stories from interviews, from gossip, and especially from Cat, J.J. felt she had written a deeply layered story. She'd chosen the words carefully. Even the headline, for once her own, was made up of words with more than one truth. "Smoke" made reference to pipes, just as "mirrors" caught the reflections revealed back to her through dreams, while "fire" also signified passion. As for "lost," the word pointed past the destructive end to the ideals of the inhabitants them-selves. And she'd splashed in plenty of local color: the hats, boots, feathers, fibers, and tie-dye apparel; the organic food, relying on brown rice, sprouts, nuts, and beans; the ritu-als of smoking with pipes, bubbles, canisters of weed; the dancing, musical instruments, songs, and games; the quirky adoption of names from a nursery rhyme.

She reread one of her favorite passages, the one about the justice circles, where the Hi-Diddle residents sat in a circle by the fire to resolve problems—in this case, the behavior of someone who was no longer conforming to com-munity beliefs, so they asked him to leave. Moon, expelled from Eden and sent to exile on "the farm."

Needing a break from writing the rest of Moon's story, J.J. headed to a diner a couple of blocks down Ukiah's Main Street, past the Mendocino County Courthouse, where so many hours of drama had ended with Moon's conviction. Walking by the modern square building constructed a cou-ple of decades ago on the spot where the original Victorian had once sat, she thought about the way she'd explained its role in this drama, and how that ambitious young D.A., Richard Martinez, had wrested the Moon case from the feds, who had successfully brought O'Reilly to justice. The D.A., angry that one of his sheriffs had "gone way off the reservation" as he put it, was determined that the rest of the story unfold right here in Ukiah, right under his nose, with his name visible in every account.

Hope I got that right, she thought, then continued down the street, picking up a copy of the *Ukiah Daily Record* to fan herself. It was already warm. May 1, she noticed. May Day, May Day, the international call for help. Saigon had fallen for good yesterday. She stared at pictures of the helicopters lifting off the roof of the embattled American Embassy and suddenly felt that Guy had lifted with them, as though he were no longer simply left alone in an anonymous forest...

Remembering herself again, where she was, she ran over the opening paragraph of the Moon story in her mind.

> Tensions ran high in the Mendocino County Courthouse as the jury delivered its verdict of guilty against Quincy Abernathy on several counts: arson, second-degree murder, bribery, growing and trafficking illegal drugs. Mr. Abernathy, a well-known local hippie who goes by the name of Moon, arrived in the courthouse in handcuffs and prison garb. With his once-wild hair cropped and his bushy beard shaved, he seemed uncharacteristically subdued. Only his darting dark eyes, hot as heat-seeking missiles, offered a window into his tumultuous soul, at once angry, fearful, defiant and perhaps threatening. Cries rose from the crowd calling out "murderer."

As J.J. hurried down the last block, eager to escape the rising heat, she felt those eyes, as if they were still watching her. At first she had figured that Moon, like a character in one of the nursery rhymes, was merely a buffoon. But with each subsequent encounter, he'd changed, going from simply weird to menacing to evil. Now she wanted to nail Moon and his story more than any other. Except for Melanie's, of course.

A chill ran through her as she stepped into the diner, and she knew it was not the air conditioning. Grabbing an ice cream to go, she rushed back to the B&B determined to finish what she had started.

Hours passed. The sun began to sink over the hills to the west; J.J. stretched again, then paused to look at the pages she had torn from the typewriter, riddled with cross-outs and corrections. *Move up*, she had instructed herself on the section describing the reopened investigation.

District Attorney Richard Martinez, learning from the conviction of former Mendocino County Sheriff Melvin O'Reilly about the aborted investigation into the burning of Hi-Diddle House, a commune in the woods off Little River Road, immediately reopened the case. Fire investigators determined that the fire had indeed been deliberately set and that someone—an adult woman—had perished in that fire. The body was so badly damaged, however, it was deemed impossible to identify.

J.J. paused, rereading that sentence, just as she had gasped when she first read the investigators' report. "The body of a young woman was found in that fire," she could hear Mama Cass say the first day they had met in the Bread & Beads Café, not understanding that Mama had gotten the low-down from Moon. But surely it was so, J.J. knew, even if the dead woman was not the one Moon intended. The facts, at last, were coming soon. Natalie, against the wishes of the rest of the Hart family, had requested that the coroner revisit the "impossible to identify" determination. She had provided Melanie's dental records. He would make his report public shortly, probably in a couple of days.

But J.J. couldn't let herself think about that. She had a story to finish.

Mr. Abernathy, having recently attempted to flee illegally into Canada with Sheriff O'Reilly and, due to a tip from a local informer, having been captured in a remote area near the Hi-Diddle Farms (a large plot of federal forest riddled with marijuana plants), immediately became a suspect. According to D.A. Martinez, not only was Mr. Abernathy known to be an estranged member of the Hi-Diddle House Commune, but there were disturbing rumors of a failed romance turned threatening. With several credible witnesses willing to testify, the D.A. named the young and fiery Loretta Canady to prosecute the case, while seasoned attorney James Mulligan defended the accused.

After reviewing this paragraph (*rework wording re. romance,* she wrote in the margin), J.J. carefully went over other descriptive parts. The depiction of the modern county courthouse amidst Victorian cupolas and sleepy store fronts seemed fine, as did capturing the feel of the courtroom: wood paneled, solemn with its flags, its judge's bench, jury box, witness stand, and open benches for the public, away from the mob of press, TV cameras, flashbulbs outside. *Shorter,* she'd written by the section where the two attorneys began sparring over jury selection.

Right length? Enough drama? she'd scrawled next to the beginning of the real heart of the story.

Using the investigators' report that the cause of the Hi-Diddle fire was in fact arson, Prosecuting Attorney Canaby built a case upon statements of witnesses, some of whom testified about Mr. Abernathy's character, and some of whom asserted his likely guilt—often based on his own words—not only in setting the fire but in doing so with the intent to murder. Public Defender Mulligan, however, attempted to discredit the witnesses as biased and unreliable and insisted their testimony was "a pile of fact-free opinion" and "the so-called evidence" was strictly circumstantial.

The back and forth continued even with the most persuasive witnesses, such as in the following dialogue between Prosecutor Canaby and Ida Swig, a cashier at the local Mendocino General Store. It was followed by Public Defender Mulligan's cross-examination.

Ms. Swig testified that Mr. Abernathy had come into the store before the fire to buy several canisters of kerosene, whose discarded remains were found at the scene at Hi-Diddle House. Those canisters were determined by fire experts to have been used to cause the fire. She further said Mr. Abernathy had returned the night of the fire, roaring drunk and said: 'Trouble In Paradise. That old house is now exploding, kaboom, and I do believe the little bitch fried."

When asked by Ms. Canaby what she believed he meant by that, Ms. Swig replied, "He meant he burnt the house down with his girlfriend inside."

Then, when Ms. Canaby asserted that this was a serious admission and asked what she did with the information, Ms. Swig answered: "You're damn right it's serious. That's why I took it directly to the Sheriff's Office."

"Shorten and paraphrase," J.J. wrote above the next section as she reviewed it.

Finally the last, and as it turned out, star witness, was called by the prosecution. Ms. Katerina McNealy—known in the community as Cat—took the stand. The young woman with dark, long hair, gentle eyes and a regal bearing who wore a flowing skirt and billowy blouse immediately commanded attention.

Prompted by Ms. Canaby, she told her story: "I come from the mountain country of Carolina where I learned my trade, midwifing. Often I make home visits, but also bring my practice to a small clinic in Fort Bragg where they believe in my work. I came here because, like most everybody these days, I heard about the path of love and sharing and living in harmony many folks try out in California. I found such a place to live, at least for a while, in the Hi-Diddle House Commune."

Ms. Canaby went on to question the witness about how one lived in the commune, and what went wrong. Ms. McNealy spoke persuasively about a life of harmony, equality and sharing—even of sexual partners "if everybody feels good about it," and also about the right of refusal. She described taking up with a new fellow who went by the name of Sport, but that one member of the house who'd been sweet on her but "whose favor I never returned, objected mightily. Being a founding member of the house, I guess he feels he has the right to power over me, but it doesn't work that way."

Ms. Canaby asked Ms. McNealy to identify that person, and she pointed at Mr. Abernathy. She went on to describe his wrath and the destruction that followed: his eviction, threats to her, even messages left at the clinic, his warning, "You're going to pay a heavy price for this, Hillbilly Woman"; then the fire; the rumor that a woman had died in there; the realization, "My sweet Jesus, that was meant to be me, but I was away at the time and some poor soul died in my place." She described her attempt, after the fire, to seek protection from the sheriff, and her eventual understanding that "the sheriff and Moon Boy were in cahoots, and I was in mortal danger and better take to hiding."

At the end of her testimony, Mr. Mulligan declared he had no questions, a tacit admission of defeat, and Ms. McNealy rose from the witness stand erect and dignified, then turned toward the accused again. "Come on now, Moon, you best have the courage to face me, look me in the eye, because I'm going to declare before all these folk that I'll be praying for you and asking Jesus to forgive you, but you got to do some asking and praying yourself."

Mr. Abernathy was never called to testify, and within an hour, the jury rendered a verdict of guilty on all counts and the judge gave a date for sentencing. Before leaving the courtroom, Ms. McNealy paused briefly on her way out of court to look into the unexpressive face of Mr. Abernathy. This time he returned her gaze with one that seemed to burn. According to Ms. McNealy his meaning was perfectly clear, she told this reporter: "He was saying 'From me there will be no prayers nor asking for forgiveness, but only this: the promise that if I could, I'd try to kill you all over again.'"

Depleted, J.J. turned off the desk light and moved to the window to catch the last streak of red in the sky before night claimed it. Of all the wonders of this story so far, one of the greatest was that Cat, now safely home, had won the trust—and no doubt the hearts—of the jury so completely that they found Moon guilty of everything. And even greater: Cat had managed to do so without ever bringing up Melanie nor baby Jazz, who was still out of harm's way, alive and well and living in Gran's house in Pasadena.

And that was only part of the untold story. The rest was on her: that she'd shirked her duty as a reporter to disclose a clear conflict of interest. *How should I put it?*, she'd asked herself. Disclaimer: in the name of full disclosure, this reporter has been secretly harboring the key witness in her home, while helping to provide her with legal advice. *Don't even think about it*, she told herself, and curled up on the bed.

Chapter 46

J.J. stood at a pay phone in the corner of the courthouse dropping in enough coins to connect with Alice.

"J.J. Ace Reporter. At last you're calling. How are you holding up?"

J.J. could visualize Alice, glasses askew on a chain. "Fine. Okay. It's hot but I'm hanging in. Hope my piece got there okay."

"You knocked it out of the park, my dear. Huge success. Himself is out of what passes for his mind with the series so far. What news on the coroner's report?"

"That's what I wanted to tell you. They've moved it up to this afternoon."

"Oh. I see. I was actually going to offer to come back up to, you know, do a little hand holding. I know this is a tough one for you, even though you're fully prepared for the results."

"Thanks, but no, not necessary. I've been gearing up for this all year and trying to make my peace with it. Natalie should be there, but of course is invisible so far. Anyway, it's far too late for you to get up here."

"True. So once it's official, why don't you do the Hart story first? Whatever angle you want will be fine. Then take your time with the big one. Melanie."

"Thanks, Alice. I will. It'll take me a couple of days to get back. I'll check in then, okay?"

"Take your time, my dear. There's more than enough excitement around here."

⟶

WALKING INTO THE dingy coroner's office, J.J. scanned it for Natalie. Far from the splendor of the courtroom, phones rang, people came and went, officers' walkie-talkies blared, and a buzz of voices pushed in from the corridor outside. As if it were a normal day. There was no sign of Natalie. Finding a metal chair in an obscure corner, J.J. wiped the sweat running down her neck. Two o'clock came and went. Then at nine past the hour, Natalie, dressed in her signature black and hidden behind shades, pushed in the door.

J.J. stood to wave to her. "Natalie, over here," she called out, making her way to where Natalie stood, looking bewildered.

She stared for a second through her kohl-rimmed eyes. "So you're here."

"Of course I'm here. Can I join you when you meet with the coroner?"

"Why the fuck not? You can stand in for the family."

"That's what I was hoping."

They made their way to a battered desk with a sign saying "Coroner" and pulled up two chairs. J.J., who had so much she wanted to ask Natalie, could find no words. Her heart pounded and the perspiration flowed down her back like a river. Natalie stared at her lap, twisting a tissue around two fingers with jagged nails.

Both started when a pot-bellied middle-aged man plunked himself behind the desk.

"Miss Hart?" his voice boomed.

Natalie nodded.

"As you know, we reopened the examination of the remains from that fire down by Little River. You the one who made the request and sent the dental records?"

Natalie nodded again.

"Well we've just got the results back from the lab. The dental records you provided us do not match those of the victim of the fire. She is still classified as a Jane Doe."

J.J. did not remember when she began breathing again. Natalie turned to her, eyes for once wide with surprise.

"Look, want to go somewhere for a cold drink or something?" J.J. asked.

Natalie followed wordlessly as J.J. led her to the ice cream parlor. In minutes, large floats sat in front of them. Natalie finally spoke.

"So this means she's alive?"

"No." J.J. stirred a long spoon in the drink, trying to find words. "No. All it tells us is that she didn't die in that fire."

"Well, is she? I mean, what do you think?"

J.J. stopped stirring to look directly at Natalie. "I honestly don't know. This whole year I was so certain she was dead. That she was the one they found. It was the only thing that made sense given all the other facts... Tell me Natalie, what do you think?"

"Me? I never had any facts. Just the cockamamy ideas of my parents who were so eager to bury her in their own way so they could control the 'scandal.'" Natalie mimed the quotes with her fingers. "I guess because they decided she was dead, I decided she was alive. At least I really, really wanted her to be."

"Then where do you think she is?"

Natalie's eyes started to fill with tears, then leak onto the kohl, which ran in black streaks down her face. "Look, I can't. I'm out of here." She jumped up and crossed the room, before turning back to J.J. "Thanks. For being there," then bolted out the door.

Trembling, confused, dissatisfied by the unfinished conversation with Natalie, J.J. knew she needed to talk. She needed a friend. She needed Alice. Instead, she left for Mendocino and pulled up across from the Bread & Beads Café for the last time.

J.J. pushed open the door, to be greeted by a curly-headed young woman with a flower tattooed on her upper arm. Pigeon's replacement. She wondered for a second how it had all come down for that weasely piece of shit.

"I'm here to see Mama Cass," J.J. said, and picked a table by the window.

In a moment, the large torso in a muumuu shook silently beside her.

"Well my oh my, if you ain't a sight for sore eyes. The lady who took it all down."

"Hi, Mama. Sit with me a minute. I just, well there was another coroner's report today. They reinvestigated the body in the fire using dental records. It was requested by the family of my friend. It wasn't her." J.J. tried to keep her voice from wavering.

Mama's soft, warm hand reached to cover hers. "No shit. Wonder who... So where do you think she is then?"

"I don't know where she is... I just know she didn't die in that fire."

They sat in silence for several minutes, attached by one hand inside another.

"It looks like all's going well with you in the end," J.J. finally said.

"Yup. Sonofabitch O'Reilly, FBI, Big Turd, little Weasel, all those fuckers a thing of the past now. I'm firmly on my own two feet in my own little establishment. And from here on, I'm relying strictly on humans of the female persuasion." Mama began one of her earth-disturbing laughs.

J.J. felt her breathing return to normal.

Mama's voice turned conspiratorial. "Working on a new business enterprise, a network of woman power trading establishments. When the heat cools down completely. So what's up next with you, reporter lady, now that you've brought the house down around here?"

"Well I'm going back down south to finish these stories. My business is wrapped up here."

"Is that so?"

———

ON THE ROAD again, the deep rhythms of Coltrane moving her forward, Mama's farewell still rang in her ears. "Don't be a stranger now, hear? Always a laugh to kick around old times and those jackasses who thought they could mess with the likes of us."

At Gualala, she stopped in front of her familiar motel, deciding to call it a night. Soon, washing down a carry-out burger with a glass of coastal pinot, she watched the last rays of pink sunset play into summer night as waves rolled white beneath. Then she folded herself into an armchair facing the sea and tried to make sense of what the day had brought. Her daytime self would immediately begin to probe what other foul play had taken Melanie's life. But another reality was taking place within her nighttime self, one where Melanie was always alive.

Other thoughts began racing through her confusion. How she would approach the Hart story, now that there wasn't a dead daughter, but simply a criminal charge of bribing a sheriff in hopes that they wouldn't find one. How things would go once home. How she would hug Gran on whatever planet she was inhabiting that day, wave hello to Jazz who would be racing like crazy between Cat and Fleur, or maybe Gracie. How she'd likely find Annie concocting some vegan wonder on the stove, or Dad with a new toy he'd just made, or maybe even Tom, who stopped in when he could, coming and going to the San Gabriel Mission. How Gran's house as she pictured it now was an ark, harboring so many species who needed a place to survive and then to blossom. It was in the best sense a home again, filled with life, nurturing a human family.

She remembered she needed to call Alice first thing in the morning and ask for the latest update from the paper, hope for the newest tidbit on Himself busting his britches with importance. Then she needed to set a time to go in, clear her desk, and plan her final story.

Melanie. She let herself say the name aloud, and it lingered on her lips as she crawled into bed.

With the twenty-watt light still casting its anemic glow, J.J.'s lids firmly shut.

COLORS, ORANGE, RED, yellow, then a psychedelic poster, zoom in and out. A road comes into view. A brown country road, trees lining each side, and the sounds of feet, marching. March, march, march. Louder. The street narrows, the sounds of feet soften and are swallowed beneath the sounds of a city. Horns, a siren, a bus changing gear. Buildings. Traffic signals. The lights dim, orange red yellow to dusk. An arm, shadowy at first, appears from around a corner. The scene, shot with a jerky camera, shifts, then rights itself. Backlighting glows around a figure, clear as day. Both arms now visible, a gun in one, the figure crouches, moving in shadows up the sidewalk toward a bank. His bandana glows red. His head turns toward the camera as he looks behind him. J.C. His other arm waves, a signal to someone out of sight. An accomplice. The camera jerks, then refocuses. A small figure in dark clothes and a wool cap follows. The camera sweeps closer. Strands of blonde hair escape the cap. The figure, holding a gun, turns, and a face appears. Melanie. Her transparent eyes dance in the light. She is smiling. At J.J.

Chapter 47

At the pay phone cross the street from the motel, J.J. again dropped a fistful of coins to call Alice. Shaky, she knew she would again only tell part of the story. The part about the coroner's report.

Alice didn't pick up. The call reverted to the receptionist.

"Ah, J.J.," she said. "Alice isn't in, but I do have an urgent message for you. A priest, a Father Yves, said he needs to talk to you immediately and to call this number right away."

Her fingers numb, J.J. slid more coins in the phone. In two rings, the receiver picked up and a reassuring voice announced, "Father Yves."

"Tom?"

"J.J., thank God you got my message. Listen, there's been a new and disturbing development. My network in the South has come up with another photo from that bank robbery. It seems J.C. had an accomplice. No identity has been made yet, but it looks like—"

"I know, Tom. It's Melanie. She was wearing a hat and carrying a gun."

J.J. didn't register how the call had ended, or whether she or Tom had been more surprised. She was shuddering now, from shock, from cold. There were only a few coins left, and she jammed them into the slots for the last call.

"Hello," Jocelyn answered, sleep in her voice.

"Look I'm up the coast. What was Dru telling me about your disillusionment with success? And how I'm like you? And how I didn't get the meaning of dreams? We've got to talk. I'm on my way. Be there in a few hours."

The receiver went silent. She left the phone in a shroud of fog, beginning the journey south for the last time, letting her mind fill with Melanie. She understood now what Eve had been telling her—that the answers did not lie in the bones. The ones inside the burnt-out house only told her whose they were not. Inside sources—those inside her own head—would have to give her the rest. Only with the help of her dreams could she at last write Melanie's story. But could she believe them?

Melie, in all her costumes, in all her states of mind, whirred around in J.J's head like a merry-go-round on speed. She heard Moon's voice. "We all got aliases, but Fiddle, she got more than most." Then she heard the sounds: Hans's symphony, lullabies, Woodstock, Joan Baez and Dylan, Janis Joplin and Jimi Hendrix. J.C. Calhoun and his clarinet wailing out Miles Davis.

Hundreds of miles in, wanting something different, she switched on the radio. A station from L.A. was playing only the Stones. The signal, faint but audible, filled the void. And as she turned from coast to crowded freeway through the coastal range and the outer spill of the city, it came in better and better.

She had nearly cleared Burbank when that song from *Exile on Main Street*, "Sweet Black Angel," came through loud and clear.

A new image filled J.J.'s brain. The big poster of Angela Davis, the sweet black angel of the song, that J.J. had seen on Melanie's wall. Or had Melie merely mentioned it? Or had J.J. only seen it in a vision? Maybe it didn't matter. Fact or fiction, it's a thin line.

Then the image of Angela Davis, clenched fist, gave way to another. Melanie in the knit cap creeping behind J.C. to rob a bank.

"Now de judge he gonna judge her," began playing in her head. But who? Who's the judge? She felt like yelling in protest, *Not me!* Knowing that of course she was. *I'm the writer. I'm the judge. Keep it together until you get there*, she told herself. Not far now.

⟶

J.J. SAT ON the orange couch facing a hazy view through the sliding glass door, glass of juice in hand.

"Okay," Jocelyn finally said. "You go. From the beginning."

"I, well, so I'm about to write the biggest story—correction, series—of my life. All centered on trying to figure out what happened to Melanie in that commune up the coast. It becomes a story of police corruption, huge illegal drug operations, and at the center of it the capture of crazy-assed Moon, who not only ran drugs and was in cahoots with the corrupted sheriff, but three days ago was found guilty of burning down Hi-Diddle House and attempting to kill Cat—only he killed somebody else instead. The whole year you know what we all feared: that he'd got Melanie by mistake. Only yesterday, we—that is her sister Natalie and I—got a second coroner's report based on dental records. It wasn't Melie."

"Oh my God."

"Yeah. From the beginning I believed—knew—that Melie was dead. That she died in the Hi-Diddle House fire. It just fit the facts, even though increasingly my dreams contradicted them. Then yesterday I learned from the coroner that she didn't die in the fire. After that came this dream…"

"Hold it right there. Let's work this the way you do, using the facts first. We'll call that fact one: Melanie didn't die in the fire. What else do you know for sure?"

"Well, there is this photo Tom brought me. Like I told you, he's a priest but a lawyer, too, and has deep connections to some activist Catholic underground. He came over with this picture a contact sent him. It's of J.C. Calhoun, Melanie's lover and the father of Jazz, somewhere in Mississippi. He's creeping down a street with a gun in his hand, about to rob a bank. I have that photo."

Jocelyn drew in a deep breath. "Okay. J.C. became a bank robber. Fact two."

"Even worse. A teller was shot in the robbery. They think J.C. is also the killer."

Jocelyn paused a full minute before speaking. "Wow. Right. But at this point still a supposition, not a fact. Is there more?"

"There is. Last night Melie came to me again in a dream, clear as if she were sitting where you are. J.C. is creeping up on the bank and motioning to someone. An accomplice. Melie comes into the picture, dressed in black, a cap on her head, blonde hair sticking out. She's holding a gun. There's a hidden camera and she turns toward it, smiling. She's smiling right at me."

"My God," Jocelyn's voice raised.

"True or not true?" J.J. asked. "You're the dream person."

"Well it's a fact that you had this…vision of her. It's a

fact that in the vision she was smiling at you. It may or may not be a fact that she was really an accomplice to J.C."

"But get this. Just before calling you, I got a message from my office to call Tom. He told me another photo of the bank robbery had turned up. J.C. had an accomplice. It appeared to be a woman. She was wearing a cap, carrying a gun."

"He told you this?"

"No, I told him."

Jocelyn's eyes turned from green to dark blue. "What did he say?"

"I can't remember precisely, but he was as stunned as I was."

"So fact three?"

"They haven't identified her. But yes, as far as I'm concerned, fact three."

"My God. She's still alive then?"

"I'm certain of it."

"So she left the commune and her son to end up a radical extremist and bank robber?"

J.J. sat silent for several minutes, arms wrapped around her knees. "You could say that, but those are just labels and don't tell the whole truth. The truth that leads intelligent, just people, who have courage, to find themselves in dangerous, violent places where they wouldn't go without provocation. People like J.C., like Guy. Like Melanie. I don't think we know the end of her story. And what I do know can't be proved. My vision of her wouldn't stand in any court of law let alone court of opinion, except yours and other people like you who've done intensive dream work. Besides, the Mississippi police haven't identified her and most likely won't. Tom said on camera they'd got only a partial profile. Hard to identify."

They sat in silence, side by side on the orange couch, each trying to capture the words to go forward.

Jocelyn spoke first. "It's not a fact, but probable that your dreams, like so much else in this quest, came from Melanie to guide you in a certain direction."

"Like where? And if we're back with the dream business, I suppose you're going to say next this is about me, not Melanie."

"Of course it's about you as much as Melanie. She's been a total preoccupation since you started getting messages from her. I mean the physical ones, journals, letters, testimony from the rest of us. But then moving into your subconscious with all these dreams and visions, it's like a collaboration between you."

"You sound like Ivan when he found that packet of letters and said, 'it's a sign.'"

"Well, he was right. But when she moved inside your head, it became something more than just telling her story. It became the need inside you to write what you really know, write the way you can, starting from facts, then giving space for your imagination—your dreams—without leaving more than half the damn story out, the way you have been."

J.J. exhaled slowly. "Write the way I can? The one story I wanted to write most, I can't even begin."

"Why not?"

"Why not! The basic thing I wanted to discover when I started out a year ago is what happened to Melanie. Where she is. Now I don't even have that, other than that she didn't die in the fire. And I now believe she's alive."

"Hold it right there!" Jocelyn twisted her long hair and closed her eyes. "For these last several months you've been telling me the most astonishing discoveries about Melie."

"You mean like her maybe being a fugitive, then an accomplice helping J.C. rob a bank?"

"Yeah. Like that."

"I can't write that! I can't write most of this stuff."

"You mean it can't be contained in a newspaper article.

You can damn well write it, J.J. It's a fantastic story with multiple layers. Multiple endings. Write the script. We'll put it out there for the world to see. You, we, owe her that much. We owe it to the others, too. Melanie is the best of us, and maybe the worst of us. Her story lays bare all the ways we might have gone, might still go."

"You mean like you quitting the movies?"

"Yeah. Like that."

"Okay. Your turn. What's all that about?"

"It's like this. I'm a 'Screamin' bitchin' over-the-fuckin'-top success,' Dana tells me. But the more lights, camera, action—the more acclaim—the emptier I feel inside. Always playing a role, somebody else's part, based on somebody else's plan. But, like you, I've got the real thing, real talent somewhere inside. I need to stop playing to the lights and find what I really am."

"That's pretty much what Dru said. Only he said you were in a crisis state, a depression."

"He said that? What else did he say?"

"He's really worried about you. I think he loves you, actually."

Jocelyn turned around, startled. "He told you that?"

"Yes. He also said he feels responsible for your desire to switch to the stage. Something about the Pasadena Playhouse."

"It's true. Just going there, even if it's closed up, made me start to dream about live theater. I want to be in that world, on a small, decent stage, making and directing something genuine of my own choosing, being in dialogue with a real audience without a safety net."

"So this brings us back to Melie. You want to direct a play about her? What do you know about directing?"

"Enough. I've been acting all my adult life, I picked up so much from Dru, and I'm a fast learner. Just like you, J.J., with your gifts you can learn to write a play. And yes,

I want to tell Melanie's story. It's so complex, so real, yet so mysterious. She is all of us, more than the sum of our collective parts. And, like you, I'm convinced she's alive."

In the kitchen next to Madge's orange juice squeezer, J.J. slowly dialed the phone.

"Alice? It's me. Look, I need to tell you, I've made a big decision."

"No surprise there. I know the offers are pouring in."

"No, it's not that. I've been thinking hard. The Harts' story—their daughter didn't die in the fire any more than she did in a boating accident. And they've already been named in a criminal case. They've been punished enough. I can't write it. And the big one, as you call it, the Melanie story, I can't write that either. At least not for the newspaper. I'd have to leave too much out. I'm asking for a leave of absence. To write a play…"

At the end of her conversation, J.J. turned back to Jocelyn, who lay stretching on the shag carpet, eyes staring at the ceiling.

"So," J.J. cleared her throat.

"So," Jocelyn replied. "Alice is good with this?"

"Alice will be okay. And as for us, we'll figure it out as we go. The only thing I do know is who should play Melanie. She's an actress actually, though you wouldn't know that from when you met her. You couldn't tell that she's an exact look-alike either."

"Oh? I met her?" Jocelyn looked up.

"Well, you saw her. At the church service. The one all in white with the kohl-black eyes who sang the Janice Joplin song at the end. That's Natalie, Melanie's sister."

"An actress? Really?"

J.J. paused. "Really. You were dead-on about so much of this, Jocelyn. If we do it right, the truth about Melanie—of her being alive—will be more convincing than any judgment in a court of law. And you were right about the multiple endings, too. So many of them, with Melanie out there somewhere writing even more. All those shifting faces, like a kaleidoscope with her at the center. Maybe the truth lies only in the possibilities, the changes. One vision that comes into view of course is her in that hat, hair streaming down, helping J.C. rob a bank, holding a gun. But one ending can't define her. Another vision I've seen so often is equally true. She turns, smiling. She's reaching for her baby, wanting to hold Jazz."